C. S. Godshalk began *Kalimantaan* while working in Southeast Asia. She is also the author of a handful of short stories, of which two were selected by Mark Helprin and Richard Ford for *Best American Short Stories* of 1988 and 1990 respectively. Of one of those stories, 'Wonderland', Joseph Coates wrote in the *Chicago Tribune*, 'this story, a small Flaubertian masterpiece, alone is worth the price of the book'. Ms Godshalk lives north of Boston.

'Like being taken to a magical unknown planet, yet suddenly realising it all takes place on this globe, in mysterious Borneo and Sarawak: a beautifully written, elegant and rich dream' John Fowles

'A heroic yarn' *Daily Telegraph*

'A novel of epic scope ... Godshalk revels in jewelled phrases, gorgeous landscapes and butchery ... utterly compelling' Allan Massie, *Literary Review*

'Adventure and the exotic seep through the pages of *Kalimantaan* like luscious juices' *Independent on Sunday*

'A plot summary can't hope to do justice to the richness and complexity of this extraordinary novel' *Observer*

'Vividly evoking the humid tropics as well as the authentic mixture of imperial arrogance, innocence, anxiety, dejection, irony, recklessness and cold courage that one finds in so many contemporary accounts, it carries one deep into that lost world of the Victorian British Diaspora, especially the female half. Godshalk is not only Sarawak's Garcia Marquez but also the memsahib's Conrad' *Sunday Times*

'A first novel of formidable imaginative power ... the work of a born storyteller' *New York Times*

Kalimantaan

C. S. GODSHALK

An *Abacus* Book

First published in the United States of America by
Henry Holt and Company, Inc., 1998
First published in Great Britain by Little, Brown and Company, 1998
This edition published by Abacus 1999

A CIP catalogue for this book is available from the British Library.

ISBN 0 349 11069 7

Map by Jackie Aher, adapted from *A History of Sarawak*
by S. Baring-Gould and C. A. Bampfylde

Printed and bound in Great Britain by
Clays Ltd, St Ives plc

Abacus
A division of
Little, Brown and Company (UK)
Brettenham House
Lancaster Place
London WC2E 7EN

AUTHOR'S NOTE

A hundred and sixty years ago a young Englishman founded a private raj on the north coast of Borneo. The microcosm that resulted, boasting three Christian means of worship, stone quays, great swaths of lawn, a recreation club, and musical levees, eventually encompassed a territory the size of England, its expansion campaigns for decades paid for by the opportunity to take heads. This novel draws from that history.

PHYSICAL MAP
of the
MALAY ARCHIPELAGO
by
Alfred Russel Wallace.
1868.

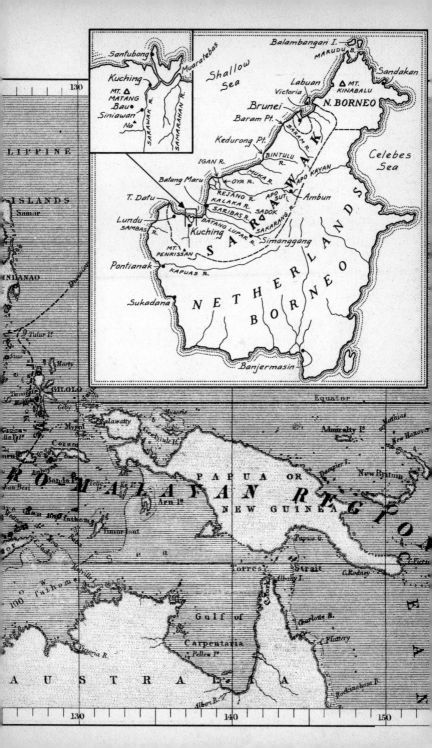

His mother died in a place he put between the red of the Punjab and the rose of Uttar Pradesh on the great relief map in the library, mostly because he remembered her in that color. Later, they corrected him, fixing his finger a thousand miles to the east, down the long Malay peninsula, then right, to the huge blot of Borneo in brownish violet. There, across the violet, he found the word. Her vague smile, her bones, her cloud of bright hair lay there. He would come secretly to stare at it in late afternoon, tracing the word strung thinly over the paper with his finger. He repeated it in his room at night in what he remembered was her soft cadence, holding the lacquer bull that belonged nowhere in this house and so must have come from her, *Ka-li-man-taan, Ka-li-man-taan, Ka-li-man-taan,* the walls reverberating with the sound, the alders lifting with it, until he slept.

The two things he remembered most clearly on the last morning of his life were his mother's skirt, with the little horse heads sprinkled equidistant across its folds, and the moment, the exact instant when, walking down to the sea, he found to his utter amazement and delight that he could whistle. The subsequent seventy-two years, the mystifying ease of achieving the impossible and the agonizing impossibility of just living, of linking days together, were wiped out. A blank.

*H*alf the face sags as if something has pulled down on it, the shoulder sloping oddly from the chair. She circles him, then slowly folds herself to the floor and takes the wrist in both her hands. Sunlight slides across the wood and climbs her knees. Her thighbones ache as they ached in her first pregnancy, but she does not move. It is the first time in forty years that she has sat alone in a room with this man without some strain. It was in this room with its few thick pieces of furniture that he mortified her beyond reason, she standing naked but for a little rose-veiled hat.

No one can tell this story. Every time you nail it to earth, it stares up at you with a different face. You think you know; then a word, a phrase in a letter, an expression on a face long dead says it was not that way at all. Lytton tried. He, perhaps, would have been best able, a natural observer, a professional accumulator of information. He wrote ten pages and gave up.

In one of his notebooks there is a description of the Yellow Insurrection in two sentences in the margin of notes on the family of pitcher plants. Two sentences to describe that month of hell and thirty-seven pages on a plant.

Yet the story appears most clearly in the marginalia. Guilt, remorse, rage, desire, sorrow that defies description appear most fiercely in postscripts, addenda. The horror described in the margin of a minor botanical discovery; sexual paroxysm along the edge of a recipe; bastard notes to no one—paper stuffed in cupboards, chests, boxes, written in solitude, meant for no earthly audience—come closest to a true chronicle. Some songs, too, may have escaped with their pure message, and maybe Dawes' dissertations, for the maniac faced everything head on.

She opens her eyes and breathes in the salt air, the fist like cold lead in her lap. There were singular conditions to that life, holding sway in that place and nowhere else. The eerie speed of some things and the wretched slowness of others. The speed with which one sickened and died. The eternal lagging of a letter. The months it took to work through those forests and the blinding velocity of the rivers, a flash flood carrying you sixty miles in a day. The almost daily attendance of death and the violent inrush of life.

There were other things. The electromagnetic spectrum extended well beyond its known range in that place. It simply kept going, sending out tentacles at either end and these crossing, merging. Colors seeped through the fingertips, the soles of the feet, warmth coated the retina, a throbbing sexuality pounded in the ear. Chairs moved, birds spoke, trees commanded courtesy. And love—blind, skewed, intense— bloomed and bloomed.

There was the currency of heads, their removal and collection, cherished coffers of semanggat.* There was the flow of merchandise, medicinals, light luxuries, rotted dainties, youth disposable as water. Then the mesmeric beauty of the place, its people, its rivers, its music resonating in the bones of the skull, the symphysis pubis.

She hears voices. The night before, she heard Gideon's laughter as if he were as near as he is now, resonant between rows of daylilies. They stood in her mother's cutting garden at the start of her life. A large female child and the Rajah Barr in dank wool. She gazed at the gloves in that fist, an idiot's idea of proper attire in midsummer, and he laughed, tossing them on the hedge.

She had gone with him, out to those rivers and airless forests and plains of mud. A big girl, eyes wondrous, easy to water, one of those women who is, in ways, a natural embarrassment, standing at the brink of it all with a box of watercolors to record her impressions of tropical flora and aboriginal life.

She heard other voices. She heard Dickie. She saw that long muscled body and gilded head, the crooked feet propped on the porch at Lingga. She saw the broad back turned to the memsahibs, the glistening yellow arc singeing the lily beds with a contempt he could not put into words. His cousin, twenty years younger, a more brutal, efficient version of himself. She sat between them in her bridal years and realized she sat between halves of a single organism, their distaste for each

* *Malay and Dyak glossary, beginning page 469.*

other not impeding a queer synergy. It was wondrous how imperfect, incomplete beings accomplish, in the end, more than the rest of us.

Sunlight floods the floor. The wood is dark. She remembers it light, honey-colored beneath the shoes with little kid inserts, like children's shoes in a huge size, "very French," her mother said, deciding them, deciding them on all the trousseau—the hat somehow too small but meant to be cocked to the side, a rakish bit of glamour, on her merely unbalanced. The imbalance continuing, clumsily, always deferring to advice—on cambrics, muslins, dumpy summer frocks, the hiatus of absurd sarongs—never ever appropriate, least of all when naked.

A breeze shifts all the light things in the room. Beyond, a line of people approach along the strand, their clothes lifted in the wind. Some wave to her, smiling. A tall savage in the red of the Lancashire regiment, a boy with an extra pair of eyes in his small jacket, a black man holding a sunbeam aloft. There is a Malay prince of great beauty whom she does not know and a Dayang, her head high as a water snake. All languid, mute. The vestiges, she realizes, of his last dream.

Charlotte referred to him in his youth as a phenomenon. Of that time there were only letters, those of friends and his own in that lead box. *"Surat-surat sudah tiba!"* the slap of the mailbag. Letters were all that were ever left. They were never thrown away. They were read and reread, eventually by eyes that had no knowledge of the sender. They were treasured and saved, not just letters but anything produced from a distance by the human hand—bills of lading, prescriptions, recipes. She could still see Lavransson bent over one of her mother's pages, embarrassed by the description of a hard birth. "Emerald green," he mouthed in wonder, at the report of a purchase of French taffeta. She often shared letters with the old sea rover, who could read in three languages but never received mail.

The door to the cottage had been open and she had stepped in. At first, she didn't see him, faced away from her as he was. She circled the chair and stared down at the still bulk. Did she too look this hideous? She had thought herself old at forty, and she had been. Not now. Now she is simply wearing one of those disguises humans wear, as he is disguised, a radiant boy housed in that ravaged box. It is this boy whom she kisses, long and deeply on the mouth.

7

I

Barr

Surat-surat

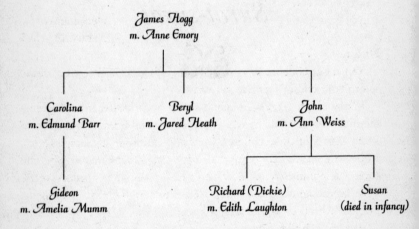

James Hogg
m. Anne Emory

Carolina
m. Edmund Barr

Beryl
m. Jared Heath

John
m. Ann Weiss

Gideon
m. Amelia Mumm

Richard (Dickie)
m. Edith Laughton

Susan
(died in infancy)

Denninghay
August 11, 1845

Dickie,

You ask of Gideon. Why in hell does it matter? You commit yourself to your cousin's service as I write.

In any event, I knew the child and youth, not the man. Carolina left him with us when he was six, when she and Edmund returned to India. Tribes of these children were shipped home, to escape fevers, to begin the only schooling that made any sense. They still are. He took it uncommonly hard. What can I tell you after so many years? That he was an obedient child? That at puberty he remained obedient, but with the odd, passionate outburst?

At Norwich they gave similar odd reports, though he was counted an unexceptional student. He would "disappear," sometimes for a day or two, and then reappear at matins, neither informative about his whereabouts nor contrite. Part of this time he apparently spent on the Wensum in some half-rotted scull. He liked boats. They said he'd often have a friend with him, a tall, fey boy who followed him about like a tail. At Jesus, he was finally sent down, leaving not secretly and in shame but in an open phaeton with bouquets and someone's sister.

Jared Heath to his nephew Richard Hogg, a newly commissioned district officer under the Sarawak raj.

Your Aunt Beryl loved him, I suppose, in her puzzled, birdlike way, but when he became big—and he became very big, much like you—she shrank back. For his part, he never showed much affection as a child but would sometimes lean against her like a little board. When he became older he seemed to hold her in some vague disdain, perhaps because she so closely resembled Carolina in coloring and voice and height, yet with no semblance of his mother's cold loveliness. It was as if, before they were born, raw stuff for the two sisters was set out in pots—the pigments, the long bones, the quavering vocal cords—and put together, once with genius in his mother, and once as a joke in Beryl, whom you know I loved dearly.

Carolina occupied the deepest recesses of his heart. He seemed always to be saving himself for her, a cold little nut to the rest of the world. He asked after her incessantly in the beginning, and Beryl, not knowing what to do, made things up. Small things, a description of a hat, a fictional picnic, a red boudoir—things in which he took so much delight that she made up more. She hinted that Carolina had a special love for nature: hence, I believe, his lifelong cockeyed interest in botany and birds.

He missed her terribly and for an astoundingly long time. He seemed to have devised a list of things that, when done scrupulously, would draw her back. He would be a good boy. He would love no one else. He would be patient. He would write. He did all these things, and still she did not come. She sent the occasional gift. These—an elephant on wheels, a wooden cow—he animated, adored.

When he came into his manhood, females noticed and he was heartless. What tenderness he showed seemed reserved for the odd, the misfit forms of life. I don't know why you want to know all this or, frankly, why I ramble on, except there's little left to me at this age but the pen. You've committed yourself to his service and, more than likely, it is to a totally different individual from the one I'm describing.

Yet perhaps you're right to ask. The East, especially such a god-forsaken corner, forces up all kinds of buried fare in a man's head. He has the same mental baggage he hauled around the Cape, but now it is roasted and set on gimbals. Complex souls do not do well. I remember my own early days in India. I clung to what Beryl called my two-dimensionality like a raft.

Gideon, to my mind, had no dimensionality. Perhaps that's why he was able to squeeze out of so many disasters here. It probably had something to do with putting him on that crazy throne out there.

He was about your age when he first went out. Nineteen, heavily built, watchful in an unnerving way. He went as part of the Company's spring contingent of third sons, clergymen's issue, and simple rascals, all full of their new commissions. The East India built on bones like those and younger. Little boxwallahs, half of them dying of ague or dysentery the first year, but the survivors turning their miserable trading platforms into the likes of a Surat or Madras. One could bolt forward. There was little bolting to be done at home, strung between a gentleman's name and no funds to support it. At first, I thought he chose this route because of his father's judgeship with the Company. I was wrong.

When he was small, he used to stare at an old relief map in the library when he thought no one was about, stare and stare, and then place his hand on it and close his eyes, as if receiving heat from a point on the paper. Carolina was buried out there, not in Sarawak but Sandakan, in the northeast, where her brother was part of one of those aborted attempts at setting the Company's foot. It was a voyage she and Edmund planned before returning home. He never spoke of it. She died there, and for him the place had the same connotation as hell.

The rest you know. Gideon returned seven years later. The youth had dried on his skin. Yet in a certain light those eyes still betrayed something of the boy. He had spent most of his lieutenancy on an East Indiaman, then moved himself, on Company wheels, into the Burma wars, where he was issued the steel in his chest. He never said anything about these campaigns, except once, gazing at a display of aspidistra, he said he began his "botanical education" in Burma. His friend out there—he used this word in regard to one man only—was a "naturalist."

He returned amazingly advanced in rank, his lung damaged and so on permanent pension, and set himself up, literally *up in bed,* in the same little room, cluttered with maps and charts and navigational texts and still all the nursery things—wooden figures Carolina sent back, paper lanterns, cabinets of birds' eggs, mountains of *The Boy's Own Paper,* rotted riding leathers, Indian erotica of a kind I never discovered in all my years out there, and the steel pellets that Norris, the naturalist and some form of surgeon, pulled out of his chest, arranged on the chimney piece. The two had served their first lieutenancies together and developed one of those friendships that only happens when young and at sea, drawing close, guarding each other's back. Harry Norris was also the only man who almost succeeded in killing him. He treated his lung in Pondicherry and did a terrible job. The man's surgical knowledge was weak, but he had a remarkable hobby, one that seemed to endear him to Gideon all his life. He could identify and discourse on hundreds of species of flora and fauna indigenous to the Malay peninsula. Norris' mother, a widow in Penang, chose to educate him herself rather than send him to England with other children coming of age, and the two would take lengthy excursions in the Cameron Highlands, returning with notebooks containing hundreds of drawings of plants, animals, and fish. The man carried these little binders everywhere. Gideon once said they provided him with his only diversion while recuperating at Pondicherry.

The week he returned, he said something offhand but odd. "Everything looks so small, Uncle. The basin, the windows, even the trees. All except the bull." It was a little funeral bull, one of the cheap painted kind they burn with corpses out there, and it alone was magnified for him. His mother, of course, was always magnified for him. He continued to write to her long after her death, macabre little letters in a small, stiff hand. Norris once told me he continued the habit at sea. As a child, he would stuff them in queer places—an old boot, an empty tobacco tin—viaducts for some telepathic post. I found one and saved it. It was like a little poem.

> It will be like this, a huge banyan all wide and sloping and a
> palace beneath with thick rugs and parrots and a great maranti
> bed. You shall be my Queen in the Trees. I shall come home
> in the evening and tell you of my adventures. "You have been
> marvelous," you'll say.

After five months of this invalidism, he appeared one morning at the library door, dressed somberly and immaculately, and asked his father for funds to buy a third interest in a small merchantman. Edmund, of course, refused. A week later, for some idiotic reason, he relented. It took only six months for the inept little partnership to forfeit both the ship and her cargo at a miserable loss. Edmund traveled through the house in grim vindication. *He* seemed unperturbed. After meeting him in the gun room one evening with a fistful of maritime listings, I realized he was about to approach his father again. Edmund had been ill and I spoke up.

"It would seem," I said, "war's a stronger talent of yours than trade."

"It would seem so," he answered. "I was lucky out there with the one, but I'm learning the other."

"You're set on a damnably expensive education!" I retorted. "John Company has invested roundly in you and would take you up again with pleasure rather than lose on his investment. Leave the trade to him. He does it well and you do not."

His face changed. It assumed an expression I had not seen before. "I'll not ship out again in that way," he said. "Not in this life. I'll not hold her down while he does the raping and casts me a guinea."

"If not the Company, then what? Where?" I said. "Farther east? Out where that maniac has drawn us all into quicksand?"

"Raffles was no maniac," he replied. He described a vision of the Singapore roads, a vast, thriving harbor crowded with more merchantmen than Malacca and Madras combined. Beyond, he said, the whole archipelago lay untouched except for the Dutch, who sat like a bunch of hens, an occasional man-of-war clucking forth in a daze.

That was the end of it. Except later, in the same place, when I asked him the real question. "Why go? For what?"

"To chart, to survey—" he replied, but I interrupted.

"What do we have the bloody Navy for? They've nought to do but protect the trade and draw pretty pictures. If you're going to hold some brown bastard by the throat and pick his pockets, I'll back you. Say it!"

"I'm going to chart," he said coldly, "to trade only enough to provision, for I too know my weaknesses. And, if I'm fortunate, to somehow invest my life."

"You're going," I said, and as soon as I said it we both knew it was the first piece of truth spoken that day, "to her."

Edmund died in the spring. He took the full thirty thousand pounds left him and bought his ship, a small overgunned retiree from the Royal Yacht Squadron. He had devoured Raffles and some other madman named Earl or Hunt, who described a journey round Borneo a decade before. The place had somehow become a fixed star. It was Norris who enlightened me years later. His reasoning went something like this. The Dutch were finished in Java. We needed only to use what we had to cordon off the entire region. Singapore held down one corner, Port Essington on the Australian coast another. Luzon could be purchased from the struggling Spanish and the north coast of Borneo nailed down by himself. The north coast bordered that great sea corridor and had no important piratical settlements. At least one superb harbor existed, with several rivers feeding into it. From here, trade could be developed with the interior, along with exploration to the great inland lake of "Keeny Balloo" to investigate mineral deposits. Once entrenched, he could move eastward, toward Celebes. The fact that the north coast of Borneo then harbored the greatest concentration of piratical Malays in a two-thousand-mile radius, that the Spaniards had no intention of selling Luzon to anyone, and that Kinabalu was not a lake at all but the largest mountain between the Himalayas and New Guinea didn't matter. No one else knew any better.

He spent October recruiting crew, his friend thumping chests. The ship's banner gave little information: "The *Carolina Barr,* schooner, 182 tons, for three years' exploration, scientific survey, and charting of the Eastern Archipelago." No one interpreted it as any more than marauding through Dutch waters. The pay alone was inarguable. I estimated he could keep it up for eight months and then have to meet with phenomenal success "charting" or drown every last man in his sleep. I was wrong. It took only six months to send back that terse little note from Singapore regarding foremast refitting and a sprung topmast. *Uncle,* I still have it, *please honor bills drawn on you to two thousand pounds, and I've arranged for deposit of insurance on the vessel as security for repayment.* Yet I was wrong twice over, because it was the only debt with which he ever encumbered me, and it was repaid in full.

He'll shorten your life, but the way you've been living it, you'll do that anyway.

Affectionately,
Jared Heath

Denninghay
July 30, 1838

Dearest,

It is my birthday. As you know, at five this morning I was twenty-seven.

I have my ship. I bought her with Father's death, yet I am reconciled to this as I believe he would be. She is a 180-ton topsail schooner. Aloft she is two-masted, and her sheer rises in a clean and handsome fashion. She carries thirty-eight men and is well gunned for her size. I have named her, my darling, the *Carolina Barr.*

I charted her course in my head all those years on the *Murdoch Castle,* and on that filthy cot in Pondicherry, and then in the little room surrounded by all the trees. I am there now, in this room where you held my hands twenty years ago. My *hands.* You promised nothing with your vague, sad smile, so I promised everything. To be brave. To be good. To be a king for you. They said that on the morning you left you kissed me as I slept. What good was that to me? That day the sun went down horribly. I began those years of night journeys out to you, traveling in boats I designed and redesigned, in

---

Gideon Barr to his mother, Carolina Hogg Barr.

carriages of great speed, in magical shoes, all breaking down and falling apart or sinking.

I didn't believe them until I saw Father riding alone beneath the trees. If you had been with him they would have dressed me in stiff clothes and set me in a window to wait. There would have been a carriage and boxes and shouting. I knew, seeing his hulk beneath the trees, you weren't anywhere anymore.

I am writing to tell you of my ship. She is a cockleshell with guns and so can travel anywhere with impunity, yet without casting threat. She is like her master, fitting nowhere and everywhere, to chart, to trade, and to fulfill my promise in this room where you kissed me. Or maybe they were lying.

G.

South Atlantic
December 22, 1838

Darling,

We departed The Lizard four weeks ago and sailed down through strong westerlies. The company think me strange, aboard more or less as my own supercargo. Sutton, the master, does the brunt. He's small but amazingly strong, like a monkey's fist with legs. He moves in little jolts as if his limbs were wired and screwed and affects a derby hat. His type comes up "through the hawsehole," berth by berth, shipping as seaman for seven years, then as mate on a Navy frigate. He sorely misses Her Majesty's tools. He started a man on our second week out. I allowed the whipping but later set him straight. We have no authority to press runaways. As for the rest, cook's a loss, and a young mid who is simply too pretty. Great blue orbs and rosy cheeks. How could a mother let him go?

I make progress with my Malay, Harry helping, although I fear I'm developing his queer turn of phrase. It was fourteen days to Madeira. Yesterday, we fell in with a large Chinaman, the *Hortensia*, and by dawn left her well to leeward. These great merchantmen sail clean enough, but in the southeast trade cannot hold on the wind as we. The company is settling, a sour one or two rising like gas. It is best to keep peace until the Cape.

G.

Indian Ocean
March 26, 1839

Dearest,

All hell broke loose on the swing round, a white gale burying us for three days. At one point it abated for half an hour, a sick little sun above, and I saw Sutton crab to the bow, his arms and legs spread, when we were hit again, yawing violently. I was certain he was gone, but when the sea washed off there he was, braced like a fat spider, that hat still on his head.

It was a birth, this rounding. The gale eased to a hard breeze and the green pastures of the Indian Ocean spread before us in sunlight. A following wind has pushed us for days. We passed Ceylon off the Dondra Head last evening, continuing under a moonlit sky. I spent much of the watch gazing into our silvery wake. It seemed I was once again on the broad highway of my dreams, though not collapsing and sinking but running in lustrous shoes, making great long strides. One doesn't feel this sweet slippage on an Indiaman. The *Murdoch Castle* plowed through the ocean like a festering city. Wind continues light. I feel a nearness.

G.

Nicobars
April 19, 1839

My Darling,

This morning, we watched for several minutes the peculiar spinning flight of a fish. At one point, a bright eye and smiling lips appeared beneath our cutwater. The creature was soon joined by others. It was our first greeting in your waters. They are yours, now that we have passed Ceylon and beat to the great corridor. You, in your narrow shoes, came this way before me. I remember your shoes. Brown with six brass hooks. I suppose when one is small and close to the ground, one remembers shoes.

I am learning to work lunars. Harry and I have discovered several flaws in the Admiralty charts, even for these well-traveled waters.

I kiss you and to bed.

— G.

Singapore Roadstead
May 19, 1839

Dearest,

Five days ago we cleared the passage at Banda Atjeh and entered the Strait. Then everything stopped, as if something in the ship or in the sky itself had broken down. We drifted like a carcass toward the center of the corridor, the heat setting us all on edge. At sunset the second day, the wind rose abruptly and slammed into our stern. We were lifted, flying, the coast of Sumatra rushing past to starboard, the ship's agility surprising even Sutton, as if she had finally sensed her true waters, past Selangor, past Malacca itself, past Bandar Maharani, prahus now slipping northward in the night, once a gong striking in the dark from nowhere and everywhere on the wind, then with dawn a huge junk ghosting near shore, her main flat. We overtook her, passed Bandar Penggaram, Pontian Kechil, then, almost without warning, cutting up through the morass of shoals and coming to rest in the eighteenth hour of the eighteenth day of May in the Singapore outer roads. We slipped between two Chinamen, set anchors fore and aft, and sank into the sleep of the dead.

We are but a speck of the traffic lying off. At least twenty merchantmen and as many junks lie at anchor in our neighborhood, along with two men-of-war and one twenty-two-gun corvette down from Penang. More of the Strait's squadron is said to lie round the point.

The town is handsome from the water, although, like all eastern ports, it takes on a different hue and smell up close. The river mouth is lined with shophouses traveling upstream as far as the eye can see, and beyond, a bank of low hills. Did you put in on a morning like this? You would have liked it, although then nothing, not the bright green esplanade nor the row of merchants' houses nor that Palladian wonder on the hill, existed. Just the start of a dream.

Raffles' dream. If you were to conjure the most natural entrepôt in all the world, you would conjure this. A superb harbor on a narrow channel through which most of the shipping has to pass, the winds themselves commissioned by those gods of greed on Leadenhall Street. Six months of the northeast monsoon to blow in the junks with their silks and porcelain and tea, then six months of the southwest to shove them back to China and pull in our heavy-bellied boys. He gazed at a miserable fishing village and saw this.

We have been noticed. A lightboat with Her Majesty's ensign repaired alongside this morning with an invitation from Government House. It seems that my uncle, that sour old corpse who has so testily written us off, has, with the same hand, written ahead to ease our way.

G.

Crosscoate Farm
Essex
May 4, 1880

Tommy,

Of course I remember him that summer. Even forty years ago, one remembered him. I don't know where you were with your specimen boxes and pressing plates. Sumatra, perhaps. I was twenty-seven, resigned to being buried out there, an old maid, forever. I had already begun to act the part. I carried an "embroidery bag" to evening gatherings with Father and Mother. I checked for mildew in cupboards, ran my fingertips along moldings, sniffed chamber pots for lye, and generally drove the house amahs mad. There was an overwhelming sensation of tightness about everything, my clothes, my shoes, even my fingernails.

Two of them came to dine at Government House. The Rajah and the ship's surgeon. I stood in the doorway between my room and the ladies' veranda and watched those tall figures wind their way up the garden stairs, the last sunlight catching first one bright head, then the other. They were beautiful, Tom. They climbed lightly, as yet untouched by the climate.

———

Charlotte Lytton Norris to her brother, Thomas Lytton.

The sense I have of that evening, even after all these years, is very rich, not for anything astonishing done or said but because it was a turning point in my life. Faces, conversations, materialize with ease. I remember Bishop Fuller's carriage arriving below the garden, our Sikhs rushing to assist. Then, directly under the portico, the Rajah's voice—Gideon's voice, for then he was merely a young man, brash and fine but still mortal.

Father looked like a child between them. "Young dogs," he called their kind, small adventurers on small ships. Normally they would never have been invited, but someone had written, a friend from his Delhi years. The three stood with some *Trident* officers on the terrace.

Father had started his stengahs early and was in his frank mode. "In ten years, there'll be an Englishman at the mouth of every river in the East," this little speech began. "And the worst will be a vast improvement over the black leech who squats there now calling himself sultan or tunku." It was reserved for evenings without Malay guests.

There was, as usual, too much Navy at table, Mother trying to dilute it with people like the Bishop and his wife and a Dutchman up from Batavia. I was seated between Hemmings of the *Superb* and the *Carolina*'s surgeon. This man seemed a lighter, gaunt version of his friend. He was very fair and his eyelashes too were blond, giving him, I thought, the gaze of a sheep. But he turned out to be very pleasant and bright.

As for Gideon, you know what he was like. You came to know him far better than any of us. There was nothing about his physical appearance that was extraordinary except perhaps his stature. It was only after he left a room that you became aware of something else being suddenly absent, an energy of some kind. He had one of those faces that, when unfocused, is almost ugly, but when animated by some emotion can be amazingly attractive.

He described their voyage as a charting expedition. This was acceptable. Anyone venturing eastward was soon in Dutch waters, and there was a Dutchman at table. Yet for some reason Father persisted. "Charting what?"

He spoke of the isles and shoals of the Sunda Strait, an area that had taken heavy toll of shipping, and the Bornean coast, uncharted in the north. "Belknap, I'm told, started up that coast in 'thirty-five," he said, "but gave up to weather."

"Belknap didn't give up to weather," Hemmings slurred. Mother looked at him sharply. She was vigilant at her table. Certain subjects spiraled downward, sometimes hellishly. Yet it was Father who picked up the thread.

"It's not shoals that'll cut you down, if that's your mark. You must be aware of that or you're a total fool."

I don't know why he was so pointedly rude; it was not like him. Perhaps because the other was young and yet had the aura of one senior. It *was* off-putting. Everyone began talking of Admiralty policy, and I let myself drift into a stupor of wine and heat.

I remember thinking, Everything must appear charming to him. The orchids, the candlelight, even *I* could not have looked half bad, sallow as I was, after a five-month journey out. Yet he never looked at me except when I spoke. I felt he instinctively knew the danger of looking at an overripe European female out there. Years later, Harry told me he looked at no one white in those days.

Despite Mother's efforts, the conversation screwed itself down. They spoke of that region to the east, a zone that ate ships. The few times our ships had gone in on the Bornean coast, they had been scuttled or refitted and used against us. Crews were sold on the Brunei or Sulu blocks, the strongest used belowdecks in their war prahus. "The Dutch have lost ten times more shipping," Hemmings said. "Gelderbloom here can tell you. Your *Carolina* would be a marvelous piece of luck for them. Shallow draft for those estuaries, yet fast and well-gunned. Perfection!"

"Luck for whom?" Gideon asked.

Hemmings gazed at him. "Bajau. Lanun. Balignini from the Sulu and Mindanao. My God, man, *pirates*." He described the huge fleets that ran down that coast before the northeast monsoon, cutting under Java and then north through Sunda with the southwest monsoon. "I don't believe *they've* ever run aground there," he said. These ships were armed with cannon, powered by sail and slave oar. They took every trader in their path and raided coastal villages in between. That year, Hemmings said, they had been active in the

Natunas, carrying off over six thousand captives, half women and children.

"Sweet Christ." The Bishop gazed up from his plate. "Why don't we do something?"

"They're in Dutch waters, your grace." Hemmings smiled. "They belong to Gelderbloom."

The Dutchman had been more or less silent all evening. "They're our problem," he said, through those thick gutturals, "as long as you don't mind losing one of your own now and then. These people are untouchable." He turned to Gideon earnestly. "They slip in and out before our men-of-war can catch the scent. And when they do, they can pull within two hundred yards of a fleet in one of those coves and see nothing. *Verdwenen!* The few times we've caught up with them, they do as much damage as possible and then run, and of course you cannot give chase."

"Why the devil not?" the Bishop cried.

Gelderbloom glanced at Mother sadly. "They almost always have captives aboard. They slit a throat every three minutes and drop the body off their stern. They start with the women and children. It is a bitter wake to follow. Our men have no stomach for it."

Gideon listened to it all with polite attention. I wondered, suddenly, if he were unbalanced. It was not unusual out there to meet a socially adept individual with pockets of dementia.

"Gelderbloom is right," Hemmings conceded. "We're not immune." Conversation turned to the recent loss of the *Charybdis,* one of our own corvettes come down from Canton to join her squadron. It was a mystery as to why she ventured so close to that coast.

"Perhaps she was assisted in," Hemmings said. "Or perhaps it was weather and then assistance. The Commander, in any event, was furious, but they would not release him for a policing action."

"It might give Kilcane rare pleasure to cut over now that he's in port," Father mused.

I don't know if you ever met Kilcane, Tommy. Who knows whom you met traveling your peculiar circuit? He was a great original. Rajah Laut of the Indian Ocean and South China Sea squadrons. His officers often dined with us while he was in port, but he almost never came. It was monstrous for a fleet commander to snub Her Majesty's governor, yet he was allowed all kinds of behavior. They had no one to replace him and he knew it. He used ships of the line like personal yachts and survived three or four court-martials. No one knew where he berthed when his squadron was in. It was rumored that he kept a Chinese in Changi.

There was the usual heat gathering over the table, and Mother swept up the females.

I was to meet Gideon once or twice again, then not until a decade later, when I was married to the surgeon whom I had so completely forgotten that night and pregnant with our third daughter, and he had his young Ranee on his arm.

You are right to ask of beginnings, you who have studied them so long. His own never fit the life. He said he went out to chart, to survey. He was terrible at it. Harry once said every coastal survey he made on his own was filled with errors. Trade was worse. From the loss of the *Deborah,* before his father's death, to the last shipment of Bornean antimony thirty years later, he was pathetic in trade. He said he went out to explore. After twenty years, he couldn't work his way down the largest of his own headwaters without a guide. His notebooks on flora and fauna were full of contradictory descriptions and childish scribblings, well matching that absurd little museum with its stuffed tapirs and hamadryads. He went out as a child would go, a brilliant child with powerfully neurotic instincts. He went out to be a king. Not a pandering bureaucrat for the East India. Not a mincing lieutenant governor. A king. Medium-sized. Absolute. In a way, it's what he was best suited to be.

Harry always felt he was drawn to Borneo because *she* was there. His mother. He never in all his life finished with her, his idea of her. You asked about this obsession. What was she like, so to direct and define a life like that? Old Anna Dean knew her in Benares. She answered simply enough. "Nondescript. Auburn hair, tall, and, from all accounts, quite stupid." What she was, of course, had no relation to what that small boy saw and felt. That corpse under the mud at

Sandakan had no relationship to the woman he carried in his heart. She was imbued with wondrous qualities in her silence, her remoteness. Of this, his creation of her, I believe he was somehow aware.

Harry once said, "My God, what an engine that woman put into our machine! If she had been less stupid, if she had even feigned affection for him, he would be running a small copra plantation in Johore and I would be practicing bad, lucrative medicine in Kent."

Of course Raffles, his writings, took up any slack. Borneo "untouched in her fecundity." "A political vacuum." What he hadn't counted on was time. Enough had passed to fill the vacuum. By the time he arrived, the place was a hellhole of piracy, swallowing anything that came close enough to devour. For a ship to put in to the north coast in those years was insanity. When he realized the truth of this, it was too late to turn back. Turning back was not something he knew how to do.

By the middle of that summer, he was brittle with worry. There was not money to continue the voyage beyond another three months. They had seen ample signs of the black trade in contraband and stolen cargo over those weeks. It would give a desperate man hope. He was intrigued, but he would never partake in it. The only transaction he effected in those weeks was to hire a "guide." A little pimp approached them at the bottom of the river road, half Tamil, almost blue, and while conversing alluded to having spent years in Bornean waters. A creature no sane person would hire as guide to a neighboring pasar was "enlisted" for the next leg of that voyage.

In truth, he was at the point of giving up, of selling the ship and settling with the crew. Then something happened, one of those things that make one contemplate the great joke underlying all of life. In August, the crew of the *Charybdis* was returned, spewed back by that maw to the East. Four days later, he met Kilcane.

It is of these times that I dream. A dinner of the dead. A handsome man escorting a large-boned girl on his arm. Now, at a time when the paper I scribble on is a blur, I see with crystal clarity the green flowerets on the Ranee's dress as he presented her ten years later. I see her broad young face, the sweat-beaded upper lip. Of all the faces that come to me, I see hers most clearly. I see her standing in her bewilderment and courage, a child rigged out as a matron. A young inter-loper in that temple of rivers and forts and mines he erected to some vapid corpse. I sometimes feel that all of it, that dinner with its mor-bid conversation and the world he created over the next decade, was, in an odd way, only a preamble to her. A tender-hearted usurper.

I am old and wish to see you.

Charlotte

Angin

July was a time of wind. Flying boxes, monstrous butterflies, and undulating dragons wheeled and dove, the rice-paper squadron soaring over five hundred feet. Women squealed, clutching spools to their stomachs, and officers aided the navigation. He and Norris had slipped into the social round with ease.

Hampers were hauled up by syces, and tea was spread on the high grass. They joined Hemmings and some *Superb* officers, seated with four sisters, all blond and fat.

"By the bye"—Hemmings smiled, eyeing the tumult—"if you're still set on an eastern landfall, there is the 'other shoe.' Not fare for Lytton's table. You might inquire of the Dutchman." He pointed a gherkin at a heavy figure sprawled below them on a little hummock.

Gelderbloom sat alone under a planter's hat. "Dyaks," he said, with odd melancholy. "A singular form of life. Those Bornean rivers are infested with them. Van Lutyens can fill your ear with Dyaks. He's our new Resident in the south. The old one was murdered with his wife and children on their way to Pontianak. They killed her and the children in front of him, and he died two days later. The north is worse. We have nothing there, no control. Their ballehs, their great war flotillas, leave those rivers regularly for captives and heads. Between the Lanun fleets from the north and these abominations, there isn't a fishing village left on that coast. And when you consider the size of it, three thousand miles, *verwonderen!*" He waxed into a description of weapons, of instruments of torture, at one point offering half a chicken, before two of Hemmings' blondes fetched Barr back.

There was a burst of female laughter above, a cloud of skirts passing along the upper ridge. Kilcane was at the hub. As usual, all eyes were on him. One could not help it; he cut an absurd figure, Commander of Her Majesty's Squadron in the Indian Ocean, Chief Guardian of the Straits—a little, red-haired wooden bird.

"Who's the man with Miss Peel's kite?" Barr asked, leaning back on an elbow. "It seems about to launch him over the harbor." At that instant, the figure turned and gazed at them. It stood for a moment, then, handing over the spool, it began picking its way down in a stiff, jaunty stride. All the men jumped to their feet.

"Lovely morning! Who, pway, have we here?" it was a childish voice with an absurd impediment. He greeted each woman individually, offhandedly saluting the men. When introduced to Barr, the copper eyes narrowed. "Small schooner off Hilliard's yard?"

"The very same, sir." He beamed.

"I've sailed on one like her. Almost as pwetty, but not as well gunned." The fox eyes scanned the harbor, locking on to the slender hull. "Too small for twansport. What are you doing with her?"

"A charting expedition, sir. We plan a circuit of the eastern archipelago."

Kilcane sighed. He withdrew a handkerchief and pressed it to his forehead, his lips. "And how many lifetimes have you to complete this junket?"

"One, sir, and that half used." It was the right answer. Light, modest.

The small face broke into a genuine smile. "I'm sure they've filled your head with Bugis and Dyaks and all those mewwy gentlemen below the wind. In that hull, you'll make their acquaintance all the sooner. They afford a unique kind of 'floating education.' "

He looked up at Barr keenly, then, bowing to the ladies, pinched his elbow in a vise and turned back with him over the heath.

"She's a useful size for some things, your *Carolina*. I'll wager I'm not the only one who thinks so this fair day. The fact is"—he stopped, releasing the elbow—"we've had a bit of news. You may be hearing from his lordship the Governor shortly. An invitation to tea, perhaps. See me after." In three strides he was gone, wedging that absurd body between two giantesses in white muslin. His officers rose and set off down the hill behind him.

Lytton was a middle-aged man who knew how to care for his person in the tropics. He used the few cool minutes of dawn and dusk to take exercise on a well-schooled gelding, changed his linen thrice a day, ate sensibly, taking greater pains with his cooks than with his secretaries, and had a good relationship with his wife, requiring no permanent mistresses. He had met the likes of this one before and knew he had a number still to endure. They were all out there for the same reason, but the cut of these new dogs was somehow more offensive. He was pleased to be able to send one directly to hell.

"We've had some remarkable news." He waved his fingers at the subaltern, who left the tea tray and sank into the shadows of the great library. "Four days ago the entire crew of the *Charybdis* but one, who died of fever, arrived on a nakodah prahu in paramount condition. Their story is singular. It seems they ran southwest to avoid a squadron of Lanun and were driven onto the Bornean coast by a squall. They grounded at the mouth of one of those northern rivers, and the local rajah sent men downstream to gather them up. He then proceeded to treat them like visitors from the third heaven and, at the first opportunity, ship them back. At his own expense! All salvageable cargo was shipped back as well. We are, needless to say, dumbstruck."

"That is indeed happy news." Barr sipped his tea.

Lytton gazed at him. "The man, it turns out, is not just some river rajah. If our informants are correct, he is the Rajah Mudah, the legitimate successor to the Sultan of Brunei. The Brunei sultanate is the only valid power east of us. He seems to be a man we would best be advised to cultivate if we are going to extend trade eastward." He rose and circled the desk, sinking his buttocks on the edge. "This may be a fine opportunity to get our toe in the door. Extend our heartfelt thanks. Gifts in appreciation. Extend, in short, our hand in trade. Our Chinese are very keen."

Barr said nothing. A breeze lifted all the door nettings, and the afternoon downpour began.

"An English vessel without much show of force, yet enough presence to be taken seriously, is what's warranted at this stage. Not Royal Navy. It would be immensely useful to us, to Singapore and Her Majesty—indeed, we would be indebted—if you undertook a survey of the mouth of this river and extended our compliments to this monkey in so doing."

Barr replaced his cup. "I'm gratified, sir, by your confidence in my ability to pass through waters described in such bloodcurdling terms only three weeks ago. I am gratified and, frankly, amazed."

Lytton controlled himself. He decided on a different tack. "Brunei is an unknown power, but that she is a power no one can deny. Nothing passes in war or trade without her knowledge and consent. Even here, when some god-rotting emissary passes through those doors, I'll be damned if I know who first uttered the words he's delivering. I believe I've been in several conversations with her without realizing it. In any event, we know the Sultan is essentially non compos, and this Mudah Aziz must be or soon will be the true power there. He has made a markedly friendly gesture to an English stronghold, and we have every reason to believe he will back it up by extending his protection to an English vessel arriving on its heels. You should, by both our own and our Malay estimates, be given clear berth. Quite honestly"—he leaned forward, distaste finally seeping through—"not many of us thought we'd be making your reacquaintance after the expedition you outlined. This is a rare piece of insurance. I'd grab it."

"I'm taken for a fool, Harry," he said that night. Yet he didn't look angry to his friend. He looked happy, and very young. There had been a period in those last few weeks when he had begun, dryly, to speak of other possibilities. Of armed cargo runs up the Strait, much desired by the Chinese, anxious to protect their trade. Of selling the vessel and investing in a camphor forest, a coaling station. Then this "opportunity." *I don't know if it was ordained,* Norris wrote. *He believed it was.*

He accepted Lytton's crazy proposition. Yet what he took away in that afternoon downpour was not just an implausible chance thrown at him but the room, the room in which they sat, the shelves of books, its high-ceilinged grace, the billowing door nettings. He could see "her" as Lytton spoke, brown shoes placed together, ensconced in its shadowy glamour. He would one day construct a facsimile of this room with native materials, years before he had any books.

"Mawning! Mawning!" the Hilliard foreman bellowed up from the lighter, a man they had been trying to bribe, to "find," for a fortnight. "Hoo! Hoo!" he said, admiring the bit of gold leaf striking the bowsprit.

Their refitting progressed with sudden vigor. New cargo was consigned, the bulk contributed by the Chinese, eager to extend trade eastward. Gaudy silks, stamped velvets, nankeen, tea, gunpowder, opium, and confections made their way into the hold. To this, he himself added several musical snuff boxes put aboard at Deptford.

A few evenings before they sailed, he saw Kilcane. Homer Kilcane was deeply attracted to him from the start. He may have seen something in him that resembled the best in himself, a fifteen-year-old mid come out to Madras, proceeding to climb through the ranks with dazzling speed. The man's own tragedy was that he became too good too fast. Commander of Her Majesty's Squadron in the Indian Ocean at twenty-eight, entitling him, as he himself once said, "to be pulled in four directions by politicians for the rest of my life." He was at heart another wild boy, one who had given up his black chance. He would love Barr all his life for not doing the same.

They dined in the *Golden Grove*'s beautiful aft cabin and talked through first light. It was a remarkable dialogue, both for its length and for the monumental areas untouched. The reason for taking up the voyage, what he would do when he got to where he was going, the fact that he was already Lytton's pawn, bought at no risk and no cost, his "smallness" and vast ignorance of the game—all went unaddressed.

Instead, Kilcane spoke of weather. He described the winds that powered the squadrons dropping out of Mindanao. He spoke of Dyaks, outlining the precise characteristics and accoutrements of their war boats. He spoke at great length of silhouettes, how to recognize individual silhouettes on the horizon; he seemed to think this was very important. He must have known he was dealing with a force instead of an intelligence, that the major moves had been called in some private madhouse and all he could do was prepare him on the course. He also understood Lytton. Throwing a small noncommissioned ship at such an opportunity was inspired. It was unlikely to be a diplomatic breach, just some queer incident, the place almost certain to swallow him up. Yet if there were something, such a specimen could well be the shoe in the door, rotting away more or less at a point when it was no longer needed. He understood but did not concur. He did not concur because he had made some effort to know the man. When they emerged at first light, he pulled him back.

"The Chinese will have bought at least one of your cwew. They always send an eye with an investment. It might amuse you to think on who. Cook? Whore? It helps to know, but it's not necessawy. It can be as useful to you as it is to them. No need to cut lines of communication. Always wegwet it."

He backed off the rail and watched almost tenderly as the other descended to the pinnace. Then, in a cheerful voice, "Good-bye! Good-bye! Scwew yourself in and I'll come for tea! I'll bwing my bwoom and help with the housework!"

That's how they left. With chisels and syrups and toys in their hold and a little pimp on deck. The Lyttons watched them weigh anchor that morning. They sat in the same garden where Norris was to court the spinster two years later, still thick with the scent of night-blooming flowers. The small hull barely moved between the heavy junks and merchantmen; then her topgallants caught the breeze, she heeled, cut round, and disappeared in the yellow steam.

Voyages across deserts, across water when you are young, always seem something else in memory. It was insane to be traveling that way, cast out on a hook with little interest in what was caught. Yet all his life he would feel the half revolution of the hull through his legs on that morning, the town drifting away, increasingly delicate, like some image a Frenchman painted on a cloud. The amazing fact remained: He was going where he wanted to go. Those rivers and plains and mountain ranges and tribes belonging to him like some medieval fiefdom, the cantilevered house in the crook of that stream, his mines and experimental farms, those armies raised up as if by incantation, dissipating into the leaves, their gory "pay" tied to their waists, would inspire none of the exhilaration of that half revolution through his legs. He faced seaward as the outer winds caught them.

The crazy points of Kilcane's tutelage were revisited, one by one. Inchi Bawhal, the Tamil pimp, had approached them for more reason than whoring on that broiling afternoon. The little man belonged to the Chinese. Of that he was certain. As to the rest, there was a new carpenter's mate and a Hainanese cook.

The Tamil stayed to himself the first days out. He carved a lewd little lady out of a piece of satinwood, which he kept in a box. When they questioned him on the huge island to the east, he stared at the Admiralty chart. He placed his hands on it, then removed them. He sighed and rewrapped his sarong. "It is not like this, Tuan," he said at last. "It is fat here, and thin here. It is a clever picture, never mind la, but it is wrong." Then Barr taking the stylus from those blue fingers, drawing several vertical lines, bolting the rest of them out of their stupor. He described those rivers falling from the central range northward to the sea, the only traffic ways, the powerful bores, rising well inland, the bars at the mouths, continuing, as if turning pages rapidly. Some of his information was correct and some was not, and it didn't matter.

Four days of open water, startlingly empty except for the eastern-most Tambilans. They came upon the place as one does in a certain nacreous light, seeing nothing, then a long white spit looming and receding. After several hours, a green haze appeared above the white, which extended across the entire eastern horizon. Massive peaks rose above the haze and vanished. They paralleled the coast until midday, then rounded a sharp promontory, the sea turning rapidly green. Sails appeared far to the north but disappeared over the horizon.

There was the paradisaical crossing of a great bight, a white starfish-encrusted bottom. On the ensuing three nights, they put in to coves on small islets studding this bight, traveling northeast. On the fourth morning, they caught sight of three fishing vessels rounding the head of an islet to the east, but these continued out of sight.

Both the islets and mainland were covered with swaying casuarinas. Inland, the clouds evaporated, revealing sunlit hills. By noon each day, the land breeze died and they hung suspended in green glass. Men went swimming. The horror tales told at Lytton's table were slowly deemed imbecilic. Then again, what better way to protect a valuable resource for future use than by flinging a veil of horror over it.

The place had given warning, yet in a rhythm they could not comprehend. On the fifth day, as they prepared to move down the coast, two fishing prahus returned along the line the others had traveled. These boats held their course, although with obvious caution. When fifty yards off, they stopped. Efforts were made to coax them in, and, after much hesitation, they approached. The men in these boats were small and unarmed. The bows of their prahus were carved in fantastic figures. A youth in the nearest held up a basket filled with tortoiseshell. The fellow looked terrified, so that his basket shook, but on more friendly beckoning, they neared the gunwales.

Some chisels and a bit of cloth were placed in a lowering basket, and these they handled but did not take. A greater effort was made to speak with them. Barr moved to call up Bawhal and, as he did so, his eye grazed the point of the islet from which these boats had appeared. A glint, and then another, winked out, a mirage of sunlight on water. He turned toward the capstan, withdrawing his pistol, indicating silently that Norris and Sutton do likewise. Sutton caught the movement and was about to remark when Barr swiveled back and shot the foremost native through the temple. The rest jumped up screaming, withdrawing parangs hidden under mats, flying aboard, the air now filled with a measured bellowing, as if one's head were stuck in a barrel and the barrel struck in a steady murderous rhythm. The sound came from two huge war prahus gliding smoothly from behind this islet, closing with a speed they had never before seen on water.

They succeeded, with injury but no deaths, in clearing their decks of these people. Sutton was wounded, and at Barr's urging the topsails were cleared, swinging them toward one of the prahus which had turned broadside to fire. A rising breeze pushed them to the point where a collision was inevitable. They rammed the forward prahu, folding her over their bow and carrying her for several yards in a crush of timber and then, coming apart, the glint now clear in iron shackles attached to limbs below water, these wretches sinking in gasps and bubbles, one agonized pair of eyes of a clear English blue that would haunt him all his life. The two aft boats surged forward, looping hawsers round the split hull, pulling her off while her crew scrambled to either sound deck, cutting loose the flotsam, human and otherwise, and sweeping away as they watched in horror and admiration at this unspeakable seamanship.

He gave no order to pursue. Instead, he retched onto the deck, a luxury he had been known to give himself after such things. Norris went below to tend the injured and within two hours returned topside. The beauty and silence of the place had once again closed in. The whispering of casuarinas, the rising fragrance of a land breeze. It was as if a sweet melody had been interrupted by a howl from hell and then sweetly resumed.

This violent dichotomy was to distinguish the place. The people, the very weather, embodied it. Rain fell with such intensity that one could watch, midst the deafening roar, water strike the earth and be driven up in a thousand fountains; then, abruptly, it would cease and one heard a bird, just one, and its single pure note in the hills.

The people seemed the most intense version of this duality. Honest, gentle, respectful of even their smallest children, cherishing their lore and tales, and at the same time methodically preparing for their gory celebrations, refining torture, training infants to perform these abominations. Yet mild. Born with such mildness of nature, living with it, even krissed with such mildness, the blade slipping between the shoulders as the condemned sat smoking a cigarette with his executioner.

The morning after, they began repairs under Monkhouse the carpenter's direction. They moved before sundown, finding a little cove farther eastward. Barr took the dogwatch, something he liked to do. He was uncommunicative yet calm, as if a pin had been withdrawn from his spine.

The two of them, the island and the man, both were inaccurately charted. Over the years, they would correct this, one with the other. He, standing on deck that day, the glint biting his eyes, chose. He chose before he thought, the glint and the bullet connecting before reason confirmed, firing, and in firing throwing all of them, the boat at the rail, the ones behind the spit, minutely "off." The place rewarded choices made like this and no others, reinforcing behavior that in England would have marked a lunatic, yet out there merely identified a well-adapted intelligence. After such a day, and there were many in those years, he did as he did all his life; he said his prayers. Norris once asked him what he prayed, hunched over his bunk or roll or, later, that great burlesque of a bed. He said he prayed what he always prayed. He asked God to forgive him and to take his soul if he should die before he waked.

His character was not something definable then. He was something in flux, in the making. For all his acuity, his alertness, he had a monumental naïveté. He "believed" in things. He believed in some cockeyed destiny, and he drove toward it with such momentum, maleficence simply lost its grip. When he faltered, Borneo herself buoyed him up. Yet of this first encounter, when Norris asked about killing the native with the shell, he said it was Kilcane who had warned him. A war prahu slipping along the horizon can look, the little man said, due to careful artifice, like a fishing boat or trading nakodah. Yet there are signs. She will reduce her speed, but the precision of forced oars creates a subtle jar, a moment of motionlessness that you can see if you do not look too hard; second, there can be the complete absence of deck cargo or cargo placed too far forward or aft; third, and most reliable, a glint, short, repetitive, that you can only see with the sun at your back and can be made by nothing in this world but shackles pulling past an oar slit. Only war prahus use slaves in this fashion. "If you think you have seen any of these things," the little man said, "you have. Attack. They will either wun, and then it's of no consequence for they will outwun you easily, or they will fight, which means this was their intention all along and now you have the initiative. It is wemarkably unnerving for them to lose the initiative. It's peculiar, weally. It's like putting a cat in a bag. For a few moments you can do what you want. I've never understood this vacuum in their seamanship."

Their courtesy is like a warm shower. They flinch at the bold compliment, the direct question.

There are tricks of the eye over water that are amplified in those latitudes. A bank of clouds on the horizon can turn into half a squadron, a man-of-war fracture into a thousand small birds. They had passed through that murderous doorway. Then, four days later, the "Civilized Person." He glided toward them, a golden egg transmuting, in the sunlit haze, into a yellow umbrella tottering over a man who stood upright in a little skiff. The apparition lay to under their gunwales and the man, Chinese-looking with rich Malay clothing, was helped to board. This was their first meeting with the Pengiran Hassan, a man who was to restore their faith in civilization and hospitality in those first days. He was nephew to the Sultan and half brother to Mudah Aziz, and the men who became visible on land and in two bangkongs just rounding a spit were his.

The delta and the river, they learned that day, was his province to govern by adat, or sultanate decree. He identified their attackers as Bajau. "We prayed for your safety but had no means to ensure it ourselves. We were impressed by the strength of your ship." The coastal waters, he said, were plagued by these piratical tribes, and he thanked Allah for allowing them to get through with as little injury as they had suffered. He said it was the Rajah Mudah Aziz who sent him upon their sighting and who now waited up a neighboring stream to greet them. It was this Rajah, his lord, who had returned the crew of the British ship. Barr noted the uneasy eyes on his own deck.

At midday, several new bangkongs arrived manned by sea Dyaks, short well-made men of slightly darker complexion than the Malays. They were led by these boats to an estuary farther down the coast and guided over the bar. This they cleared, and soon rounded the first bend of a broad river. The glittering universe of sea and wind abruptly vanished, as if a door had been slammed, replaced by an airless green wall. A tightness filled every chest. He stood in the bow, his eyes, his every nerve, poised upstream.

Malay water villages are all of a piece. Near dusk, a rotting hodge-podge of palm huts on stilts came into view on the starboard side of the channel. One of the huts was larger than the rest, and outside it, under a kind of portico, several richly dressed Malays stood gazing at their spars. A middle-aged, tired-looking man in a cloth-of-gold sarong stood in their midst, a handsome ivory-handled kris protruding from his waist. The Rajah Mudah Aziz's only other adornment was wire spectacles.

That evening, midst the sweet smell of grass mats and the drone of mosquitoes, this man courteously introduced his seven brothers, all nephews of the Sultan, who had no sons. They ran the gamut physically, having different mothers, the oldest so hideous it pained one to look upon him; the youngest, the tall, haughty Selladin, so beautiful he set one's mouth ajar.

There were the usual polite speeches. Barr extended Her Majesty's gratitude for the Rajah's hospitality to the crew of one of Her Majesty's ships. He explained their purpose was one of scientific exploration. He admired their river and town and shields and krisses. His host praised the ship and the gaudy trash displayed, and then everyone smiled and gaped. It was not until the fifth evening that true communication began. The pace of such things never alters. It is like a dream in which everyone walks and talks and gestures through water. If one imposes any acceleration, things fall apart, sometimes horribly. They learned that Mudah Aziz was indeed nephew and chosen successor to the Sultan and heir apparent to all regions north of the great watershed. He was in this territory at the behest of Brunei, to assist the Pengiran Hassan in putting down a small rebellion.

There it was. The single word one wishes to hear. The reason for it all, the crew returned, perhaps the destruction of the ship itself, rising like a fish from the depths. "We are against a handful of peasants and a larger number of Dyaks who have fortified themselves twenty kelongs upriver," Hassan said good-naturedly. It was an exercise no one took too seriously.

Stripping and lowering himself into the scuppers was a ritual of Barr's under way, and he did not abandon it on that river. He stood naked in the dark, sluicing water over his shoulders. It was suffocatingly hot, and Norris joined him. They climbed back and lay on the warm deck.

"What do we care for their poxed little war?" the surgeon asked finally. "Not once have we spoken of trade. Why risk the ship up this river otherwise?"

"Ah, Harry"—he laughed—"if luck were to throw both lovely arms around you and press you to her breasts, you'd shove her away. If we're to screw ourselves in, it is with war. If it is a 'poxed little war' all the better, for we've not got a bloody regiment up our sleeve. They need us. It's been four months since the *Charybdis,* and so they've needed us for at least four months. Who are they to call on, the Dutch? They're already in the south and would overrun them like the plague. For four months those gentlemen upriver have had time to dig in. Aziz and his mates are up against it."

He stood up, glistening in new sweat.

"We'll lend a hand. 'Tis the Christian thing. That sour-looking god Selladin is their temenggong. We'll have a chat and see how prepared for battle they truly are." He dropped down, straddling his friend's body, grabbing his ears. "The question"—their noses touched—"is the 'extent of their gratitude.' " He kissed him.

Malmsey

The kris is a beautiful and savage weapon. Certain ones are said to have a will of their own. The blade, the mata keris or eye of the kris, is the seat of this power. It was such a weapon that the Pengiran Selladin possessed, a personal daimon between his flat, smooth stomach and sarong. The hilt was carved in the shape of an ape in embrace with itself. It was called Berok Bergayun, and it was said to have killed through several lifetimes. He had been given the weapon by his mother, and he was never without it. This woman, Hassan said, was a Lanun of rank, and this had gained him both the respect and suspicion of his half brothers and of the Sultan himself.

This young man would not come at Barr's invitation but invited him aboard one of his own bangkongs. He stood waiting at the gunwale with dignified coldness. Yet in the course of the afternoon, he asked intelligent questions regarding the strength of their guns, the maneuverability of the ship. After determining distances and a thorough description of the rebel stronghold at Siniawan, a battle plan was drawn up. All during these talks, a woman was present. She sat in a lightly veiled cubicle on deck. She did not sit huddled, as Muslim women do in the male presence, but with her back straight, her head lifted. This was the Dayang Ajar al Selladin, one of Selladin's wives, then about twenty-eight, older than her husband. Their relationship was unique, for she was said to accompany him everywhere. Her profile was haughty and lovely, although Barr took care not to look at her directly.

He promised to assist them. Five days later he withdrew the promise. "The question," he said, to Norris' violent objections, "you do not listen, is how much our help is 'worth.' Such information must always be forced." He had somehow anticipated this, a dialogue that, if he had been perspicacious enough to sift through the possible outcomes, would have resulted in the hesitation that destroyed him. He praised the preparations made by their temenggong. He said he had decided his presence in the balleh was not necessary "to take so small a thorn from the paw of so large a tiger." That same evening, in that open hutch with its thick grass smell and drone of insects, they offered him the moon.

The province, of which the town of Kuching and the river were only a part, territory belonging to the Pengiran Hassan by adat, was, at the successful conclusion of the conflict upriver, to be "left in the hands of Tuan Barr," who would, in turn, pay tribute directly to Brunei. Mudah Aziz explained that he, as heir to the Sultan, would return to Brunei after the action was completed. His brothers would return with him to help him stake his hold. Hassan could no longer hold this province successfully and would be forced to comply.

In the days that followed, they threw themselves into battle preparations. A cockeyed, tragic little battle. The balleh swelled en route. Chinese from the gold mines inland volunteered to join them, as well as six bangkongs invested by a local sharif. This was a tall, lean man with strong Arabic features. As sharif, he was descended from Arab traders who had entered those waters centuries before, claiming descent from the Prophet and, with it, immunity to law. They were almost always in league with the piratical tribes, supplying them with salt and ammunition. The Sharif Jaffar had an outstanding talent for organizing squeeze and blackmail, strengthening his requests with murder. His boats were included because he wished it.

The battleground was reached on the fifth day. It seemed to consist of a mud and stick stockade besieged by several movable bamboo fortifications. These people appeared to fight only from behind walls. From time to time, gongs were beaten, followed by shouted threats and an occasional shot from two decrepit Portuguese lellahs. Amazing rules held sway. No night attacks could be made by either side, and an amount of time was allowed on each side for meals. "Sweet Jesus," Sutton said. "We'll be here for years."

Breakfast was served separately for the three Dyak tribes accompanying them, who, when not allies, were enemies and so ate their rice at some distance from each other. Barr was delighted with it all. He decided to lead the advance himself and preceded this by a stroll up to the stockade to gauge the range of the guns that had fired so ineptly on them on their arrival. And this was the pity of it. Those poor wretches had never seen an organized advance before, let alone one led by Europeans and covered by accurate fire. After a short burst of cannon fire, they rushed down the backside of their stockade, to be cut to pieces by Dyaks and with them almost two hundred women and children.

Before sunset, their Dyaks spread into the territory and slaughtered every living thing, including two or three hundred pigs. There was no way to stop the butchery or the head taking that followed, the sole payment extracted by these people. After two days, they proceeded downstream with a miserable column of prisoners and the few upriver Malays who led them. Some of the Chinese asked permission to stay behind and were already mapping out a crude town on the ashes.

That's how they did it. The broad swaths of lawn, the orchards and gardens, the astana, the gunboats, the interlocking system of forts, the mines, the young district officers—their dewy brides arriving at dockside with crates of crystal and plate—wax seals melting in the sun, tiffin, chintz-covered sociables, the vast shipments of purgative salts, antipyretics, and love letters, all began with that miserable little massacre.

It was not much different from the way any other river and slice of watershed was seized in those three thousand miles of archipelago. He had the wit to throw himself on the right side of a pitiful little war. He then applied "the recipe": the usual promises of increased revenue to the local tunku, to be furnished by improved security and open trade, this in turn causing adjoining river systems to drop into one's lap. If they didn't drop, they were encouraged, as violently as resources permitted. It was used with boring effectiveness from Madras to Celebes, although rarely by individuals. There were some.

In later years, he and Kilcane would recite the names of this small, colorful tribe over their gin paheets. Rajah Hare, sovereign prince, mass murderer, gifted cook; Rajah Spring, the only American, small, almost a dwarf, pederast, sublime fiddler; Rajah Hausbuch of Saba, whaler in the Bering Sea, possessor of an Austrian baronetcy, former manager of Dent Brothers, Hong Kong, who convinced the Sultan of Sulu, for five thousand pounds per annum, to designate him Rajah of Sandakan and Datu Bendahara, a man murdered in his seventieth year for a two-acre guava stake in Makassan, all he had left.

The only thing that perhaps separated him from the bulk of ersatz rajahs, tunkus, and small- and medium-range megalomaniacs who sparked and faded over two centuries in that region was his amazing naïveté and the unfailing neurotic source of his energy.

What happened in the weeks and months that followed has no logical chronology. It cannot truly be attributed to what was done, what successes were accomplished on what dates and to what cumulative effect. It lay rather in the interstices, in the set of an eye, the commitment to violence displayed in a lower jaw.

He was curious about the wretches they had brought downstream, imprisoned for days in a rude stockade. "Who are these people?" he asked Selladin one evening. "Truly."

The Malay gazed at him intently, and then into the trees all round. Seeing they had stopped, his men encircled them at some distance. These people were as vigilant over their prince in Kuching as they had been upriver. "We are pengirans," he said. "We are taught to expect submission from all living things. It is thus. We accept it. Hassan carried it into the realm of hell. He extracted everything from these people, leaving them nothing but debt. By law, they then must forfeit their lives or their children as slaves. They are a simple people and try to think on what to do. At first they will part with a child, usually a female infant."

Darkness had dropped, and clouds of fireflies filled the trees. "What if they refused?" Barr asked. "Not rebelled, but simply refused?"

The fine eyes scanned the river. "These people are easy to punish. Those of one river do not speak with those of another. They say 'We of Sadong'; 'We of the Sut.' Hassan would simply invite another tribe, a warlike tribe like the Sakarang or Saribas, to claim heads on their river, to burn villages and take slaves. Other spoils would be his as their lord. Here he does not stand alone. It is a way of life for the Sultan himself."

"But that's monstrous! Why in God's name—"

"Why?" Selladin smiled. A finger almost touched Barr's chest. "Because of you. Outside, on the great seas, the Sultan himself has been forbidden. The Portuguese, the Spaniards, and the Dutch allow trade only from their ports. We have nothing left to eat but ourselves. We start with the feet."

He glanced backward. "These people have no warrior blood. They fought with the strength of their despair. Hassan had run out of tribes to set against each other. The Dutch are already in the south and would finish us. The English are cautious in their initial forays. He expected, at most, a small frigate. It would be bribed to do the work at hand and then disappear. Ships disappear all the time."

It was, of course, what even Lytton expected out of the odds. He had, in effect, been pitched from one little nest of intrigue, over five days of water, into another. That he survived was due to the man himself, for no one counted on his species of life turning up. But it was also due in some real measure to this young Malay.

Selladin, haughty and circumspect, in those days together lost his coldness. He became over those weeks and months, because of some natural sympathy and a deep curiosity about the world beyond his own, a friend. *He speaks to Gideon from the heart,* Norris wrote, with some jealousy, *the way, heretofore, only we spoke.* Pleasant afternoons were spent on Selladin's deck, hours when Barr felt enough at ease to ask questions he would not have attempted with the others. One question had lodged in his skull.

"With the piratical fleets prowling these waters, trade has all but ceased," he said to this prince one day. "Yet Brunei, Sambas, Sulu are not dead ports. How, without trade?"

"There is always trade," the other replied.

"But even black trade can't account for it. A few tons of antimony or quicksilver by night, a pirated cannon, can't pay for it."

"Not quicksilver or guns," Selladin said. "Two nakodahs were captured off east Java last month. The crews arrived on the Brunei block. The Malay captives are, as we speak, making their way back to their relatives overland, from sharif to sharif, bribing each in turn. Other captives go into bondage. When a sultan needs slaves, he notifies the left, and they eventually arrive on the right." The main commodity in that commerce was people. Thousands of men, women, and children. Their backs powered those great war bangkongs, their hands pruned the royal gardens in Brunei and Sulu, their thighs spread in the pengirans' harems, their heads hung in upriver longhouses. Two tribes in the upper Sarawak were gone.

"Tell me, my friend," he said, on another afternoon, "of the old man in Brunei."

Selladin's handsome face slowly changed, taking on an almost aged aspect. He spoke of a man who sat in a great stilt house, a place from which, for seven hundred years, all measurements in that universe were taken, a universe that once ran beyond Celebes and northward into Mindanao, an old man who loved sweets and torture with equal intensity, who was not Iang de Pertuan and would never be "he who rules" because of one small thumb too many, a man suspicious of his nephews, swayed by venomous mouths.

All coastal rajahs controlled at least one river. Any trade between the interior and the sea passed through their hands. Brunei was the colossus, with several rivers running into her bay. The inland tribes brought down their camphor and plumes and diamonds, and the old man took his share. What he could glean from the sea accounted for the rest. It was this young man who explained these things and others on those afternoons, leaning gracefully against his gunwale, the little veiled cubicle occupied by its silent shade. It was this man, in the end, whom they would rob so thoroughly there were no bones left to pick.

Aziz deemed it Barr's right to dispose of the prisoners from Siniawan. Against Selladin's advice, he entered their stockade alone one evening and, in the middle of that rank, sullen crowd, began to speak. He spoke at an idiot's pace, using the Malay and some Dyak he had begun to acquire. He said *we:* "We will care always for our obedient children. We will see no harm comes to those who seek our protection." He was wearing a coronet of lightning bolts on a stage at Malmsey. Yet something happened. Those glowering eyes were raised. He realized it too and, somewhere, he began to absorb the claptrap he was spouting. He spoke with authority and "love"; there seems no other word. The energy was undeniable. One was disgusted by it, by the process of it, and touched.

He was invested with his river. After a formal little speech under torchlight, Aziz embraced him and commanded each of his brothers to follow suit. Hassan was no longer among them. This man was a cipher. He was the first to extend welcome to them after passing through that door, and he revolved away, only to turn back over the years with a cache of different faces.

Barr traveled back to the ship that night in a mood of distilled euphoria. "When I get my crown," he said to Norris, standing in the pinnace as it glided through the darkness, "I will give you my hat." It was a hat he wore at sea, black and rusty and molded to his head, and give it to him he did.

Water is everywhere in Borneo. Hundreds of streams flow down the central range. Rain drenches the earth daily in the wet monsoon. The animals themselves have aqueous souls. There is a tribe of insects that imitates a distant waterfall, the bulbul trills like a rivulet, and the wah-wah sounds like a drowning woman.

I did not have his nerves, Norris wrote. *I had not realized how much fear had paralyzed my senses until it appeared we all might live. I looked around in the days after that proclamation with the joy of an infant. I was in love with not being dead.*

The surgeon would row ashore each dawn, and one morning spotted an Argus pheasant, a beautiful bird, crossing the bank. He took out his notebook and attempted to sketch it. Scithers, an old quarter gunner signed on at Deptford, was already mending sail down the bank, and he trudged up after a while and peered over his shoulder. "Be the gent who strolls beachy path," he said. "Right proper toff! Terrible screechy voice!" Norris looked into that toothless grin and laughed, a strange sound on the air.

All was sunlit. The ship rested mid-channel like a bright apparition. Strolling upstream, he came upon five bangkongs neatly aligned along the shore, bow to stern. The first was tied to a stake before a little tent. Two Malays were seated beneath; one was armed, and the other seemed to be some sort of scribe. Men from the boats waded in as their turn came and had quiet words with these two, who, he learned, were men of the Sharif Jaffar. They were extracting payment from the boats for their participation in the recent balleh upstream. These men, apparently, also kept rigorous tally of extortion and thefts in the district, exacting squeeze with great precision. Nothing seemed to change hands that morning, but much was painstakingly written down. He mentioned this river bookkeeping to Barr, but it did not seem to interest him.

He, he said, had spent the morning seeking a suitable site for his astana. From the awkward sketches he produced, this was to be a massive construction of nipah palm and baked brick with several outlying buildings. Gardens in the West Country tradition were also roughly sketched in, as well as a stone balustrade encompassing an elaborate quay. Norris burst out laughing, and he laughed too.

"Of course, all I can get them to begin is the main structure," he said. "But it pays to plan ahead, to know what the rest will be like. It avoids tearing down and restarting."

Realizing he was serious, Norris said nothing.

"Would you have me in some nipah hut?" Barr snapped, suddenly vexed. "I'm not some river trader, and I damned well better not look like one. We must look *permanent* before we can do anything. God knows there's enough for ten lifetimes." He had also, he said, initiated a search for a yellow payong, a royal parasol, which he planned to have carried aloft by a chamberlain sort of character wherever he went. He shared a litany of plans that day, which lasted well past sunset and into the night.

The surgeon meant to set his foot gently to earth, to say, Don't take this quite so seriously. The Malays have a polite turn of speech. Bequeathing this river may be, for Aziz, a gesture. Put out your hand and you lose it. They meant to offer him, he felt certain, no more than residency and trading rights on the river.

Norris didn't say it. He didn't say anything. The man's plans were so powerfully fueled they would have flattened any point of fact standing in their path.

In the days that followed, he somehow procured an inventory of the river's revenues from Mudah Aziz and closeted himself with it. "Antimony is worked in Bidi and Penrissan," he said brightly, when Norris entered the fetid cabin. "The forests are full of gutta, camphor, and cutch. There are several kinds of rattan and large reserves of hardwoods and oil nuts. The Chinese don't seem to have much success with gold washing, but they do a capital job with pepper and tapioca above Bau. Sugarcane would probably do well in the valleys eastward, coffee a little higher, maybe even cotton." His face glowed. "As much as ten thousand piculs of antimony, sulphide *and* regulus, can be packed off before the monsoon. Coconuts, dye woods, plumbago, tortoiseshell, pearls—it's amazing what the Chinese will pay for bezoar stones!" He pulled his friend over to where he had mapped out a crude system of forts, extending east and west.

"My God!" Norris said. "These are hundreds of miles beyond this river."

"We can build two a year. Kilcane has a dozen men due for release over the next three years who could man them with native fortmen."

Norris eased away, but he continued, barricading himself first with two "stewards" extracted from Aziz, then the hapless Bawhal. The surgeon reentered the cabin the next morning, tripping over the Tamil, curled up like a prawn. Barr sat in the same place, pale as death.

"Nothing." He rose, giving the papers a vicious swipe. "I've been reading *history*. The fiends neglected to say these lists were ten years old. All that's left of open trade, taxable trade, is a bit of sago pushed about by night. The only thing of any value is opium, and that's controlled by the Chinese. God bless Hassan," he said bitterly. "The man had a knack for squeezing rocks."

He had extracted that crazy inventory, gone wild with it, then reverted to bleak reality, all within two days. "Perhaps we can still leave our mark," Norris offered feebly. "There's room enough for improving the human condition in this place."

"The human condition!" He laughed. "Slavery? Heads? They're the mainstay of the economy! Even here, the sharifs take half!"

"This is so," Bawhal mumbled from the floor. "It is all Allah has provided in His wisdom." This was a favorite phrase of the Tamil and was, at best, annoying, yet Barr looked at him queerly.

"Bawhal," he said softly, gazing at him. He bent and lifted the little torso and kissed the oily mat of hair. "Now get the hell out, there's a good chap."

The bank of an eastern river at twilight is awash in shifting light. A figure stood in the mutating air, spotless caftan skimming the sand, the lean face gazing at the ship. The Sharif Jaffar had been invited. The pinnace was sent in and he was welcomed aboard, and in that same hour, belowdecks, he made that dignified murderer, that quiet squeeze-taker of all black commerce in the district, his chief of police.

Jaffar could not believe the man's lunacy or his own luck. He had been offered license to eliminate all competition in the district. He may have puzzled over it, he may have doubted its legitimacy, but he sunk in his teeth. In the weeks that followed, he set about systematically destroying all other black alliances throughout the region. The man's reach was astounding. He was more thorough than a dozen seasoned district officers. Barr figured that by the time he finished cleaning up his opposition, roughly by the monsoon change, he himself would have only this man to deal with, and the answer as to how to do this would, he hoped to God, congeal before him.

It was his habit to stroll the deck in that brief time before nightfall. He would stop amidships, light a cheroot, and rest his arms on the rail, gazing at the little knoll he had selected for his astana. After a while, he'd ease around and regard the line of Chinese shophouses on the far bank, crooked, filthy, yet with new construction at each end. The segments turned mauve, little tendrils of smoke rising from the upper stories into the darkening sky. At Bau, the Chinese gold camp upriver, the same thin spirals would be rising. After fourteen hours of digging in hell, a man would crawl to his pallet, stuff his pipe, and draw himself into paradise. He blew out the smoke of his cheroot and watched it too curl in the evening sky. He would not rack his brain weaving through pitiful sums of camphor and cutch on some defunct list. They were nothing and paid these pengirans nothing and would continue to pay nothing. What he would tax—royally, regularly, and with precision—was opium.

He had asked for a certain amount of help from the pengirans in those days, and after a fashion it was offered. Yet at every turn, they continued to exercise their outrageous rights, undermining whatever progress he made. They showed no inclination to return to Brunei.

"There's too damned much nobility about," he complained to Norris. "No one knows whom to obey. The only thing is to cart them back to Brunei myself. Our excellent sharif will spend the next three months murdering the last of his opposition, so I needn't worry up a police force yet. Opium revenues can wait. We'll negotiate with the Chinese when we get back. We'll be in a stronger position. They'll deny its existence, then try for the best rate. The important thing is they are Chinese. They will hesitate at least six months before moving against us, and we need four to screw in.

"Of course," he said, a few evenings later, "we need to leave a few bones of government in place. This lot will leave a hole that will be filled by worse. We need a code of law. I think I have one."

To pull a system of jurisprudence out of the air for a hundred different tribes, some their intellectual equals, others residing in trees, was insane. Yet he did have one. With Selladin's help, he had exhumed the Ondong ondong, an ancient Muslim code from which the pengirans vaguely drew their power. Seated on a straw dais on a steaming morning and holding it in his fist, he proceeded to reinstitute the old order of the four wazirs. There were the Datu Pattingi, his chief adviser; the Datu Imam, leader of the priesthood; and the Datu Bandar. He asked those people to choose respected men from among themselves to fill these ancient offices. For the fourth, his Temenggong, or chief military adviser, he chose, at Selladin's suggestion, a man from Siniawan, an individual who fought with singular ferocity on the ramparts upstream. To this man, Si Tundo, he presented a sash cut from his only dress waistcoat and a tin of potted cherries.

The man held these objects gravely, then bent to the ground and pronounced the somlah. Norris was ashamed. This creature seemed an honest fellow who had suffered, and he didn't like him made the fool. Yet the surgeon would come to feel differently. What the Siniawanese knelt before on that morning was not a brazen charlatan. Over time, he and others like him played a part in transforming Barr into what they supposed him to be.

In retrospect, it's hard to say what he actually achieved in those months. He had snared his river and slice of watershed, but almost at once the corruption and murderous nature of the place closed in. So he did something absurd, something a child would do with tin soldiers when the game became too lopsided. He made rebels his wazirs. He made the number-one criminal in the territory his chief of police. "He knows where to look," he said simply. And he made the main contraband the base of his economy. He taxed opium, he encouraged its use and taxed it heavily, and in doing so made an enemy of the Chinese, one of the worst things you can do out there. But he was buying time. And he was becoming a remarkably good judge of time, not punctual or methodical but able to judge how long something, good or bad, needed for ripeness, for fruition. Yet even then there was something missing, a brutal follow-through that was not part of him. There were moments in which he seemed to recognize it himself, and he spent these hours, sometimes days, darkly.

He had put off his planned voyage to Brunei, yet the presence of the pengirans plagued him. They continued to give orders and claim privilege, undermining his smallest decisions. He resolved, at last, to appeal to Selladin.

"Selamat pagi, Tuan Besar." The young man gave an amused glance at the payong held aloft at the back of Barr's skiff. He extended a hand, helping him to board the bangkong. "You have set upon interesting solutions to your problems. In Jaffar and the Chinese you yoke two tigers to your cart."

The two spoke of Jaffar and of the hostility between the Chinese and the tribes inland. "Selladin," he said finally, with feeling, "you are a newfound brother to me. But the others undo all I begin. You must take them away. Only then can you depend on a stable friend on this river."

The Malay gazed over the water, watching its ruffling surface. A dugout approached from the far bank and, laying to, two women disembarked. These were the Dayang Ajar and a slave. The Dayang dropped her veil as she stepped over the gunwale, and Barr gazed at her. He had done this, embarrassingly, on one or two other occasions, but had quickly turned away. This time he did not turn away. The women disappeared into the aft cabin, and the dugout swung away.

"You are right," Selladin said, as if there had been no interruption. "But it is too early. Our people in Brunei are preparing for our return. If they have sufficient time, it will be safe, with our backs guarded. To go before their work is done would put the Rajah and my brothers at risk."

"I cannot wait," he said coldly, rising. "I will take you all myself in ten days' time. I will deliver you under my guns."

Selladin said nothing. His eyes followed the wake of the retreating dugout. There was sadness in the face, and something else. He looked then like a man who gazes at something he cherishes deeply and which is receding forever. For the short time they knew this man, he was an anomaly. His nature could not be explained by race or privilege. He was one of those who carried Islam not in his head or in his words but in his blood. It was as much a part of him as his beautiful eyes and strong teeth. His fault was one frequently found among them: a monstrous dread of shame. When he spoke of the danger to him and his brothers if they returned to Brunei without preparation, a place controlled by a man whose paranoia and cruelty were legend, the other did not listen, and Selladin would not speak of it again. He was, at bottom, a man whose wife was coveted by another.

Barr's attraction to the Dayang Ajar amounted, over time, to physical pain. How he planned to disengage her from this man, he never consciously addressed. He knew Selladin treasured her and would have the forethought and intelligence to protect her if his own life were at risk.

In the end, he did not have to transport anyone. On an overcast morning, ten bangkongs and twice as many outriggers dropped downstream, the only sound the soft whimpering of females below-decks. Selladin had organized this fleet quietly and gathered his brothers and their households. Barr watched from the bank until they cleared the lower reach and were lost to sight; then he turned and helped Monkhouse shift a riser.

There were times, Norris wrote, *when he peered into my notebooks, when he straddled my chest under those stars, when he gave me his hat, that I was his. I cringed from this new vision.*

Young Mrs. Goldpastures, newly ensconced in her universe, will say, "The cutting gardens will be thus and so, the orchards there, the stables and spring paddocks to be set here." Joy will rise in her face, the implacable joy and novelty of ownership, a life of fecundity and fruition spreading before her—"the hives at the bottom of the wall," a ringed hand pointing to a little gazebo under construction among the fruit trees. He, no less proprietary, enthusiastic, no less disarming, no less *pretty* with those blue stones and sun-blackened face, pointed to his estuary, his forests, his mountains, giving each its Dyak name—Matang, Na, Santubong—passing on, holding forth on rain, its power and idiosyncracies in that place. He would be pushed, twelve years later, toward this same estuary and then sucked out again by the worst early monsoon storm in four decades at the moment when, upstream, his first child was being born, the deck sliding back and he cursing every square foot of mud, but not then. Then all was sparkling and sunlit.

Clouds hid the inland range, and he explained how these would soon vanish and return as showers in the afternoon, a phenomenon characteristic of every mountainous island on the face of the earth, yet in the light of such enthusiasm his guest feigned fresh interest.

Kilcane paid his first visit that autumn. He had learned through his multitudinous sources that they had indeed "screwed themselves in" and decided to see for himself. He had come, ostensibly, to force the release of two British subjects bought as slaves from the Sultan of Rhio. Such individuals would not usually be given this degree of attention. He made it an affair of policy. It would do as well as anything to set half a squadron on a lark.

The *Golden Grove* waited on the tide, then crossed the bar, two frigates remaining at the mouth. Only he would have risked a ship of her size up that river. He enjoyed the rediscovery of his young friend. He showed no amazement at the niche so artfully carved out but solidly approved everywhere, making a few critical suggestions. The man, Barr realized, somewhat astonished, was "on holiday." Watching Kilcane do anything—drink a cup of tea, cross a garden, disembark from a pinnace—was intriguing. On his arrival upstream, two crewmen slipped into the water and made a chair of their arms for him. All his life, he had a violent dislike of getting wet. He could not swim. He hated water, even to drink. His men deposited him gently on shore and returned to the pinnace for two large baskets. One, they would learn, contained the mechanism for watching an impending transit of Mercury; the other was a picnic hamper. He took picnic hampers everywhere. There was no campaign or action in which he took part that a picnic hamper wasn't part of the baggage of war.

He admired the great roof propped at the juncture of the river and a small stream, the beginning of Barr's astana. The tide and rains sloughed off any filth in the area so that it was always clean, and water rilled perpetually, giving a sweet hum to the air. "I might be contented here for a time," he sighed. He set up shop on the naked veranda, in a squat little folding chair of his own design. It was a peculiar gimbaled affair, and apparently he toppled backward endlessly in several prototypes before getting it right. Seeing this individual reclining in that contraption, pulling little cakes from a hamper, somehow brought all of it back to the realm of sanity. The man could make anything seem normal. There would be moments when Barr suspected the man himself had not really arrived at all, but what the Dyaks call his semanggat, his dream self, had climbed that river while the true bag of bones called Kilcane sat four hundred miles to the west on some collapsing chair. He was often reported to be in two or three places at once.

He had, he announced, been made Rear Admiral, and his real and true reason for coming across was to celebrate. His first evening ashore, he withdrew potted herring and a superior brandy from his basket, filling their cups under the stars. "To the Wajah!" he said.

"To the Admiral," Barr retorted, still numb with the apparition.

"In eight months, that's not half bad." A small paw rested on his wrist.

In the early stage of this visit, a gunboat climbed the river, the flag of the Netherlands fluttering at her stern. They watched her ignore the two ships in channel and put in handily at the stick wharf.

The Dutch. What breed are they? From what planet? They are further removed from the English than the Dyak. Who can fathom such ruddy-cheeked wholesomeness and Calvinistic depths in the same skin? They are the most inappropriate form of life ever to take up residence in the tropics. Everything about them is wrong: their clothes, their language, their religion, their food. A Dutch meal on the equator—sausage, pickles, schnapps—should kill you outright, yet they pile it in for breakfast. Their women deliver babes through withering heat and monsoon rot like rolls from an oven, and these slough off dengue fever as if it were summer complaint. They will break. But it is usually under some vague malaise of the soul. They sin with unparalleled conviction and beat themselves with a heavy theological bat the while. At the time, they were in the south, barricaded by those mountains.

"You must live with this damned cheese-eater at your back," Kilcane warned. "Be at your gwacious best."

A very large pink man drew himself out of the gunboat's companionway. He had a thick cap of blond hair, and his white shirt was set on his shoulders with the sleeves hanging empty so that he resembled a disheveled angel. He grinned at them, holding a pan in one hand, which he began beating with a spoon. The two officers on deck looked distinctly embarrassed. "Welcome, Tuan Rajah!" the angel

70

bellowed. "I apologize for my cooking pot! I've nothing else with which to greet you!"

They had heard of van Lutyens, the Resident at Pontianak, yet suspected he didn't exist. So much of the European presence in these waters didn't exist from one season to the next, sickened to death or murdered and the event marked only by silence. Van Lutyens was very much alive. He had sailed around that arm of coast to investigate the new rajah on the Sarawak River, he said, and, after noting the frigates at the mouth, to register an official protest on behalf of The Hague. Protest he did, on the spot and with great vehemence, holding his frying pan over the water and letting go with a torrent of Hollandsch. When he finished, he reverted to English. "My God, it's good to have a neighbor. Gelderbloom wrote something like you was headed my way. But he predicted I'd be making the acquaintance of a corpse, not a little rajput."

Van Lutyens was, in all but looks and appetite, "un-Dutch." He was never dour. As long as they knew him, he never wavered in his good humor or natural zest. No one, European or Malay, thought poorly of him or his large red-faced wife. Barr came to like them both enormously. For decades, the Dutch waged a spasmodic war with the tribes in the south, and these people often asked him for help. His answer was always the same. "The Dutch government is a powerful one, and in the end it will prevail. The best thing you can do is to get, as soon as possible, the most favorable terms from Tuan van Lutyens." Van Lutyens returned the favor.

In the early days, it was good to have a man like this beyond those mountains. The huge range to the south was always shrouded in clouds, looming and vanishing with weather. Sitting on the astana veranda at any hour of the day, all was serene. The broad river glinted to the north; to the west, Matang lifted its verdant face. The east fell away in soft hills. But to the south there was that range. As you traveled toward it, you traveled back in time. There was mute terror in the direction. This was dispelled in no little way by the knowledge that van Lutyens' garrison lay on the other side. On the other side of that barrier, Birgit van Lutyens, her reddish braids fastened to her nape, was bent over her vegetable patch, the leather strap of her revolver slung over her shoulder and between her big breasts. Yet one came by sea from Pontianak. Only the Dyak traveled over that range.

Van Lutyens kept them company for two days, departing for Pontianak on the dawn of the third. For a man, a Dutchman, in whose company they had spent so little time, they were oddly sad to see him go.

"You are, of course," Kilcane said one evening, stabbing at a jar of pickles, "no more secure than a tent on a beach." He said no more. He was right. There was no army, no navy, and no treasury. There was no trade to speak of. The pengirans had sucked the country dry, and the raiding tribes had done the rest. His visit created a layer of ease, but his departure was inevitable. There would once again be one ship in channel, a small one.

The Saribas and the Sakarang, the two most powerful raiding tribes, had not vanished. No one seemed more disturbed by this than Norris. He felt their presence behind the first wall of leaves, watching. They would not watch forever. He was gratified to find that Kilcane concurred. The man believed they should move against these tribes while he was with them.

Yet the thing that Barr decided to work on in those days was a revised system of weights and measures. They took it to be some sort of mental exercise, a warm-up before tackling the obvious tasks at hand. It was not. He was to work this way all his life. A revised system of measurement, the design of flower borders for imaginary promenades, an improved cookhouse smokestack often took precedence over vital campaigns. A quarter-mile riding path along the river was completed the day before the massive balleh departed for the Sut.

He may have been right to work this way. The Dyaks marveled at the straight, short road and the vicious little pony that bolted with him back and forth. They liked the curved sundal borders, the rectangular patch of lalang grass, the triangles and swirls of canna lilies. Geometry was for them the footstep of the Deity. And that parasol, an embarrassment to the rest of them, they greeted with raw delight.

He could have levitated to the roof with it, and it would have surprised none of them.

When he finished with his weights and measures, making a mess of them, he began to plan, to their great relief, for the business at hand. He turned toward it, obliterating all side vision, his concentration as fierce as with his kati-to-stone conversions. In the six weeks that followed, he and Kilcane proceeded to find and burn out these two raiding tribes with a cold and systematic fury. They destroyed strongholds in the interior first, where the local fleets were formed. These tribes were sea Dyaks under Malay leadership. They resided on different rivers and called for separate expeditions, to be led by Europeans, captained by Malays, with the main fighting force Dyak, paid with heads. When Norris reminded him of his original horror of this practice, he reasoned with him. "We must use the currency at hand," he said, "until we are strong enough to replace it." They never were, or, if they were, they never did.

The Saribas were the first to be attacked and burned out. This campaign sinks into the bog that is formed by all such expeditions. A place, a face, materializes but is soon mired in the same endless tracking through mud. The years blur it into one long journey. The balleh against this tribe was successful beyond words. The pattern was repeated, working eastward. After this, no notable encounters were made, and the campaign was considered a success. In actuality, what happened was a studied retreat. They did not know it then. They thought they were striking terror in the hearts of some aborigines. The greater proportion of the enemy was, in fact, never seen but deserted their villages and disappeared into the forest. The expedition against the Sakarang was carried off in a similar, bewilderingly successful fashion. Except for two initial skirmishes, these people, too, simply vanished. The plan was to regroup and form a seagoing balleh against the coastal raiders, but Kilcane had run out of time.

He was bitterly disappointed. Yet with these inland forays, he had bought them a few years' grace. And he was to return over and over again with his broom. Part of his mandate was to suppress piracy. If he chose to do it on this young lunatic's doorstep and, in fact, up his rivers, it was his business. His brilliant successes in the Indian Ocean gave him such leverage.

In reality, these expeditions were more than a lark. Over the years, they would become a vital source of income. Kilcane needed money badly all his life. There were a wife and daughters in London and rumors of insurmountable debt. It was the reason many talented Navy men stayed in the East. The suppression of piracy could be amazingly lucrative. By Act of Parliament, twenty pounds was awarded for every pirate taken or killed during an attack and five pounds for every "piratical person" on board the vessel at engagement. The act was designed to target West African blackbirding. Yet it was the Navy men in eastern waters who wrung it dry. Barr once confided his fear to the surgeon that this would eventually do them true damage. It was a moot point, for he would not let down such a friend.

Kilcane and his officers were in the habit of coming up to the half-finished astana in the evening. They were pleasant, cheerful guests. Mess during those short days was an odd combination of curries and shrinking contributions from the ship's stores, highlighting the impending pulling apart of their worlds.

"I'll come again to sweep your coasts," he said, on one of these last evenings, "but sooner or later you must buwy them. They can only be surpwised by wegimental attack for so long. Thank the Almighty Chwist none of them took it into his head to turn and fight, or we would not be sitting here eating this mess. Your life will be one of buying time."

Kilcane's appetites—intellectual, culinary, sexual—were fastidiously nurtured by living on the country. He was immensely curious about the Dyak and the way he functioned in his environment. He was fascinated with the importance of heads, an idea he traced, unfathomably, to the Greeks. He became intrigued with the Dyak language, which he maintained he had heard twenty-two years before in a coastal region of Madagascar. He was especially interested in their ability to fish and hunt with poisons, yet avoid poisoning themselves with the meat. Indigenous ingredients for his own stews, casseroles, and ravigotes would include all species of fish, the diminutive deer, an occasional serpent, and the fabulous thick-scented fruits growing on the riverbanks and low hills, delivered by carefully prescribed porters, all female and no older than fifteen.

During those final meals, discussions took place as to who would throw in their lot with the new enterprise. Some of Kilcane's officers expressed interest in returning after their commissions were up, and a number were as good as their word. As for their own company, while every man was given the choice of leaving, all but five stayed on. Those remaining, together with a handful of men scheduled to be released from Kilcane's squadron in a year's time, would allow Barr to begin securing one or two outlying areas with rudimentary forts. He could thus think of eliminating Jaffar.

This individual had done a remarkable job. With the exception of his own person, the river system had become a virtual vacuum of criminal activity. The power and scope of the man was astounding. The subject of Jaffar came up in those last days. They had entered that brief, leaden period before a monsoon change when the air is thick and everything hangs suspended, waiting for the great reversal of winds. It was an evening one remembered for, if nothing else, its weight. Limbs refused to move. Iron beetles bombarded the lamps.

"You can't kill a shawif," Kilcane said, apropos of nothing. "They'll be all over you." This was a disconcerting habit of his. He would course along some silent line of thought and then burst into words, assuming by some clairvoyance you had been coursing alongside. Only Barr seemed untroubled by it. The general turn of conversation took possession of the group once again, and Kilcane joined in. During a discussion of improved lateen rig, he slammed down his fork. "By God, you can send him on the haj! He hasn't gone alweady, has he?"

Barr gazed at him. "I don't give a damn whether he's gone or not. He'll go again!"

"Wight. He must go if you ask him. It's not so much a wequest as an honor. No Muslim can wefuse. It will be a *gift*. Send the wascal to Mecca. And make it clear that when he gets back, it can be no further east than Singapore."

"I can't enforce *that*!"

75

"Not now. But by the time he weturns you can. By then, you may kwis even a shawif. Of course, you must have his weplacement in the cupboard." He crossed his legs and leaned back. "What's next?"

"Revenues."

"To eat!"

A lid was lifted, disclosing something floating in a glutinous broth. He pushed back his chair and hailed a small midshipman from the stair. Within half an hour, a hamper was delivered from which he withdrew smoked eel, baked soda wafers, cheese, pickled onions, canned peaches, and a stone bottle of porto—the last of his picnic stores.

Kilcane ate with his usual appetite, but, glancing at his friend, he sat back. "You have no more idea of business than a cow a clean shirt," he said tenderly. "Get yourself an agent in London. Form a company to back you. A knighthood can be huwwied along in this way. More to the point, for no one will knight a headless man, arm yourself. This is an *island*. A well-armed gunboat is worth ten wegiments. And get yourself another ship. The antimony and the Chinese should pay for it in a year. Don't fwet about the Chinese, you'll never wing them dwy!"

He rose, then sat down, rubbing his thighs.

"One thing more. The thing neither Spwing nor Hare nor any of those others had the bwains or inclination or means to do. A thing you must do for it will give an 'air of permanence,' a key step to a pwotectowate, which will mean help even if I'm called north." He leaned forward, his eyes sparkling. "A *bwide*. An English Wanee. A titled, bwoad-hipped May or Maude or Adelaide." He glanced about. "A bit of chintz and flowis water. Babies"—he wriggled his fingers distastefully—"little wajah mudahs cweeping wound the garden, that sort of thing. Nothing café au lait, mind. Plow a bloody black hawem if you like, but wed an Englishwoman." He sat back and grinned. "I'll send some cwystal for a wedding pwesent. Ladies love cwystal. I'll send some to that maniac up the coast as well."

On All Hallows Eve, the *Golden Grove* was turned about by hawsers and they accompanied her down to the sea. She gained the estuary at noon, her gig hauling her over the bar. She loosed sail, drifted out; then the great boom surged over and she was sailing, the frigates falling in.

Those on the beach took care not to catch each other's eyes. He, too, looked forlorn. Yet forlorn because his friend was going. He and Kilcane would take outright joy in the sight of each other all their lives. If he had reflected on his position at that moment, on the absurdity of it, it might have created a vacuum in which the whole matchstick edifice would have collapsed on his head. He didn't reflect. Except for a few drunken nights, he never did. He turned and strode up the beach and heaved himself into his prahu, directing its bow upstream.

A row of anemic primrose seedlings lined the mud walk, and the Sharif Jaffar bent his elegant torso to peer into a little shoot. He straightened in the noon glare while a slave inquired within. He had been invited and had been kept waiting for twenty minutes. The man did not wilt. He seemed to take quiet interest in the things around him, in Monkhouse's carved risers, in the line of wash, a Guinean parrot in a cage. Barr waited another ten minutes, then had him waved up the stairs by a filthy cook boy.

Accustoming his eyes to the gloom, the man found he could sit nowhere but on a dirty mat. He inclined his head and remained standing.

"Last month, I made an interesting discovery," his host began, without greeting. "I discovered that my people have an inadequate supply of salt. Salt, of course, is vital to their lives. Happily, I have just now located a source, which I will make available to them cheaply. All revenues will be deposited in our treasury and used to expand our efforts against smugglers, efforts that you so effectively initiated."

Jaffar stood in silence. The dark eyes glimmered. Salt was one of his prime sources of income. He had supplied the Saribas with salt and ammunition for decades, exacting payment in slaves and raids, and Barr knew this and he knew that Barr knew it.

"Tuan Rajah," he said quietly, "there is no lack of salt. There is a reliable source."

"There is now. A second thing. For your good service to me during these past months, I have thought long on how to reward you. I have settled on what, I believe, will demonstrate my gratitude best." He leaned back, exposing both soles. "I make you a gift of the haj."

The man swayed, as if a wind had entered the room.

"As haji, you will have no need of weapons. You will forfeit your guns, your lellahs, muskets, and powder. You will disband your forces. Forces"—his voice softened—"to whom I am most grateful and whom I will personally recommend to the Dutch Resident in Banjermasin for employment."

Jaffar's face remained expressionless. Yet it seemed he was suddenly closer to the veranda doors, telescoped not so much by movement as some trick of the eye. He was said to be a magician.

"Where are you going?" Barr heard the trace of panic in his own voice.

"To obey your wish, Tuan Rajah." The man's eyes burned, and then, regarding one doorway after the other, he saw there was no way to leave. Si Tundo had placed a man at each exit.

"There is no need to trouble yourself," Barr said, in a more natural voice. "All has been brought to my house. We have collected your agents. And we have collected your sons."

It was true. He had been isolated most effectively in a short amount of time. All those loyal to him within the town had been arrested. It was Si Tundo who executed this, placing the snares and pulling them in remarkable synchrony while this man peered into bloodless little flowers. That same day, Jaffar began his journey. He was escorted by sea to Pontianak and from there on a Dutch man-of-war to Singapore, where he was not detained for a single night but placed on a westbound frigate, courtesy of Kilcane. One did not interrupt the motion of these things. It would have been easier to kill him. But killing a sharif would have turned his own Malays against him in those days. Jaffar's removal was a coup. His replacement was an act of genius.

. . .

Of all the Englishmen filtering into that territory in the early years, no one was more suited to his work than Bigelow. Bigelow served with the Madras Engineers and, while with them, stepped into a policing action by accident. Through common sense and courage, he did well with it and stayed with the work. He was shifted to Malacca and, later, Penang, where Kilcane found him. He was short, powerful, and a confirmed bachelor, from the cheap Bombay black leaf that permeated everything he owned to his unalterable biweekly visit to the same Hainanese on Water Fairy Fire Cart Lane. Bigelow didn't like change. When he found a pipe or double-bore or whore that suited, he was faithful as a bride. He was uncomplicated and competent. It was as if a solid block of Ayrsford stone had been transported through space and now existed, with equanimity, in the middle of the jungle. If he had a shortfall it was loneliness, a quality he himself never consciously identified. Occasionally he thought he was "off," but no more.

The new chief of police was quartered in a little bungalow next to the fort. His presence was betrayed, early on, by the clatter of his typograph, one of the first east of Malacca, its fury impressing the Dyaks enormously. The first task he set himself was recruiting a small force of native police. It turned out that he had a gift, despite appearances, for the inspirational touch. After the selection and rigorous drill of raw material, he personally designed the little cocked hat he had these gentlemen wear. It was made of red-dyed leather with a hornbill feather stuck in the brim, and more esprit de corps was elicited by this device over the years than by any communal bloodletting. His only requirement for his men, other than intelligence, stamina, and reputation among their own people, was height. None could be taller than five foot seven. Bigelow was five eight.

The post had been coveted by another. Sutton, the ship's master, not a man to be bitter, was bitter over this. He would have relished the work. As it was, he helped with the small number of district officers recruited by Kilcane, their briefing and assignments, but they were most often gentlemen and he was never easy in his authority. The policeman's job, carving out his own force, an extension of his own arm, should have been his. He watched Bigelow go about the work in his stolid, bull-like fashion, without finesse, without a particle of art. Yet he had to admit, over the first two years, no extraneous energy was expended. The man was not stupid and never second-guessed himself. There were ways he could have done better, ways he could have improved on a course, and when he perceived this, the master would mentally jump into the job, once or twice almost uttering advice, hanging back with acid in his gut, until one day he heard himself say to the back of that thick neck at the typograph, "Christ, Abang won't do it! He'll pretend to do it, which'll be worse; you can't send a Murut to discipline a Saribas!" Bigelow continued stabbing at the machine, then turned and looked up with an infant's gaze. "Ah, Roger, thank you, by God," he said, and with those words the two embarked on a three-decades-long friendship.

They were friends the way two bull rhinos can be friends, grunting and shoving dangerously, yet unfathomably in each other's company. Sutton was the more poetic, the more insightful. For an uncritical man, he went straight and pleasurably for Bigelow's throat, although, over the years, he would allow no one else to do this. "You know, Frank," he would say, "you've got no tact. 'Tis a serious problem unless you plan to travel wide of the gentle sex." Bigelow would rouse, but Sutton's finger shoved him in the chest wall. "You be blow and bellow and cock and no tact and no wit and not much intelligence, except to kill or save your skin." In later years, one would become deaf, and five years later, the other, and they communicated over the next ten with little notes, sitting on the constable's crooked porch, the floor littered with bits of paper. They would save common queries, comments, and insults, searching around for them on the table or at their feet. "How?" One would stoop for a paper and slam it on the other's knee. "Why?" "Wrong!" "Senile bastard." "Yes, true, true." On a rare moon they even talked of love. "A bit thin-boned," Sutton commented on the C of E's wife. "Should feed her marrow cream like Cook on the *Elizabeth Guerre.*" "Well," Bigelow said, interested, "she's a bit thin-boned, but she's a nice female little woman and he must love her pocket, for the tribe he's producing," but he said it sweetly, like a boy. They never discussed matters of policy. They both had unsettling thoughts over the years, and voicing them and agreeing only increased their unease.

Bigelow was the first white man to be recruited from the vast outside. A trickle, then an amazing stream, would follow.

The number of headwater Dyaks coming down to trade in those years gave him his deepest pleasure. He had corrals built for their livestock and extended the pasar for their up-country goods. He would stand in his dugout in the morning light and watch these shy, silent people approach from the water. The Chinese submitted a steady number of applications for commercial building sites along the river, and an influx of gold workers from the Montrado kongsi was reported. Two upriver tribes came down to wash sago, something that had never happened. The very flow of the stream seemed faster.

He rode the crest. He affected then what was to be his uniform for the rest of his life: white linen trousers and shirt, the tails loose and the whole belted with a thin kain. With his stature it was becoming, and when washed in the yellow light of that parasol he was damned impressive. A crazy confidence permeated him then, a sexually tinted zest, a charmed immunity.

His astana was completed, and, even before, life began to revolve around it. Monkhouse liked the new building. He liked the long curve of veranda, the soft rill of water. It was the first land-bound dwelling the ship's carpenter liked and, when asked to finish it within, he set about the work with originality.

It was, in fact, a handsome house, the large nipah roof resting on four whitewashed arcades. His living quarters were above and consisted of a few large, open rooms surrounded by a veranda. They remained virtually unfurnished in the early years except for a few pieces of native furniture and his charts and guns. The gentle rill and the variety of birdsong in the area kept the place pleasantly furnished. There was a library in the rear, the first room completed, empty except for a volume on tropical diseases and Laplace's *Mécanique Céleste*. A little journeyman clock, its glass encapsulating a green, living cloud, sat on a split palm table. In front was his saloon and a long narrow dining room. Here, Monkhouse spent the better part of the winter carving a shallow frieze depicting mermaids and mermen and several forms of Bornean water life. Into their outlines he rubbed a white paste, prepared by Bawhal, a cache for all sorts of recipes, that caused turtles, dugongs, sharks, and sawfish to jump out with manic life in the light of a lamp. This bestiary was a great source of amusement for the Dyaks. Monkhouse's coup, however, was a pair of life-sized crocodiles carved out of satinwood. When finished, they stood on their tails on either side of the entrance to the saloon, regarding each other with mute hilarity. Later, when the Ranee's kapok and chintz were placed about, these buayas lost their magic, their bold, happy faces taking on an aura of confusion and sadness.

He loved his house. After it was finished, he worked on diagrams for an orchard, lawns, and a scheme of footpaths bordered by jasmine and sundal and other night-blooming flowers, for he liked to walk about in the evening. Bathhouses and servants' quarters were planned nearer the river, and bungalows to be used for men on leave from the interior.

His bedroom was no more than an empty square with a large maranti bed in the middle. Like the other rooms, it had an opening between wall and ceiling to allow for air, the great overhanging roof sheltering from rain except in the northeast monsoon. The datins, the wives of the datus, had elected themselves his ceremonial housekeepers and spent much time examining and arranging the few articles of his toilet.

He had a boy in those days, a child, who took special pride in his personal effects. His name was Unggat. He was a wiry, intelligent fellow, and Barr acquired him in a singular way. The child was found after a Sakarang raid, not as one of the victims but as a member of the attacking party. He could not have been more than eight, but his father was a chief, and they often took sons on these forays, however young. The Rajah's force had come into the village just as the attackers were withdrawing, and in the confusion the boy was left behind. At first, he was grouped with the victims, but one of the women who had a daughter murdered in the raid pointed him out hysterically. They were at a loss as to what to do with him. To take him along was impossible; one might as well take home a small tiger. Yet to leave him would have meant his death. It was hoped that someone in his party would return for him, so he was left in a conspicuous spot on the riverbank. He was given a basket of food and ten scraps of paper and told to stay where he was and to throw one scrap away at each sunrise, and by the time they were gone, his people would claim him.

The boy, who was strangely unafraid, apparently did this, but no one came. On the eleventh day, he left, heading not toward the Sakarang but toward Kuching, "to return," he said, "the basket of apai rajah." Three weeks later, he materialized at the door of the astana cookhouse.

He was a wild-looking thing, given to stealing and shoved away by everybody. It was finally Njoman, the Saribas umbrella bearer, who took him in. Two more unlikely individuals than the old warrior and this child did not exist. They were fifty years apart in age and from enemy tribes. Yet Njoman, in his silence and soft movements, had the habit of the forest. While one never heard them speak, Unggat was always in Njoman's vicinity. At night he slept anywhere—the cookhouse, a godown, the kebuns' shed near the river. One morning, the Saribas waited at the bottom of the astana stair.

"Tuan Rajah," he said, "the kebuns' shed is in some seasons the house of the buaya. If he enters and finds the child, he will eat him." This was an explanation. From that night, if one peered through the cracked palm door of Njoman's hut, one could see the outline of the child against the old man's back.

Over time, Unggat was admitted to the astana itself and given work. His true employment, however, seemed to be to imitate all the forest sounds in the area and stalk and kill domestic animals. He was a fierce little spark, flashing by or dead asleep. He carried a small knife, the only servant in the household allowed to do this, and he owned a red jacket, which came from the Datin Amina, the old Datu Imam's wife. He taught the baby maias to put her arms in the sleeves of this jacket and the two would walk this way down the mud paths, the richly attired orang utan and the naked boy.

The Chinese cook threw him out of the cookhouse so savagely one morning he never went back. Instead, he was mysteriously promoted to the job of valet, keeping track of Barr's personal articles. He was immensely proud of this new work. He would recite a list of their possessions in a high singsong, his back against the wall, his kurap-infested feet sticking out, his face dwarfed by a great turban. "Eleven pairs of socks; five good guns, one small devilish one; six seluars; seventeen kains; the jumping needle box; the stone arak bottle; the hide-covered malacca stick; three topees; one iron medicine box; thirty-eight rusi jars behind the bathhouse": The song rose in triumph.

When Barr thought back on those days in later life, the early campaigns and annexations would form a morass in his brain. Yet faces would appear with brilliant clarity. Not just the important ones, the chiefs and datus, the criminals and saints, but little people, sometimes people met only once. The face of a blind man sitting on a log at Lemanak; a young nonya bent against the wind at Serikei. The face of the boy Unggat came to him like this. And with the face of Unggat came the old sour one of the Datin Amina, who made the red jacket and brought ointments for those feet. One had, from those years, not so much a story as a string of heads. He would pass from one to the next like an old penglima in his longhouse, affectionately, reverentially. He'd think first of Dawes.

Youth creams, Swatow love potions, three sizes of enameled basins, Indian double-bores, and steel scythes expanded the meager wares of the pasar pagi now that the pengirans weren't lifting off their share. A little nut had swelled and burst.

A new species of life arrived on the heels of this small show of prosperity and industry, as bizarre as the enterprise to which it was attracted. The sudden increase in Chinese made them sniff the wind. Rumors of open trade and the absence of an overriding colonial fist set them in motion. A small army trickled in, more or less one by one, consisting of the lost, the criminal, the unprincipled and free-swinging, the madly talented, and the simply mad, each with peculiar gifts if you dug through the callus and decay to look for them. Yet no individual member of this tribe was as classic as what appeared before Ramadan outside the shophouse of Heng Fo Peng touting a dubious gusi bulan.

You couldn't truly tell what form of life it was, but it had an ingratiating expression. Albert Dawes, "Peachy" to his friends, among whom were counted several thousand Kayans and a half-score fellow truants from Moreton Bay, extolled the virtues of the big blue jar to the suspicious Chinaman.

Everything about Dawes flapped, like a tent with feet. He had all sorts of things he liked to keep on his person, and it required a kind of huge shirt. He was no beauty, and he wasn't healthy. Three or four diseases gnawed at him more or less continually, although they never seemed to affect his overall progress. He had developed a way of "using them against each other," he once explained, malaria burning off the kurap, alcohol keeping parasites at bay, certain skin molds relieving depression. He was the only man ever heard to describe cholera as "a touch of the plague last spring." He did have one thing. He had beautiful eyes, blue as harebells and twinkling. Later, after he lost the one to infection, the good one, in moments of reflection, would stare at its neighbor, a cheap glass facsimile bought in Banting. His feet were covered by a reptilian skin, the only white feet known to successfully go unshod in that country.

Dawes had gone abroad at the Queen's expense, at twelve, spending the next two decades of his life in the Australian penal colony at Moreton Bay, breaking out, a tourist on that vast macabre coast, twice. He had several bones broken and mended on their own, resulting in an interesting gait. The day before his thirtieth birthday, he broke free a third time in a borrowed longboat and began the two-thousand-mile flight into that northern universe, crossing the Great Barrier shoals with twenty-seven eggs and a dying shipmate, the latter, he once confided, turning out to be fresher fare. He made astounding speed, changing boats thrice, a flying skeleton on the wind by the time he reached Timor, and a vegetarian for the rest of his life.

After an initial tendency to throw him in the brig whenever he turned up, Barr came to value the man. He was untrustworthy and had a criminal mentality, but he was a consummate diplomat and he was "kind." One finds that quality rarely and in the damnedest places. If Peachy liked you, and he liked all sorts, he did his best for you. He was niggardly with money and wildly generous with his person. He knew the country and traveled through it with the impunity of the insane. He came and went, crossing borders and river systems without the by-your-leave of any sultan, datu, or tunku. He was forever developing things, seams of gold, camphor trains, all on rivers to which he was forbidden access. He would occasionally emerge on the coast to beg a stake. On the odd chance the pieces looked like they would fall together, he'd lose interest and move on. It was not an uncommon tendency among that small brotherhood of fugitives scattered through the three thousand miles of archipelago to bail out when things were working and stick when they were not. He had side interests. One year he cornered the Chinese market on gutta-percha, the next on swallow nests. He always did a bit of trade in opium and firearms, a third of his rifles exploding on their maiden shot.

There were other facets to this man. Dawes was a fierce autodidact and natural scholar. All his life, he scratched down his observations of the interior tribes in the penmanship of a six-year-old. These descriptions were eerily complete. If someone sang a song, he wrote down all the words; if they cooked a meal, he gave all the ingredients and amounts. He described the cleverest way to pull a brain through the nostrils and named the best wood for smoking the gutted result. Once he actually published some of these "notes," after considerable editing, in the *Journal of the Indian Archipelago,* the filthy, yellowed sheets being rightly identified by a Madurese assistant editor as brilliant sociological observation. He wrote extensively on the Kayans, one of the most feared and little known tribes in the Bornean interior, and it was largely through this that the world learned of their complex culture and skill at torture and music. "No one lives with the Kayan," Si Tundo said, when he was told where Dawes had spent the winter. "Even the Kayan cannot live with the Kayan."

Barr tried to control Dawes' activities in his territory without success, so he offered employment. Dawes didn't want a job, but for twenty years he waxed in and out of service as the mood moved him. He was unruly, unpredictable, and undependable, and worth ten district officers of the highest caliber. His main value was in the remarkably accurate and timely information he provided. He never stayed in one place long enough to lose perspective. He recognized the dynamics of incipient disasters and passed them on with time to do something about them. It was Dawes who first told him of Mua Ari, the inland rajah, a mirror image of himself, residing in the Ulu Ai. "Why, the bugger's as real as your own mother! Nice chap, given to disguises. I tried to sell him some Miniés before Hari Raya but he wouldn't have them. Knows his ordnance."

"You what?" Barr was stupefied.

"Before our deep and abiding friendship, your grace." Peachy grinned.

He was the postman. The Ear. It was Dawes who'd loop off two hundred miles to check on the mental health and state of the larder of "the Infant" at Serikei; who brought news of Dickie Hogg when he passed through the Second Division, for, while that individual kept meticulous records, his reports were almost nonexistent. It was Peachy who checked on the beautiful boy dying of guilt in the Rejang, and it was he who headed off the second Saribas massacre. It was also Dawes who confirmed the existence of the priest. "Fat," he said, "with one convert, a half-grown liar. Now this, I says to myself, is a pitiful thing. So I let him baptize me. Albert. That's my name anyways."

Peachy was, after all was said and done and the crust of sin rashly or desperately committed scraped away, a good man. He possessed that peculiar morality which forms late, a version which, if it actually takes root, never measures anything. He simply had several things done to him at an early age that he decided he would do to no other human being. He thus had a roundness. He was often happy.

"You know the odd thing about Dawes," the C of E once said. "I mean above and beyond the fact that he looked and lived so damnably queer? The one thing that distinguished him from most other human life was the constancy of his happiness. And if this scuttling wreck, this rotting little bag of aches and schemes, was happy, you wondered why in hell you weren't delirious every day of your life."

It was Bigelow and Dawes who set the standard for the rest to come. Such bedrock often made the difference between a burgeoning little microcosm and a few blackened sticks in the wind. It was Dawes who suggested Barr visit Bau. The Chinese were admirable, he said, his blackest compliment.

Two little balls rolled on the silk. "Chia-kou-le." The Chinese smiled, folding up the Pen Ts'ao Shih Yi, *the supplement to the Book of Herbals. "They will do well in the Sadong basin, Tuan Rajah."*

The nutmeg trees were a gift. There were always gifts. There had been jars, a piebald horse, dwarf pears, and a twelve-year-old with circles tattooed around budding breasts.

The Chinese were his main source of revenue in the first decade. Without them, any attempt at establishing a viable entrepôt in that archipelago would fail. They were the merchants and financiers. Hordes of Hakka and Hokkien provided the only reliable labor force. They were paramount farmers and miners. They controlled the sago refineries and the gold mines.

For years before his arrival, Chinese migrations from the mainland had come in evenly spaced waves. Contingents of Teo Chew, Hokkien, Hakka, and Hainanese would appear intermittently, as if boxed and shipped by some Nan Yang P & O terminal in the sky. A few would join forces to wash gold or work antimony, and the next year there was a village, growing quietly, paying taxes.

Their largest settlement was the kongsi at Bau, the main company mining gold in the interior. It was in existence when he arrived, and its efficiency and solidarity impressed him. In addition to gold, Bau silently served as the center for a network of enterprises throughout the eastern archipelago. The most lucrative of these was opium.

He taxed them heavily from the beginning, yet he always yielded when he pushed, allowing them to open a new mine under the aegis of the old and, every now and then, to contract for a new block of shophouses in Kuching. It was, in essence, very "Chinese." They caused no trouble and were helpful when it did not subvert their own interests. The kongsi used Pontianak as its gold port and had its own invisible lines of transport, banking, and communication, which were, on occasion, made available to him.

Despite its straggling appearance, Bau was run with strict discipline. The towkay, Chan Kho, a thin, ageless man, greeted Barr with a friendly, cringing demeanor. He lived in a low sooty house with an altar table and tapers at one end. It smelled always of rotted fruit and incense.

Barr was alert to their needs and allowed them to keep their familiar customs, but forbade the most distasteful ones. Chan Kho would reply with deep assurances, followed by amnesia.

"He's an oily devil," Barr would say, in admiration. "He knows we can do nothing without his little lacquer revenue boxes." Yet he persisted in one area. "You may not buy and sell children," he warned more than once. The Chinaman assumed a tragic face, protesting that this had long since stopped. On one visit, the blatant lie made him explode.

"Nan Yang is full of Swatow and Teo Chew who will float on leaves with their shovels to mine gold here!" The momentary look of horror that passed over that yellow face was not lost on him.

"I'll be damned," he said, slamming his gunwale as they slipped into the stream. What the Chinese feared most was more Chinese. Massive immigrations, unauthorized and therefore uncontrolled by the kongsi. This threat was a weapon, and he would use it to great effect over the years.

The industry seen at Bau, their gambier and pepper farms at Siniawan, their betel nut, Indian corn, and sweet potato fields, their padis at Paku and Tegora, were impressive. A new gold mine and a recent attempt at diamond mining assured him that they would not fail because they never failed. Yet their unflagging energy, their mysterious lines of communication and organization, chilled him.

The Chinaman gazed, dead eyed, as his guest's prahu dropped downstream. "We must be watched," he said to the leaves, the air. "We are corrupt. We must serve the Dyak in the sunlight so we do not cheat him in our shops. Our junks traded here when his kind lived in caves."

Ajar

*I dream in broad daylight, riding in the Jalan Singh, of arms around my
waist, breasts against my back. The illusion persists in my tub, a dugout,
a chair. She slides naked into my lap even on my judgment seat.*

Three Englishwomen were in residence by the summer of the fifth
year, two wives and a child's nurse. The bones of a little society were
emerging. It appeared timely to think about Kilcane's advice. Yet
time passed and he seemed to make no effort to secure an agent,
much less explore the possibility of marriage. When Norris asked
him outright, having wed himself in Singapore the previous summer,
he said he didn't have a pig's idea about where to find an agent. As
for marriage, he was thinking of writing to a "cousin." He said this
offhandedly, as if he were thinking of ordering more ordnance or a
new gunboat.

"I've written to Deanstown," he volunteered that winter. "I don't
know any eligible women in England, nor do I have the time to cultivate any. My cousin is, if I recollect, an attractive, healthy widow
with one child and still of bearing age."

The surgeon said nothing.

"I can't waste time wooing some infant! Sometimes I think you've
been put on earth to torture me with that blank slate you call a face.
Raffles married a woman ten years his senior, and it brought him

advancement, children, and the love of his life!" It went no further than this. He would miss Norris deeply, the man spending less and less time in Borneo as the years passed, his wife unwilling to reside there.

Except for his widening circuits up-country, life began to take on an almost colonial hue. Up at five, canter the little bajau down the river path and back, after which the animal had to be hand-cooled for an hour; two hours of work; breakfast; the bureau and courthouse in the afternoon; dinner; cheroot; work; bed. On some evenings, he invited a Resident on leave or a local nakodah to dine. The Nakodah Dullah was a welcome guest. He was the wealthiest merchant in Kuching: fat, amiable, omniscient. He knew the black trade intimately and fed on every link. He started his fortune by faking ancient Chinese jars, rubbing them with sand and tapping them with hammers, selling them to the Dyak at outrageous profit. The Dyak valued old porcelain above all other possessions, counting his wealth in jars. A coral and cream gusi tuak, part of the dawn sky, cured infection and soothed the mad for decades in the Ulu Ai. A gusi bulan commanded the price of eight slaves. Dullah's negotiations were always conducted well up-country. "I take care of my traders," he would say, when one of the wretches he employed up some remote stream was hacked to pieces, "far better than your great Company, which sends children out to do its work. Pardon me, Tuan Rajah, but this is so. Two-thirds of those little chaps dying. An English boy in his hut, a little boxwallah dying of fever and his dear mother not knowing. Unnecessary sorrow!" Barr enjoyed this entertaining crook and frequently dined with him, as well as other nakodahs from more distant parts, men who often would be identified as enemies on the high seas.

Other evenings, he labored over a Dyak vocabulary compilation and maps of the interior with Sutton. He had started schemes for European investment, and correspondence with London had produced one or two responses. In between, he wrote letters dissuading various missionary societies from sending representatives. When he took up his lamp, a heavy-thighed Melanau awaited in his bed. He stayed clear of Malays and aristocratic natives. Before the Melanau, there had been a Kelabit, who slithered through the house like a pretty serpent, and before her a

Murut with a regal walk, and a Dusun with nothing save a musical laugh. He seemed to be constructing an ideal in pieces.

Part of his week was spent in the tiny courthouse on the opposite bank. The datus had instituted a simple system of justice with him at its head, but for most cases they presided alone. Some things he did not address. Slavery was endemic and vital to the economy, and he did not interfere except in cases of violent abuse. He forbade the taking of heads. He forbade it being done privately, while his ballehs for decades were paid for solely by the opportunity to take heads. Yet the distinction was made and kept. If anyone took it on himself to sever a head on his own, he was subject to severe punishment—for a chief, death. This was not true for simple murder or "change of life." A man could kill for a variety of reasons and still be a good man.

There was one instance in the early years in which the ruling on heads was imaginatively challenged. It was said the Orang Kaya di Gadong, a chief of the Saribas, had ordered heads taken. Dawes, abiding in the area, confirmed this. Barr summoned the chief to Kuching. He was an old man with elephantiasis in his legs, and it took him several weeks to arrive, carried by his sons.

"Selamat," Barr said brusquely. "You have come."

"Yes, Tuan." The old man was supported by a lean square-shouldered youth. "I heard that you sought me."

"Do you know why I have called you?"

"My sons say it is about the Sakarang heads, but I wait for you to speak."

"You ordered the taking of heads when I forbade it. You know the punishment," he said.

It was the young man who responded, in a quiet voice. "Tuan Dawes says, across the sea, men kill our brother dog and hang his head within their houses. Tuan Dawes says in Java there is a white man who collects the heads of the maias, who harm no man but travel through the forests quietly and care wonderfully well for their children. My father ordered the heads of two men who killed his wife and small daughter."

Barr gazed at this youth who stood like stone. It was not so much the argument but the force of its presentation that gave it odd weight.

He rose heavily. "Old man, for not coming to me to settle this difficulty, for trying to come to an arrangement out of my sight and taking heads, you lose one half of all your jars." The Orang Kaya made as if to speak, but his son turned him away. Barr was said, on that day, to have tempered justice with hati baik, good heart. The youth was named Jawing, and in later years he would be much sought after by the regime for his prowess as a tracker.

Grievances of the weak against the strong were often not brought to court at all. From the beginning, these people had taken to standing in the shadows of his veranda at dusk. They would wait silently until he finished his dinner and lit a cheroot. The cigar became the signal for them to shuffle forward out of the darkness and take their turn murmuring into his ear. He encouraged this communication and, through it, gained information that often would have come to him in no other way.

Increasing signs of commerce and reliable revenues from the Chinese set the enterprise on a course of expanding dreams. Then something happened. It was not a gradual thing, a slow withering away, something he always feared. One morning, all traffic on the river vanished. The pasar and alleys emptied of life. The place fell under a pall, as before some natural disaster.

Si Tundo sent men downstream and by evening confirmed what had crossed the bar. The little fort was put on alert and the ship's cannon were trained downstream. Shortly after dawn, eighteen Lanun war prahus swept upriver to the deep pulse of gongs. This daylight visitation amazed any who dared to look. It was assumed to be an advance party for a larger force at the estuary, yet no other vessels had been sighted.

In effect, these men, all Lanun of the first rank, had done a remarkable thing. They had taken care to balance his strength, neither threatening by sweeping up in too large numbers nor drawing attack by appearing with too few. They thus created something unique: a fragment of time during which they could converse.

These were splendid vessels, ninety feet in length, double-tiered and armored in sheet lead. The Lanun were from Lanun Bay in Mindanao and the islands to the north. Their squadrons were powered by sail and slave oar. Their officers were lean, athletic men who wore chain-mail vests and carried the long kampilan. They had been cruising for eight months, they said, and would be glad to get home. Some of their vessels had been taken from the Bugis. They confirmed that they started down the east coast with the northeast monsoon, returning home by the southwest winds, a two-thousand-mile circuit. They spoke politely from their decks, answering all questions put to them, and might have been sharing clever ways to braid a hawser or caulk timber. Yet a glance into the oar slits, and those miserable eyes within reset one's bearing.

As formidable as these vessels were, they were not easily maneuverable and, Barr realized, could not possibly stand the ramming of a screw steamer in shoals. He noted with even more interest that these men smoked opium, revealing a huge untaxed market undoubtedly supplied by the Chinese.

He liked them. He liked their fierce appearance and their courteous speech, their shields covered with small rings, which chinged in a sensual rhythm as they walked. He liked their forthright approach to conversation. When he showed an interest in their flagship, he was invited to board. Despite warning looks from his own men, he deposited his revolver with an officer and passed to the deck.

Beneath a canopy, an elderly man sat on a raised platform within sight of the double bank of oars. He was introduced as a senior lieutenant, and he greeted Barr politely, with a touch of amusement in his black eyes. He was dressed in a plaid sarong and mail fighting jacket, though his fighting years were long over. His features were pleasant and sharper than the Malay.

In retrospect, Barr felt he asked imbecilic questions, yet they proved to elicit an astounding amount of information.

"Yes, I enjoy pirating," the old man said in remarkable English. "It is the only ennobling trade left." He laughed at his guest's astonishment. "I speak *hollandsch* as well, Tuan Rajah, and *espagnol*. We have met your brothers, verily we have made their acquaintance.

"Do you know, Tuan Besar, who made the pirate?" He leaned forward, his eyes dancing. "Not Allah, my goodness, no. Not the devil.

You made the pirate"—he sat back, a shadow passing over his face—"and you made him of our best men. We traded freely with the Chinese for two thousand years. A pleasant arrangement, and good for both. Your brothers do not approve. They forbid the Chinese to trade with us." His fingers took up a small leaf and placed in it a drop of sirih.

"Have you ever seen a green sea of pepper?" He folded the leaf into a neat little packet and offered it delicately. "It is very marvelous to the eyes. When burning, it makes a great wall of black smoke stretching for miles on the sea. This too is marvelous, unless you are the grower of pepper. Your brother Hollandsch burns the pepper and spices his ships cannot hold. He forbids trade in opium, pepper, and spices under pain of death, and, to his credit, he does what he says. In Java, in Kalimantaan, our ships may sail only from ports where there is a *hollandsch* penglima. Junks may come into Batavia and Banjermasin alone. Our people cannot pay this double carriage. Our boats return with their cargo, and in that year our children starve." He helped himself to sirih. "We were good traders, Tuan Rajah, and now we try, with Allah's blessing, to be good pirates."

Every question he asked on that deck that day received an answer. He inquired about their vessels, how they could navigate so successfully through straits and in shoal water, and the old man called for rudders. Hundreds of islets and villages were delineated that were never known to exist. He asked about some strange little loops, and it was explained that these marked the habitual routes of the new steamers.

"Why do you tell me this?" he asked finally, flabbergasted not only that such information would be shared but that someone of his rank had the authority to do it.

"Because you ask, Tuan Rajah." The old man smiled. "And someday, we too may have a question and we will ask it of you."

He was strangely moved. "You have done me a courtesy this day," he said. "We are not friends, but I wish that we may meet like this again."

The Lanun regarded him candidly, then turned to where his fleet was coming about in the stream. "I am old," he sighed. "An old man wishes many things. I wish for less pain in my bones, for the strength to plant more sons. I wish to grow rambutans by my door and to fall asleep in the shade with other old men. It will not be. But I wished to see the Inggris rajah, and him I have seen!" At this point, an officer approached and placed his forehead to the deck. He spoke one or two words, and the old man answered. The command was, upon regaining the estuary, to remove the left hand of five men whose boat had pulled too slowly in their display upstream.

At dusk, these visitors took one long look at the *Carolina*'s guns and proceeded downstream. It was the strangest naval review ever witnessed. For a long time afterward, he found himself half wishing for the company of that terrible old man. He would not meet the laksamana of the Lanuns again, although he would be in killing range of his sons at Batang Maru. The English would come close, a capture undone, at the last, by "guilelessness." An old man would be interrogated three years later at Bata Run, caught with other piratical persons by the frigate *Io.*

"My God," the lieutenant of the *Brest* cried when the other one, the freckled one, volunteered the story in the P & O bar. They had stumbled upon the great prahu with three others in shoals at Bata Run. They killed half and interrogated the rest. "What is your place at sea, old man?" the mate asked. "Cook? Priest? Sail mender?" "Laksamana," the man said, a quiet face, light slipping in and out of the eyes, and the freckled officer, the man who would carry the moment into eternity, put him with the rest, the flotsam to be traded, dutifully making the switch at Changi, so much garbage cast off and two British officers and four crew ransomed from the dead. "Laksamana"—the lieutenant of the *Brest* rammed his forefinger into the greasy Inggris–Blanda–Melajoe dictionary atop the copper bar—"a Sanskrit word meaning admiral."

The Rajah Laut with his English fleet could now be drawn into those waters on a string, and the Lanun had met the man who held the string. Their visit and departure, without the horrendous wake anticipated, did as much to increase his stature in those years as Kilcane had done.

In November the monsoon changes, and there begins a fortnight of raging wet winds. Water seeps everywhere. It is a time when people sit quietly and wait for the worst to pass. One evening during this unsettled time, he and Norris smoked, their lamp surrounded by blackness, when Si Tundo was announced. The man entered silently with a strange look on his face and placed a small bundle on the floor.

Barr gazed at him quizzically, then stooped and unwrapped the thing, revealing a melded piece of metal the size of a fist. He turned it round offhandedly, then went pale. Just visible were vestiges of a figure, stretched and distorted, an ape embracing itself.

"How?" he asked hollowly.

"By fire, Tuan Rajah," the man replied, tears glistening. With a quiet voice he told how they had murdered Selladin. The brothers had been scattered at night under their separate roofs. The signal, it was said, had been given by Hassan. Two hundred men pulled silently in the darkness, moving against all at once. Selladin and two of his men were caught at the entrance to his house.

Barr stared at the lump of steel. "How did you get this?"

"A slave. The boy escaped. He is a child and was afraid. He hid among his people on the Suai, then worked his way down the coast."

"Is there no one left?"

"I think not, Tuan Besar."

"Are you certain? No babe? No one?"

"The Dayang Ajar was not found. It is said that the Pengiran Selladin placed her to sea. Yet I do not think this is so, for there was no warning." Tears streamed down his face.

The boy repeated what Si Tundo said: He was with his prince on that night when his followers were cut down. Selladin fought until his shoulder was opened so that his right arm could not move. He was still able to fall back to the house and bar the door. The boy said he bade him bring a keg of powder and crack the head, and with his one good arm he strewed the powder around himself. He placed the child through a small opening in the floor to pass into the water. The boy swam thirty yards and heard the explosion.

Mudah Aziz escaped, wounded, across the river. He tried to barter for his life but, when he found it was useless, put a pistol in his mouth. All the brothers and their families, save Hassan, ceased to exist that night.

The time of this massacre, the description of it written in his own hand, rests in that lead box. He wrote that he never betrayed a man before and it made him want to sleep. When he slept, he dreamed. He looked up from his bed and a figure stood barefoot on the floor, head high, a lewd smile on her lips. He pulled her to him and she came. *I am base,* he wrote.

Runners were sent to Lundu, Sibu, and the new fort at Semunjan. Strange sharifs and tunkus had slipped into the territory. Brunei had been quietly fomenting rebellion for some time. Kuching was forti- fied, and he sent word by rapid prahu to Singapore and from there to Malacca. Kilcane was in Madras, but he had given him discreet prior- ity and this was honored by the temporary command, a youngster named Dylan.

The *Phlegathon,* a steam-powered warship, slipped her monstrous nose into the Muaratebas entrance six weeks later. He could not fathom how he warranted her. He assumed it was a mistake, a mis- take that would cost his friend dearly. She was no mistake. With her came a dispatch announcing his appointment as Her Majesty's con- fidential agent in Borneo. It was in this capacity that the ship was placed at his temporary disposal. The look on Dylan's face as he delivered the message was one he would recall soothingly for years, recall as a turning point, not the appointment, the paper, but the look on that young face, transforming him from a fortune-hunting buffoon into a legitimate authority. They sailed together, visiting neighboring estuaries and finally Brunei. There they invited the Sul- tan to forfeit the offshore island of Labuan for attacking the ship, a single discharge from an old lellah missing the *Phlegathon* by fifty yards and embedding itself in the chest of a child on shore. This was agreed to, and Barr's sovereign rights were reconfirmed in perpetuity.

In Brunei, he did his best to find any surviving relatives of Mudah Aziz and his brothers, interviewing all important Malays himself. There was no one.

Strings lashed about made no sense, human shapes hanging in the air, enticing evil antus to one's home. Why not spread them on dry rocks close to the stream where they were washed? Nothing about these people made sense.

The Datin Amina bent to avoid the damp garments, passing beneath with a slave child. The wah-wahs heralded dawn as they approached the astana stair. She hoped they would wake him and she would not have to wait, as others rose about her. She settled on a lower step, her scarf over half her face.

Neither she nor the wah-wahs had to wake him, for at that moment Barr walked up the path from his bathhouse, a sheet around his shoulders.

"Selamat pagi, Tuan Rajah," she said, rising. He was momentarily startled by her grace, given her age. Though she smiled, her voice was strained.

"Selamat, Siti Amina."

"The Dayang Ajar al Selladin has come," she said abruptly. "She asks your protection as friend to her dead husband."

He gazed at her. He pulled the bath sheet to his face and turned away. He stayed in this position so long, she wondered if he had heard her.

The change in him in the days that followed was absurd. He dashed around; he didn't walk anywhere. He'd disappear and reappear in fresh clothes. He filled the house with flowers, then ordered them all removed. At one point, his hair bore the stiff gleam of Goa pomade.

She did not come. There was, of course, no way she could have come under his roof. She was invited to stay in the house of the Datu Imam within his small kampong upstream. These people had no choice but to offer her shelter, yet she was not welcome. Such a person had marked blood and belonged nowhere. How she made her way upriver and who it was that brought her were not made known to the Datu. She appeared one morning, a month after the Lanun, between the little spirit house and the bank, with two slaves.

> *Of all the people I came to know in that country,* Norris wrote, *I could never place this woman. She was too haughty, too strong for a Muslim woman, and even less resembled the memsahibs who were to take over in years to come. Physically, she was not truly beautiful. What beauty she had resided more in her movement, sound, and fragrance. She had an arresting carriage. She moved as if wading hip deep through water, her head high. He may have been first attracted to this remarkable bearing. One could wonder why he didn't stay with this. As Ranee, she would have helped him keep that tangle of forts and rivers together. She was capable. It became clear there was little of which she was not capable.*

Ajar had a melodious voice, from soft, deep gurgles to jarring stilettos when scolding a kebun or syce. The other thing was fragrance. It seemed fragrant things always surrounded her. The cottage at Na existed not so much as a place but as the sounds and fragrance surrounding the Dayang Ajar. She was an excellent swimmer, something rare among Malays. And she carried a kris, not an ornamental one but a well-made blade, in the folds of her sarong. When the surgeon asked once why she went armed, she said it was not unusual.

She said the special guard of the sultans of the Majapahit had been comprised solely of women.

"What did the men do?" he asked.

"I do not know." She smiled, looking at the notebooks in his leather sling. "Perhaps they were clerks."

She spoke freely if you addressed her but rarely initiated a conversation. Barr once asked her, in a black hour, of the trustworthiness of Si Tundo. "Do you know this boat, your Bujang Brani?" she said. "This boat is very beautiful, as if made by a goddess. It was made for the young son of Si Tundo. The Pengiran Hassan, who cannot swim and does not like boats, saw this one and liked it well enough. He marked the bow with his kris—two short cuts—which meant it was admired by this pengiran and therefore must be delivered up to him in two days' time. The boy was killed at Siniawan. Si Tundo retrieved the boat and made it a gift to you. It is a gift of the heart. You need never fear this man."

She told him other things, imparting anecdotes and information with a winning grace. She was brilliant and sensual, and it would seem her affection for him was real. Yet there was something uncertain about her, gliding with her. A Muslim woman in her position was removed from the world. Yet in those early years, some of the most vital pieces of information he received were supplied by Ajar.

There was a time when great shipments of tea were being directed to the Lanun by the kongsi. "What in hell do they do with it?" he asked. "They don't drink it!"

"They drop it in the sea," she said. "When the Lanun ask for tea, they prepare for war. It is the chests they want. The lead-lined tea chests. Out of these they make the armor for their ships." With two desperately needed gunboats waiting in Singapore unpaid for, she put it in his head to tax the Chinese on the tea they sold for the lead chests. And for the chests. And then she counseled to wait six months for their blood to cool, and to extract five times the opium revenue he had been receiving. "You tax nothing," she said disdainfully. "Bau supplies opium to the Lanun, but also to the Balagnini and the Bajau. You must tax the double carriage, and then again for the trouble."

"You'll turn me into a bloody pengiran," he said, and she heard the coldness and instantly softened. She'd slip from harpy to queen to child with the ease of a witch.

He told the datus he could not guarantee her safety upriver and sent for her. Two months after her arrival, she floated down the river and came to reside in Kuching.

He went a little mad. Buoyant, remote, garrulous by turns. It was not clear if he loved her. Could one love a species so different? Yet his feelings were deep and all-consuming. He ensconced her as an avatar, an exotic focus of all his yearnings.

He had them build a little pavilion near the brook that ran north of the house, and here she vanished to the outer eye. In the evening, however, after the business of the cheroot, he would step onto his veranda and she would be standing there. She would place her hand on his arm and walk with him in the night air.

While she did not live under his roof, her influence soon permeated the entire household. Things were always being done to please her, and she always expressed her gratitude, although this was met with silence and strained faces. Sharp words passed in the cookhouse, and meals became suddenly superb. Wonderful fish appeared, perfectly prepared: pomfret, barbel, sole, mullet, crabs, prawns, oysters, turtle grilled lightly by a Madurese she had placed in the little smoking shack. Lim, his Chinese cook, retreated silently. Roots and stalks never seen before were served, delicately seasoned. Sweet black-rice puddings appeared with great frequency because he liked them, but whatever was uneaten was immediately thrown away, for this confection, she warned, turned poisonous within hours. Over months, the astana servants, the amahs and kebuns, the jagas and syces, were replaced by people of her choosing—silent, subservient shadows.

The only member of the household over whom she held no sway was Unggat. He encouraged the child's wild spirit, and she recognized this and let him be. Yet, over time, Unggat too fell under her spell.

Barr came upon the boy one day, sitting perfectly still behind the doorway of the two wooden buayas. He had never seen the child immobile and asked if he was sick. "They talk to each other, Tuan

Rajah," the boy whispered. "The buayas. They tell jokes to each other and laugh, but only when no one is here."

"Who told you this?" He smiled.

"The Dayang Ajar al Selladin."

He took hold of the stick shoulder and jerked him up roughly. "*The Dayang Ajar,* simply this," he said.

In those months, a small kromang was installed under a lean-to against an outer wall, and in the evenings the little gongs melded with the rill of the stream. Flowers appeared in all the rooms, floating without their stems. She took an interest in the garden, especially in the English flowers whose shoots had come on the new mail packet. She showed the kebuns how to coax them into growth, and under her guidance they met with surprising success. Yet her methods were brutal. One day Unggat, who had picked a few anemic stalks of larkspur, walked around until nightfall with his hands wrapped in his sarong for she had threatened them all with loss of both hands if one seedling died.

On Barr's suggestion, a garden was begun beside her pavilion. The area had been the site of an old Muslim cemetery, and, once the earth was broken, bones worked their way up during the rains. The kebuns were sickened by this, for nothing came forth in that place except it was called forth.

Having her there was a consummate mistake. It was easy enough to keep his Muruts or Melanaus or a low-born Malay, and to couple with as many as he wished on circuits. But the Dayang was a noblewoman, widow of a pengiran. It was the Datu Imam who firmly warned him. And so he built the cottage at Na. It was at Na that Ajar came into her own.

In the house of the sumur gamelan, orchids grow inside the walls. It sits on a spur of Na, sloping eleven hundred feet to the river and plains below. Here the air is cool and pure. The vista is of distant mountains, forests, and, here and there, a gleaming strip of river.

One traveled nine kelongs upriver to Lida Tanah, a small landing place on a branch stream. A little Malay house stood at this juncture. After disembarking, one passed through several hundred acres of Chinese gambier and sweet potatoes. Halfway up the mountain the trees became immense, branching only at the top, the ground clear. Because of its position and the forbidding aura surrounding high places, Na, even in the earliest days, was considered secure.

The cottage was reached by a succession of little ladders and bridges. It was constructed on a cascading brook and was called the sumur gamelan, or musical spring. Water flowed beneath rocks and emptied into natural pools below, the whole like entering the abode of a water nymph. Antus, Dyak spirits, dwell near falling water and she, like most Muslims who did and did not believe, propitiated them with miniature houses placed on poles and filled with fruit. These spirit houses drew birds, and the area was full of birdsong. It was a queer place, its serenity regularly interrupted by violent atmospheric displays. Thunder would roll up the valley in the afternoon, and one could watch sheet lightning below. He once told Norris that he knew, even as a boy, this place waited for him, a place where weather revolved crazily and a beautiful woman soothed him to sleep.

While Ajar's hand was in evidence at the astana, Na radiated her presence. It was hers as the realm of a sorceress is hers. As soon as her foot touched the mud floor of the cookhouse, pans were said to slide to her hand, knives quickly chopped everything placed before them, meat turned itself on the brazier.

Superb ikat weaving covered the interior walls. Mirrors, large and small, some mere slivers, were placed everywhere, so that you repeatedly found yourself turning a corner and meeting yourself. At first, tiny birds like dragonflies would fly inside and thrash their reflections, leaving small iridescent corpses on the floor. He complained about this, and the next time arrived to find all the mirrors equipped with little doors. In the morning, when he opened one of these to shave, he met his reflection through a vague luminescence of wings.

"They imprint their souls," she explained offhandedly.

In the whole place, there was only one ugly note. At the entrance were two dull brown jars about eighteen inches high. Both were filthy and one was cracked. He once asked her why she didn't find something nicer for so conspicuous a place.

"These are *gusi*!" she said in genuine shock. "They have great power. Certain ones heal sickness. The witch Farida has gusi that anything placed in them overnight will double by morning."

"Well, by God"—he laughed—"let's fill them with gold bars."

"These are different," she said coldly. "These are gusi tuak. They speak."

He never heard them speak. Once, he leaned over a mildewed lip, but all he detected was a sickening stench. The kebuns crawled in their presence. The Dyaks did not value them.

Over the years, he brought guests to this retreat. Each, in his own way, cherished his time there. At Na, you lived a life, for a few days or weeks, totally unlike that lived at lower altitudes. You read, swam, played chess, breathed in the cool pure air, and talked of things you had not realized occupied the remotest corner of your brain. Conversations were often strange. No one stayed within his sphere. Hogg, the warrior, expounded on a tender form of pantheism; the priest, on wit; tight, perfect Lytton, on sex.

When there were guests, Ajar was rarely seen. Once or twice, in the evening, she passed through a room where they sat. She had, by then, discarded her widow's weeds and wore the kain-di gerus, a luminous Bugis cloth. She'd pass through like a candle in a dark room and disappear, and they were once more three or four mortal men sitting on rattan chairs. "Circe," Dolan said once, watching her vanish.

She swam in distant pools, her voice was heard outdoors, in the cookhouse, but that was all. In the evening, he retired early. In the mornings, there was an ease, a languor about him that was not present in Kuching, but to call it happiness would be perhaps to go too far.

All those who spent time in that place were aware that it was not the hideaway of a mistress or concubine but the realm of a ranee.

"Ah, the Dayang," Fitzhugh once remarked. "She was his little general, his Nur Mahal, worth as much as Dawes in the beginning." Barr himself may have found this out by accident, one day mentioning a nagging problem to her and finding, a few weeks later, it had resolved itself. He would bless his good fortune. Months later, he may have mentioned another cloying annoyance; perhaps he didn't mention it, but it kept him from sleep and she inquired as to the reason, she was solicitous of his health. Again it dissipated, and so he persisted, over time, never quite acknowledging the cause-and-effect relationship until he literally came to depend on her. Dian, a Kayan chief, a thorn in his side for a painful eleven months, suddenly fell dead into a bowl of broth. His eldest son "went away," and the Gat tributary was cleared for annexation. He depended on her and then, vaguely, over time, began to distrust her. But, and this is the queer thing, in all those years he never asked. He very much liked going to Na, the mystery surrounding the extent of her power serving perhaps as an aphrodisiac.

"The cousin," during that time, had become a joke. Yet his correspondence with the woman continued. It was the way he got by, for he would never, even inwardly, ignore advice from Kilcane. When asked by a European—or the one man of God who managed to wedge himself in-country—if he planned to marry, he would allude to this mythic creature.

In the running assessment of the humanity trickling into his territory in those years, nothing seemed so utterly useless to him as the clergy. Men appeared as stones, something to be judged, hefted, and set into place. Even useless shapes, undersized, could be rammed somewhere. Sometimes one hit a bonanza, as with the huge well-fitted boulder of Bigelow or the awkward, dangerous, but amazingly useful flint of Dawes. Proponents of the Word fit nowhere. He referred to Kuching's one man of God in those years as "that ass with his cow," and Semple was aware of it. Despite his vehemently discouraging any missionary inquiries, Semple and his wife arrived under the auspices of the Christian Knowledge Society of Madras with a trunkload of cheap Indian Bibles. The only other ecclesiastical presence in-country was said to be an Italian priest, reputed to be somewhere in the mountains to the southwest.

From the beginning, Semple displayed a keen interest in the moral health of the four Residents. He climbed the astana stairs a month after his arrival and announced his success at convincing Cakebread, the Resident at Banting, to marry the Dyak woman he had been living with for three years and with whom he had two children. "It sets a good example," he said. "Now in this case I cannot marry by banns as I ought and, not being a surrogate, I must marry them upon your good license, sir."

Barr was staring into a pail of fish left on the stair by the cook. He pulled out a red, muscular tail. "Have some ikan merah, Semple."

"Thank you, no."

He let it slosh back and stood up. "My district officers are forbidden to marry during the first ten years of service. Kindly undo what mischief you have done."

Semple backed off but did not retire. Over the ensuing months, he increased his proselytizing among the Malays. This made for much misery, for these people did not wish to reject the Rajah's priest.

Barr invited him to tea. "I allow no missionary to meddle with my Muslim subjects." He did not lift the pot. The man was not foolhardy. He withdrew to the higher ground of Sunday matins and evensong for the small European community and bided his time.

If Barr didn't like Semple, he loathed Delia Semple, a great, fawning slug of a woman. She greeted him always, in the pasar or padang, with displays of deference and maternal solicitude.

"We have gathered a group of native women for embroidery and Bible study," she said one day in the Jalan Singh. "Perhaps your little Dayang would like to come downstream and join them. These girls are so naturally talented."

He was dumbstruck. He had no idea Semple or anyone like him had knowledge of Na. He grunted and brushed past, knocking her wide bonnet awry.

The Semples could not be dislodged. Arthur Semple employed the barnacle glue of faith to astounding effect. The extolations and threats from that rickety pulpit had already set hooks into a dozen simple hearts, including that of the head fortman and poor Scithers. The only way to flux him out, Barr decided, was to replace him. He set his jaw and rewrote his latest denial, one to the Society for the Propagation of the Gospel in Foreign Parts.

This particular petition had included the application of one David Martin Dolan, Calcutta See, Anglican clergyman and medical doctor. Two professions invariably meant some dunce was inept at both, but since there was no physician, with Norris in Singapore, he took the chance.

"How in hell do these leeches sniff you out?" he asked, and Dawes, who sometimes passed through to the Apo Kayan at the start of winter and was now perched on the veranda rail like a damaged jackdaw, swung his head in wonder. Barr rose as the packet entered the reach. "We must pick up the boob and be pleasant." They watched her churn up mud, her transom dragging dangerously as she swung in. No one got off but Lavransson, the captain, a Tamil with the mailbags, and a dismal-looking trader—a large unshaven man with a big roll and rifle case. A handful of this type combed the reaches of the archipelago, usually truants from Australia's penal colonies. They'd drift ashore and drift out again, often with a theft, a corpse, or a new human being in their wake. It was Bigelow's habit to truss them up before both feet touched mud, offering accommodations at the fort and outward passage on the same vessel.

"Club mate, Peachy?" Barr asked. "Let Bigelow know what's come up."

An hour later, Monkhouse and Scithers came upon this same individual sitting in the middle of the river road, drinking water from a coconut. He smiled up at them. He said his name was Dolan.

"Dolan," he said, as if it were some happy signal. They regarded him. He lumbered up and bent over the roll, rummaging around, finally withdrawing a limp piece of white cloth, which he slung around his neck. Bone rasps, saws, and ball scoops glittered at his feet.

"Caw," Scithers said. The crates sinking the aft quarter of the packet were the property of one Mrs. Dolan and contained crockery, pots, pans, chairs, bureaus, linens, and a cast-iron field stove.

Dolan was big, not just tall but well-muscled and larded with an uncommonly positive disposition. He was to spend the next three decades in Kuching as clergyman and much-needed physician. He was not much of a clergyman, he had the unfortunate habit of always seeing the sinner's point of view, but he was a decent physician. The dual professions were the result of love. Dolan had twisted his whole life around for the woman he married.

Maureen Flaherty had vowed to marry only a clergyman, and Dolan, mad with love, screwed himself into the shape of a man of God. She was a pitifully thin young woman with an almost pretty face. Her glory was her hair, deep red with translucent rainbow glints. One could not help but wonder how a man like Dolan made love to such a stick. Yet he did. And whenever he could, it would seem, because Mrs. Dolan was always pregnant and even then, if she waddled out from the cookhouse or across the veranda of their tiny vicarage, his eyes followed her appreciatively. It was a source of amusement to the rest.

Mrs. Dolan arrived three months after Dolan on a Company frigate, big with their first child, having given him time to build a little nest. He was waiting at the dock and, after embracing her with embarrassing tenderness, propped her in a sago barrow atop all her rug bags and pushed her, a man transporting his weight in rubies, from the landing to the courthouse, where they had been allotted two rooms until a bungalow could be constructed behind the Chinese. She sat atop her mountain, a little *mater eterna,* giving high, clipped orders all the way.

"Shut up and get down, darling," he said when they arrived. "T'isn't a proper home, but I'll do my best to give you one before the year is out."

Dolan always did his best, and his best was damned nigh wonderful. He couldn't cook, that he made a mess of, but he was amazingly competent at just about everything else. He was a good companion hunting and a superb shot. And he was a decent hand with a boat. He had spent six years at sea, and he never forgot this first love. He had four dogs, and he named them Spanker, Pusher, Crossjack, and Jib, after sails on a bark. A fifth, the great yellow animal Rejang, came later.

The Dolans were his first legitimate "family," an event he would look back on as a small, bright christening.

Kandjeng-Tuan

When one thinks of them, one thinks of Reventlow, the picture of Reventlow behind the foot-thick wall at Betong, naked in the sweltering heat, a shaft of light through the gunport illuminating the long muscles, the sex purple against his thigh, Martini under his knee. Dead, yet not dead, just dead asleep after three nights of raids, eyes opening, asking for a drink, drinking it, expressing thanks, never waking.

The *Jared Heath*, a native-built sailing gunboat, rounded the cape in heavy swells to search for the packet. A ship had been sighted. Barr was often aboard on these excursions, anxious for a response from possible agents. They cast eyes for the overgunned tub but, instead, sighted a man-of-war on a bead for the estuary, a bobbing little cork in her wake.

"Only one man sails like that." He laughed. "The flash! Cracking everything on but the bed linen!"

It was the *Golden Grove*'s fourth crossing. The gunboat careened in as she entered green water, dropping sail, the yellow payong shooting up, almost whipped away.

"If you insist on using that thing," Kilcane bawled from his fore-deck, "Her Majesty will stick you behind those black wajahs at one of her levees, and you'll deserve it!" He gamboled aft. "I have a pwesent!"

"What is it?"

"A phenomenon of science!" It was a little steam-driven gunboat. She had a paddle wheel on each side, looking somewhat like a duck, and over the years was to cause more problems than any other vessel in service. In the lightest chop she'd lift a foot, but was worth her weight for intimidation. "Take care of her," he warned. "If they capture a steamer, even this wee one, who knows what they could not do. They are by far the better seamen."

It had been two years since his last visit. These brief sojourns were almost always unannounced, squeezed between campaigns and a source of joy. In the early years they were invaluable, reducing the possibility of coastal raids for a considerable span. Kilcane poked around like a boy, lifting every lid. He was delighted with what he found. He was delighted with the heavier Chinese revenues and with Brunei's continuing passivity. He was delighted with the number of junks and trading prahus in channel, and with the increase in interior tribes coming down to trade. He was delighted with the tidy line of district officers' bungalows and the primrose walk and Bigelow's tough little brigade. He was especially pleased with the continuance of "open house" at the lighting of the cigar. He had, he said, six weeks and he planned to enjoy himself.

"Who is she?" he asked on one of their first evenings. He was seated in the newest version of his chair, which had little brocade arm sleeves. "This black cweature you've installed upstweam?"

Barr rose and lit a cheroot, stifling his rage. "The Dayang Ajar."

"Selladin's widow! By God. You sent that beggar packing a bit early, didn't you? Doomed by all. *Kecelakaan.* Fancy she survived. Well, keep her, but shift her well upstweam. A West countwy lass and nothing less, and you damned well better get started."

He felt bad for scolding him. He produced another present, ordering several heavy crates ashore. They contained books. There was a colossal dictionary with its own rosewood stand that would collapse from worms the next year, *The Posthumous Papers of the Pickwick Club,* a compendium of *Birds of the Indian Subcontinent and Malay Peninsula,* and fourteen tracts on America.

The steamer and books were to herald two decades of gifts. Over time, Barr would come to suspect that all of it—the books, the musical instruments, the furniture, the windows, a small observatory—were not so much gifts as provisioning for Kilcane himself, deposits against a future day when he would give it all up and park himself on that broad veranda until death dragged him off. The man disliked his relatives. He basically had no home.

He also delivered, on that occasion, two newly conscripted officers for the Third Division, men newly released from his squadron. They were desperately needed.

A rudimentary system of residencies was established during that first decade to accommodate forts on four neighboring rivers. The fort at Lundu served as the seat for the first outlying district. These were nothing more than thick stone or wood structures in the middle of a thousand square miles of forest, housing boys, turning them, over isolated, dangerous years, into adept, queer men; boys passing through no middle phase, simply awakening one morning, dangerous themselves; desperately craving, above all, their leave, their holiday, a commodity of time which, when gained, was invariably misplaced; at a loss when faced with prolonged conversation, a woman in a hat, roads and road signs; boys, able to make a five-week journey through unmapped mud, trembling at the back of a two-penny tram—Reedy sitting for a whole day in Piccadilly Circus, his brain frozen; relieved beyond reason to be back, beginning, almost instantly, to await the next reprieve—at heart savages, yet in the middle of their own deaths calling their mothers. They were, in such vast areas, innocent. They were selfless and brutal. There was Beard, giving up his own rations to his wounded Dyak lieutenant during the seige at Sut, the next winter burning this same man's longhouse to the ground for cheating on his rice tax. They were required to concentrate so fiercely on survival, normal maturation went by the wayside. One found pockets of pure infancy in a retiree. One would meet the wreck of a DO in later years at a bar in Malacca or Penang and marvel at the childlike gaze.

In the first five years, half died. Three were murdered, four died of fever, two of infection. Then there were the mysteries. Dylan, the Resident at Tigh who, at little over the age of a choirboy, had lived through most of what a man can live through in Burma, was done in,

Sutton wrote in the Death Book, by a tree: *Martin Dylan, killed by tree, Sadong basin, Whitsunday, 1845.*

"A tree?" Barr asked. "Why in hell put that?"

"Because it were a tree." Dylan spent three weeks tracking a head party in the Sadong basin and on the twenty-second day, a week into fever, had come across a kapok, its great roots uplifted, its branches buried in the earth. "It's something they do up there," Sutton said. "There's a reason, but I don't know it. Coming upon it at the wrong time can be bad." Dylan was found, without wound, at the base of this thing.

Walter Campbell, died sort of by drowning. The whirligigs of the ence-bung, the betel flower, a tri-petal with a dartlike shaft, spun into Campbell's stream in the Apo Sut, a pink blizzard. It reminded him, in his malarial dreams, of young ladies at the spring ball at Spars, and he waded out, spinning over his own rapids. Death, it was agreed, could be worse.

Then there were incidents of unsuspected health. If a man was not heard from for three months, one assumed he was dead, but there was the rare happy surprise, as with Hayden in '48, his family notified, his death allocation made, walking through Cakebread's door at Hari Raya Puasa, having "gotten lost."

How did one do this for ten years? "Time contracts or expands around the least you need to do to fill a day," Smythe, a long-lived type, once explained. With fever or dysentery, you could easily fill a day with sleeping or shitting. If the least was to preserve your life and those of your men in a drawn-out raid, you could fill a day with considerable work, going, as some did, three days and nights without sleep.

The Resident, the Kandjeng-tuan, was the chief judicial officer of a division. He was responsible for revenue collection and expenditure, public works, police, and a mystical department called "general affairs." He was assisted by one or more district officers, along with Dyak pengulus and Malay tuahs, the arrangement lifted en bloc from the Indian service. Aside from a short apprenticeship with a senior man, recruits were not subjected to any but the leanest entry education. This was bestowed by Sutton and finished by Barr in the form of a little speech.

"Good news travels fast and bad news uncommonly slow. No one wishes to file a negative report. It's damned depressing. So good news piles up like gas. I have found myself sitting on a wondrous mountain of it. Discontent, extortion, smuggling, graft, false accounts, must find their way into ink. Do not converse about it, *write* to your superior, even if you share meals. A chat can be changed, denied, and mucked up in truly amazing ways." Thirteen years later, preparing recruits for the Batang Lupar, he would say, "Talk to each other. Give no fear or speculation the validity of ink. Allow diplomacy a chance, and again." When Sutton reminded him of his original speech, he said, "That's impossible."

The younger they were, the more they took him at his word. Old hands used to layers of hypocrisy marveled at its absence in the reports of these children. And he read them. He could not grasp six out of ten items in committee, but he recognized when something wrong or astoundingly right or ingenious stared up at him from these sheets. "I say!" he'd exclaim. "How in hell did he do that? What a capital approach. Dunn, you say? Not Dunn? Reventlow? All the more remarkable. Send my felicitations. One of the new double-bores."

He stressed accessibility. "Move around. Don't fix your route. If a man comes to you for a trivial reason, hear him. These people do not come for trivial reasons."

Kilcane was the main supply for recruits in the early years, but word eventually spread to Singapore and the Straits Settlements, and it turned out not to be hard to find English gentlemen with naval or East India background willing to spend ten years up some remote river. It had much the same appeal as the Company's service, only more so. A Bornean river was one step beyond the East India in romantic attraction and possibilities, and you did not have the heavy Company hand and cut. You could wind up with something. Then again, ten years does not look like eternity when you're nineteen, although for many it turned out that way.

Requirements were minimal. You had to be clever enough to pick up the language and customs of a primitive people, and of a bootstrapping disposition. You had to be between eighteen and twenty-two, unmarried, and to remain unmarried through your first ten years of duty. It was assumed you would take Dyak mistresses but breed up-country, not exposing these natural families to European life in Kuching or transporting them in government vessels.

For the most part, intelligent choices were made in these men.

The most successful and, in many ways, peculiar recruit in the early years was a young cousin of Barr's, Lieutenant Richard St. John Hogg: "Dickie." He passed two annual sojourns in Sarawak while on leave from the East India's marine, before joining the enterprise permanently. He was a silent young man, large and fit, with golden moustaches and eyes like flint. He had put to sea at eight as a gunner's boy and had known no other life. His superiors thought very highly of him.

Who can categorize those who are made to cast off their childhood before they can walk? They grow into strange organisms with great gaps that you fall into if you step the wrong way. Hogg was appointed for ten years to Lundu, the loneliest, most godforsaken outstation. He was twenty-two. Yet he went about his life up there in a bloodcurdling, matter-of-fact way. He learned the language of the Dyak and their habits and superstitions and simple aspirations as no other. Over that decade he established a mysterious bond with them. They became *his* and he became, in those years, no more nor less than a blue-eyed sea Dyak.

He had a seaman's sense of order and catalogued everything: ordnance received, fruit trees planted, cows purchased for the fort, heads confiscated—these aligned in the bottom fort room, labeled as to who and where and when taken and by whom and how and where and when they were punished for it. For leisure, he taught himself to read French and sang little ditties he composed in that language. He made remarkably accurate drawings of his surroundings and neighbors at Lundu. There was a wonderful series of sketches of a wasp and her nest that he recorded over several weeks. And he fornicated non-stopping.

The first time Dawes passed through Lundu he was nonplussed. "Do you know what he's doing up there?" he said to Sutton. "Do

126

you know what he's doing three hundred miles up-country, sur-rounded by twenty thousand heathen, dysentery, barmy solitude, anything female having more than two feet or wearing thirty pounds of brass coils and earlobes to her armpits? He's teaching himself French. French like no one's heard in this world. He's got all these little books. And he draws. Pictures of bugs. That's all I saw, but Reventlow says he has a whole 'curriculum' worked out." And he was single-handedly proving his thesis of the races. "They should be *mixed*." Peachy grinned, grinding his fist into his palm. "Breed until nothing's left but blond, blue-eyed Dyaks as far as the eye can see!"

Hogg never, to anyone's recollection, showed fear or pain. One got the sense that he had not so much conquered them as never had them. He addressed himself to the problem or assignment at hand, and anything could be stripped of its terror, its hopelessness, by pro-cedure. Procedure was his rod and his staff; he invested all faith and love in it. His rod was procedure and its handmaids were French, sex, and entomology. He seemed beyond ailment. To get himself through fevers, he would recite passages from *Bowditch,* his blistering feet slowly feeling the cool bedrock of the words. *The earth revolves around the sun, and since the direction of the earth's rotation and revolution are the same, it completes a rotation with respect to the stars in less time than with respect to the sun.* "How much less?" he screamed one night, at a malarial peak. "Three minutes fifty-six seconds mean solar units," he answered, and felt himself sink from the burning heights, limbs cool-ing. Through the arctic segments, he'd imagine a fat lady he saw when he was six in a tent show at Romney Bridge, huge and pink, with a thin film of sweat her only true attire, a spectacle of fat, cost-ing him five pence for two minutes of viewing, immense breasts bursting a little silk halter, monstrous thighs, the crowded tent all heat and tumescence, nothing again ever cold. He had these tricks. Later, he didn't need them.

The man was not cruel, but over the years he developed the habit of power and it made him awful. Within his vast inland territory, he was used to complete obedience. A sudden fixity in those pieces of flint was enough. He had a violent temper and when he tried to swal-low it, it made him physically sick. Consideration was reserved for the

Dyak. He had no illusions about them, but he took pains to put himself in their skin. He was tenacious with enemies and had a long and dangerous memory.

Many of his successes could be explained by the fact that all his life he continued to be at sea. No one took advantage of the waterways, tides, bores, freshets, and other liquid phenomena like Hogg. Over time, the country entered his every orifice. All his sinews and blood ways and the taut neural web that he considered himself were invaded. He breathed it, ingested it, pumped it, and defecated it. He had one or two bouts of wretched loneliness in the first two years. After five, he no longer wished to come down.

His great talent was for war. No one could muster the Dyak for battle like Dickie Hogg. He used what ordnance and personnel were issued and took sublime care of them both. For two decades, the Tuan Mudah, as he was called, and his thousands of sea Dyaks became a formidable force at his cousin's disposal, fighting with Dyak cunning and the discipline of a marine brigade. The cogs would begin to turn in a relatively unimpressive way. He would send his calling-out spear with a string of knots for the number of days before these people must join him. In this way, he could raise six thousand men in a remarkably short time, the only payment being the opportunity to take heads. It was a maniacal way to keep order. With heads as payment, feuds were strung out for generations. Yet more and more rivers were opened, and these were kept safe for Europeans to travel a hundred miles upstream.

While Dyaks continued to take heads in government ballehs, he followed Kuching's directive, dealing with them severely for taking heads on their own. If they even consulted omen birds for an expedition, he sent his Sakarangs to burn their longhouses to ash.

His internal record-keeping was meticulous, but his reports were odd. One came away intrigued with what wasn't in them. "The conversation was a little stiff," he'd say of a meeting with chiefs from a newly annexed tributary. "It was interrupted by them going away from time to time, and many casualties." Another account of this incident, gleaned from one of his Dyak lieutenants passing through on leave, included a longhouse burning, an execution line, and two strangulations under nets.

"I hate these things," he said, when he was questioned at the astana a year later. He refilled his glass and settled into a chair. "I hate interrupting decent maneuvers with conversation."

He had what he called his small crises, described by others as bouts of violent paranoia, after which he would sleep—in a chair, a boat—and wake up totally refreshed. At these times, he was known to seek company.

He was not completely alone in Lundu for his full ten years. Reventlow was sent up the last year to assist him. The boy was bright and eager, and Hogg taught him everything he could absorb. He showed him how to keep order and discipline among the native fortmen, how to dismantle and clean all the firearms in the station, how to bake tapioca root and roast dragonflies and the big white slugs the Dyak pried out of dead wood, and how to bore and weight a blowpipe and develop the upper arm muscles necessary to use it. He showed him the wonderful way a mud wasp makes her home and how to sexually please the Dyak. For diversion, he made love to him once or twice himself.

While Barr came out unfinished, Hogg came out complete. He acted as the complete act, superimposing himself totally on the place in which he existed in time. Lundu was never Lundu when he was present. It was "the land trod upon by the Tuan Mudah."

One speculates what it would have been like if their appearance on the scene had been reversed. Barr was a romantic. His decisions were romantic, abrupt, attuned to the air he sniffed, and in that place, in that time, unerringly correct. Only a romantic could have cut out that cockeyed kingdom, and only a flat realist could have held it together and methodically expanded it. This was Hogg. Yet it was he who looked the romantic. He, in fact, looked demented, with his flowing blond hair and chawat. Dolan called him "a Dyak with English information." Depression, a chronic problem for young district officers up-country, was unknown to him. If he felt depressed, he looked around for the cause—a long wet period, the start of ague—and usually found it. Each year he gained in autonomy, rajah Ulu of his subrealm.

"He's doing a damned fine job up there," Barr confided to Kilcane, "but I can't stand him."

"Oh, he's all wight," the other replied. "Just don't make the mistake of ever asking his opinion. He'll give it, and then he might twy thinking again, and with six thousand sea Dyaks behind him that's unwise. You must keep on the wight footing with your cousin. You are dealing, at bottom, with a nine-year-old gunner's boy."

Later, after his decade was up and he stayed on, Hogg found it even harder to pay calls on civilization. His arrival from the interior always had something preposterous and sinister about it. "Have you seen him?" Dawes asked. "*Wow-wow-wow!* Comes in with five hundred personal guards. Head high as a topsail. Switchin' to ducks at the armory. Don't know if you're beholding a penglima decked out as toff or vice versa."

When down-country, Hogg billeted at the fort. He took care of his business, picked up supplies, and left, his men waiting on the outskirts of the town until his signal to leave. In '54, however, walking upstream from the fort to cross to the astana, he passed a small but particularly orderly garden, die-straight rows of cabbages with strong wire fencing, pea vines tied to bamboo trellises with rattan bows. Returning in the dark by the same route, his eye drifted to a slice of light from a doorway above this place, in it a very pregnant woman who seemed to gaze straight at him, although she could not have truly seen him in the dark. This image returned to him at Lundu, so that he found, on his sortie down fifteen months later, he walked past the garden several times until he met its owner.

Oddly enough, Hogg came to feel at ease with no one white in those years except Mrs. Dolan. She never really spoke back to him, in the beginning, and looked annoyed at being addressed by this strange creature, half Englishman, half savage, while she tended her vines or melon bed. Yet after a while, because of his obvious harmlessness to her, his "need" to converse, and the peculiar innocence in those flint eyes, she let him rattle on. Unlike anyone except Dolan, he addressed her as Maureen. "Maureen," he'd say warmly, shyly, but then everything else sounded like a recitation from some naval ordnance manual. He knew it. To pull himself up, he would sometimes inject a non sequitur, commenting on the weather or paying a compliment to her garden or even, once, coughing violently.

He normally conversed with no one other than to establish facts or give orders, criticism, and a rare word of praise. Even at sea, he never had conversations longer than two sentences unless they involved something sea-minded. He spoke with his Dyak lieutenants in interchanges that waxed poetic, on occasion, but never conversational.

She'd glance at him, a handsome face that seemed as if it had been battered and then healed slightly askew. She came to think of him in the same category as some of the interesting forest specimens her husband brought in on his excursions with his dogs—strange, occasionally beautiful creatures. Yet there was a day she put down her trowel, crossed her arms over her latest pregnancy, and began to listen to the shy, ragged recital. It was a description of his childhood. She could not conceive of him in infancy, any infancy, except perhaps hatching out of some steel orb.

"I entered Her Majesty's navy at eight," he said, rocking a small sphere in her melon bed with his boot. A little serpent slithered from the crater and, without seeming to reach for it, he flipped a short knife, pinning the creature below the head. "After twelve years I applied for my discharge, but owing to the kindness of Captain James Peel, I gained my lieutenant's step. They gave me two years to serve here. And then I returned. The Admiralty is glad to do this, I think." He withdrew the blade, wiped it on his thigh, and replaced it. "They feel naval officers are likely to be of service in the improvement of native states. This is true enough, I think. The discipline and obedience you take away are of great value. Don't you find it with the children, Maureen? I mean, you cannot learn to command until you've learned to obey." It was the kind of thing he said before one of his brutal disciplinary actions, yet here it was lapped in the tonalities of love. It was the only vocabulary he knew. It was rather like making a hat with nuts and bolts, odd and painful but still a hat.

"You come off ship with a sack of useful things. A little soldiering, knowledge of the artillery drill, care of ordnance, navigation, carpentering, an eye for management and order." He looked admiringly at the evenly spaced rows of beans, the neat line of wash. "That fellow may have a mate. I'd keep an eye out, Maureen."

"Aye," she said, and began again with her trowel. In the almost horizontal light, her hair wore a fiery halo, and before he knew what he was doing, he reached down and touched it lightly with his fingertips. She flipped the trowel around her head without looking up and continued to work.

"There you are," he said to himself, walking upstream. "There you are, you poor, fucking fool. You've made love, true love, for the first time in your life, to a pregnant woman who thought you were an insect."

For eight years, Mrs. Dolan had no idea of the altar erected to her in that fierce heart two hundred miles to the west. No one suspected this formidable individual who bedded Bidayuh, Melanaus, Dusuns, Muruts, and Sakarangs had fallen into irredeemable and timeless love with the C of E stick. Madness comes in all forms. "But this," Dawes was to say, "takes the cake."

Hogg would love two things in his life: the savage Mua Ari, a worthy and entertaining opponent for a decade and a half, and Mrs. Dolan; and here he loved purely, deeply, like a young, young boy, this doyenne of laundry wires and bleach solutions, this remarkable shaper of spaces—legumes planted not only in rows but in concentric circles of increasing radii giving the Dyak final conviction that she was a witch, this field lieutenant of a crisp little army—amahs, children, husband, animals—all adhering smoothly to her will. She was "the distant thing." The distant thing he could never touch, antipode to all his dark accomplishments. She had hovered just out of range, in other forms, all his life—a light-filled, forgiving thing. She was all fragility. She stamped her foot and it was laughable. If she had been robust, she would not have pierced him so. Yet his was not an ethereal love. What flesh she had burned him fiercely, the hundreds of brown spreading thighs across his forests drying into dust. The delightfully warm course of blood, when he spoke to her of things he could speak of to no other and not feel the fool, reached an organ he could not place. From here, it was but a little leap to the ruby aura of her hair, the nubs

132

of breasts, the cool, efficient hands that he imagined, in the months and years ahead, wantonly caressing his long body. He wished her to suckle him, to croon to him. The only "faith" he ever betrayed was the belief that someday fate would kick out the bulwarks of both their lives and they would flow together.

In the meantime, in his oddly domestic dreams, she would lift her chin in a doorway, a garden bed. "There you are!" she would say, her eyes drinking him in. "Heart of my heart," she would say these words.

The handful of district officers recruited in those early years were of a more or less straightforward mold, with two exceptions. One was Hogg. The other, two years later, was Bobby Fitzhugh. Fitzhugh arrived while Barr was at Pontianak. He had left orders with Sutton to take the new man's measure, brief him, and send him to his station. If he had met Fitzhugh himself, he wouldn't have sent him anywhere.

The man, as they say, defied description. He was one of the rare paper referrals, but it had come through Kilcane and so was automatically accepted with thanks. What was expected and what arrived were comically disparate. Fitzhugh had been captain in the Inniskilling Dragoons and was the son of an earl. He had a settled estate, and so it was assumed he must have done something fairly hopeless to seek employment in that corner of the world. It remained a mystery. No one ever effected such a complete obliteration of his past. With a title in one's background, it was an impressive accomplishment. He seemed to have disappeared down a hole at a garden party in Surrey and resurfaced at the astana wharf five months later in more or less the same attire.

Fitzhugh was deposited by Chinese prahu, rather than the mail packet, on a June morning and stood in the sunlight all pink and tubby. He seemed extremely young or maybe ageless, the way some idiots are ageless and some stupid, happy men. The hands, however, looked strong and somehow did not fit the body. In any event, he was written off, by Dolan in a state of mute collapse on the aft quarter of the launch and Sutton with a ball of saliva over the rail. No one went down to greet him. He was observed, a fat, foppish young man with a handkerchief tied over his head, directing the placement of an enormous kit. One counted three fancy gun cases, four topees, and what turned out to be the most impressive supply of fruit salts, anti-leech pastes, and mosquito oils ever imported by a single individual. One shotgun was a custom-made Purdey. What in hell did one do with something like that, Dolan asked, when the bore rotted out in four months and it would not suffer a replacement from a mortal weapon? The bore never rotted out. Something, Fitzhugh once explained, to do with aguar gum.

Sutton, a reasonable man, sent him to Simanggang. Simanggang was the newest up-country station. It had only native fortmen and would normally never be given to a recruit, but it was the place most likely to brace him up or finish him off in quick fashion. This may sound like a joke, but it wasn't. You could not cajole anyone into efficiency in that space and time. The only one who seemed to like the pink balloon, to love him really, was Dolan's dog Spanker, and no one liked this animal.

Fitzhugh left in six dugouts, trunks and boxes packed five feet over the gunwales, with some miserable-looking Kanowits securing them down. It was a journey for which most DOs would not use space up in three. He had been offered three, and came up with the others at his own expense.

Nothing was heard for five months. Sutton and a regular circuit party finally passed up the Batang Lupar before Christmas. His report was astounding.

"It has *curtains*, by God! And he's made those monkeys plant a garden. A *flower* garden! Best call him down as a bad job and be done. Don't want some bloody earl round our ears."

That was a month before the attack on Simanggang. The Saribas burst out of their river and set upon the closest station to check any interference with their raid. Word of the attack gradually filtered downstream. Nothing was heard from Fitzhugh.

No one wanted to go up. You knew what you'd find. It was hard. You arrived three weeks after one of those things and were met by only unbelievable stench and clouds of flies. Seven weeks later, a little scroll wrapped up in string was delivered by two Chinese gold diggers on their way downriver. Sutton handled it delicately, knowing it was the last mortal words of a man they had all so coldly given up.

The thing was a request for fruit. Fitzhugh explained that his trees were not yet bearing and he would love, he used the word *love*, a delivery, he used the word *delivery*, of fruit if they could somehow manage it. No mention of a raid. He got his fruit. Cakebread and Smalley brought it up. When they entered his last reach, he was waving from a neat little landing. He must have had damned good communication, they said, for he stood with all his fortmen behind in smart salute, looking as pink and inept as ever, his feet in blazing white socks. He had at least fifty pairs of socks.

Fitzhugh not only fought well but with no loss of life to the fort, except for a cook boy. He had "strung bombs about the shrubbery," he said, and this killed or maimed the first three waves. The boy had run out to grab a chicken, and this made him sad. They had taken eighty-seven prisoners, and these were "about the place working."

There was a border of something like hydrangeas around a little porch he'd had them build. And he had real butter on the table, not the rancid tinned stuff. He'd "found" a cow, a scrawny thing with fistulas on its hocks, and he produced a little churn. His fortmen would take turns pounding it, storing the precious slabs between pandamus leaves in a swinging locker. Cakebread and Smalley turned over the green fruit.

"Oh, I say," he said happily, picking up a durian, sniffing it, pressing it as if in sexual paroxysm. "Terribly grateful."

It was Hogg at Lundu and Fitzhugh at Simanggang that more than anything else secured the territory in those years. He had the country between a pair of bright hard pincers. Through them, the years of grace granted by Kilcane were extended to the interior. It was not secure, but it was quiet. He could leave with reasonable hope of finding the whole illusion still levitating in some form or other when he returned.

He allotted himself thirteen months to go back, charter his company, and gather up his bride. A cousin required no lengthy court-ship; indeed, over their peculiar correspondence, the woman had stayed remarkably constant.

"It is time you have your ranee, Tuan Rajah," even Bawhal had said. As guru of English to the sons of the datus, the Tamil had thrived and become cocky. "It is dangerous not to do this. What is 'titah in perpetuity' if there is no perpetuity?"

Bawhal was dismissible, but Si Tundo was not. "The Rajah Laut will not support you with a Malay ranee," he said simply.

Yet it was not the stability provided by Hogg and Fitzhugh, or any advice or personal resolve that finally put him in motion. It was a pic-ture, the tenacious image of Maureen Dolan atop her rug bags on the day of her arrival, snapping orders as if elbowing her way through market day in Marley Street. The absurdity and power of that vision, her swollen stomach, the damp violet patches beneath her arms, a white woman not so much as taking a breath before ordering this strange universe to conform to her needs, spelled out the success of his enterprise in ways that piculs of antimony and opium revenue could never do. A thousand years of British civilization astride a sago barrow. Kilcane was right. The bastard was infallible. Having made his decision, he crossed the floor through an insistent thrum and gained his bed, giving in to the malaria that had been nudging his shoulder for two days.

Movement, especially over vast distances, put him on a plane where he could take up that ancient correspondence. He no longer wrote as a child, but his innermost thoughts were still nakedly revealed and no subject was taboo. It was a bizarre communication, one he would never relinquish. The letters were filled with color and anecdote, the kind he had so desperately wished to receive as a boy.

Batavia Roads
February 27, 1850

Dearest,

I am bound for England via the *Paarl,* a Dutch East India-man. She has put in for a diplomatic pouch, and it is here I have caught her, for I have had business with their sago car-tel. Only after two days did they deign to see me. One is taken down among them. I am addressed as "Mijnheer Barr," a rapid slide.

This is a handsome town. The buildings are all white, with canals and little drawbridges everywhere, yet in truth it is nothing short of a living hell. Disease carries off a quarter of the population a year. It cannot be blamed on the Javanese. They would never have set a town here, by God. But the Dutch like their water carriage, it reminds them of home, so they built on this swamp. No one puts in except under orders; no ship careens here unless she's up to her gunwales in water. I am told during the past five days over three hundred men have died while anchored in the roads. They die of fever and flux, from eating anything or nothing. Great saltwater crocodiles prowl the shallow bar for corpses.

The *Zwart Vin,* a Dutch man-of-war, has been here a fortnight. She's come down from Kapal Island, where they all refit, and lies alongside. Forty men sick, seventeen dead, the rest too weak to work. Ashore the poor wretches buy fruit, they cannot afford much else, and it takes them off.

In port also is the *Red Dog,* a Yankee brig, flying that carnival flag of theirs. Americans are the damnedest people, astounding for their bottomless audacity and good luck. Her cargo is "aer batoe" from the Penobscot River, wherever that is, packed in hay below the waterline. They are said to favor iced drinks. We are supposed to prefer warm lager, God knows why. I'm told they have the governor eating out of their hands by offering a free half ton. Well, it's hard, it's cold, and it takes a damned sight longer to melt below the waterline than we imagined. Her master informed our officers that we are welcome to as much as we like. They are an openhanded tribe.

We carry teak and pepper. I do not look forward to Dutch sea meals—salt horse, pickled cabbage, potatoes, potatoes, potatoes. The green turtle is splendid store, staying alive for weeks without food or water, yet they pass her by for *aardappels.* We've hoisted colors and signaled for a pilot. I am that happy to stand out.

G.

Capetown
April 17, 1850

My Darling,

A rapid voyage. We put in at Anjer Lor, then out into the southeast trades, making eight hundred miles in a week, long seas running. We passed under Madagascar the last day of March, on a bead to the Cape.

Here we are a Batavia ship and so lie in quarantine a quarter mile out. A doctor boarded at sunset for the smallpox check. They have true terror of it here. I travel with one friend, a Bidi diamond nestled in my pocket. I will go to Wakefield and Kemp to have it set in a ring.

This is a bothersome journey for what I fear will be a bothersome woman. I do not need a "helpmate," whatever Kilcane's ideas. No man needed one less. But I need sons. And perhaps a daughter, I wouldn't mind.

G.

Hampstead
July 1, 1850

Dearest,

Transshipped on the merchantman *Charlotte Latham* second of May and began to lose the southern stars. The twelfth, anchored Saint Jago. Two days ago we sighted The Lizard and moved up-channel in a steady rain, past Beachy Head, finally abreast of Dover after an absence of eleven years, seven months and ten days.

I cannot tell you how misplaced I feel. To see the old victualing wharves, the bleak quarantine island, and all the big-nosed bloodless faces, I half doubt who I am or where I came from, that place receding in a waxy dream.

I have rummaged all morning in my bags, looking for the appropriate thing to wear. To wear! I fear I look hideous, burned black as I am. Harry said I looked like the Devil himself. I hope not, for I do not wish to take any more time with this business than I must. Would that I could couple with my cousin on her parlor rug and return in nine months for my issue. This, at least, I'm assured she can do, for she has borne one sound child. And so I will package myself and commence to drool and flatter, all to enter some tight, bony vestibule.

I am expected at Deanstown in a fortnight and will spend the intervening days trying to secure an agent. Kilcane, miraculously, has his own business and may follow by a month or two, which gladdens my heart.

G.

II

Melie

Měngail

The eye, large, luminous, was too high in the crack. He had envisaged her shorter, and not so oddly mannered as to peep out at him in this way.

. . .

Bathingill's Lady's Daily Diary

> *July 14th, 1850*

The Rajah of Sarawak has arrived. He arrived this broiling morning in black wool and top hat. He emerged from an old cab with leather curtains yet looked quite splendid, not in dress for that was queer, but in his person, big and fit with sun-blackened face and his teeth a nice surprise for one come from the tropics, crooked but all there and very white.

"Tell Lady Mumm, Rajah Barr is here," he said, Budding taking his hat, gaping like a fish. Mama, of course, described him quite differently. A tall, quiet young man at his father's wake. She has been very excited all these months we awaited his return. She has been at loose ends as a widow. This morning she changed her dress thrice, deciding finally on the gray silk, a poor choice I think, for what little color she has was already drained by nerves.

It was horrible. He looked at her blankly, framed in the doorway in her pale skirts and fichu, his eye traveling over her as if she were stock in a meadow, returning from her shoes back up to her face with the consummate rejection of a cow beyond her milking years. This before saying a word.

Iris Mumm regarded him as well, on that sweltering morning. She had expected the half-score years in the tropics to help span their difference in age. Yet what stood before her, eyeing her so coldly, so "innocently," was not a malarial wreck but a man in his sexual prime, shoulders bursting out of black wool, absurd kid gloves clenched in a fist, an aura of steam and discomfort surrounding him, and her own flat rejection in his face.

She did not detest him for it. She did not detest him, though his letter of intent had arrived three years to the month before the wretched man himself, her bearing organs drying up, her child now a head taller than she. Later, when he rode out with Melie, saying, as she told her, nothing at all but quietly seeking the child out, she was numb. For one long solitary afternoon she wept, a roil of bereavement and fury. In the second week, she turned her mind to practicalities. Things, queer and painful as they were, were falling into some sort of place.

She had deep affection for this awkward girl, her only child, so unlike herself at this or any age. For seventeen years she had catapulted between ridiculous rage and warm surges of love for this child. Rage because she was slower and plainer and so much more vulnerable than herself. Love, she guessed, for the same reasons.

The quality of certain flesh, lambent, moist, infused with youth, the creature standing before him in dark bombazine was in full-blown possession of this.

Amelia was broad-browed, not pretty, the head set nicely onto square shoulders above full breasts. He helped her mount, her boot in his woven fingers, and felt, with some surprise, a stirring in his groin. By the fourth morning of hacking out, watching the ample haunches rise and fall to the trot, the fresh young face turned round to him, he was planning her life.

In the afternoons, they walked down turf paths and peaty corridors where she had stumbled as an infant. They visited the stable and paddocks, the decaying carriage barn, a little temple buried in a copse, a leftover from the place's original Catholic owners—Saint Eustace standing in a small, windowless apse, Saint Eustace with all his hunting paraphernalia, his oven, his stag with crucifix between its antlers. She sometimes sat on the foot of the hoary little deity. He told her of that country, a strange, fantastic portrait that seemed to range further and further from the truth despite his best efforts.

She had an athletic walk and they covered much territory. When they reached the sheep-faced lions at the start of the drive, they traveled back, past a little wood and the starved lawns, here and there glimpses of verdant tunnels and lichen-covered putti. She listened, a flood of sensations washing over her, aware not of his words but the smell of him, the breadth of his shoulders, a smile, a moment of pensiveness transforming that face. There was the long, low turn and then the great rotting columns of the carriage porch and the house itself. Here was wealth on the wane, a wavering female hand, the father and husband a financial disaster.

He sat between them eating their delicate food, peonies and fans glinting up from the bottom of his soup. His eyes grazed the pots of cream, the pear compote, the fine gold hair of the girl's lip. She might die in the first wet monsoon.

>Deanstown
>August 20, 1850

>I shall marry. My cousin is too old, but near the hen there is a chick who is altogether acceptable. Melie sits a horse admirably and does not rattle on. She is of a sympathetic disposition and she is "musical." There is some heaviness to the chin, but believe I like it.

He did not ask for her hand until a month later. He was spending a day or two a week at Deanstown while negotiating for an agent in London. He hoped to attract one who would actively support him with the Colonial Office, pressing for recognition and eventual protectorate status. He found he had little talent for the business.

By the third week, Iris Mumm was leaving them alone in the music room. The girl sat at the piano, her fingers shuttling stiffly, feeling his presence in her papa's chair. She never asked what he would like to hear but continued from one wooden performance to the next until, one evening, she felt his hands on her waist.

"Marry me," he said. Her fingers continued loudly, rigidly. "Marry me." She felt his breath in her ear. She rose and rushed from the room.

He followed her out and through the hall and up to her room at a quick, silent step. He closed the door and took her in his arms and kissed her, she pulling around wildly, resisting yet sinking, a miraculous heaviness rising from her thighs into her throat. He stopped. Pale faces stared out of the gloom from every quarter. He gazed about, releasing her, then turned slowly on his heel, leaving her disheveled and seething.

She woke in sunlight, still in her dress, the faded roses and cornucopias, the shelves of huge German dolls, afloat in golden motes. At breakfast, she sat mute over her egg. When they finished, he stood behind her chair and formally asked for her hand. Iris Mumm rose, her eyes brimming, and kissed her.

The girl was not unhappy. She would have fluttered about, then backed away indecisively, she told herself, if he had not wrenched her from her nursery comforts. His presence in the days that followed made her feel strangely out of control. He was her true sexual awakening, and the sensation was vast. She believed she had found something wild and fine. Maybe she had. But the dank black wool and the cowherd's inspection of her mother and the stinginess of her honeymoon were just as real.

Among the collection of wonderful, useless things her father had brought into her life—before a life-sized Chinese doll and after a great velvet opera cape, which appeared one morning on her bedstead like a slice of night—were two circus horses. The circus was a small rural one, disbanded after years of traveling, its animals passed on to farms or shot. They were the most beautiful things he had ever seen, he said, and he knew she would feel the same, and she did. They were unloaded on a freezing morning, tentative, powerful, the huge gray flanks backing off the van, nostrils snorting smoke. He told her mother they would pull one of the plows. She smiled dismally and went back to the house. They would, of course, pull nothing. They would eat and sleep and surge together like two storm clouds. In that year, the already flagging place had the aura of unkempt magic. She and her father began to shyly take up each other's cause. When she dreamed of him, dressed in his failures, these absurd, lovely shapes drifted behind. They now reappeared, a silvery backdrop to this man.

There were small, queer things. She had been told by her cousin Peggy Sears that he had been seen purchasing lace in Dunlop Street and a large amethyst at Wakefield and Kemp. She waited to receive these engagement presents, but they never materialized. She surmised that Peg was wrong, as the gossiping young matron often was.

At Wakefield and Kemp, he had the diamond set in white gold. Standing before the glass cases, his gaze drifted into a familiar spectral pleasure, violet nipples over a shallow bowl. The lace would rematerialize in an exquisite kebaya; the amethyst, set in silver talons, jammed on a small thumb.

Through the offices of Spottiswode and Bloch, Broad Street, the Borneo Company was established with capital of sixty thousand pounds. Its published aim was to develop state-controlled monopolies of coal and antimony mines in the territory, to organize the sago and gutta-percha trade, and to finance further commercial enterprises, paying royalties into the state treasury. None of this existed. Raymond Bloch understood this. He did not care whether Borneo itself existed. This self-styled rajah existed, for the press was full of him. The publicity was enough to float a public company of moderate size. Many a profitable enterprise was started with less. They discussed antimony, cassava, and timber, which were deemed of growing importance, and copra, which seemed pointless. By that time, Kilcane had arrived, but Barr declined his offer to meet with his agents, feeling the need to stand clear of his mentor in this arena. Kilcane did accompany him to purchase another small steamer on credit. And he accepted his friend's offer to put a man-of-war at his disposal on the return voyage.

"Warm chestnuts! Little gloved hands. Mawwied ladies! No virgins. What were we about on the other side of this planet?" Kilcane was happy. He accompanied him to Jordan Haas, who was painting his portrait. For these sessions, Barr dressed in a midshipman's jacket and gazed into the distance against a backdrop of cardboard palms. When it was finished he could not pay, and so Kilcane had the portrait placed on his account. Haas, in fact, was never paid and the portrait never delivered. They moved on to the Admiralty and, later in the autumn, made a round of country visits.

A few clubs and city companies paid him attention. Occasionally he'd see a face that brought to mind a distant life. At Clewes, he glimpsed a tall lank frame moving along the wall, much the same as it had moved along the wall of a Norwich corridor. Biverts had been one of his few school friends, his timid crew on the Wensum. He had not really been a friend but a boy beseiged, a boy whose sexual inclination was used against him every day of his life. Barr sometimes kept the others off, and Biverts thanked him with a dogged faithfulness. He lent Barr money and often did assignments for him, for he was quick. Once, in a rush of gratitude, he kissed him and was knocked unconscious.

"It's so overblown!" Biverts exclaimed happily. "So extravagant! Why couldn't you come up with a little copra plantation like Grosset? A private raj! *Headhunters!* I don't believe it. You have made it up as a romantic investment for rich ladies. I shall ask Maman to buy shares. Why, it should have a theme. 'Oooo ladies, sweet ladies, open your—' "

"Shut up, Frank," Barr said amiably. "I must go. I'm late for a sitting with Haas."

"Haas! May I come? Do let me! Will you have a macaw perched on your shoulder? A negress draped over your feet? May I come out? Who knows, I may be of use!"

"Good-bye, Frank. Take care of yourself."

"You know," Biverts said, as if to no one in particular, "I really must go somewhere." Barr looked at him. The other drew himself up and smiled. "Good-bye, your majesty!" The egret stride bore him quickly into the crowd.

With his marriage settled and an agent secured, he went partridge shooting. He took four days to fit out a small cottage in Devon, inherited from his aunt, planning to use it for his honeymoon, later sending half the furnishings back as inappropriate expense. He caught fish and saw the races at Fairbairns. He became enamored of croquet and ordered a first-class set stowed aboard the *Terror.*

"*Twill,* my God. Muslin, muslin, muslin!" Peg collapsed on a trundle cot. Sunbonnets, shawls, crinolines, parasols, gutta boots, medicinal kits, two paramatta riding costumes, and a set of prayer books, bound in white kid, covered beds, bideaways, and chairs. The tropical trousseau was easily gathered, Iris Mumm having purchased many of the articles over the past two years. The girl spent the rest of her time attending farewell teas, fixing her teeth, having a great variety of shoes made, and spending one wet afternoon with a sad boy in a velvet waistcoat. She had a long visit with Spaulding, her mother's physician. And in the evenings, or whenever she had a few moments to herself, she wept, emerging swollen-eyed to meet her mother, who had often spent the time in a similar fashion.

On her eighteenth birthday, he presented her with the diamond and twenty pounds of stationery with HH THE RANEE OF SARAWAK in demure gold leaf. She sat on her bed, staring at a sheaf of this paper. She rose and gazed at the large, milky girl in the glass and burst out laughing, then watched the face crumble.

She convinced herself that a new life was beginning, wondrous and strange, and the only way to free herself from the old one was to hurl it from her. The next day, everything—the view of the paddocks from her window, the old groom coughing in the stable yard, her mother's voice wafting unexpectedly from an upper story—would seem immeasurably precious. Watching Budding and a maid carry one of her trunks down the stairs in their careful tortoise steps, she realized that the old life was already closing her out while she ruminated whether to kick it away. She threw up.

Iris Mumm did her best to fall in with the girl's moods while dealing with her own rising panic. One did not warm to this man. In truth, they knew him no better now than they did on that first steaming morning. She herself had been almost comically rejected and had flippantly switched positions with the being dearest to her in life. She had encouraged the girl. She was hurrying her from a room still smelling of nursery paraffin into *what*? A dozen times she wanted to grasp those broad young shoulders and say, "This is absurd. You cannot go to that place. I cannot bear it."

Her own life stretched before her in a leaden void. Husbandless, aging, bereft of her child. A tangle of ribbons, a small shoe, tightened a wire around her heart. You could die horribly out there, she wished to say, watching the girl pressing on a trunk lid, but merely added her weight. The fact was she would have gone if he had chosen her. She could not, with any fairness, hold the child back. She might come round on her own. This gave such a murky, skewed logic to the decision that it was never firm and she was always wretched.

Amelia had a fyce, an animal for whom she felt no deep affection. She insisted on taking it with her. It was ridiculous to cart a dog halfway round the world, and she knew it. It would be a nuisance at best. It already was, forever tripping her up. Yet this was her first demand. He acquiesced, and this simple act somehow stopped her giddiness. It gave her a small control, however imbecilic, over her new life.

The wedding was a minor success, society diverted by the demure Amazon and her Rajah. He had done nothing in his life that surprised himself half so much as standing under a flowery arch beside this huge confection. He gazed at the unknown guests, the epergnes filled with sweets and miniature doves, the fiddles, white ribbons snapping, and wondered what in the name of hell they, this day, this hour, had to do with him.

I've done it, those eyes said to Kilcane. Now where's my knighthood? My protectorate? Be quick, damn you.

"She's a nice child, you know," Kilcane said, almost sadly. He had three daughters. "You're not so diffewent fwom Spwing or Hare after all, my lad. You are a blackguard, perhaps the blackest of all." They were the first and last words of disaffection he would ever utter.

Amelia, flushed in her white satin, passed through the room, Barr thought, like an overrigged ship. That an element of him hated her before they met, before he even recognized there would be a need for someone like her, he was unaware. He overheard her speaking of aboriginal tribes, the exotic flora and fauna, and materialized at her side, gripping her waist. "There's more to it than flowers and monkeys, my dear," he said and released her.

Later, in the soporific air, his face took on a momentary tenderness as he watched her from a distance. What had "she" looked like, almost the same age as this girl, in her white satin, a flat circlet of rosebuds, Beryl had said, for she was tall, a child on colt's legs. His eyes filled and his bride was at his side, squeezing his hand.

The cottage at Combe Martin was a thick little box in a water meadow bounded on two sides by the Bristol Channel. Beryl had kept it for him, a last bribe to that small, cold heart. It was the one thing she had that was hers alone. The newlyweds arrived in the evening, and a cold supper had been set out by the day woman with a small fire in the grate.

He regarded her standing in the middle of the room in her traveling dress and little rose-veiled hat. He made a slow circuit of her, then slipped the gloves from her hand. He lifted her shawl and, by the light of the fire, began to undress her. She did not move, not looking at him, not shrinking back or helping. When she finally stood almost naked, the little hat still on her head, she laughed nervously. He laughed too, a lewd laugh, staring at this big naked girl with the tiny hat, and she let out an animal sob and began to grab for her clothes. He put his arms around her and held her tightly. When she finally stopped shuddering, he bent down and lifted her foot and placed his lips on the broad instep, then glided them to the back of her knee.

She was sickened by the episode, by her humiliation, and overwhelmed by his ardor. Yet that night and the nights that followed, his lovemaking seemed to continue out, as she lay under him, to all female forms, the next and the next, never assuaged, never uttering, at any time, her name.

Their one excursion was a morning carriage ride up to Lofty Lynton with tea at Lynmouth, its sea-level counterpart, the six-hundred-foot journey between the two made in a little water-ballast railway. A tub in the car at the top of the cliffs was filled with water while the one at the bottom was emptied, causing them to travel down through the blue ether. Mid-mark, the lighter car passed them with a pack of screaming children. They laughed, and she thought perhaps she could stand it, that there would be moments. It pleased her, too, that he was made slightly green by the descent.

Iris Mumm wore an enameled watch pinned to her breast by a pheasant with a ruby eye. No matter what her dress, the little timepiece was always in place. As a child, Amelia would watch her mother rotate the little wafer between finger and thumb. It could signal the onset of endless cold silences or violent rushes of affection. She learned to be quiet and wait. Her mother stood stonelike in the railway din, the wafer spinning. The whistle blew, and she stiffly offered her cheek. The girl pressed it long and heavily with her lips, then dazedly hooked her arm in her husband's. The fyce began a shrill barking, and he picked up its case and guided her aboard.

They were seated, her clothes cold against her skin. Her mother's mute face slid before her eyes. A misty green soon replaced it, rushing by like liquid. Against this fluid mat, shot with spasms of sunlight, all the faces, human and animal, all the beloved faces she had ever loved and had loved her back, smiled sadly and vanished. He handed her a handkerchief.

There was a dining car, but he chose not to use it. They ate in their seats. She ate miserably, yet with appetite, for she was a big girl. She was probably the only woman in England, she thought, to ride in a second-class carriage eating cold mutton with a diamond of this size on her finger. This queer mixture of extravagance and thrift she somehow knew would characterize her life. She knew this and much more than this in her young heart. She had not snared him. It was she who was caught. That pale column of misery sliding from view had realized it too. The thought of the stationery in her trunk made her smile crookedly. It was the first adult expression to appear on that face, and it made it momentarily ugly.

A small passel of new employees was to sail with them, including Frank Biverts as his personal secretary. Also aboard was the newly named Lieutenant Governor of Labuan and his secretary; Russell was an experienced man who had been twenty years in Malaya, first as a journalist and then in teak. Lady Russell accompanied him, along with a grown daughter and a newborn son who would die en route.

At the last moment, Raymond Bloch came down to wish them bon voyage. *I do not like this man,* she wrote to Deanstown on the first sheet of what was to be a correspondence weighed in tons. *He seems exactly what he physically is, coarse and bloated. Yet the Rajah appears to be satisfied with him.* Meeting Bloch revealed a new side to her husband. Listening to the two converse, she perceived a frightening naïveté. Her blood ran cold with the discovery. How could he be taken in by such a creature when she herself, a girl who had been nowhere and done nothing, was not?

The ship was cramped and stifling, packed with seasick females and seventeen new recruits. Sex was a nightmare, any intimacy, it seemed, witnessed instantly by dozens. She succumbed to her first fit of sea-sickness off the French coast and never recovered until Saint Helena. To mark this landfall, he presented her with an ivory paper knife. She was delighted with the little gift. She sat on deck under rugs, slitting the pages of her Malay primer, mouthing the strange words into the wind. At Capetown, leaning over the rail, she would observe him presenting an identical knife to the tidewaiter as a small bribe. She would remove hers from her bag, look at it, and drop it into the sea.

Saint Helena, twelve hundred miles west of the Cape, was a place he knew and found to his liking. The isolated little island was a pro-visioning larder for upwards of a thousand ships a year. The Russell infant had died five days from port, and since its mother could not see the body cast into the sea it was buried here. She stayed with Lady Russell, and he used the rest of the day to climb to Longwood, Napoleon's prison home.

It is a pretty little manse, much like my own, with a sunken path through the garden which he had them dig for privacy. The view is splendid. Antiscorbutic gardens are spread all about the hills, bright patches of cress and onions and fruit trees, neither orange nor lemon but something in between. My bride is no longer vomiting.

She was seasick from Capetown on with only short respites in Malacca and Penang. The hill of Singapore was sighted on the first morning in March.

Ashore, she revived rapidly and took an interest in all the raucous, teeming life around her. They were greeted by the Norrises, and Barr escorted her to dinner at Government House, along with the Russells.

Everything about the evening restored her. The huge house was appointed with superb taste, the dark faces gliding out of the shadows only to provide a service. The food seemed lifted straight out of a London kitchen, but with a mysterious pungency. She began to be reassured. She enjoyed her reception as the Ranee Amelia, yet once or twice in the evening she felt there was something of the sideshow about this man she had married, and therefore about her. She read this most clearly in the intelligent gray eyes of Charlotte Norris.

Curried bouillon double froid, jugged ducks with bread, chicken croquets, ox tongue with white sauce, soursop custard, java mokka. She sent the entire handscripted menu home. She felt she looked well, she wrote, despite her sea journey. She had worn the green shantung, feminine yet not girlish.

That first evening bore a surprise for him. At cigars, Lytton rose and announced with a mocking glint that Her Majesty had been pleased to name him a Knight Commander of the Order of the Bath. Apparently, his knighthood had followed him around the Cape on a rapid new warship that had entered the roads that afternoon. He sat stunned. He questioned everything, including the actual decoration and its placement.

I am a knight, he wrote into a small pool of light, his bride lightly snoring in the bed. He wrote long and lavishly. After placing the letter in his box, he rose and looked at her, the mouth slack, the heavy limbs, a land beast once again in its element. "The girl is merely sleeping," he said, but it did no good.

She, too, wrote. In her heart, she thought of these letters as a paper trail, for she was disappearing into a universe that might swallow her forever. The whole earth was water, she had learned in these five months, serving only to separate her from what she loved best. Her letters were cheerful, informative, but with occasional small remarks that tortured the reader.

Everyone rests here between one-thirty and four. At five-fifty there is sunlight. At six-ten, everything is in darkness. We sleep early and rise early, like farmers. The Rajah is affectionate and instructive. He is so big, Mama.

Crosscoate Farm
Essex
December 3, 1880

Tommy,

Do I remember? Why do you keep asking this? I close my eyes and *see*. It is life now that is the insipid dream. I see a large-boned girl standing pigeon-toed with a fyce on a string, heat rash covering her arms like pink sleeves.

I remember thinking, My God, he's brought back a broodmare and no mistake. There was nothing in her that betrayed a woman he would have chosen, he would have desired. How do I know? I don't. Except someone small and exquisite and sensual would, I believe, have been more to his taste. But such women are not meant for breeding.

The surprise of it, the sorrow of it, who could know better than you, was that she was a broodmare by disguise. She could have raced in her own right, as you once said. A thoroughbred, forever made to pull that circus cart of his. I liked her from the start. Her intelligence, her confusion, her resolution, at all costs, to deal with things, and especially her size. We were both big women. To sit at table between the two of us was to sit, Harry once said, "on a tidal wave of breast."

We had been married eight years when he brought her out. I was pregnant and staying with Mother and Father, unable to cross to that nether world. He greeted me warmly as the wife of his dear friend.

Father was both stunned and pleased by the way things had transpired in Borneo, although he looked upon the business of a raj as ridiculous. Our Chinese were delighted with the possibility of trade. There was, of course, a problem with the Dutch. The Hague had finally taken notice of this English madman fashioning himself a little potentate in the middle of a vast Dutch sea. Van Lutyens sent him renewed warning in care of Government House, thereby putting himself at considerable risk.

The man wrote that a delegation of Dutch ministers was to pay him a visit after Hari Raya. He advised him "to stuff the place with plants and animals," for apparently he had attempted to convince them that Gideon was first and foremost a naturalist, supported by the Royal Geographic Society. One never knew when to take van Lutyens seriously. In the same transmission, he warned him not to go barefoot in his garden and to change his cooks at frequent, irregular intervals.

The Dutch Foreign Ministry had protested to London. By then, of course, they could bellow all they liked for they were weaker by the day. Whitehall seconded this by his knighthood, eventually improving his status from Confidential Agent to Commissioner.

He and his bride were to continue on, with the *Terror* as escort. It was arranged that Russell and his party would stay behind until a fort and habitat could be created for them on Labuan. Construction was to be undertaken by the officers and crew of the *Terror* after departing Kuching. All was ordered in one universe to take place in another.

He left with her in that gunboat. A big girl with twelve batiste nightdresses embroidered with little flowers and a

Savory & Moore's medicinal kit in a pigskin envelope. Her people—it was only a mother, God help her—must have thought her destination a day's sail east of Singapore, lawn tennis and garden clubs to follow the next spring. I felt guilty for years for not taking that plump arm in my grip and steering her away for a half hour's enlightenment. Nor did I contradict him when he intimated I too might be settling there after the child.

I don't know how he could have missed her, missed what he had in her. He found her, labeled her, and, for years, never looked again. By then, she had grown up without him. He had drawn her into that world, not hoping to get anything out of her but an aura of stability and, of course, live issue for which he would pay the price of always having her as part of his baggage. He would try to make something of her, a "talisman," a symbol of some kind to them. She was, at base, tenderhearted. She understood so much more than he realized. During a four-day bout of milk fever, she delivered a strange little speech that I remember more clearly than any normal words we ever had. She described him as wanting no affectionate contact with her unless sexually aroused. She used the word "revenge" queerly. I did not understand what she meant, but I do now. He never really had *her* touch, *her* caress—his mother—and so ricocheted through life, bruising things in revenge. Imagine a mere girl understanding this.

He had missed her altogether, the heart of her misidentified. She would pass blood, pass poisonous liquid feces, pass live and inert fetuses like the rest of us, placentas like great livers—"misidentified."

I will have my tincture and sleep. I sleep for great blank stretches now, getting used to what will come.

Charlotte

The new gunboat, a sailing steamer of two hundred and fifty tons, already crawling with vermin, crossed without incident. She would write of her arrival, her ascent up that river, in the romantic, lightly florid style she was to adopt in all her early letters.

Our little flotilla climbed upstream, and huts began to appear on the banks. We occasionally passed women and children, the former wearing clinging garments wrapped tightly about their breasts, their heavy hair looped in knots. All stopped to face our gunboat, which had decked itself with little flags. An iron meshwork was strung round the sides so that Binky could run free. About a mile up, a large number of native craft joined us, sweeping around wonderfully, the men standing and slapping the water with their oars. We passed Chinamen in gondolas and houseboats bursting with Malays, many sitting on the roofs and waving. A few wore two hats, a turban to signify they had gone to Mecca and a straw cone on top.

The Malays seem all of a mold to me: soft black eyes, children's noses, bee-stung lips. They are graceful and soft-spoken, always bowing and slipping around one's back. The Dyaks are a smaller, sturdier breed. Their women wear great coils of brass around their torsos so that it seems more like a punishment than adornment.

Ah, Mama, the heat. A deep breath fills the lungs not with air but with warm fluid. Everything has a scent or odor. It's as if one fell into a pot of essences, thick concentrations of both lovely and nauseating things. One wishes to do nothing but recline, waiting for night and the possibility of a breeze. Yet there are surprises. I reached out and touched a branch near shore and was deluged by an icy shower.

Around noon, we heard the boom of cannon upstream; the *Carolina,* the Rajah's schooner, saluting us. She is named after his mother. Her dear soul is very precious to him. We came round a bend and she floated before us, little puffs of smoke drifting away from her deck. There were dozens of native boats, discharging muskets, and crowds on shore waving and beating gongs.

It is a little like a play city with gaily costumed children come out to welcome a play king. The most hideous individual supports the Rajah's yellow parasol, his feet a mass of ringworm, the backs of his hands tattooed. His name is Njoman, and he serves as umbrella bearer and official state executioner. A large junk exploded crackers as we dropped anchor, and hundreds of birds burst from the trees. For a moment, I could not wait until the end of the day when I could sit at the foot of your bed and describe it all to you.

"I will deliver," she wrote that same month,

my first lesson in geography. The river at the town is as wide as the Thames at Westminster Bridge. On one side is the Malay kampong, or little village, and the Chinese kampong above it on the same bank. Below, almost directly opposite the astana, is the town itself. It consists of a line of Chinese shops with dwellings above, a few Indian stalls, and the Chinese temple, with painted gods and dragons tumbling over the roof. In front there is a quay used by native boats. Behind the shophouses is an enormous mud yard. This is the site of the pasar malam, or evening market. Lower down is Fort Carolina, also named for the Rajah's mother, and attached to it is the prison and the chief constable's compound and a little courthouse. Above, on the slope of a hill, there is an especially pretty little house with blue gables. This, I am told, is to be the residence of the new agent of the Borneo Company, a Scotsman, and farther up the same hill, behind the Chinese, is a house all on stilts, that of the resident C of E. Next to this is a little wooden church with an ironwork cross. We have two houses of Christian worship, the second that of a Reverend Semple and the Christian Knowledge Society, its thin spire rising from a grove of trees. On our side is the quay and the astana compound and a sloping lawn of coarse grass. I have made you a map with my watercolors.

I am told one mile upstream is another kampong with a large Chinese community, and thirty miles west begins the Second Division. The Rajah's cousin Dickie resides seventy miles to the west, at Lundu, and is Resident of this territory. This individual has some mysterious significance. He is called the Tuan Mudah, the young lord, although the Rajah seems not to use the name. His division is the pink blot, a little smudged, to the left. A hundred miles due south begins Dutch territory. In between are approximately six hundred thousand Dyaks and one hundred thousand Malays. To wit, my realm.

There had been some confusion coming into the quay on the day of her arrival. Her husband, she suddenly realized, had already disembarked. He materialized on the quay, greeting people under a yellow umbrella, no longer an odd species of life in dank wool but very much the ringmaster of this circus. He turned to look for her after a while and she proceeded along the deck, passing smiling faces and cold, curious eyes. She felt herself grow dizzy.

Many officials were crammed on the little quay, Malays in turbans, a variety of Chinese in blue gowns and pigtails to their heels, and behind, to the line of trees, hundreds of Dyaks. At one side, neatly aligned, stood four young men, the Residents of Tegora, Banting, Sibu, and Simanggang, all in clean ducks, topees under arms. She smiled and held out her hand to the first. Cakebread took it, his lips mumbling. She moved to the next. She felt their shyness and coldness, men barely out of boyhood, who wielded vast, solitary power somewhere in the interior, who were not allowed to marry, and yet had come down over many weeks to greet her, a girl younger than they.

One of them made a stiff little bow, she did not know which, and she found herself gazing into a black spiked forest, a waxen scar halfway across. One hand she held was missing a thumb. Her mouth filled with saliva. The Rajah's group, congealed around the umbrella, was again moving away. She swayed, and a steel grip was on her elbow. A warm English face smiled directly into her eyes. Fitzhugh introduced himself and placed her hand on his arm and pressed it there, proceeding with her up the slope.

The astana struck her not as a palace but as an unfinished dark house decked out in cheap fripperies. There were pails on the railing, and chickens clucked beneath the stair. Her heart sank. Yet two Englishwomen waited on the veranda, and the sight of them brought a rich wave of relief. A face crowded with teeth approached and curtsied in a cloud of rose water and sweat. Mrs. Semple called her "my dear" and took her hands. The other woman was very thin, with magnificent red hair. She was introduced as Mrs. Dolan. Delia Semple explained that the memsahibs in residence also included Ruth Michaelis, the bride of the new medical assistant; and Mrs. Reedy, wife of the Lupar Resident, both down with fever; and a child's nurse. Six more Englishwomen were expected in the coming months. Senior men were now allowed to marry after seven years' service, since a second tier had been recruited. She realized, as this woman spoke, she was not being addressed with the deference and shyness of her other greetings. Mrs. Semple regarded her with blunt curiosity. As she answered one or two pointed questions, she felt deep relief, the heavy mask put down for a moment in this maddening heat. She half wished this woman would put her arms around her. If she did, she might weep.

"Thank you. You've been most kind," she managed to say. "I'm afraid I am slightly fatigued."

"Of course, my dear! Forgive us, little Ranee." The woman grinned. "This lot will follow you about for a bit longer, and then you'll be left to yourself."

The parade followed them inside, where they were encouraged to sit on little stools covered with cloth-of-gold. Again, it resembled a child's game. She half expected to be given a coronet of daisies and a reed scepter. They were showered with yellow rice, which stuck to her skin. Everyone sat and smiled stupidly at one another. Eventually, her husband stood up and was immediately encircled by the throng, the whole mass passing out to the veranda.

No one seemed to notice she had stayed behind. She found the house to be surprisingly cool. She passed from one large, gloomy room into another. There was no sign of decor, of a feminine hand, yet there was a faint aura about the place. This had not been a house without a woman. He must have had someone. It would be unnatural otherwise, and he could not be condemned for it. Her mother told her to expect this and accept it, but not under any circumstances to condone its continuance. How could she condone or not condone anything? She realized, at that moment, she was being watched. A gray face blinked at her from a doorway and vanished. The wahwah, a small gibbon, reminded her of the fyce. She stepped onto the veranda and sat down, squinting into the blinding light of the quay. The officer who had offered his arm now stood with the fyce on a rope. Her husband and his clutch of worshipers were gathered below some trees.

She must have dozed in the chair, for when she opened her eyes Barr was standing over her. "There you are," he said. "Come and see your home." He lifted her by her hands and led her back inside. It was simply half a dozen cavernous rooms with the jungle pouring through openings between the walls and ceilings. There was little furniture except a few pieces of rattan. On the upper level, however, there was a room unlike the rest. Off a great empty bedroom was a little chamber with a small rattan bed at one end. It had a pretty painted Chinese table and gilt mirror and curtains, or rather lengths of red gauze draped over poles, giving the whole a ruddy hue. It seemed to resemble something between a sewing room and a brothel.

"This is your room exclusively," he said. "When you feel the need for privacy. Your sanctum sanctorum. My mother had a red dressing room in Benares." She stepped over the threshold. He looked at her and she said nothing. "Or you can use it for something else." He watched her and his face changed. "Or lock the damned thing up." He walked away.

She did use the little room. It would, in the years to come, become the nub of her universe, a place of agony and sweat and supreme joy and despair. Here all the children but one would be born. It was here, for three days and nights, she would lie dying. It was the room in which she would rise one morning, not a corpse, as everyone expected, but a ravenously hungry woman.

That evening, she placed her prayer book and diary in the drawer of the Chinese table. When she heard nothing on the stair, she lifted an oblong package from a trunk, unrolled several layers of matting, and withdrew a large doll. She gazed at it tenderly, then placed it in a corner behind the gauze. She wondered why she hadn't expressed pleasure with the little room. It was a thoughtful and surprising gesture. Yet she could not bring herself to thank him. Gifts were an uncharted zone. She had not received the jewel or the lace. She had seen the tidewaiter finger the knife.

From the first, she was made familiar with a litany of diseases, bites, stings, rashes, ague, and malaise that commonly affected Europeans in those latitudes. To this was added a lexicon of plants, roots, insects, and land- and water-dwelling animals she was to avoid at all cost. She was to look where she stepped below, and under what she passed on high. She was to shake out her gutta boots, never go barefoot, never go without her topee during the day, and stay indoors from eleven to two.

"Do not cultivate the young district officers," he said. "It will breed rumor." She thought of the pleasant fat face that had smiled at her on the quay, the arm braced under hers, and let it drift away. To this, she added her mother's warning to confide in neither female friends nor servants. The whole crushed her heart.

Her position in that place was defined early on. The first week, he had ordered a prescription of quinine to be kept on hand for her, and it was delivered the same day and placed on the little dressing table. He noticed it when he entered in the evening and picked it up as she was undoing her hair. "You must keep this on hand, Melie," he said. "Fevers come on damnably fast and they can do real damage." He was about to put it down when he looked at it more closely, then strode from the room. She could hear him shouting angrily in Malay from the stair and someone running out of the house.

"What is it?" she asked. "Is it the wrong medication?"

A half hour later, Michaelis, the young man whom Dolan had trained to the apothecary, appeared on the veranda. The poor fellow had come at a run and was breathless. "My God, Rajah, is it not quinine? I opened the jar myself five days ago. I gave my Ruth a dose and she's right as rain! My God," he said again, seeing Barr's face.

"It is quinine. It is the patient who is incorrect," he said frigidly. "There is no *Mrs. Barr* in Sarawak."

The man looked bewildered, then blanched. "It was an oversight, an absurd mistake." He snatched the thing back and jammed it in his pocket. "It's just that we thought—that is, it was supposed that the Ranee might take comfort in the informal address, everything being so new and strange. Mrs. Semple—"

"Ah, I might have known that cow was at the bottom!"

The bottle reappeared an hour later with *Her Highness the Ranee Amelia* in handsome script with an overlay of wax. She stood by the lamp, the smell of rotting fish and flowers on the breeze, and contemplated it.

In addition to the matched German saddles, embroidered tea sets, clocks, silver plate, salvers, sugar dredgers, mustard pots, and inkstands transported on the *Terror,* wedding presents continued to arrive.

> We receive all sorts of things, some alive, some dead, some fragrant, some stinking. They include several beaded ba, or baby carriers, a little owlet, a cage of lovebirds, and, today, a muddy sack of something crawling. They join a growing collection of jardinieres, the ugliest displayed most prominently for it comes from an important 'towkay' upstream. The datus and their families have sent rich batiks and a pretty plaid cloth not unlike dress Campbell.

No Malay women were presented on the day of her arrival, but he explained that a reception was planned by the female relatives of the datus and would be held at the astana in a few days' time. Weeks later, when she had all but forgotten this, great baskets of food appeared at the cookhouse door. At midmorning, a line of small boys staggered up the stairs under stacked lacquer boxes. Cushions and betel boxes appeared in the saloon. The Datin Aisha, the first wife of the Datu Pattingi, never moved without her betel.

By noon, she was informed that these women were assembled and waiting. She wore a long-sleeved frock to cover a tenacious rash, buckled her leather sandals, and descended into the smell of thick coffee and soft murmurs. The datus introduced their wives, daughters, and nieces and then departed, as if depositing children at a birthday tea, the only man remaining being Bawhal, judged harmless and left to translate.

The Datin Aisha, an older woman in a rich sarong, slipped a hand under her fingertips and guided her to a little dais. Once seated, the others sat around them, dropping their veils. Sweet, dense coffee was served, along with a variety of little cakes. "Makan, silahkan," the Datin urged. "Minum! Jangan malu!"

The woman regarded her in some detail. "Only virgins wear gold ornaments," she said in a slow idiot's Malay, "but a ranee may as well." She glanced at the great white feet in their sandals. "Her sarong should be very long, for the feet should not show." Bawhal translated painfully. There was tittering. They were making sport of her.

"But how can one walk in skirts that long?" she asked pleasantly.

"A ranee does not need to walk. The wives of the Sultan of Brunei never secure their kain tapes, because they have no need to rise."

It was a stilted, hellish session, the second and third wives always asking permission of a first wife before speaking. In bidding goodbye, this Datin's voice was mellifluous, her expression dead, and the others followed suit. There was no friend to be had here. She stood at the doorway smiling, trying to hide her feet. The door was finally closed, and she rushed to the small red room and collapsed on the cot in sobs. She willed herself away, willing as she had as a child, not away from that room with its faded fruits and cornucopias but back into it with all her heart.

He arrived back from Lida Tanah that evening. He was delighted, he said, the reception had "come off." Glancing at her frock, the thick sandals, he suggested she might select some "light Malay clothing." Before bed, she gazed at her dresses hanging limp from a pole. As she looked, a tremendous roach crept out of the bodice of a gray tea gown and passed into its sleeve. Her gorge rose and she dropped to her knees, groping under the bed for the wretched pot.

The bulky figure and peculiar, delicate stride struck her as funny until she recognized the rescuing angel of the first day. Fitzhugh stopped to take his leave before returning to his station. This was one new face she recalled with pleasure. Knowing it would occasionally be part of her life heartened her. Now he had come to say good-bye. He saw the expression on her face.

"Ah, you'll do splendidly," he said warmly.

She turned away, her eyes filling stupidly. "I've already made a hash of it. The datins think me a fool."

"That lot!" He laughed. "You'll find a way round them. If they truly get under your skin, ask the Rajah to pack you up to Simanggang. I've a very nice place up there, if I do say so." They spoke of country houses, of London, of the social habits of wah-wahs. An hour later, she watched him pass down through the canna, feeling more bereft at this stranger's leaving than for any friend she could remember. She would conjure Fitzhugh's face and cheerful voice often in those months, a little wedge against advancing misery. Then, in summer, another visitation served to fortify her.

A very young boy came down from the Sakarang on temporary leave and she found him one morning, quite by accident, sitting outside one of the DO bungalows. She had been walking up from the bathhouse with an amah and the fyce and was struck by an amazingly beautiful boy cleaning a rifle in the shade of a doorway. His name was Connor Doherty. He and his brother had joined the service two years before, at eighteen and nineteen years of age respectively. Both had been midshipmen on the *Superb,* Hemmings' ship. Brothers were rarely placed aboard the same man-of-war, but these two had campaigned so desperately that Hemmings allowed it. They were released into service at the end of their sea duty. Sutton assigned them to the Sakarang but Barr reversed the order, saying they could bloody well sell themselves as a duo to Hemmings, but he would have none of it. "Split them up," he said.

"In a way"—Sutton scratched his ear—"they be sort o' 'alves. What one misses, t'other battens on. They don't do well apart. Like swans."

"Jesus Christ," Barr said, and dropped it.

A fort at an outstation in those days was a thick wooden or stone stockade with a few smooth-bore guns. It had an armory and crude living quarters for the fortmen below. The Resident or district officer berthed above. The Dohertys were assigned to one of these in the middle of forty thousand Dyaks. Their main support was twenty native fortmen and the small Malay population gathered around the stockade. It was an energetic way to begin an interior education. The tribes of that region, the Sakarangs, the Batang Lupars, the Undups, and the Lingas, had been at war with each other for decades. When the first Sakarang penglima walked out of the forest with eight hundred warriors and empty head baskets, Connor Doherty pulled up a stick chair for him. Two days later, this man returned upstream with all his warriors and empty baskets along with a tin of Epsom salts for swollen knees. Neither boy could remember much of what transpired, but for years afterward, shades of an Irish quick step were said to surface in Sakarang gawais. The two continued to make curious, undocumented inroads. There was Pa Atok, a colossal thorn in the side of every DO in the Third Division, yet never giving these two trouble, his raiding parties of a thousand or more circling twenty miles wide of their station, losing both time and heads to do it. This man, one day in conversation, had expressed an envy of the canopy creatures who could poke their heads above the leaves and see "the world of light, even to Kinabalu." It was Ross Doherty who, for two weeks, worked on a rattan hoist that eventually lifted the savage above the highest branches, the man almost dying of vertigo and wonder. Getting him down, they cracked a humerus. Pa Atok carried the crooked arm proudly for the rest of his life, a memento of this vertical journey. Sutton opined, years later, that the brothers survived because they were young and they were idiots. "There's no immunity like that. Except," he added sorrowfully, "they didn't, did they?"

The boy rose to his full six feet and rested the gun against the wall. "My lady," he said with a shy, glorious smile. He was almost her age.

She wound up spending a full hour talking with the young Resident from the Sakarang before she remembered her husband's warning.

Once you accept racing through clouds of mosquitoes to your nets in the evening, once you accept checking your shoes each morning for the little white three-step and automatically refuse second helpings of black-rice pudding; once you accept that disaster is reported with a smile and good news with a sort of balmy melancholia; that supplies, mail, kebuns, and kulis move with remarkable torpor while vermin, rashes, and septicemia move like lightning—life takes on a semblance of normality.

This normality was abetted by an English clock. He still spent the cooler hour at dawn riding the bajau, after which he bathed, saw a handful of petitioners, and joined her for breakfast. He would then walk down to the landing stage where his datus awaited, and the small crowd would glide to the other bank, ascending the slope to the courthouse.

This building had a peculiar charm. Mythical animal heads peered down from each corner of the ceiling, dragons or dogs with square teeth and condolent expressions. An aromatic wood was used for the rafters, giving justice a light medicinal scent. On some days, she found it a pleasant place to spend the heat of the afternoon, more restful than a fitful nap. Chairs were set for him and his four datus on a little platform, and the public sat on mats in front. She was struck by the dignity and fairness of these four men. If one of them had a private interest in a case, he was absent.

Otherwise, she spent the hours between two and four resting indoors. The remainder of the afternoon she studied Malay with Bawhal and wrote letters or saw an occasional visitor. They dined a few minutes after nightfall. There were sometimes one or two guests, usually Residents from one of the other rivers. She came especially to enjoy the company of the Nakodah Dullah. He always greeted her warmly and admired even the smallest new accoutrement to the astana's decor—a little marquetry table, a lacquered bowl. In truth, he spent so many mercantile hours praising trash, he no longer knew what he liked. Except women. It was said the best of the white female captives taken over the years in those waters—there were six—went to him. One, kept in Rhio, when given a chance to gain her freedom, would not take it.

Dinner was the most pleasant time of day. It was the hour after dinner that she hated. At the first puff of her husband's cheroot, the veranda came to life with roiling shadows, the first shapes creeping to the edge of the table, leaning into his ear. She would rise and slip away.

"This is where my true power comes from," he snapped one evening, coming in and finding her already under her nets with candle and book. "These voices out of the dark are my ear to the ground."

It sounded so pompous, so melodramatic. She wanted to say, This is no palace! This is no center of government! You are standing in a roach-infested, leaking house at the edge of a jungle! But she didn't. She realized, at that moment, she feared him.

On one of these evenings, slipping away from table, she almost fell over a crouching figure on the stair. She gave a little cry and the man looked up, a Dyak face.

Lim, the cook, appeared instantly. "This man is from the Sadong, Rajah Ranee," he said. "He is a chief. He wishes to ask the Rajah for help with attacks on his river, but he felt ill and so I gave him permission to sit on the stair."

"What's the matter with him?" she asked.

"He has a pain in his head, Rajah Ranee."

The yellow eyes were half closed in pain. She gathered her skirts and climbed the stairs, snatching a bottle of eau de cologne from her Chinese table. She went back and sat above the creature on the stair, sprinkling some drops on her hands and massaging his temples. The skull felt dry, like a nut. After a moment, he leaned back into her skirts as if this was the most natural thing in the world. When she stopped, he rose and pronounced a beautiful somlah, an odd thing for any Dyak to do, and left. She did not mention it to her husband. She thought she had done an unwise thing. The next morning, when she looked for the little bottle, it was gone.

While she did not cultivate the datins and stayed clear of those night-time specters, there were some things in which she began to take an interest. He had begun an experimental pepper farm at Tegora and often went up during the first year of their marriage. Farming was somewhat familiar, and she would inquire about its progress. In the autumn, he began work on a scheme for a national bank with the aid of Lim, who had graduated from cook to a sort of plenipotentiary regarding the Chinese. She would sometimes sit silently at their sessions with her needle.

Lim was a marvel. Always a step ahead of his master, anticipating decisions, smoothing alternate paths if they were needed, and doing all silently. He was a genius at managing kulis. He had been a kuli himself the first third of his life. "Wah! I can see the stolen chicken in your pot!" he would hiss. "I can see through your bowels into the earth below!" and some poor brute would rejoin a workline with renewed energy. Barr found himself wishing he had a dozen Lims to spread about. He no more wished it than Lim produced duplicates of himself—cousins, nephews, uncles—all carefully tutored by the cook.

The Rajah has a singular method of government, she wrote at Michaelmas. *He discusses revenues with his cook and cuisine with the Datu Imam and religion with his master-at-arms.*

She did her best with these letters, yet found the effort, the effort with everything, cost her more and more. She saw herself steadily flagging. At times, he saw it too, in the dull eye, the nervous hands.

Pontianak

A large tureen, with a thin crack between a little blue shepherd and a little blue sheep, and a long *driedtfleisch* sausage wrapped in oiled muslin and slipped into a canvas rifle case arrived by gunboat that winter.

He had planned for any bride of his to have, as her first journey, one to Pontianak. He looked forward to seeing the van Lutyenses yet was uneasy about introducing this girl to them. Dirck had too much natural courtesy to find fault in her. And the idea of seeing her side by side with Birgit depressed him. Then again, what more helpful experience for a young bride than to show her what a white woman's intelligence and will could do in that country. In June, using one of the gunboats as escort, the *Carolina* sailed round the great elbow of coast without incident.

Both van Lutyenses were on the beach, along with a group of officers. He knew most of them on sight: Klopperburg, the naval attaché; Wenderholt, the surgeon; the military officers van de Hyden, Stalvius, and de Groot; and a strange one in blue worsted and oak leaves whom he did not recognize but who turned out to be the new military assignee. This man, Aalbertsberg, almost immediately submitted him to a stream of specific, rude questions. He asked about his outstations, the size of his European force, the kinds of ordnance he used. The man flipped a cigar while a nervous subaltern translated. *"Met wat voor kruit laadt U Uw patronen?"* Van Lutyens pulled him away to see some sick ponies, and he vanished from the earth.

Birgit van Lutyens stood squarely over her thick legs, arms folded, taking stock of the new bride. Birgit had reddish-gold hair braided into a tight knot from which tiny snakes sprang free and, unlike most European women in the East, was lightly sunburned. She had a straightforward speech, a willingness to plunge in with any work, and an immediate, direct response to everything about her. The blue eyes melted easily, while the jaw could set like granite. She was one of those woman who, people say, would be a beauty if she dropped a stone, yet the essence of her beauty lay in her ample flesh. In times of fever, a small feral face began to emerge in the glass. She was the first to see it and doubled her ration of beer. Her children approached her straight on and kissed her full on the mouth.

They are a starched, red-faced, and kindly people. The garrison is entirely European, relying on no native recruits. They grow a vast acreage of cassava, but the main occupation seems to be the regulation and taxation of sea traffic. In between, it would seem, they eat. Our stay consists of lurching from one gigantic repast to the next. We breakfast on leverworst and cheese, ginger pannekoeken, sausage from their own pork, deviled eggs, and jam—all piled on the same plate. Tiffin holds no respite. Thick potato soup, whole rockfish, stewed chicken, curried rice, a pretty salad, persimmons, custard apples eaten with a spoon.

Yesterday, I slipped away. There is a path behind the nearest kampong, and walking here I came upon a singular creature eyeing me from beneath a tree. She was handsome and slovenly with that heavy hair they have twisted in loops with God knows what vermin within. I learned later this was van Lutyens' mistress! There were two children lolling with her, one black as ink, the other lily fair. Kuching is a bastion of civilization compared to this. Someday, I will ask Birgit about it—she seems an open, warm creature. I feel we are to be friends.

Barr had noticed the woman on earlier visits. "One must do it," van Lutyens said. "They are pleasant creatures and they provide a measure of safety as long as they love you. When they stop, you may still enjoy them, but dine at home." Barr had the sense that, despite his words, he had true feeling for this woman.

The two men were swallowed up by the garrison, while she shared Birgit's day. She became tenderly acquainted with the small van Lutyenses, four yellow heads with dark blue eyes. The older ones had learned a great deal of cooking, and each had a specialty that was pressed upon her. It was a refreshing idyll, the strange guttural tongue, the nostalgic routine of a European household. Individual objects gave small flashes of pleasure—a large painted plate, a little German vegetable knife. Best, a true Dresden rose, its heavy, fragrant head pinned to a nipah trellis.

On the morning of their departure, they were laden with smoked meats and Birgit's thick liquors and fruit syrups. "It has been lovely," she said to this woman, and meant it. "You must visit as soon as you can come away."

"Met het grootste pleizier." Birgit held out a red hand, then snatched it back and kissed her, a wet burst.

"Met het grootste pleizier," she repeated to herself, rocking out to the wind. The garrison and houses soon vanished in the steam. Yet they were there. There were now two poles to her world. Labuan to the north, where the Russells and their party had taken up residence, and Pontianak, both places in which a white woman kept a European parlor. A civilized world was forming itself about her in thin filaments. Thin, yet she knew instinctively the power behind the beaded lamp, the porcelain cup. In some deeper realm, it should be measured in tons, like ordnance. They were already on the wind, the gunboat shearing in.

These social rounds, in reality, were enormously dangerous. Traveling down that long coast, they were protected not by tangible naval might, as she assumed, but by an easily upset, ever-changing balance and counterweight, surmises of an enemy's cerebrations at a particular juncture in time and space. The monstrous weight in their favor had been Kilcane, and he had not swept the coast for four years. "They will not strike with the monsoon in abeyance or two days from a Dutch stronghold and Cape Datu fortified to the north." The truth was, this kind of excursion could have cost them their lives.

She was grateful to him for the visit. Despite van Lutyens' morals, she would come to appreciate the couple as much as he did—indeed, she was surprised he appreciated their special warmth. She wondered in what other ways she might have misjudged him. Standing at his side, she felt a queer stir of affection and put her arm through his in the wind. He looked down, and the color of his eyes and the color of the sky seemed all of a piece and she suddenly understood nothing at all.

The dawn after they arrived back, he left upstream with six prahus. It was a little voyage he had not mentioned, yet it did not seem normal or necessary. It felt to her like a slap.

Except for periods of fever, murky expanses of time spent in a drenched nightdress, she continued to write to her mother almost daily, enthusiastic little missives filled with information and description. Iris Mumm searched them for signs of her daughter's true state of mind but found nothing.

A staple of the economy is antimony ore, presently unsalable due to the disturbances in Europe. . . .

Our little bazaar is charming, the wares extending from moon cakes to serpents stuffed in bottles (a triangular head is said to be poisonous, an oval one harmless, but I cannot tell the difference). . . .

It is true the Dyaks have some abominable practices, but these he is steadily eradicating. They are a shy people and not unintelligent. . . .

We have eight hundred species of birds with brilliant plumage but few true songsters [this with her Easter pastel, a pair of kingfishers]. The place abounds in creatures which look like everything on earth except what they are: insects disguised as leaves, butterflies with the eyes of serpents on their wings, serpents fitted out as branches. Everything is in disguise, the edible to look inedible, the harmless to look deadly, the deadly to look harmless. There are hundreds of varieties of butterflies, some as large as dinner plates, and three kinds of leeches—two in grass and bushes, one aquatic, the buffalo leech, whose acquaintance I have thankfully made only in a jar in the Rajah's new little museum. Did I tell you of it? Mosquitoes, stinging flies, ants, scorpions, centipedes, and one hundred and twenty species of serpent round out this bestiary, supplied in some detail by Tom Lytton, a young naturalist who is staying a fortnight with us, brother to Charlotte.

The weight of writing these letters, echoing so little of her true life, steadily became more oppressive. In order not to dull their cheer or betray a growing depression, she began once again to keep a diary, not the dreamy recordings of childhood but a bitter counterweight, written in haste and never reread.

June 2, 1852

My body is covered with a sickening rash. Cologne stings horribly, but I must do something for it smells foul.

July 4, 1852

He has left here thrice in four months for brief sojourns upriver. These trips are just the duration for which I may be best suited. I would like to see the country. I can understand his not wanting to take me as far as Simanggang, although I would relish seeing Fitzhugh.

These trips of his fell into a pattern. He and roughly thirty men, handpicked by Si Tundo, would depart before dawn. When he returned, ten or twelve days later, he invariably had some small gift for her. Once it was a simpalili, a baby tarsier with huge eyes and tiny spatulate fingers. She was enchanted. No trace of Na clung to him, yet she felt oddly nervous around him those first days back.

Once he returned to find her sitting on the veranda, barefoot, a yellow sarong wrapped tightly across her breasts. "Splendid." He kissed her, pulling out a chair. In reality, he thought she looked ridiculous, decked out like some Indian cow.

She felt herself clothed in something that might, at any moment, pull apart and drop around her feet, but since he seemed to approve, she had several others made. She gazed at her image swathed in the soft bright cloth, artfully draped yet on her somehow concretized, resembling nothing so much as a commemorative statue. She returned to her own clothes, anemic and lifeless but suitable to her size and stride.

It was more than dress that struck him as offensive. After his visits to Na, the girl began to disgust him. She seemed to smell more strongly of animal sweat, there was always some damp patch under her arms or down her spine. At certain times a faint odor of menstrual blood could be detected. Ajar's fragrant liquidity wrapped around his eyes, and he went off to smoke alone.

Yet there were times she could surprise him. "Did you know," she said, one evening at table, "Lim and his people take all their meals from baskets brought from a relative's house? I've asked Ah Heng to share our kitchen, but she refuses. Given the nature of the Chinese, I find this odd."

"The nature of the Chinese?" He laughed. "What do you know of the nature of the Chinese?"

"I know they are greedy," she replied, as if softly stamping her foot. "I know they would not refuse free victuals without good reason."

He looked at her. "And what may that be?"

"The possibility of poisoning."

He took another bite, the plate before him changing into a coiling mass. "What a thought for a well-bred girl." The fact was, this inept child, this meaty, seasick girl, had detected the single real danger in his household. Van Lutyens had warned him, and the man's instincts were sound. Yet he had done nothing. He gazed at the broad young face, the limp, wide collar. She could harbor, he thought with some astonishment, insight, opinions, sexual tastes. "What to do, la?"

"I should invite them to take all their meals from our cookhouse. I should brook no refusal."

She was right. The Chinese were no fools, and if Lim and his tribe ate from their cookhouse he would not have to address it. "All right. See to it."

She faltered. "Me?"

"Of course."

She spoke to Lim the next day. The man declined politely, saying it was not necessary to spoil them.

"Both you and I know what I am saying," she said to the Chinese. "The Rajah has put his house in your keeping."

"Wah! Have you lost your dung mind?" Ah Heng cried to her husband when he told her. "He has no sense, and so we should join him? Are we to be his testers, something for which you use a dog?" From that week, food expenditures increased tenfold to feed the extra mouths. A little green cabinet appeared in the cookhouse containing horn cups and lalang wands and all manner of poison detectors, along with a fish bowl in which a small portion of each dish was dropped, the tiny fish watched by the sharp eye of small nephew Wang.

There were other things. One morning, shortly after he was awarded Commissioner status, she found him in the saloon with Biverts surrounded by dozens of bits of colored cloth. He would puff his cheroot, squat down, move one or two pieces, then slide into his chair and contemplate the work. She watched this. After some minutes, she bent and adjusted three blue bands atop a yellow, turning them laterally and eliminating a green. He stared at it.

"By God." He looked up at her. It was the first pure sign of approval he had ever shown. She flushed despite herself, looking suddenly as pretty as she had peering back at the trot. The blue bars and yellow field flew that summer, hoisted beside the Union Jack while a ship's fiddle played "God Save the Queen."

The flag had occupied him for months. He spent colossal amounts of time with such things. He spent days choosing the right marble slabs for his fish market and music for a little municipal band. Two breeding bulls took a solid three months of research before he finally made his selection. He persisted in having a hand in everything, no matter how small, sinking into the sweet stupor of attending to such minutiae. By then, strings had started to fray, but by then that phenomenon was entrenched at Lundu, reinforcing, splicing.

Despite these small triumphs and the antidote of the diary, by the end of the second summer, her letters began to fall out of their braced enthusiasm. Iris Mumm was gratified, hoping she might at last glimpse the true state and well-being of her child. A light sarcasm seeped into the pages, although only regarding unimportant things.

> He insisted I try durian, a fruit considered the nectar of the gods by these people. A segment has the appearance and smell of a decayed fetus.

> He grows not sago or areca nuts, but "pimentoes" in his experimental gardens. Wizened caper bushes line the laundry stockade. Little flax plants burst blue and die. He will not draw from this place what it wishes to give [this, her first direct criticism of him].

> I like Mrs. Semple quite well, she is the only woman who treats me as a human being, without ceremony. She has long since overlooked the stupid incident of the quinine.

She found she spent much time with Delia Semple. The woman had a brusque, pleasant way of taking her in hand, something dear and familiar. Charlotte Norris was still in Singapore, and Mrs. Dolan was too busy having babies. The only other candidate for friendship was Ruth Michaelis, who seemed perpetually strung out on emotional tenterhooks, whether by an infant with fever or a curdled custard. She took comfort in Mrs. Semple's cheerful, solid presence. This changed with one incident.

Delia Semple did not usually call at the astana after the quinine episode. She'd meet the Ranee halfway up the quay, and the two would cross the river and stroll through the morning pasar. One day, Melie started from the astana early and decided to wait for her friend by a small inlet where sago prahus dropped their lines. A young Dyak was bathing close to shore, and at first she did not notice him in the blinding dazzle. He stood thigh deep, cupping water over his shoulders and back, twisting languidly in the sunlit wash. She gazed at the taut buttocks, the swing of thick, knife-edged hair. She was transfixed. She found herself wondering what it would be like to have sex with someone simply because one found him beautiful. At that instant, she saw Delia Semple. She was standing on the far side of the inlet among some nipah palms, her feet planted wide beneath her belted skirt, her large cloth bag clutched to her breast. She too was gazing at the youth, and it was a look of such unadulterated lust that the other turned away.

There is a point, usually recognizable only in hindsight, when something difficult or chafing passes into a deeper stage. She felt this was happening now. For some time, the heat and density of the air had been doing small, ugly things to her body. At any point where flesh met flesh—under her arms, her breasts, her buttocks—a rash would form and a vague stink would rise so that she was always surreptitiously sniffing herself and slipping away to bathe, sometimes four times a day. She had developed a gradual edema. Her face and figure seemed bloated, especially when compared with the lithe, dark figures around her.

September 10, 1852

Today I dropped my palm leaf fan and Sarhid, a cook boy, stooped for it by my chair. His nostrils seemed to flare for a moment, and I was mortified. Why must women spend a fifth of their lives with bloody wads between their legs?

A light wash of pustules now exists between my breasts and but-
tocks and anywhere moisture is retained. I can only disgust him.

She was unaware of how powerful her disgust for her own body
had become. She slipped the little book deep into its drawer and
withdrew a sheaf of gray paper.

September 15, 1852

Mama,

A very speedy game of mahjong today with Mr. Reedy
and Mr. Ang Chew. The tiles were not lettered or numbered,
the winds were not marked NESW in the corner as in our set
in the morning room. It made the game difficult, but as for
the method of play and scoring, we are correct. . . .

Rereading the mahjong letter, its dogged cheer, its little inventive
asides, she realized her precarious mental position. Dreams confirmed
this. In these dreams, she traveled through the rooms of her childhood, becoming smaller as she passed through each succeeding doorway. They were soothing at first, moving in a world sweetly familiar.
It was only at the end, when she had passed through the last of the
doors and stood not in the stable yard or cutting garden but in front
of that turgid, brown river, that her heart contracted.

These dream meanderings always began in the green dining room
at dusk, quiet as if set for a wake, a deaf-and-dumb Mary lighting the
beeswax candles. She'd glide past her, into the music room, past the
great sociable with its woolen roses, the two brass sconces like
inverted top hats, into the hall with the small stair. She always headed
down in these dreams, her destination the basement kitchen. She'd
pass through the scullery, turning left at the japanned coal bucket, and
step onto the wide slate floor, cold in summer, where the Spanish velvet smashed in smooth yellow gobs and Mary called the dogs; past the
scrubbed oak table, the copper saucepans, the black Carron range
with its expandable sides, the line of butter molds, brass spring scales,
and tin spice boxes, the glistening conserve shelves—apple, medlar,

bitter lime. In the scullery, a younger Mary filled hot-water cans, the first for Mama's bath. She passed through the narrow inner arcade connecting the kitchen and stable yard, birds hanging by wires, now into a time when her Papa was alive. She'd catch her breath and turn the other way, round the corner, past the pudding basins, the fish tureens marked in waxed pencil TURBOT, SALMON, HADOCK (the one D never noticed, but now eerily exact); past the biscuit tin painted like a parson with the lid shaped like his hat, the black eyes following her along the sideboard—into the little alcove with its built-in bench, the smell of ginger in hot milk. She drank it down, then slipped through the door, which slammed violently at her back. She was outside in freezing air. She ran round and round, trying to find a way back inside, a way she knew existed—Budding's open crack, for he believed in fresh air at all times of year, but it was sealed, for Mama wrote that he was dead—through the icehouse, her legs on fire with touch-me-nots, the root cellar where there was a little door, but where? She moaned.

He would put an arm around her then, shake her, and finally rise and drag himself elsewhere. He'd lie in the dark and rue his senseless haste. A choice between a woman beyond her bearing years and this unstable child.

She was not truly afraid until the dreams slipped into daylight. One morning, her mother's skirts disappeared around the corner of the washhouse. On the landing, nimble fingers tucked in a wisp of hair. These were hallucinations, she knew, brought about by her poor health and unhappiness. She only began to feel true terror when palpable objects shot forward in time and space. She found the heel, white, cracked off when she was twelve, caught in a splintered floorboard. A glove she had not seen her mother wear for eight years, and assumed lost at Covent Garden, appeared in all its physicality on the Chinese table. She slipped it in a drawer. Other objects appeared, objects lost and mourned when she was a child. One morning, the dead pony Hector grazed at the bottom of the orchard.

There was no one to tell of her madness. She took long walks up the one safe path, cropped low by the kebuns. At the end there was a pavilion by a small creek, and she would sit here for hours. One day the boy Unggat was dragging along the fyce and came upon her. She looked at him with swollen eyes, not caring what he saw or thought.

"Sometimes I see things," she said dully. "I hear the voice of my mother, though she is not here."

"I also, Rajah Ranee," he said. He sat down and gazed at the stream, the expression coming into that dark face matching any misery and longing she felt. She did not make him go away. In the days ahead, when she walked up this path, a shadow sometimes followed, and when she sat down and watched the water, it sat down and watched it too.

The boy eased her. He did not slink behind so as not to disturb. His face looked into hers squarely. At times he was aloof, his mind engaged somewhere else, yet when she gazed at him, he smiled. Once he patted her arm, a curious gesture in such a creature. She taught him a few words in English, useless words, yet ones that gave her pleasure to hear in the mouth of a child: "Happy Christmas," "snow," "marzipan." Later, raising a cup or piece of fruit, she said its English name and he repeated it, then in Malay. There was, in those weeks, the first night she slept through to dawn. Objects adhered to their rightful place in space and time. One day, she opened the drawer of the little Chinese table and found the glove gone. It seemed with each new object the child named in his raspy voice, one of those mirages from hell imploded.

Unggat told her stories, stories told to him by Njoman. Most had to do with Grandfather. This was how the great buaya was addressed, for to use the crocodile's name was to call him to you; he was a courteous animal and would come if beckoned. As they sat, he told her about one crocodile who ran up bills in the bazaar. He married the daughter of a Chinaman and was a very good husband until he learned to gamble. With his winnings he bought a fine sarong and a bag of betel nuts and drank arak into the night. She laughed, and he told her another. This was how, through the boy, her burgeoning madness lost its grip and how, too, she began to learn that soft, gentle tongue. Despite Inchi Bawhal, the little primer had remained as incomprehensible as when she first slit its pages on the *Terror*'s deck. Grandfather spoke slowly and did not mind repeating.

Unggat, she realized, had an odd collection of jobs. He would attend the door in the morning, but not in the evening. He served at breakfast, but not at lunch. While his job as valet had passed on to one of Lim's relatives, he still considered himself the official inventory taker of the Rajah's personal effects. His favorite occupation, however, was ringing the dinner bell, a round brass gong, three times, evenly, not too loud or too soft but as Lim showed him, calling the Tuans to dine, and they came at his command. This was a time of mystery. Men and women eating together around a table covered with tapers and flowers as if around a corpse.

In rainy weather, she often sat with him in the saloon between the wooden buayas, and one day he told her their secret.

"Do you *hear* them speak?" she asked.

"No, Rajah Ranee, but it is true. The Dayang told me this. She knows many animals who speak and has herself a gusi tuak."

"What dayang knows such things?"

"The Dayang Ajar-only-this."

In late afternoon, Njoman would come for him. The old man would bow to her silently, and the two would depart. Njoman, the Saribas umbrella bearer, the state executioner, she knew held her in contempt. She was to him useless and ridiculous, a great cow who could do nothing for herself.

She would see the small face under its turban at tiffin and this consoled her. Yet she knew the boy was a respite and not a cure.

There is a moment in those latitudes, a pause in the great revolution of winds, when they cease blowing from one quadrant and, for the first time in months, start from the reverse. With the southwest monsoon, everything lightens, a breeze blows through the innermost convolutions of the brain. Things slammed down in temper are picked up again. Jokes are cracked. Love is made in slow and imaginative ways. In November, the universe lurches again and the reverse occurs, wet winds shrieking from the sea.

In the course of two weeks, everything was soaking and smelled of rot. The netting in the veranda doorways, sucked out and in by the wind, stayed drenched; the floors were sticky with salt blown over twenty miles of forest. Small charcoal braziers were set out every-where, but all they did was draw new forms of vermin from every crack. One evening, she sat down to write in her diary and found the pages peeling off. She held the pulpy clots in her hands and then balled them up and flung them away, the weeks and months of her life.

The wind, more than anything, drove her mad. She would get Lim and the kebuns to pull away the furniture and block the openings on the windward side, and by afternoon it would be blowing from another quarter, pouring water through the ventilation space between wall and roof. Most maddening was the fact that no one else seemed bothered. Barr was on the hind end of a circuit up-country, and the others seemed to take it in stride as a necessary annoyance.

One sodden morning, she unlocked a storage room under the eaves and found all her leather trunks covered in green velvet. Her saddle was set on a wooden rack and, when she brushed the cantle, the air was filled with a sickening green cloud. She lifted linen out of a chest and it fell apart along its folds, a strange geometry of rot. A cuckoo clock, an absurd wedding present, sat with its bird thrust out, the mechanism choked with minuscule plants. She decided to clean everything, to move it all into cupboards and seal them. The cup-boards, however, the few that existed, would not close for they were too swollen with moisture or, if they were closed, would not open. She sank down and wept, the grotesque clock in her hands.

"Rajah Ranee?" She gazed up into a black, fierce face. Njoman stood over her, the ends of his cocked kerchief hanging limp. She clambered up and rushed away.

That afternoon, she woke from a leaden sleep to loud, rhythmical banging, as if every door of the house were being opened and closed by maniacal hands, drowning out even the wind. Doors everywhere were being removed and shaved and replaced. The workmen pro-tested to Njoman that in the dryer months the wood would shrink and nothing would fit. The Saribas said nothing.

Mold everywhere vanished under his fierce eye. The saddle was burnished and oiled and would never again wear its sickening mantle. The only tragedy, he felt, was the bird. She had wept over it. He blew and brushed away the little plants with a feather, brushing and blowing until the bird disappeared with a snap. His bones trembled, but he carried it up the stairs and placed it outside her door.

She emerged onto the veranda in one of those brief lulls when everything steams. Unggat's feet slapped up the sticky boards and he sat next to her. She absentmindedly took his hand. She pressed the spider fingers and gazed at the river, a brown roiling animal. When she let go, the indentation remained in her puffy palm. They stared at it.

"So much water," he said, "means a child is coming." He yelped and bounded down the stairs.

The monsoon delayed the mail packet for weeks, but the heavily armed tub finally passed over the bar, the intrepid Kling at the helm, for Lavransson was down with fever. Crossing from the pasar, her dugout hove to, but there was nothing for her aboard. It was not until she climbed the astana steps that she saw the crate. Bigelow had brought it up, having caught the packet at Santubong. The man himself, a dull fortress, rose out of the shadows. Bigelow always mashed her hand. She thanked him and he left. That was, she thought, this individual's particular grace: He did not loiter. She had the crate hauled up the stairs and down the hall and placed in the little red room. She waited a painful, sensuous moment, then tore at it with scissors and knife, and all the sweet, familiar odors of her childhood wafted into her lap. The box contained a small universe, one of bracing air, where appointments were made for one's teeth and hair by another human being. The familiar labels of Vichy and seltzer, the odors of camomile, gum arabic, and Wilson's pastelles, Haxhurst's safe cure, fruit salts, Mrs. Ruyden's ointment, laxatives, orange pastes, and vetiver, entered every pore. Her mother's arms were around her. There was a layer of extract of beef, and one of Birds' custard powder. *Inhale the vapour of Norwegian pine* a little box of pastilles invited, and she gobbled five.

There were three pairs of shoes made on her own last, too small now with her swollen feet, and a pair of espadrilles. Boxes of starch stuck together in a crazy, caked edifice—somewhere in her letters she had asked for it; a gross of hair nets—who in God's universe would send a gross of hair nets? "You've wisps left out," fingertips brushing her neck. A tortoiseshell hairbrush slipped out of its felt envelope; near the bottom of it all, a strange, misshapen parcel taped over and over and sealed with wax, after several minutes of cutting and unrolling, a horrendous thing, the mothy fox mask labeled as to the day put to ground: VALE OF WHITE HORSE, SEPTEMBER 13, 1844, her first hunt.

There was a box from Charbonnel and Foster and six bottles of Rimmel's vinegar water in newsprint. She could see those long hands folding, wrapping. All this unadulterated love, not in words, for there were none save a note with the usual concerns and bits of gossip, but in things, in the aromas and tactile power of objects. It was as if the vast distance separating them had worked as a filter until, somewhere over the Indian Ocean, all the meanness and resentment and petty hatreds sprung up between them had been burned off by sun and wind and only unconditional love survived in the rich vocabulary of fruit salts and hair nets.

Paper lay everywhere, crumpled, rolled, bits of *The Times, Godey's, The Courier,* advertisements for the Hippodrome, Drury Lane. "Pneumatic playing cards with glider finish," she read, an assortment fanned out in a disembodied hand. A marten muff with tiny brazier; a new calèche transporting fur-wrapped beauties. Parisian colored plates predicted spring. A smooth page around a bottle advertised the circus in the Crystal Palace.

Horses diving forty feet are said to enjoy their own performance, her mother wrote of this spectacle, *but opinions differ as to their seeming to do so.* Attached was a list of January hunts and country balls. *Four hundred children attended the London Mansion House twelfth night. Chloe, Peg's eight-year-old, went as Night in dark blue silk with a crescent moon tiara.*

She lay back, an espadrille against her cheek. A small breeze fluttered the nets, as if shaken by a hand. She saw, in the gloom, her mother topping a ladder, wide sleeves pinned back as on a spring cleaning day, hurling the winter draperies to two parlor maids afraid of the height. The vision worked as she watched, hanging light summer silk, smoothing the folds. It set down a bowl of flowers, looked around, satisfied, and vanished.

She splashed some tepid water on her face, brushed back her hair, and pressed talc under her arms and between her breasts. She held up the collar of her dress and let it flop back. Disengaging two boxes of starch from the sticky mess, she grabbed an armful of dresses and hurried down the stairs, calling loudly for the wash amah. The smell of steam and starch accompanied by clicks of the coal irons rose up from the washhouse all the next day. She directed Lim's women to change the flower bowls daily and to scrub, oil, and buff all the floors.

When he returned, she greeted him in the hall, her belled skirt reflected in the floor.

"How are you?" he said, surprised.

"Pregnant," she replied.

Buaya

These places, places in which there was nothing months before but a little native settlement, could burst into something quite different with a European presence. It could happen with marvelous alacrity and be wiped out even faster, a fortnight of cholera doing the trick with so much thoroughness that all one could find twenty years later was a paragraph in basement archives twelve thousand miles away. By his fourteenth year, the place had established itself as a viable little entrepôt. The fact that a massive raid had occurred that winter resulting in the massacre of thousands, that raids were still occurring in the interior, that two Dutch men-of-war had been "lost" off the south coast, notwithstanding, something more powerful had superseded daily business. It was, in short, civilization. Its crowning glory showed up that spring.

In May, an Italian naval frigate entered the Muaratebas estuary with a mass of blindingly white uniformed officers and the remains of a small operatic troupe. The *Principessa Matilda,* her captain said, was in those waters to survey sites for a proposed penal colony. When the news reached Russell in Labuan, he immediately wrote to London of the danger from the proximity of a colony of Italian criminals. The scheme was eventually dropped. It was one of those queer visitations that happened in places like this, as if the most remote corners of the planet were lodestones for these bizarre little circuses. At first one would ask a man to repeat himself, but after a while, if a new arrival announced, while dressed in immaculate white serge, that he planned to measure the cranial capacity of gibbons or paint a complete study of the family of pitcher plants or found a penal colony, one was willing to believe him. In the course of eight months, there had been a Russian with two trained bears from Vladivostok; an olive oil salesman, his wares in exquisite blue and gold gallons—an individual who was to return a few years later with a supply of straw hats so that, for a period of eight weeks, over five hundred land Dyaks sported straw boaters before they dissolved in the monsoon rot; and an Austrian dentist.

Serafina Bassioni arrived on the *Principessa* in the last hours of May and the next evening celebrated her fiftieth birthday by singing the entire lament from *Lucia di Lammermoor* in the astana saloon, accompanied by a humming chorus of young officers. It was a natural aria for her, affecting her audiences deeply, for it was a true lament, involving her life and great love, Alphonso Bassioni, a mediocre tenor. They had been part of a traveling troupe in the Punjab, following wider and muddier channels, terminating in a triumphant concert al fresco on the Chuf Parade, having run out of subcontinent. Three days later, Bassioni died of gastric upset, and his little pigeon, befriended by the Italian naval attaché then in port, continued to flap around the Bay of Bengal and the South China Sea for a decade and a half, so full of holes the worst storms passed through, leaving her unscathed.

She had copious jet ringlets, grease-paint eyebrows, and a rice-powder complexion, yet there was a crazy authenticity about the voice. Such music had never been heard east of Madras. It changed everything minutely, cracking small locks. For months after, the wash amah mimicked the gorgeous melody in her flat, nasal twang and, hearing it, those white-clad dark-eyed young men rose up before the Ranee's eyes like flowers.

With her growing size, she wore the loose baju kurong. The edema had vanished in her fourth month, as well as her rashes, and she had bloomed. On the evening of the little musicale, she was softly resplendent. Seeing her afterward, arms lifted to undo her hair, he stood behind and withdrew the pins himself. He was surprised at the pleasure it gave him, the sensation thickening in his throat, his hands gliding from the animal-scented hair to the curve of her back, her buttocks, lifting armfuls of robia, pressing her steadily forward over the bedstead. She was appalled by the act, and appalled how it passed from livid embarrassment, over weeks, into mortifying pleasure. Now that it was more grotesque than ever, her body interested him, and she began to take a new and powerful pleasure in it herself.

Blessed Peg! She has sent the most perfect thing. A lovely copper tub in which I fit, a balloon with limbs. I place my head on the lip and my breasts pop up like buoys.

The second half of her pregnancy was filled not with lassitude but with energy. She had Monkhouse build six large chairs and she stuffed them with kapok cushions. She had previously told her mother what she was trying to do with the saloon, and Iris Mumm sent out a Dearing & Clark chintz, it all taking the lugubrious round-trip journey. *It's only things like rot and death by snakebite that are quick,* she wrote back peevishly, a healthy little jolt. When the trellises and blue morning glories finally adorned the saloon, the room would resemble an *allée du jardin* in which the buayas lost their manic exuberance. A Chinese silk salesman, cousin to Lim, emptied half his wares on the veranda one wet afternoon, and she selected a yellow silk for the nursery. There was now a whole race of Lims ensconced in shophouses across the river, and one young female was selected to be the new infant's nurse.

Iris Mumm felt the joy the pregnancy brought her daughter. A key part of that alien world now resided within her, she reasoned, and so it was no longer strange. Yet she forced herself to read the letters as if they had been written that day and not as they were, a voice from five months past. Was she now nursing a newborn? Had she suffered horribly? Was she alive? One note reverberated for months.

I learned that Charlotte's mother died on her return voyage to Singapore. This woman had such a sweet and cultivated nature, Mama. It makes me uneasy when women like this die before their time.

And Lytton, she thought, shifting her belly from the little desk. The man cared nothing for his wife. He had his Chinese on the side and a Malay, Charlotte once confided. She flung her pen against the wall.

"What is the matter, Rajah Ranee?" Unggat looked up.

"Nothing. I am just fussy today."

Those days were filled with an ease. Things she had struggled with now flowed in and out like the tide. She continued her lessons with Unggat. He had names, Dyak and Malay, for all the trees and flowering shrubs. Each orchid, even the smallest, had a Dyak name. He pronounced it clearly, and only when she repeated it to his approval did he move on to the next. She did not know most of the English names, and so he didn't have much to do.

"This Unggat," Njoman said to her one day, "is telling the names of flowers for which there are no names. They are his names, and then he goes behind the bathhouse and laughs. I have beaten him." She was deeply embarrassed, then furious, and then she laughed, seeing herself, a big white balloon, painstakingly mimicking the devil's syllables.

What in fact was happening, on those long afternoons on the veranda or propped between the buayas in the clatter of rain, was an exchange of educations. His world of lore and antus could not slip into her skull without replacing some fact-laden theses. For the boy, the abundance and energy of her world, its ships, guns, stone quays, books, the phenomenal obedience of a dog, made him dizzy. Over time, the derision in which he held this big white woman with the lost eyes, a woman who believed everything he told her, even the purest invention, was transformed into a fierce filial love. And he. The waxed-shut ears, the nauseating smell of his kurap, his small thievery were minor irritations through which her love for him expanded so that, at the end, when all she had of him was a fading memory in a black time, her most treasured possession was the word "empkening," the name he assured her was Dyak for her favorite cassia fistula blossom, and his, part of his death baya, a lace cuff stolen from her dressing table, its mate lost on the outward journey.

There was the day she heard him addressing someone very politely in the orchard. She half rose out of her chair but could see only his head above the brush. She assumed it was some ruse for her benefit, as it often was. Yet a strange feeling came over her, seeing just the one head. When she stepped off the veranda and trudged down to where he was, a small green snake was coiled on the path.

"Do not move, Rajah Ranee," he said softly. "This is mati puchok, and he is very fussy. You must say 'Selamat' and ask if he has need of anything." When she looked down again, the animal was gone. In this way, the most deadly form of life in that place slid away from them that day in a strip of sunlight.

Unggat introduced her to a great variety of smaller fauna. There was the morning he shouted to her from the kapok swing; he was always doing this. He called out again, this time with clear urgency in his voice, and she lumbered over the grass and his legs were crawling with ants. "Banya samaut," he said, clenching his teeth, and she began frantically to pull them off, screaming for the orchard kebuns, tearing off his sarong, each red creature taking a small piece of flesh. She and a syce carried him inside, prying them now from her own legs and one from her neck, which was to leave a small scar all her life.

That afternoon they sat with their legs in the same tub of salts. With those dark sticks touching her calves, she closed her eyes and heard the first of the afternoon thunder rumble upstream. After a while, the explosion of rain. She eased her back and began to count, slowly, as this boy counted, a list of the good things in her life. This child within; this child without; a new sense of well-being, her depression lifting, the edema gone; her coming into her sexual self. She had found a Malay dress that was becoming, not a small thing, really; her final triumph over lifelong constipation, the flora and fauna in her digestive tract loosening her bowel, yet not too much, unless there was fever. The rain stopped, Unggat dozed, and the sun reappeared in a bright green flash across the entire horizon, before sinking.

They resumed their lessons. The boy's English was limited but remarkably functional. He knew the words for sweets and cigarettes and money for gambling in the Chinese pasar. She had asked Bawhal to teach him some Jawi, but he did not like the Tamil, with his heavily oiled hair and western clothes, and so he learned no Jawi. He did not do what he did not wish to do, for, as he reminded her, he was the son of a chief.

His mischief was in most ways harmless. He never did anything perversely bad except perhaps stealing Njoman's betel box. This box was made of teak and tooled silver and inside were separate compartments for sirih, lime, and a small silver masher. It was a beautiful, self-contained little object and possessed, as such things do, a power unto itself. It would be missing regularly. Unggat would swear he didn't take it until it was found among his few belongings. He'd appear with terrible bruises so she thought of speaking with the old man but, on looking at the two faces, somehow held back.

The boy was so much part of the astana, a small arrow flashing by, his wild cries, his tricks. Barr clearly enjoyed him, and it gave her hope for the child coming. While they now had a curious relationship of polite routine and abrupt, almost violent sexual congress, the only glint of affection between them seemed to emerge when this small savage was present.

The last month of her pregnancy oddly resembled the first. She spent the morning throwing up, drank some tea, and then hurried to the bathhouse, the smell of diarrhea making her stomach turn, the cramps unbearable, yet it was just cramps, just diarrhea. She would adjust her skirts, checking for stains, and walk, white as a ghost, to where a chair was set for her in the orchard.

September 5, 1853

My world has changed with this pregnancy. I am looked after. Raseh, an orchard kebun, has made me a comfortable chair in the garden and here I sit for long hours. This old man came with his granddaughter a year ago, the two sole survivors of a Sakarang raid. He is a land Dyak and these people have a remarkable litany of taboos, especially for pregnancy, which he has shared with the household. I am advised not to wear a particular yellow or touch the pandamus tree or eat eggs. Small, repulsive objects are set about everywhere to ward off evil. A talisman will be placed on a path where someone has recently slipped. This morning, a bunch of dried leaves hung above my nets and a more loathesome object under the bed. I am given papaya, to thicken my milk when it comes in, and prawns to prevent stillbirth. Ah Moi was severely corrected by Raseh's granddaughter yesterday for using thread from a particular lily stalk.

I sit and watch this man work. His universe seems so small. He prunes the arc of canna. His mind is not elsewhere, but with these lilies. He addresses them and then listens. When I ask him about gardening techniques, he says, "All that is living, Rajah Ranee, is rushing toward death. All that is dead is rising to life." I have the feeling that anything may become anything in Raseh's world. The rules of greed have been suspended. In his universe, the small is limned in the light of heavenly objects. His beautifully plaited broom, his hooked hoe, the three betel nuts wrapped in his head scarf. He finds nothing marvelous in our world except perhaps the dog and O'Neil and Sill's marmalade. He is most impressed with the fyce, in reality a stupid animal who does next to nothing. The first time Raseh tasted the Seville marmalade, secretly dipping the spoon and applying it to his tongue, his eyes glazed. I caught him in this, perhaps the only sin of his life.

Land Dyaks are a farming people, shy and painfully honest. Their language is different from other Dyaks and seems to rise from a separate past. All Dyaks begin to clear forests for padi when the Bintang Banyak, the Pleiades, appear on the horizon before dawn. The land Dyaks call these stars Sakara. Bawhal says it is the Batara Sakra, in Hindoo mythology, to whom care of the earth is confided. Yet there are no Hindoos for five hundred miles. There is a plant that grows very fast, an enormous parasitical thing with fleshlike petals. Raseh calls it Bua Patma and speaks of it as if it were a person. Patma, Bawhal says, is the sacred lotus of the Hindoos. It seems in this old man, to whom Malays will not give a civil *greeting, the deepest strains of culture may be rooted. "Selamat pagi, Rajah Ranee," he says each morning, not lifting his eyes, and my day begins aright.*

Yesterday, I received the first present in this place for me alone. The gate sentry escorted a man to the bottom of the steps, his feet caked with mud, carrying a bag snapping and glistening with some form of life. It turned out to be fresh prawns from the wife of a local penglima, good for pregnancy. This woman is Dyak and very sweet-natured. The Malay women, though solicitous to my face, remain cold. I don't care. Their coldness is more than balanced by creatures like my prawn giver and Mrs. Dolan, a kind, sensible woman who has come forward with a bank of maternal advice, despite our being only five years apart in age. I visit the Dolan bungalow regularly. It's like entering a small world of European niceties and order, if one excepts the nappies drying everywhere.

Her letters and diary were melding, the letters becoming more realistic, less ruthlessly cheerful, the diary now containing a scattering of pleasant everyday occurrences. It was, she knew, a sign of health. One incident, however, was so bizarre that she rejected the idea of ever mentioning it in a letter.

September 15, 1853

Last evening I bathed in the little bathhouse halfway down the slope, Ah Moi bringing my heated jugs. As I sat in the tub, there was a soft sound, as of rain, but no clatter on the roof. Something small skittered past, and the candle on the floor went out. I saw Ah Moi, her face frozen, climb onto the stool which held my towel. The floor was suddenly alive with rats, all traveling from the open river windows to the back door. I finally found my voice and screamed. Njoman appeared in the upper doorway with a lantern. I could see the things climb up his legs and thud to the floor, passing on.

"Don't move, Rajah Ranee," he said. It took almost five minutes before this loathesome stream began to diminish and then disappear. The candle had vanished and the coconut oil in the lamp was gone. These migrations are said to be rare, but if you harm one

of the creatures, they all will attack. No one knows why they occur. I have not met any other European who has witnessed it, and I believe one or two think me mad.

He has returned from circuit. I can no longer bring myself to use the bathhouse and have asked him to build a water closet on the lower level of the house, perhaps converting a storage room. He says this kind of thing is not likely to happen again. It means he will not do it.

Next month he will rendezvous with his cousin, something which makes him uneasy. He says the two of them in one place outside of Kuching is tempting to his enemies. I have not met the Tuan Mudah, a title which this child will take from him if it is male, yet I feel I can wait. Strange information seeps from his region, rumors of massacres conducted not by warring tribes but by him. *Then there are the small "requests"—for yellow soap, a Guard's cake, a barometer.*

He plans to return well before the birth. Birgit extols the value of separation in the tropics, and I believe she is correct.

This pregnancy seemed to stretch well beyond any known gestation period for human or animal. In the last weeks, she stayed within the astana or on the veranda most of the day, watching the river traffic, a slow, languid rotation of thoughts passing through her head. After the heat of midday, she sometimes waddled off with Unggat. They avoided the kampongs. She did not wish to encounter any of the datins, with their thin smiles. They walked along the little creek behind the astana, but only as far as the pavilion and small graveyard of Malay rajahs, the little ironwood monuments askew in the tough grass. They would pass along the bank and turn at the dairy paddock, with its two pedigreed bulls. She liked these animals. She liked their hot grass scent and wide, impenetrable eyes. Barr's idea was to eventually supply all of Kuching with milk from this dairy. She did not tell him of these excursions, for, since her pregnancy, he seemed to weigh her activities, as though she were sitting on the defendant's mat in the courthouse.

Walking eased her back. The baby seemed to have run out of room, pressing under her ribs. She walked with her thighs splayed, like Sutton, she thought, the fyce scampering around her like a wild little planet. Barr had warned her against taking the dog anywhere.

"Better a brute like Dolan's that'll stand you in good stead if you need him," he said. But the fyce was jolly company, far more so than at home. The two sat, she and the boy, watching the creek, not so foul as a few months previous, or rapid as the river, at one point eddying, at another making little swirls and, one afternoon, little whirlpools—one, two, three, four—nearing the bank. She watched with dreamy interest, and then her jaw dropped.

The size of the thing, the monstrous head sliding as if greased, stopped all sound in her throat. It made a hooking motion, the fyce in its jaws, then sank back. She clambered up, unable to breathe. Laughter passed over the water from the kampong upstream. Below, where the creek narrowed, the water broke apart and stilled.

It was dusk by the time they regained the astana. She slumped on a lower step while the boy ran inside. It was midnight before enough men were organized to block and drain the narrow section of the creek. It was done on Barr's orders. She watched the process, carried on by torchlight, then sickened and went to bed. They found the thing in the foul muck the next morning. It was taken with surprising ease—its feet fastened over its back, rattans lashed round the jaw—and floated between two dugouts to the bank.

She was struck by its size and strange docility as it was hoisted between the poles. She regarded the thick scutes, the optic knobs, the great slow-swinging tail. The crocodile had been spotted a week before, a kelong upstream. This maddened her, for if, in fact, they had seen the thing, why wasn't a warning given? As she watched, they did an astonishing thing. Those carrying it placed the poles on the ground, backed away, and dropped to their knees, pronouncing the somlah.

"What are you doing?" she cried.

"He too is a Rajah, Rajah Ranee," one old man said shyly. "He has acted only according to his nature. He must be given respect, or his people will take offense."

She felt she alone was not mad in this place. Si Tundo was suddenly there and the head was severed messily, for there was no other way with such a head, the expressionless, hissing rage of it, no fear or pain visible. The crowd gathered in as they slit the belly, pulling out the mangled body of the fyce. There were two hair balls, for hair is not digested, and a glistening mass of bone and sinew, which, on closer inspection, was the head of a child. They revived her on the veranda.

She hated him for this, for the theatrical gesture of draining the creek and killing the thing this way and putting the whole of it on display. He turned everything to some maudlin use.

"Did you think this would please me?" she almost shrieked, when he came to her. "It was a *pet*! To retrieve him like this! Did you think—" She stopped and got to her feet and lumbered inside. Lying in the dark, she thought perhaps she had been wrong. Perhaps this ugly gesture was meant innocently. All he knew how to do.

A week before, Njoman had told him she walked along the creek with the boy. The man said, "Grandfather abides in this creek, Tuan Rajah." He had planned to do something about it. He had come down from Na with Na in his head and loins. He simply forgot.

The incident of the buaya brought her, as life was so often to do in that place, rising and flipping in the air and coming down as something else, blessings. One was the big stupid puppy Sylvester, son of Crossjack, gift of the Dolans. The other was the most singular acquaintance she would make in her life.

Sitting in her orchard chair once again, jarred only by the occasional shout from the river or clank of a pan in the cookhouse, she noticed, one morning, a figure at the edge of the trees. It stood the way the Dyak stands, on one foot with a languid elegance, yet it was too tall for a Dyak. This man she recognized as a well-known tracker, the son of the Orang Kaya di Gadong and one of the men who had trussed up the crocodile.

He was a friend to Raseh, and this too was peculiar, for both the sea Dyak and the Malay held the land Dyak in contempt. The Orang Kaya was Malay, Raseh told her, but the young man's mother was Kenyah. He was thus a strange animal, a Muslim in religion and manners and a Dyak in everything else. It was said he had, for an entire year, sat in the Tamil's classroom. It must have been a painful thing, for he was the only adult in a class of children. Yet he was a good student and now spoke credible English. "In the longhouses, even on the Baram," Raseh told her, "they sing of Jawing, and in the mosque he takes his place among the lords."

He has come, she thought, to apologize for the buaya. To frighten a pregnant woman was considered grave rudeness among them. She nodded in his direction, and he moved lightly over the grass, greeting her politely, and stood by her chair. He gazed at her open book, which had a picture of Canterbury cathedral. He asked of the method of building it, and what was grown in the fields surrounding it. He spoke slowly, slipping between English and Malay. When she mentioned the buaya, he did not apologize but squatted and told her something of the creature's habits. There were many stories about this animal, he said. The great ones, the saltwater monsters at the estuaries, were sometimes over seven meters.

"It must be a horrible death," she said.

"Tidah," he replied. "If Grandfather takes you, he gives you such a measure of fear that it deadens your pain. You regard the doors of death in peace." They spoke for a while longer; then he rose and glided into the trees.

She would come to see this young man often. She knew he was much in demand as a tracker by both his own people and Sutton and, at the same time, had duties as eldest son of the Orang Kaya. Yet he was very often in her vicinity. What she did not know, of course, was that he had been charged with her safekeeping, a task he would have desperately wished otherwise. After the incident of the crocodile, Barr had spoken with the temenggong and the temenggong with the Orang Kaya and the Orang Kaya had offered his eldest son for this duty.

"Raseh," she said one day, "how is it that you are friends with the Penglima Khaled?" For this was also Jawing's name. "The land Dyak and the sea Dyak are not friends."

The old man studied his hoe. "The Malay say the land Dyak is the wood on which the white man will be burned," he said softly. "This makes me sad, for I have always tried to do right by my neighbor. The Penglima Khaled says to me, 'Raseh, this is not so.'"

Before birth, a father walking under his house hears a low chuckle. He turns and sees a beautiful woman, her face like the moon, her eyes like stars, her hair vivid red. Should the fire of onions and tubars have been neglected, she opens her mouth and out come peals of laughter. Her feet rise an inch or two, and she flies swiftly past him, her red hair flowing like a comet's tail, and he sees between her shoulder blades the gaping wound of the Pontianak.

That autumn his circuit was prolonged, for there was cholera in the Second Division. Dolan, too, finally went up. During his absence, she had taken to dining with one or two Europeans in the evening. Otherwise, she was comfortable with Lim and his family about.

October 9, 1853

He has sent word from Lobok Antu and is to come round by sea. A storm has been hanging for two days and feels like it will never break. I read Black Sambo *to Unggat and he thought it very fine. Cox and the Boynes to dine.*

Glasses of diluted gin were served to the men and coconut milk to the women. In the middle of dinner, the storm broke, sheet lightning illuminating the river and hills beyond. With the first big surge of wind, all the lamps went out. Intermittent flashes revealed a roiling, tortured universe of water and branches. It showed no signs of diminishing and, after dinner, her guests decided to leave together. As soon as they stepped outside, their lanterns blew out and they vanished. Ah Moi helped her to bed. Before she undressed, the pains began. It was as if all the world were in labor, magnified by the wind, her body rising in a stiff arc with it. Midway through the night, it backed for a time and she slept, waking before dawn in a blur of pain. Through the steaming wreckage of the morning, Unggat held the hand of the maias under the porch stair, listening to her cries. She raved through a dream of being clogged for all eternity, and then, at five in the afternoon, a pale, bloody form slipped out, a dead boy.

Many reasons were given for this. The fire of tubars in the cookhouse had been put out by the storm. A lone hawk was seen above the ridgeline. Perhaps most noteworthy, although no one was brave enough to say it for she was of the powerful cook's family, the baby amah selected was somewhat cross-eyed. She was given these explanations as if they could assuage her grief. She felt no grief. She felt only the absence of pain, and emptiness.

Mrs. Dolan and Mrs. Semple visited several times. She would see no one, they were told. Ruth Michaelis came and was told the same. Semple did not ask. His face appeared as through a fishbowl, the moist eyes large, explaining to her how the child had not been baptized before death, had not been consecrated to God, and so could not be buried in consecrated ground.

She turned to the wall. She had seen him, her son, his perfect small hands. At dusk, another face materialized, worse than the first. "They will not bury him," she said, to appease this new specter. The Datin Aisha gazed at her. A brown claw rose and stroked her brow. That night, she and her sister wives returned to the astana. They took the small corpse and washed it and wound it in white cotton. They brought a little coffin and they placed the body in it and carried it to a boat and pulled to the far bank, where the old Datu Imam waited in his clean gray robes. They dug the grave themselves in the churchyard, setting the tiny feet toward the east. The Imam offered prayers for the small spirit, and they left before dawn.

Aisha returned to the astana that morning in a fresh sarong. "The Tuan Mudah is buried in his sacred ground," she whispered into her ear. "His feet are set toward Kinabalu."

She visited the grave, cotton batting stuffed over her nipples, for milk poured out of her, everything sour with it. She had not known of the great mountain to the east, Kinabalu, the Chinese Widow. It eased her, knowing it was out there in the mist and that you could see four seas from it and that the small spirit was walking there. It eased her far more than any of Semple's unctions could have done.

In the days that followed, she stayed by herself, avoiding unnecessary contact. She avoided, most especially, Unggat. She began a needlepoint canvas of Chinese blue and sat with it for long hours. When Ah Moi hovered about, she retreated to the orchard.

Barr and his party, returning by sea, rounded the cape without incident. The storm caught them off the Muaratebas entrance, in minutes increasing to a gale, sucking them seven leagues out. They regained the estuary after sunset the next day, pressing back under a reefed fore and mizzen. The launch was gone, cut loose on his order to prevent her from stoving in their stern, Fishbein, the little mid, wide-eyed in her prow.

Two cutters swept out the next morning in search of her. She was not found, but four Dyaks were spotted off Santubong floating in a milky sea, having released small bundles of bark to poison the water for sharks. The detritus of this little fleet limped upriver a week after the child's birth.

He sat below the room in which she slept, fouled by his own smell, and wondered what it was in him that made him function as he did. To plan a circuit with Dolan in tow, the only doctor, during her last month, and then come round in the teeth of the monsoon. Yet it was not so strange. He was prone to these murderous quirks. They were broadcast through his life. Aunt Beryl's sad dog eyes glimmered from the ceiling. He had known of the buaya. He let Fishbein drown. He sat below her in his rising stink and pondered on the mystery of the organism that housed him.

Little blue junks and stiff little waves stretched taut on the bamboo frame, a watchtower in one corner. She rejoiced in her empty womb and willed it sealed up. She sat as one in a trance. Minutes turned into hours and life passed and this was all she wished. The blue canvas completed, she put it aside and began a hare in brambles. The ceaseless application of the needle frightened the kebuns, who were familiar with the power of intense weaving.

One morning, she became aware of the tracker standing once again at the edge of the trees, his face regarding her and the astana and the sky itself with equanimity. He is back on the job, she thought, for by then she had discerned his assignment. A hateful job, watching this great calfless cow. Yet she did not mind seeing the figure, always at a tactful distance. It seemed that nothing in all the earth, above or below it, bothered this man. He was in rhythm with it all. This place belongs to him and he knows it, she thought. And someday it will again, and he knows this too.

The jawing is the barb of the sumpit. It was his mother who gave him this name, Raseh told her. Once she noticed him, he approached in that easy glide, appearing to move slowly, as they all did, yet covering amazing ground. Over his shoulder she could see that he carried a pole and at the end of it was a rattan cage. In the cage was a bird, a gift, he said, from the Orang Kaya. It was black, with a yellow ring around its neck and bright yellow bill and yellow legs, so that it looked like a little man in a colorful suit.

"This bird," he said in English, "speaks as a man." At that instant, the creature made a raucous noise and slammed against the cage. She laughed, and he swung the pole to the ground. "You must ask him a question. Then he will speak."

"Very well." She pinned her needle to the canvas. "Tuan Burong, will the mail packet arrive today or tomorrow?"

The creature's flat, bright eye fixed on her, cocking its head. *"Gua burong, gua tak tahu,"* the words rasped clearly from the beak. She sat back, amazed.

"What did he say?"

"He said, 'I, being a bird, do not know.' "

She laughed out loud, and he smiled, a flash of strong white teeth.

"Does this burong have a name?" she asked.

He looked at her keenly. "He is called palit-mata-sapu-moa."

That afternoon, she gave the cage to Raseh to hang in a tree. Raseh, in his spare time, made fish traps and spirit houses and all manner of small constructions, and she asked him to make a larger cage. "A pretty one, Raseh. A little rattan kraton." She was delighted with the gift, yet there was something about the tracker that left her uneasy. He was not insolent, yet he seemed to carry himself so high. She asked about him. It was the first time she addressed her husband in pure conversation since the death of the child.

"A man of many talents," he said. "Yet he has a problem. And it's more than the mixing of bloods. He seems willing to concede the white race is an impressive one, but does not quite accept the brown one as inferior."

"Raseh," she said the next day, "what does it mean, 'palitmata sapumoa'?"

"This means, Rajah Ranee, 'Wipe-the-eyes-and-dry-the-face.' "

Simanggang

The Batang Lupar has a wide spreading mouth. In its marshes birds flourish, the barbet, heron, kite, pigeon, plover, kingfisher, nightjar, and hawk. Here the wild pig thrives.

In the winter of 1854, she accompanied Barr up to Simanggang, Fitzhugh's station, to investigate a new cyanide works. He did not like taking her inland, it was a nuisance of the first order, but he felt he could not refuse. She was a young woman who had lost her first child, and she deserved a respite.

The morning of their departure, she awoke in darkness and dressed by lamplight. She would come to love the limpid air of these early morning starts, the smell of Moore's Moist Chocolate, the Southern Cross glimmering as they swung into channel. In her old age, the memory of these times, pre-dawn starts inland, would be among the best of her life.

A strong ebb was running and they sped downstream, past Santubong and out to sea, the great rollers rocking the palm-leaf awnings. It was an eight-hour downwind leg to reach the mouth of the Batang Lupar. She knew she would be sick and resolved to stay below on a mattress with a bucket. He finally pulled her topside and wedged her aft like a piece of deck cargo, directing her to keep her eye on the forward horizon. She felt immediate relief.

Batang Lupar, February 11, 1854
Crossed bar through warm downpour. Thunder rolling up astern
for hours, gibbons answering in the hills.

She wondered, on this ascent, what their Dyaks thought of her. Her food must be carried and prepared like that of an infant, while their own women took on these tasks and more when traveling. She could not proceed along one of their narrow log roads without slipping. Fresh paths had to be cut for her daily to relieve herself in private. Yet they seemed always well-disposed and patient, extending their arms, falling in before or in back to assist, once or twice quietly amused, but never meanly.

I sometimes think they fear us terribly. And sometimes I feel we are a great joke.

My baggage contains dry clothes, but by the time I put them on they are already sodden. His kit—his guns, cheroots, brandy bottle, spyglass, medicine box, and sleeping mats— somehow seems so much more compact than mine, which contains only a few changes of dress and a book or two.

We keep strict pace. We start exactly at daybreak so that I rush from my water closet of branches half done. I am convinced my bladder is permanently enlarged. Rains come daily at two and we continue through, the sun emerging and drying clothes on our backs so that one may peel them back like paper. Yet the rashes and wet are made up for by the magnificence of the country.

Even here, there are the Chinese. We pass their padis and pepper vines, their lotus, pink and white, which they feed to their pigs. They have expanded to the eastern bank and are asking for increased protection. A new gunboat is soon to be deployed here. It is hoped Brunei will blink.

Above Seduan, the river narrowed. They didn't see the sun for five days but only a green, watery light, everything soft and heavy. They passed through a green vault whose floor was water, now brown, now clear, a film of vegetation soon over everything—the lungs, the tongue, the surface of the eye. Here, she found, some senses deadened while others became unaccountably acute. One began to hear things that made no sound: the crackling of the cells of the skin filling with water; the drumbeat in the chest of the stern oarsman. She found she could predict, easily—"Around the next reach there will be a boat," and there was—and once the bowman turned to her and smiled, having had the same vision.

She had the sensation, below Undup, of hundreds of small glasslike fish running beneath their hulls, and a little later the bowman leaned over, his ear close to the water, putting in a belaying oar. They broadcast a pouch of white powder over the water, sculling to keep position, and suddenly the surface glistened with small fish, which they scooped up and broiled that night.

She would be torn, on these journeys—which she would insist on repeating when she could for the rest of her life—between a revulsion for the regimentation and lack of privacy and general bodily rot and the little string of mysteries that revealed themselves to her as salesmen on her doorstep.

Lingga was Fitzhugh's lower station. The man himself stood on the dock, rosy and beaming, and handed her out happily. She watched with some embarrassment as his men struggled up the bank with her dressing bags and rugs, yet he seemed delighted with all the paraphernalia.

Lingga, February 16, 1854

I am to be left here for three days in the keeping of an old man, Tunku Ibrahim, while they travel up a branch stream to attend to business. They will then fetch me and we shall proceed to Simang-gang. I am dropped and picked up like so much baggage.

The Tunku is a sympathetic man, very tall and thin with a hooked nose. He has in his possession a camera obscura and this morning gave me a picturesque explanation of how it works. How it came into his possession he does not say. They say a two-ton Keneally boiler was found above the Pelagus rapids, and several tins of lavender talc in the baya of a Kayan chief.

I have nothing to do. I give out digestive salts to those with stomach problems and quinine to a cook boy down with fever. At night, I retire to the gun room, with the Tunku stretched outside my door. In the morning, he presents me with a cup of very good tea. It is raining.

The third morning, she rose to blowing sheets of water, the whole little stockade moaning. When she stepped onto the veranda and peered into the deluge, a flotilla of war boats stretched downstream as far as she could see. The Tunku stood at the end of the landing and, turning, hurried up to her. "These men say they have come to join the Rajah, Rajah Ranee," he said nervously, every part of him drenched. "These men say they have come to help him." His eyes darted from her to the river.

She knew nothing of the politics of this river, but she knew the description of a large raiding balleh. A group like this, without a European or Malay at their head, was dangerous. When she tried to question the old man, he seemed to withdraw into a terrified trance. She went inside and retrieved her small target rifle. She walked to the end of the landing, the little rifle held low.

"You will wait!" she cried over the water. The Tunku rushed up with an umbrella and repeated the words in Dyak. A man in one of the boats rose and spoke angrily and for a long time.

"This chief says they will not wait," the Tunku said. "This chief says they are going to join the Rajah."

"He *will* wait," she said, trembling. "Tell him this is the Rajah's wish. He must obey the Rajah's wish."

The Tunku related this, his own voice a little more forceful.

"If you disobey," she cried in Malay, "our guns will destroy all your boats!"

The Tunku leaned into her ear. "I think we cannot do this, Rajah Ranee. I think we do not know how to fire the guns of this fort," he said. "I think they have no bolts."

"Surely you can fire just one," she hissed, "just one, just one time?"

He said nothing.

She walked briskly back and sat down facing the river, the rifle on her knees. The Tunku followed and stood beside her holding the umbrella, a pointless gesture for she was covered by an eave. The rain eased off and the afternoon wore on with this crowd sculling in the stream. Twilight descended, and then, half dead with strain, she noticed, one by one, the boats turning and drifting downstream. When the last disappeared, she began to shake. The Tunku spoke, but she did not hear him. She could neither release the rifle nor move and sat on in the darkness.

A large figure approached in the pitch black. "There's a good girl." Fitzhugh was lifting her gently; she smelled his strong sweat. "The Tunku told me how marvelous you were. And with that little rifle. Really! You have been brave and marvelous." Her legs gave way. His body servant brought her brandy.

Barr arrived the next afternoon. "Stood your ground," he said, patting her hand. "Probably nothing to it. Most likely Kanowits coming to join us." Fitzhugh looked at him. "They were Kayans," he said, incredulous. "The Tunku knows the bloody difference." He apologized, after a moment, and went out. They moved upstream the next day.

Simanggang was unlike any other station. Except for the gun emplacements, it could have been the domicile of a dotty maiden aunt. Batik curtains hung in the gun ports; trellises weighed over with flowers bedecked the outer walls. Fitzhugh's personal quarters contained a cot and hammock, a rotting camel's-hair chair that seemed to have levitated from some Bavarian parlor, and a table bearing a nosegay of plumbago in a shell casing. Some form of blossoming vine, sprouting out of a dead tree, had been painstakingly trained with a wire to travel up and over the sill and run along the wall, where it burst into an explosion of white stars over a rack of cartridge belts. The man touched her heart.

Traveling wreckage in this part of the world was common, but Fitzhugh's was peculiar wreckage, punctuated with tender civilities.

He seemed miraculously adapted to the place. This was not true from the beginning. In the beginning, he had come closer to succumbing than any other new man. He developed recurring malaria and lived his life by a febrile clock, fitting work in the hours he knew he would be most able to function. They all did this to some extent. Yet he found, one day, finishing an ordnance check as the first sweet, murky wave swept over him, he was experiencing something like anticipatory pleasure. He was looking forward to the next four hours. He did not enjoy the frigid convulsions that would follow, but he enjoyed the delirium, the accompanying dreams. He had favorite ones. He found he could trigger them as one triggers an entire song by singing the first verse. He would start with an image, and the whole dream would roll over him. They were like fairy tales in which he played the key role. All kinds of magic was available at the drop of a hat. He ate his favorite foods. Animals spoke. A white, languorous arm sometimes rested around his neck. He began to plan his daily life around these hallucinations. At four, he would taste the fever on his tongue and hurriedly finish the work at hand and lie down. He began to fear not the malaria or his growing weakness, but the madness that had reared its head. He had, by accretion, chosen to live more in this macabre state than in the real world. It was his boy, Talip, who became truly alarmed. He would hover over him with a wrung-out rag, continuing a low, fervent, one-sided conversation. It was the boy who pulled him back.

Fitzhugh gave them his quarters and put up with his fortmen. The first morning she woke to a rapturous song, a low gurgling, rising as if boiling up from the river, continuing in a series of whoops and a great dive. The eerie melody went on for several minutes, ending with three vibrant descending notes. Fitzhugh brought breakfast: tea in a chipped Staffordshire pot, coddled eggs, sweet bread with real butter, tiny bananas, and jackfruit.

He had all sorts of fruit. Touring the station, she was given three lime-colored smooth-skinned balls by the child of a Dyak fortman. She put one to her lips and Fitzhugh grabbed her wrist. "It will turn your bowels to water." He colored. "I'm sorry. I've lived too long alone."

"You've saved me!" She laughed. They strolled about. The place seemed half fortress, half little park. Within the mud yard, he had a small smelter and its half-trained Dyak machinist, awaiting two steam rigs due to climb up the following month. Beyond the yard was a garden. A honey bear traveled contentedly on a wire; a large cage with something very energetic hung high in the leaves. Three little Dyak girls stared at her, then turned and fled into the trees, their movements sensuous, gliding.

Simanggang, February 27, 1854

The females are lovely, like their fabulous flowers, bursting forth full of pigment and juices, only to dry up in a day. They all chew betel and are stained scarlet by it on the mouth. Once mature, their work never ceases. Their heads transport massive weights; their small bodies shudder with the huge rice pestles. I wonder they do not dislodge some organ. Perhaps they do, for there are not many children. Consumption is common. Their thick hair falls out in tufts at the first sign of sickness. And yet they are always elaborately adorned, their little torsos bound from hips to breasts in heavy rings of brass. They sleep in them. Fitzhugh says they drown in them as well, unable to save themselves. When in mourning, they discard these rings and may readorn themselves only when a head has been brought into the country.

Barr, too, was impressed with Simanggang. Under the crazy decor, the place was in paramount condition for what it was. Yet what it was was useless. No stockade could hold a territory of forty thousand Dyaks, the nearest help two rivers away. The thing that held Simanggang together was not the well-ordered station or the carefully chosen, regularly drilled fortmen or the peaceful neighboring tribes. What held Simanggang together was the genius of Fitzhugh, a man for whom he felt a natural distaste.

They made one excursion while at Simanggang. It was to dedicate a new longhouse, and for this they brought gifts of gin and copper wire. When she objected to the gin, Barr laughed. "It is lemonade to their arak."

*A longhouse is a nice dwelling. It is sumptuously large and airy,
sitting at tree level. There is the ruai, a long veranda in front, maybe
six hundred feet, where bachelors and widowers sleep, and compartments in the rear for thirty or forty families. All the people you have
ever loved or will love sleep in it with perfect discretion. A notched
pole is drawn up at night and you are secure in the leaves. There are
vermin, but there always are.*

At Ran, the site of the new building, they were greeted by the wife
of the chief. She was a handsome woman of about forty, her heavy
hair caught up in silver combs. One leg emerged from her high split
sarong as she walked, blue with tattoos. This woman sat at her feet
and began a litany of questions addressed only to her. She asked the
number of children she had; how their farms were faring. She
expressed a desire to see the Ranee's mats and weavings, at one point
pushing up her sleeve to examine her skin.

Her guest soon felt comfortable enough to ask questions herself.
She asked after the young boys and girls standing in the shadows. She
asked about their carvings and the spirits that influenced their daily
lives. "Do you speak with these antus?"

"Spirits do not answer men," Liang Balu answered. "If they did, I
would ask the road by which my little daughter went." This was said
with such sadness, the other asked no more. When they departed, she
gave the woman one of her earrings and the other undid her necklace and placed a single blue bead in her palm.

She woke in the night to the sound of someone urinating. She
rose, slowly feeling her way to the rail. Everything below, the slope
and river, the great rice mortar, the boats pulled up on the sand, was
bathed in silver. There was the scent of sundal, of something rotting.
A woman sighed.

"Where was the chief?" she asked Fitzhugh, as they passed downstream.

"You met her. The chief died five years ago, and his widow is now chief to thirty thousand. There are many important ladies in the forest."

She deluged him with questions about these people. She asked after their marriage rites, their food, their hunting paraphernalia, their dances. Many jars of considerable beauty had been lined up on the ruai, and these especially intrigued her. Rice brandy and rice wine were stored in some, he said. But the most beautiful were empty. One, an exquisite T'ang, stood alone in a far corner. This, he told her, was reserved for a grandmother who had chosen it as her burial urn.

"But how will she fit inside?" she asked.

"She will," he replied curtly.

"How?"

He gazed at her. "They will cut the top off, fold her up, and stuff her in. They will drill a hole in the bottom for the fluids and let them drain through the floor."

Simanggang, March 7, 1854

At Ran the men danced, their muscles coiling and springing to the kromang gongs, the sapeh and gampang. An old woman danced, her arms snaking out as she slowly rotated, her head cocked coquettishly. Bobby rose and twirled after her, and everyone roared. The men are all brilliant mimes and outrageously obscene. Children rouse and sleep everywhere, little potbellies bare. These children, surrounded, day in, day out, not by symbols of death but death, heads hung from rafters, corpses dissolving in jars, are happy. They are gay and mischievous like children anywhere. And they are loved. These people are not monsters, I think. Rather, at a tender age, they have melded monstrous acts with love. It is perhaps the key to all monstrous things.

She asked Fitzhugh of heads. To take a head was not easy, he said, used to her now. It usually required several strong chops. It was then wrapped in leaves, the jaws bound with rattan, and the brain removed.

225

Later it was smoked. A severed head was treated with great affection. One conversed with it, imploring it to turn from its old home and adopt its new family. In a Sakarang legend, the first male lover brought his lady the head of a maias after she had refused all other gifts. This too she refused, but less forcefully, and so he brought her a human head. This delighted her. "See to what cruelty thou has forced me," he said, drunk with love. Fitzhugh threw his heart into this, elevating his voice for the part of the damsel, the warrior given an Oxford sheer. It sometimes seemed she had come straight from her white satin and wedding fiddles to the gorgeous company of this man.

Simanggang, March 13, 1854

To Fitzhugh, the Dyak merely responds to his world. In this place with its wild cycle of rot and regeneration, life can only come from death. Before he marries, before he gives life, he must pay for it. In all his myths and legends, it is a woman who taught him this. A life force animates every living thing—himself, his padi, the womb of his wife. He is deeply attached to members of his family. If one dies, he must make up the deficit in this force or remain in mourning and the beloved will have no attendant in the realm of shades. If the dead was beheaded, it is worse. One cannot perform funeral rites over a trunk alone, and so "exchanges" occur, deficiencies made up with slave heads. The head of a woman or a child is especially valued, for great risk must have been taken in approaching so close to an enemy longhouse to take it.

This force, the semanggat, whether in a plant or a man, is a lively thing. It can leave its dwelling place and go walking about. It is usually during dreams that it slips out. One sometimes will meet it on a road. When residing within the head, it is small, but when strolling about it is the size of a man and looks like a normal man. The trophy head contains a wealth of semanggat.

"Why a *head*?" she asked. "Why not a liver, a foot?"

"Well, it's portable for a start," Fitzhugh said. "And, when smoked, it doesn't rot. You have something you can hang on to. Preservable, portable, identifiable. Then, too, if you set out to do your neighbor a bad turn and you're met by a gaggle of eye sockets, you might think of moving on."

Van Lutyens had once talked of heads. "The Dyak gains semanggat by destroying the life of another." He poured schnapps into Birgit's little green glasses. "It is a limited commodity. We Dutch are not so very different. For us, wealth is a limited commodity. What spices our ships cannot carry we burn, and the price for pepper shoots up in The Hague. You English, as usual, are more adept. With your black-birding head tax—my God, you even use the right name—you take more pirates whole than these poor brutes ever take heads!" The observation made him merry.

They left Simanggang on the first day of April, Fitzhugh standing on his quay in blinding socks, making wide, sad sweeps with his arm until a bend in the river obliterated him. This man, with his consummate courtesy, his tender greetings and partings, pink eyelids fluttering, lent a precious civilization to those years.

"If ever there was a born family man, Bobby is it," she said on their downward leg. "Perhaps it's time he came down to inspect the spare dovecote."

Barr lit a cheroot and gazed at the bank streaming by. "I don't think you quite have the riding of it."

Three years later, coming around a corner of the veranda in Kapit, everything in shadows, she would behold Fitzhugh bent over his boy, who sat in a chair, their mouths pressed in the deepest, most sensuous kiss she had ever conjured in all her young girl's imaginings.

Fitzhugh loved, she would write to Charlotte Norris after his death. *He didn't like people and animals and things. He loved them. He loved his fort, his flowers, that little Ching device on his door. He loved his butter churn and he loved his boy Talip. He loved everything but a woman sexually, and this, knowing that vast and extravagant heart, doesn't seem important.*

The bead rolled in her palm. It was not blue but violet. It was, she realized in the slatted light of the little boudoir, Venetian glass. How had such a thing come to rest in such a place? It rotated, revealing deep striations, a twinkling star. At this moment, those people existed somewhere to the east, in the twilight. This bit of glass said she had been among them. She had entered their world, if only briefly, and was welcomed and asked forthright, tender questions. From time to time, she found herself speaking silently to that woman up-country, seeing the comely, attentive face. When she would hear, five years later, that this widow had died, she would find herself grieving.

Barr mused over their journey. He thought of her and that absurd little rifle, her cold-blooded questioning of Fitzhugh. Who was this girl? He felt her muscle stretching his constraints. The lesson from Simanggang was clear. She had a clairvoyance and empathy with the place. While her presence did not seem to affect his progress with Whitehall, it might turn out to have a quiet yet important effect on his hold in-country. On inland trips, his simple presence was enough to strengthen his authority in an area. Yet he would find in years to come, if he brought her, a different bond was created with these people. He could depend more deeply on them. Her well-meaning, interested presence, her tender eyes, were remembered. Tribes sending representatives down-country with some difficult request or complaint sometimes sent them through her. Once or twice, as with a desperate appeal for quinine in '67, it came only to her. Above Simanggang, her earring was placed on a priceless ikat mat.

The Dolans and the Parks, a new couple with the Borneo Company, were invited to dine upon their return. He described Fitzhugh's success, allowing her to interject wherever she wished. It was a pleasant evening and she enjoyed herself. He came to her afterward with a new, tentative warmth so that she waited, venturing nothing, suspending herself to see what would come. The next evening was the same. She felt they had set upon some new and fragile course. For a week, nothing he did disappointed her. She could see a thin rim of happiness just beyond her normal vision. The next day, and the next, did not prove her wrong. At the end of the second week he left.

She gazed at the space his boats had deserted at dawn. She watched the brown mass moving smoothly before her eyes and made, for no immediate reason, a tacit connection between these small kindnesses, these rare shows of affection, and his disappearances upriver. She, who had no gift for mathematics, suddenly recognized a precise equation balancing one with the other. She sat very still. The trees on the far bank blackened against the dropping light. A kingfisher skimmed over the water and rose, its green and turquoise suddenly afire. Information poured into her, the bird in its flight pulling taut a sinew round her womb, disclosing it occupied.

The place spoke to her like this and she accepted it. She felt it belonged to some unfamiliar end of a legitimate spectrum of sensation. She instinctively respected it and called it by its right name and did so from the beginning. It was a very Bornean thing to do. She had come out, in large part, a child. She "slipped in," a young, open creature, fingertips uncallused, tongue moist and darting. She slipped in in her youth and natural openness; none of the others was like this, not Maureen or Birgit, the most competent, whole people she knew— their competency, their wholeness, setting limits, blurring all they could not identify and encompass and use. Dreams. Birds. These were not strange. What was strange was their blindness and deafness. It was to drive him mad over the years, that this wide-eyed girl developed, without seeming effort, such a peculiar rapport with the place. "She can be duped by anyone," he would say, and, in the same week, "If you want to know whether the monsoon will be early or the samaut eat the new coffee plants, ask the bloody Ranee!"

She had searched herself, searched for the lack in herself, for she had been taught to look there first, and she had found it in abundance and it had tortured her. The lack! *He* had come to *her,* climbing out of that hideous carriage in his dank wool. She had searched for the lack in herself and agonized over it when he had already flung his heart up some river. He was the crooked one. She would, sitting there with life again inside her, travel beyond him.

The one benefit of pregnancy was her menses stopped. She suffered with a heavy flow all her bearing years. It would appear, much later, that here she entered a period of life when her body was no longer hers, existence merely a series of steaming lulls between parturitions, the inefficiency of the process maniacal with the sepsis of the place. She had somewhere, listening to carriage wheels, watching a black-clad phenomenon emerge, staring at a blurry wash of trees, given her body up, not forever, but when she would get it back it would seem of little use. This fecund middle period, what she later would think of as the great scorched plain of her life, was alleviated, more than anything else, by new faces: a new district officer, the occasional bride, "visitors"—a form of life still belonging to the outer world, sounding and smelling of it. At the least, they amused; at best, they deflected the heart from madness, murder, suicide. In the years that followed the death of her first child, these individuals, some she didn't even like, kept her, in divergent ways, from sinking.

The Italian frigate and its preposterous cargo heralded a new era. It was as if a seaborne plow had come in to loosen the ground for all sorts of dainty, implausible things—*Godey's* catalogue, bassinets, enamel commodes, romantic novels, drum stoves, bath cabinets. Increased stability inland and the modest wealth riding the coattails of the Chinese loosened it further. Five Christian marriages were conducted that winter. Mixed-breed families were shifted to more distant streams. The first rape of a European by a European occurred, the cordwainer's wife losing her mind over the exquisite fifteen-year-old son of the Boynes.

The flush of marriages continued into summer. It would eventually culminate in a bona fide bride packet and a swelling of the dovecote, a cache of unsolicited females—governesses, nannies, sisters—come out to net husbands farther than the Indian fishing grounds. Perhaps the most improbable marital arrangement, however, was that struck by Frank Bigelow.

Bigelow had stayed a bachelor with seeming equanimity, and why he suddenly decided to marry, no one knew. Marriage for a man in his profession was basically unsound. "He's dodged along for so long he doesn't realize everyone doesn't live this way," Barr complained to Sutton. "The idiot says he 'fell in love.' "

Bigelow did fall in love. In Penang, beginning the only four-month leave of his life, he stood on the P & O pier in the blinding light of a Sunday morning and gazed at a queer, picturesque trio dragging up the strand. Tannes Hewitt, the widow of a civil servant killed by summer cholera in Calcutta, her two small children, and half her luggage—the other half having sunk in transit from Madras on the *Mata Bombay,* a floating miracle of rust—arranged themselves in sodden display on the pier with a dozen or so fellow survivors. The woman would spend the next two days trying to negotiate transport for herself and her children down to Singapore, where she had a cousin. She had booked passage on the Indian wreck with the idea of joining the fishing fleet farther east, but with those millstones around her neck it would have been absurd. Her predicament did not interest him in particular. A sixth day into his leave and already bored, he bought a coconut and was sipping its water on the jetty, watching, for want of anything better, four-year-old May Hewitt play with a rag doll. The program involved much altercation, and over that hour it was with this child that he first and foremost fell in love.

May played alone, above the beach where English families up from Malacca made their picnics. As he watched her, so thoroughly engaged, her small, determined expression, the fluff of gold hair in the breeze, he found himself acutely sensitive to everything around him. He felt the salt breeze in every pore of his skin, the hot rail burning through his forearm, the cry of gulls thrilling his nerves. Tears blurred his vision. He wanted a child, a family, with a desperation that confused him.

He thought of seeking out the hapless woman to whom this child was attached. There had been a boy, too. It was clear there was no man. He spent the next morning pacing Weld Quay, reflecting on life and realizing that this sort of reflection was something for which he had no talent. One and one made two, and if there was more to it he could not comprehend it. Occasionally, in his solitary life, when he had a "feeling" he wished to share, he went dashing about with it until it cooled in his hands. At those times he knew despair. He got drunk and, for a year in Lucknow, took opium.

He had almost forgotten the trio when, at dusk of the day he was scheduled to move up the coast, he saw Mrs. Hewitt at the window of the Star of Amritsar Freight Bureau arguing through a hole in the glass with the Indian agent. She seemed at the point of nervous collapse when she turned away. "Come, my chicks," she said vacantly, "put on your shoes. There are horrible things in the ground."

After a bribed introduction by the purser of the *Mata Bombay* and four days of courting with the children in tow, they were married in the little C of E annex off Bloom Road. He gave over his leave and shipped with them down to Singapore. There, she and the children put up with the cousin while he returned to Borneo to prepare a place for them.

The new little family arrived in Singapore on the eve of Deepavali, the Indian festival of lights. He sought out Norris, and Charlotte invited the new bride and her children to lunch at Government House, festooned lavishly with colored paper lanterns. *The new Mrs. Bigelow is a thin, breathless creature,* she wrote to the Ranee. *She has a pretty face with eyebrows like little Chinese bridges. The children are robust, a boy and a girl. They hunted cecaks all afternoon and filled the place with their merry noise.*

"The man is a natural mark," Barr said, "and the woman and children will be, too. The bungalow's large enough to house a boarder. One of the company clerks, I think. A white male who can handle a gun. A clerk will be around continually, while he will not. It's the best we can do for him."

Cox, a tall, balding clerk and a decent shot, moved into the Bigelow compound three weeks later. He occupied a room made by constructing a new wall and punching through a window and outside door.

Cox was a dull, kindhearted man. Although Bigelow wondered for a full six months if he was, in fact, a man, given his willingness to take the children at any time of day and to pull the laundry off Mrs. Bigelow's wire. He was one of those people who, their whole life through, seem to slip between other people's lives, never quite touching anything. Yet the children sought him out from the first and, for want of other companionship, he was glad. Cox didn't know how to talk to children, so he addressed them as adults, and they liked this quite well and repaid him by talking to him as a child. To hear him chatting with the six-year-old Herbert at the end of Heng Fo Peng's dock was rather like listening to two people speaking totally different languages and understanding each other completely. They spoke of horses, death, policemen, and the Godhead, Herbert having a most detailed idea of this last. "He has one thousandth of a hoof in Him, and one thousandth of a feather, and part of every animal that ever lived, and His head can go around like an owl's," he volunteered one afternoon. "Do you like counting gutta and percha and piculs of antimony all day, Cox?"

"Not much."

"Why do you do it?"

"It's what I know how to do, I suppose."

"Well, how will you learn to do something else if you spend all your time counting piculs?"

"I wonder." Cox smiled.

"All you see is the rattan outside your window. You never go anywhere!" Cox pulled in his neck.

"Don't sulk." Herbert slapped him on the back. "Nothing comes of it. There's a genuine manang come down from Sibu. The Rajah's doorwallah told me. He will fix you up. You are too much on your own. My mother was all sheets to the wind until she found the policeman."

Herbert was right about this as he was about most things, as he was right when he advised his mama to marry Bigelow and stop dawdling for it was bloody hot on that beach with half their fortune drowned.

Cox's world began each morning with the small tonnage of import-export equations, equally useful in the long run, he suspected, if he instead counted the number of hornbills clacking over his roof. Once, in a flash of despair, he did count the birds and thought of transforming this number into copra tonnage but did not do it. He liked his new habitation. The little room stuck on the side of the policeman's domain was the closest he had come to being part of a family since he was twelve. He liked the sounds of the children, of crockery being stacked, of Tannes's sharp and tender words. It was the first time he had been daily around a grown woman since boyhood. Tannes, so queer, her gestures tentative, pretty. He soon fell in love. At night, he lay on his cot on the other side of the nipah wall listening for Bigelow's first grunts and moans, the vivid torture of those barrel thrusts, her soft cries, and his own desperate hands. After six months of this, death was better.

She was an effusive, hysterical mother, often unable to cope. He tried to relieve her of the children with little excursions, although they had already learned to keep themselves to a surprising extent.

Herbert was cruel to his sister. May's plump little arms were always full of black-and-blue spots from his pinches. When she followed him, as she often did, he shoved her with force into the nearest and most unpleasant thing around. Yet the boy was strangely attuned to her. When she was truly frightened, and once when she was ill, he acted before any other. "It's all right, Mayo," he said, wrapping his arm round the small, burning shoulder, half carrying her back to the bungalow, where he pulled off her shift and covered her on the cot and ran for Cox. The first day of her complete recovery, he blackened her eye. Their conversations were disturbing, unless you were used to them.

"I will," he'd say malevolently, "kick you to hell. And I will kick you every time I see you from now on."

"All right." She'd reach into a string bag and hand him the smaller of two moon cakes.

"Thank you, Mayo." He'd pop it in his mouth and grab her hand, and they'd run off to watch Inchi Statoo set up his chapati stand.

Cox loved best their mother's company when she was feeling well. She had sweet moments, and in these her flighty, breathless conversation was a titillating balm. She would try to convince him to marry, sometimes reviewing, one by one, the poor clucking specimens in the dovecote. Once, by accident, though he wove it through days and nights endlessly otherwise, she brushed against him with her breasts. For days he counted gutta, dammar, sisal, and aloe, his fingertips caressing his chest at the point of impact.

Bigelow traveled through his domesticity with a benign brutality. When he mucked it up with her and the children, he withdrew into his house of muscle, despairing. The soft gesture, the loving word, danced about in his brain but never found an exit. She and the children rallied more and more around Cox, who for the first time in his grown life was happy.

From the river, the town looked to be divided into six sections: the wharves; the Chinese shophouses and pasar; the two Malay kampongs; the astana with its outbuildings, district officers' bungalows, gardens, and dairy; the fort and jail compound; and the European bungalows massed together on the hillside behind the Chinese. This was to the uneducated eye. The educated eye saw a great deal more—indeed, all manner of moving strata, concentrations and diminutions of energy, momentary shifts, producing little spurts of wealth, of ruin, of calamity that were largely predictable.

His route on Tuesdays, when he ditched May at Mrs. Minjoot's—for his mama usually had sick headaches on Tuesdays, Bigelow returning from his three-day circuit on Monday evenings—was up the Po Li Pi, the-side-of-the-police, onto Kreta Ayer, past the Indian sweet stalls, the windowless office of the Bau kongsi, the dog urine and curry smell of kampong Melaka, onto Poeh Keng A, eight-small-houses-lane (only now there were seventeen), and up "Bukit Dawes," named privately because on this hill Tuan Dawes had given him two proper shells for the eye sockets of his Kelabit head, now hidden above the munitions keep. From this small rise, Herbert Hewitt Bigelow surveyed his kingdom with the terrific, intimate knowledge of a seven-year-old.

Herbert knew things. He greeted the jaga at the astana gate in sea Dyak, the kebuns in Cantonese, Riduan, the lieutenant at the fort with a three-pronged question in Malay; and cursed the chapati stall owner in Tamil. No one took much account of him. He passed in and out like a fly. He knew some things that would weigh heavily on the chest of a grown man. He knew, contrary to the belief of the Rajah and his datus, that the Tien Ti Hueh did most verily exist, not just in the territory but on this river; he knew the signal the secret society gave when an important member was visiting from the mainland; he knew where to buy the best yeast biscuits with which to turn sugarcane juice into arak jelu; he knew the location of four of the five Teo Chew gambling rooms and how Siti Aisha herself passed money through the greengrocer and sometimes small pieces of spinach jade when joss was bad; he knew all the bean-cake factory workers and the workers in the sesamun oil factory and the tiny ironware and crockery factories on Blue Lotus Lane, greeting each in their accustomed tongue. He knew how the finger was sewn on and began to move in the dhobie house behind Jalan Singh, inviting the guilty party to come forward; he personally felt the sharpness of the long nail on the C of E kebun's pinky and knew the six ways you could kill a man with it; he knew the horrible meaning of the cuttlefish tattoo; he knew there was a kechil in the garden of the sour Tuan Park and the gelatinous, pear shapes of Mrs. Semple's breasts when she washed them in the bathhouse behind the kapok tree; and the best way to cure a head, this again from Tuan Peachy. He knew too that the priest had arrived. He had crossed into Division One in the company of a single Dyak. This man, as much of a myth as anything else in that place, was now sitting on the shady side of Heng Fo Peng's wharf.

Ignazio Paoluzzi fanned his face and stared at the large house across the water. "I will wait until I am invited," he said aloud. It was a habit he could not break, although it embarrassed him. He tried to whisper, but his voice soon did what it liked. It was a habit of solitude. He had been sitting for almost two hours and Joseph, his convert, had not returned. The boy had disappeared as soon as they entered the network of alleys.

"I will tell the child to say I am here," he said, for he had also grown accustomed to seeing things, however well hidden, and so saw Herbert behind the water cart without looking in that direction. "I will ask the child to bring me water and to say I am here and wait to see if I am invited. If not, it doesn't matter. I have come for salt and sugar, not a rajah."

"Of course," he said, twenty minutes later, "there may be a letter. Perhaps with a European rajah, there will be a letter. The Holy See will remember"—the Holy See long since one with the disinterested aqueous universe girting them all.

Herbert walked up the astana steps, slipped into the hall, and stood outside the library on one foot. The Ranee was always pleased to see him, so that the gate jaga only spat when he caught sight of the small weaseling form. When Barr looked up, the boy pronounced a deep somlah and announced the arrival of the priest.

"So the papist exists," he said. "That's what we need, another bloody man of God. Tell Tuan Dolan to give him supper, little man. Or Semple. Then pack him off. How in hell does he exist up there?" (This to the air.)

"Why not ask him?" She stepped in and placed her hand on Herbert's warm head. "You must wear your topee, Mr. Bigelow."

"All right," Barr said. "Not to dine. Cigars. One."

Paoluzzi sat very still as the dugout glided with him across the river. He looked about like a child, a big, soft man in a greasy soutane. Paoluzzi was, she would think twenty years later, the single organism most misplaced in that universe. Nothing like him should have existed in those hills, much less survived as long as he had with all its flesh and illusions intact. When he climbed the veranda stair, he smiled at her and opened his hand. There was a small clam on his palm.

"I found it with my foot in the mud," he said. "It makes wonderful soup. But truly superb!" He wiped his upper lip. It was the most vulnerable face she had ever seen on an adult.

"I have been in Borneo fourteen years, or maybe fifteen," he said, staying, after all, to dine. "I am sixty-four years old. Sixty-four. Sixty-four less fourteen, so you see I came out when they said. I spent five years with the English in Candy, at Regina Mundi. So five years and fourteen is nineteen and I am sixty-four. It all works out. I have come with Joseph, my convert, to buy salt and, maybe, sugar. Joseph is gone. He has done this before. I will beat him when he returns. I don't really know how to get back without him. Perhaps Peachy will take me up. He sometimes passes through"—he smiled as if conjuring that simian face—"sent by Cristoforo the Blessed."

Men like this were often less crazy than they sounded, Barr knew. DOs come down from the interior sounded balmy for three or four days, their conversations often entertaining. When they began to make sense, they became boring. The priest, however, seemed demented.

"The first?" He smiled at her question. "I am not the first! Antonio Vintimiglia established the Catholic mission in Brunei in 1691. There was the Spaniard Cauteron and two Italian priests in between. So I am the fourth, you see. Although I have found no sign of the others. Nothing. I am very fortunate to have brought with me an altar stone and the blessed statue of Saint Theresa of Avila. They have given her hair and teeth, the fiends. But they are children. I do not wish to insult them. They are easily insulted. One must welcome what spark of faith appears and be content, not grind it out in hopes of perfection." He looked into each face. "I thought perhaps there might be a letter. If one comes, I would appreciate your giving it to Peachy. He is my friend. He comes through the Apo Kayan. He is the only one."

The man's secret was simple. The inland tribes would not harm the mad. It was about the only immunity one could stumble upon that worked. Maybe, Barr mused, there is something to grace. "Maybe," he said to Paoluzzi, "with two mail packets, there will be a letter soon. We will send it up to you and post any you wish."

She was repelled by this man, yet felt unaccountably sad when he left. His convert, a sullen unkempt boy, did at last return. Sitting in the dugout, the priest looked like a fat roach on a junket. They swung about, Paoluzzi sitting too far aft, rising, rocking the boat dangerously, sitting down apologetically. He settled himself, looked about, and, spying her, raised his hand and blessed her.

That autumn, the Ranee had high fever and a miscarriage. She was ill and remained so through the New Year. In April, she was pregnant again. Dolan prescribed a sedentary spring and summer. Unggat kept her steady company. He could read to her now, simple things, his pronunciation often more amusing than the text.

Unggat does not seem to grow. I feel he is to become one of those men, more common among natives, who remain boys in size, yet with a mature intelligence.

She had the leisure to do nothing but observe her most immediate world. There was an increase in bungalows on the far hillside and a new kampong of wooden bungalows for the dozen or so colored clerks and their families. A little hospital annex had been completed, as well as an extension to the jail, painted white, the color of sadness, by some Punan prisoners. That spring, Cardhu and MacMahon arrived, swelling the Borneo Company's allotment of Scotsmen to seven. The little navy now included four sailing gunboats, three armed screw steamers, and five heavy river launches.

How could it happen so fast when everything, taken separately, happened so slowly? To put one block of wood atop another and hammer it in that heat leeched a man's life. There was something not right about it, something wafted on blue smoke out of a bottle. Yet there it sat, a small free port drawing increasing tonnage. Tonnage that now included a burgeoning array of items for the small but swelling group of memsahibs.

Key to the contentment of the white women living in Kuching was the fact that there was now "another place," another enclave of Europeans within a brief sail. A bonnet could be put on one's head and a call paid on an Englishwoman in her nipah parlor thirty miles over water. This knowledge did untold psychological good. Yet when she asked to visit Labuan once the child was born, he denied her. "You'll not be going there," he said flatly. "You'll see the remnants of Claire Russell's 'view' on your doorstep in due course."

Labuan Island, off the north coast, was half forest, half swamp. The *Terror*'s crew had built bungalows between the high tide line and a low, wet plain, the site chosen by the Russells because it had a pleasing view of both the sea and a little valley behind. The harbor was immediately christened Victoria. When Barr arrived that first winter, he was speechless. They had created a miniature Batavia.

Sickness plagued them, but never enough to draw up stakes. The spring of the Ranee's new pregnancy, fever took half the population. He sent Dawes, who was in the territory, and thirty men to move the survivors to higher ground. They rebuilt, but it would take five years before the place could offer any kind of port facilities. The prospect of a coaling station faded away. For a decade, despite Russell's endless committees, Labuan would show no signs of becoming more than a way station for coastal traders.

Barr's little entrepôt to the west, meanwhile, thrived. It did so not just as a growing port, boldly situated. The place seemed to pull together in queer ways. The Chinese were running their affairs with supreme efficiency, providing uninterrupted revenues and often resolving problems, Chinese and non-Chinese, before he got wind of them. To his surprise, the clergy, more specifically Dolan, also played a hand. The man had a quiet way of mustering the flock, though rarely to spiritual ends. Whether constructing a dam or organizing a fire chain or transporting Martini-Henrys to a rifleless station, he was on the spot. He had a deep love of firearms, possessing a personal arsenal, which his wife referred to as his "hunting kit." He had also become adept with the sumpit, the only European besides Hogg to master this weapon.

The Dolans were frequent guests at the astana. Maureen spoke an elemental, broguish Malay, which, contrary to the efforts of other memsahibs, was never misunderstood, nor could one feign to misunderstand her for, as she herself declared, she spoke clear as a bell. The pan was warmed, not scorched; the water closet disinfected with a half dipper of lye, no more, no less; the baby cornstarched before she was nappied: There were no misunderstandings about directions or method. Maureen Dolan was unfit emotionally for that place or anything like it, yet she proceeded to bend the whole country to her way, to Mrs. Beeton's way, the thick tome of Victorian cookery and household management her only true bible.

"She says no and it's *no* or yes and it's *yes,* by God," Dolan would boast. No Hokkien grocer or Malay fishmonger ever got an extra rupiah out of Mem Dolan. Dolan, on the other hand, was a disaster linguistically. It took no time at all to tie up his tongue. He would sometimes get to the point in the pulpit where English itself flew out of his head and he'd gaze down at those upturned faces for a full thirty seconds before mumbling the closing benediction.

Their speech with each other, on the other hand, was a study in the remarkable communication of good marriages. A thought rarely had to be completed before it was understood. In the early years, love whipped them around like puppets. At odd moments in the day, he would drop a speculum or depressor, wash his hands, and appear where she was— he always knew where she was—kiss her, and vanish.

As a girl, Maureen Flaherty had a queer introduction to sex, bequeathed by a maternal uncle who caught her by accident, at fourteen, in her drawers and nothing else in a bedroom of a summer cottage in Kilkeel. Profoundly affected, he lunged for the child and found himself midair, having exited a low window, hanging for a moment in a strange zone, then breaking both kneecaps. On the day she saw her Uncle Aidan lurch forward and disappear into a square of blue, the jarring sound on the air was her own laughter. If it had not occurred, she knew, she might have kept her knees glued together to the grave.

She did not tell Dolan about this. She told him few things of real importance. She did not tell him of the miscarriage of what would have been their firstborn, occurring while he was in Dublin seminary, a bloody little mass bearing the name she secretly gave to it, so that he never understood the names of uncles and grandfathers given to his sons, but never his own. "You are a rare bird," he would say, in jest, in anger. He never knew how rare.

She was a good Irish girl and she played the game. When they married, she came equipped with four muslin nightgowns with little bone buttons from her waist to just above her knee. The first she wore as a muffler on her wedding night, Dolan keeping off the damp channel air with his long, burning body.

When she first arrived, they occupied two rooms attached to the courthouse and, later, a bungalow set on a hill behind the Chinese. It was built entirely on stilts, for she had a horror of vermin. It was a place with nothing native about it, no stick of furniture, no decoration not transported by ship, and was decidedly spare.

Maureen kept house in a violent sort of way. Milk left to spoil, an animal tied in the sun, and her steps shortened to vicious little clicks as she lashed out at the offending amah or syce. Birdsong stopped. Mistakes rarely happened twice and, if they did, the criminal vanished. Peace settled with equal suddenness. She'd smile a lovely, apologetic smile, brushing the anger from her skirts. Barr drank her in. In the early days, he would often go to observe Mrs. Dolan bathing a child or basting a roast. He'd show up on some pretext merely to inhale her industry and restore his faith in the universe.

Her roasts were superb. Dolan, with his slew of dangerous dogs, filled her larder with exotic game to which she gave prosaic, familiar names as they were slung on her table. "Woodcock!" she'd exclaim or "A fine brace of guinea fowl!" and then proceed to look it up in *Mrs Beeton's,* transforming an Argus pheasant into roasted game hen, a lemur into an acceptable Wellington. She alone succeeded in producing firm gelatines in that climate.

"She's a dab hand with ikan merah," Dolan bragged. "Waves Mrs. Beeton's wand and it's *saumon fumé.* Kick off, damn you!"—this to Spanker, the slow animal. He was a man in his castle, rolled over and back by a tide of contentment. When it was at its ebb, he would go off to smoke with his friend Heng Huat, modest dispenser of Sumatran tobacco.

In the early years, Dolan kept his dispensary on the other side of the pantry, and she found herself involuntarily privy to the medical histories of many of the Europeans of Kuching, histories that often overflowed into a broader realm, given Dolan's dual vocation. She was amazed at some of the things seeping through that nipah wall, beating an egg wildly to clear her head, checking her garden in the middle of a downpour.

Dolan was a conscientious minister of the Word, but from the beginning he set limits. Among the non-Europeans, he thought it sensible to concentrate on the town's Chinese, conversion to Christianity for them being tantamount to political advancement. He left the rest to Semple and the mythical priest up-country.

The Ranee greatly admired the efficiency and thrift with which the Dolan compound was run, old sheets cut into singlets, day-old pudding sliced and steamed for tea. Decor was minimal: a few thick pieces of oak, pastels of Donegal, the *Dublin Times* Christmas spread of a milky Mary and big-headed child pinned to the wall. She would sit at Mrs. Dolan's table with a cup of black tea and marvel as this woman ordered her day. Now and then, Maureen shared a letter. It was usually from her oldest brother, a stolid account of human and animal cycles on the other side of the world, at the end a strangely tender parting, as if tacked on by a different individual. "Ah, Brothereen, tell it," she would say, misty-eyed. They all had dreams of home. Not home as they left it but pink and gilded temples, a home of one's early years, years bathed in someone's love. Simple yards became bowers, sunshot and breezy, places in which one thought more lucidly, lapped in a future yet unfolded. The light warmth of the sun against the chest, the cool of orchard stone at one's back, delicious phenomena of another world.

Maureen dreamed of a special lushness, the cool, lovely fiction of Ireland. With the children's fevers, O'Boyle's Medical Hall appeared before her eyes, an unapproachable beacon, the clear blue liquid filling gorgeous bottles in the window, always gorgeous, always blue, coming away with a packet, the wax string stiff in her hand, the contents improving a life. Through McShanney's, wet hydrangeas against her skirts, a skirl of blackbirds overhead, small decent birds that imparted no message or curse.

Letters of the potato famine did not diminish the brilliance of these dreams, even with their tally of the dead, everything brighter, more glorious; the seasons—the seasons of heaven, O'Boyle's blue bottles the blueness of Chartres, of Egyptian gates.

Maureen had a boy, a sort of general factotum, whom she scolded from dawn to dusk for his slovenliness, his extravagance with their supplies. *"Tengok sini!"* she'd cry sharply. *"Njang pertama, pagi pagi!* Ah, I'm destroyed." Nothing could be wasted in that household, nothing used just once.

Yet in all her niggardly pinching and halving, there was, deep in her soul, a secret, full-bloomed appreciation of the luxurious. When the Ranee invited her to look over extra dress yardage arrived on the packet, she came in a small fever of excitement. "Oh," she said, reaching for a piece of violet tarlatan, caressing it tenderly. Yet she would have none of it. Nor the crepe, nor the watered silk. "There's my navy cord for spectacles," she said. The afternoon rain started, and the thin figure trudged down under its green waxed umbrella. That evening, she fed them and, after all was scrubbed and put away, the amah berated, and heads checked for vermin, she walked down to the empty cookhouse and pulled out the pilfered scrap of silk, its silvery threads like an insect's wing, gliding it slowly across her breasts.

I almost love this woman, the Ranee wrote, *yet in England we would have been hard-pressed to find an inconspicuous time to entertain her.*

Once again huge, she kept to the veranda, the orchard chair, listlessly watching life around her. Living organisms had surprisingly predictable clocks. The wah-wahs heralded dawn; the bulbul trilled at half past six; Semple's tinny bell rang at noon. At seven each morning, a great water bird emerged from the end of the bungalow line, its long legs lifted carefully, its beak pointed earthward. Biverts lived in eternal fear of stepping on something deadly.

It always amused her to see this figure. Barr spent two hours with him each morning, not in his library but in the dining saloon, taking advantage of the great expanse of table. One morning, she came upon the two of them surrounded by piles of her Persian wool. The waxed basket Raseh had made for her was upturned and the skeins were everywhere, piled in mounds. She was angry, yet the expression on their faces made her pause. Each little hillock had a label. A purple, SAGO; gold, PEPPER; coral, SISAL. OPIUM identified two pounds of ivory wool she had been saving for a window bench for Deanstown. A gray pile was labeled ARAK; pink, ANTIMONY; black, SUGARCANE; green, COFFEE; GAMBIR, TAPIOCA, COCONUT, and ALOE, one yellow strand each. Imports were relegated to a sideboard, its legs sprung by moisture.

Barr took up a large skein of flaming scarlet, pulled it apart with his fingers, and flung it over all the rest. "The Celestials!" he spat. It was, she knew, a description of the truth. The Chinese held a major stake in every successful venture in the territory. It was more than their greed that gnawed at him, it was their solidarity, their intense xenophobia. At bottom, they would never truly have allegiance to anything non-Chinese.

The two had, that morning, come up with the beginnings of a solution, a way to curb their voracity without diminishing their value. Pepper and gambir were to be the test. Land for pepper and gambir would be owned, he said, from that point on, only by the raj, though it would not own the plantations using it. The planter would obtain his land wherever he wished, for almost nothing. He'd run almost no risk of losing capital if his venture failed. It guaranteed that land would be kept under cultivation and at the same time rein in the Chinese. He was delighted with the scheme, which, in effect, had been suggested by Biverts. Four years later, with land for sago and sugarcane also included, he would find it was not the effective curb he had hoped. He would resort to a different maneuver, one he had considered in the past and always rejected. Opium came to the Chinese from Singapore via the Natunas. There was no reason why balls of opium should not come directly to the government and thence to the Chinese. He would sell it to them for distribution, levying a tax on his own price. There would always be smuggling, but he could force them to take an increasing number of balls each year. They would scream to heaven, then comply. It was the curb he sought.

She skirted the wool, passing out to the veranda. The wide sweep of boards and the river glinting beyond gave the impression of sitting on the deck of a boat. A line of prahus swung off the far bank. On the near side, a child sat with fish traps, puffing a cigarette. These days had a pleasant emptiness. She invested in nothing, strangely immured from things. She slept like one drugged.

In the afternoon, under a yellow web of bougainvillea, she and Unggat read from a book of fairy stories. He was too old for such things, yet they both enjoyed them. She would get annoyed when he sat blankly through the most exciting passages, then laughed when nothing was funny. "Aha!" he would cry at a place where nothing was revealed. Yet even this fell into a rhythm. His favorite story was about a little girl with matchsticks in the snow. He knew nothing of freezing and yet felt some inner torture at this child's plight and a great release at the paradise toward which she was drawn at the end.

She, too, came to have favorites.

> Summertime, how lovely it was out in the country, with the wheat standing yellow, the oats green, and the hay all stacked down in the grassy meadows. And there went the stork on his long red legs, chattering away in Egyptian, for he had learnt that language from his mother.

It was a pale blue volume from one of Kilcane's consignments. She could smell the grassy meadows, feel the sweet dampness in her toes. Who was this Dane?

Her only discomfort was cramps in her legs, and it was Aisha who showed her how to stretch and remove them. She would lean on those thin shoulders and stretch her hamstrings as the datin pushed. She relished contact with this woman, an enemy turned into a friend by her dead son.

> *August 12, 1855*
> *An immense crystal rosette lies glinting on the lawn. Kilcane has*
> *uncrated a colored window, and it sits like some massive jewel in the*
> *lalang grass. This man brings such queer things.*

Kilcane visited at the end of summer. Her memories of him were not favorable. She did not like the proud, strutting demeanor in someone so basically unattractive. She felt, at bottom, her husband valued him well beyond his worth. She believed to him she was no more than a piece of equipment, relegated to a category barely above concubine and below a good gunboat. In all likelihood, it was what he thought of most women, save some Chinese in Singapore for whom, for years, he was said to collect jade and Selangor silver.

The window he brought was Venetian glass. It was to be set over the astana stairs, rendering the dark center of the house light and airy. This thing, which had made a sea voyage of eight thousand miles unscathed, shattered completely when maneuvered up the slope, and the two of them sat midst the shards laughing. *I believe this friendship exists,* she wrote, *because they are deranged in the same ways.* A duplicate, commissioned in Murano, would be shipped out the following winter and, once installed, give the gloomy hall the pink and orange shimmer of a pre-Raphaelite bordello.

The *Spectre,* a new and deadlier model of frigate, had accompanied the *Golden Grove.* She had consigned to her a large Sarouk for the astana saloon, a gift from Iris Mumm for her daughter's birthday. Kilcane had ferried it out from the P & O agent in Singapore. To it he added a thick brick of the London *Times, The Illustrated London News, The Spectator,* a copy of *Burke's Landed Gentry,* and a stereopticon with a set of slides on the wonders of America. In the evenings, they drank stengahs and viewed Sioux and Cheyenne aborigines.

The man had taken to wearing a haji costume as his house garment, its skirt pinned up between his legs, looking like a lewd grandmother. For several nights after the aborigines, he sat hunched over a book he said was written by an American, his eyes sometimes red and tender. For years, he would search for more publications by this Mrs. Stowe but was disappointed. He always brought books, this time a handsome set of Jane Austen, whom he admired enormously, and, for Barr, several filthy Indian *Parrot* books in green leather. The burgeoning little library was entrusted to Pa Tek, a kebun removed from the pomelo orchard and promoted to librarian. No library was better kept than by this savage, who lit little braziers during the wet monsoon, tending them through the night so the books would not rot.

Nepenthaceae

Wind already blowing from the west. Other signs indicating monsoon will be early. Almost impossible to dry anything properly. The porter Abdul died at seven p.m. of gastroenteritis. Packing up my collections and will steam to Sarawak and commence on the maias.

Visitors continued to be an unguent to that life. Italian sopranos, naval megalomaniacs, demented clergy: All had their salubrious role. The autumn brought yet another, totally unlike the rest, a man, she found, made solely of air and light.

Lytton was a perfect small statue, a face of classic dimensions and a boyish, earnest expression. He physically seemed as remote from his sister Charlotte as one could get and still emerge from the same womb. He was one of those men who "came into his own" only in his specific area of interest, of devotion. When he spoke of his work, his face filled with light. His wild, speculative flights took place within this envelope. He was, by then, a well-known naturalist, working on the theory to be simultaneously proposed by Darwin. Starting his research a decade later, the young man outlined his ideas and submitted them humbly to the colossus, work in some ways more brilliant and thorough than anything Darwin would postulate.

Over the years, Lytton visited the astana in Kuching several times and was always made welcome. If he never succeeded in convincing his host of his kinship with his arboreal neighbors, he nevertheless entertained them both with an intelligent flow of talk. This was the elixir of life. Good conversation could supersede even sex in such a place. Barr was intrigued with the wealth of information this individual carried between his small, perfect ears, yet Lytton's personality could rankle him.

"I've never seen a freer way of life in someone so shackled up!" he once said, and she was mildly astounded, as she was to be from time to time, by such insight winging from so dense a place. Lytton, in turn, found his host perplexing. Barr seemed to be one of those queer specimens that, at odd moments, works against itself. Yet the man's tenacity was remarkable. Lytton had once helped him collect a sizable menagerie of Bornean life to be transported to Germany, where it had been commissioned by a private zoological society. After two months of work, they watched the vessel load, journey downriver, cross the bar, loose sail, and sink fifteen hundred yards offshore. Barr stood in the surf as a rare pigmy tarsier floated in, still in its bamboo cage. He turned and made the upriver journey in silence. "Where's that furry brute you brought in three days ago?" he asked, when they arrived in blackness. He grabbed the terrified marsupial in its crate, drew *Number 1* on the slats, and went to bed.

Lytton's main purpose in coming to Borneo was to study avian life and the maias. He was given permission to travel to Senmunjan, where there were thick concentrations of orang utans. He was offered the little bungalow at Santubong to cure his birds and prepare for the expedition.

The naturalist was also one of the select visitors invited to Na. Barr thought it might offer the young man a broader menu, that he might enjoy investigating the flora and fauna of higher altitudes. Yet the sensuous, eerie nature of the place and its chief occupant had the opposite effect. Ajar shocked him. He had met the Ranee, and found her superb, and this black whore revolting.

A rude wooden lodge on the side of a crystalline basaltic cliff
twenty miles upriver where the Rajah is accustomed to go for

relaxation and fresh air. Finest subacid fruits, mangosteens like large hearts. Noisome streams and a black chatelaine.

While at Santubong, he rode the tide up once a week to dine. On one of these occasions, a packet of mail awaited him, having followed him about for a year and a half. His dearest friend was a young botanist who had devoted his life to the study of liverworts in the Amazon basin. Lytton would get letters in a small, crowded hand from this individual, letters so long in transit that the writer had to have changed considerably to the eye since the time of writing. Indeed, he died a year before the last of these was delivered, of appendicitis, above Manaus.

There was one afternoon Lytton sprinted up the stairs waving a single letter, misdelivered at the fort. "It's from Darwin! He agrees! Completely! He has worked on a similar hypothesis and thought of most of it. He elaborates on it beautifully!" She was struck, watching him stride to and fro, by how oddly selfless he was.

"They are stealing it from you," she said quietly, when he finished.

He gazed at her. "On the contrary, it's a collaboration."

She sighed and put down her needle. "What will you do when you're old, Tom? What will you do when you cannot traipse about the earth as you do now? What will you live on? No one pays you for your labor except some stipend from a naturalist society now and then." She marveled that she could speak this way to him. Yet the fine face, its pale, high brow, seemed so vulnerable, she felt she must.

"Oh, I'll go on for a long while." He laughed. "I don't need much. I'm healthy as a horse." He gazed over the river. "I had an offer just this winter for my beetle collection."

She looked at him.

"From one of the most eminent names in entomology. It is the finest collection in the world." A small flash of pain crossed his eyes, seeing her face.

Lytton was in awe of the universe. He was happy with the smallest discovery. He felt no fear of being superseded or undercut in his work, the workroom was simply too vast. On some evenings, Barr would pump him for background information for his new little museum. It was all Lytton needed to launch himself into his favorite sphere. "This is not an 'interesting island.' " His face gathered light. "It is another planet. Species have existed here in isolation for thousands of years. You have over eight hundred species of birds alone. You have toads that are nine inches in height and other creatures so small, so *small*—" He seemed to see a wondrous lilliputian menagerie marching before his eyes. "To the east, everything changes. It is as if a wall exists between here and New Guinea. It passes between two small islands only a few miles apart, yet with flora and fauna as different as Europe and the Americas. In one hour, you can sail from one zoological universe into another. Pass on to Celebes, the Moluccas, and the difference is even more remarkable. Your forests are filled with a great variety of monkeys, deer, wild cats, civets, and otters. To the east there are none. Here, I am convinced"—the handsome face waxed beatific—"we have the beginning of man as we know him."

Barr listened, but he had reached his limit of attendance. She, on the other hand, seemed to follow adroitly. He liked the way she looked when she listened, her hands folded over her swollen stomach. She found the young naturalist pleasant company as well. He had such fresh enthusiasm, such an eye for the natural lesson. It became habitual, while he was at Santubong, for him to appear at least once a week in the afternoon, when he was likely to find her alone. She would wait on the veranda with the tea tray and they would chat animatedly for an hour or two, rain or shine.

One afternoon, however, climbing the steps under a heavy downpour, the fifth day of continual rain, he found her sitting dully, her face slack. A stiff gown was spread over her knees, her fingers twisted in a sleeve. "How lovely," he said, extracting the frayed fabric.

"They were supposed to be bell sleeves," she said. A small Eloise, a dressmaker's model, lay on the floor. It was indeed dressed in bell sleeves. He laughed.

She gathered herself up awkwardly, her eyes blazing. He touched her shoulder and she stiffened.

"Go up and rest," he said gently. "A little lie-down under the nets. You'll feel better. The child and this weather are a trial."

"I don't want to lie under *nets*!" Her eyes were hard. "I want to lie in a cool room with an English spring outside! I want to walk through my mother's cutting garden. I want to see the green of first shoots, not these huge, leathery abominations." She kicked at the heavy leaves blown in by the wind. "There's no *beginning* to anything here! If I died on that grass, a tree would sprout from my stomach within the hour and as quickly begin to rot. 'Flowers,' when they are fragrant at all, are fragrant to the point of putrescence! That filthy Rafflesia with its scent of rotting flesh is only the logical culmination. I hate it! I hate it all!" She rocked where she stood, shocked at her own display.

"But it's magnificent," he said, stunned. "It's fully a yard across. It can hold over eight pints in its nectary."

She stared at him blankly, into that perfect, earnest face, and then burst out laughing.

"If you knew what you have here." He smiled, relieved. "The wonder of it. In some areas almost every tree, every bush, is a new species."

He started, on that afternoon, with the primitive flowers, ordering their species and subspecies on paper. On each of his following visits he brought new specimens, displaying the loveliest epiphytes, aligning them on the little tea table, the sound of his voice and the peculiar subject matter strangely titillating.

"The petals of a primitive flower are in rings, like the magnolia. Later, triggers and levers develop. This lady"—he held up a pale lavender orchid—"is the most complex of all. The male ichneumon wasp copulates with her. It grasps her abdomen. The orchid can only survive with this wasp. It is a perfect replica of the female of his species."

Her face burned. She felt absurd, sitting there enceinte, with this young man expostulating on sex among the flora.

"Your flower beds are a display of genitalia," he said. "You find them beautiful and they are!" He brought her, on the next visit, a false water spider—a ghostly, leafless orchid—and, one rainy afternoon, the *Coelogyne pandurata*—voluptuous, ice green, with golden darts in its throat. At night he wrote, next to an entry on Nepenthaceae:

> Poor sleep sets violet crescents under her eyes. Edematous dimples form above her elbows. One looks at that skin and knows its feel, the half-sweet, gamey smell of its deeper reaches. She is open, generous, and cheerfully disposed and he is changing it, like the maimed rider of a fine horse.

A throbbing sexuality flowed from his pen, although all he could bring himself to do physically was, one afternoon, to bite her knee. He was seated on the Sarouk at her foot, a line of little tree ferns spread before them, and, in the process of rising, he briefly sunk his teeth through the muslin. It was an absurd gesture, it "hurt," the fire rushing into her groin, her breasts. He continued to rise and walked out of the room.

She told him one day of Simanggang, of Fitzhugh's zoo. She told him of the strange song she had heard before dawn and he immediately identified its perpetrator, *Hylobates mulleri*. He told her some of the habits of gibbons, their diet, their mating behavior and gestation. She was intrigued, yet afterward felt the mysterious rhapsody had somehow been stolen from her, its magic drained away.

One afternoon, he arrived in the wet and a little leech clung to his boot. He pried it off with his knife and flung it over the rail. He saw the expression on her face. "Things you find horrible can be exquisite."

"Like what?"

He sat down. "There's a flatworm that lives on the forest floor. It looks like a beautiful piece of red and yellow porcelain if it doesn't move. When it moves, it turns into something quite other." He stretched his legs. "It's actually an interesting animal. When it runs out of food, it digests itself." He was not sure she heard him.

"What does it eat first?"

He looked up, surprised. "The reproductive organs. Last, the nerves."

Thunder rolled up each day a little earlier and resumed in the evening. She felt the low rumble in her flesh, her breasts huge and tender. Any movement was disagreeable.

"Are you so very unhappy?" he asked one evening, for she looked unaccountably sad during these rumblings. They were alone in the saloon, a thick, hot blackness enveloping the house to the rim of the lamplight. The first pelts of rain began, and she closed her eyes. "When I was little, we spent summers at the seashore," she said. "Once, I couldn't have been more than eight, I was swimming, diving off a little skiff. The sky was gray, you couldn't see the sun, and suddenly, after diving down, I couldn't remember which way was up. Every direction was the same dull gray. I panicked. I swam wildly in one direction, then another. I tried to let myself float up, but it didn't work. Finally I gave up, I was close to passing out. And I suppose I floated to the surface, because I remember swallowing great gulps of air and sobbing."

He sighed. "Perhaps you should try it here. Go limp and let the natural forces carry you. You may find you float upward."

She gave a little snort. "Natural forces! If this lamp went out we would belong to them! You can't let anything carry you here."

He sat silently, his eyes grazing her tortoise comb, the rich hair in its teeth.

He arrived in the afternoon deluge with a small cage under an umbrella. Inside was a tiny animal with a tail like a plume. "May I introduce *Ptilocercus lowii*," he said, "a gentleman who is only found in Borneo and who has thus been allowed a genus to himself."

As she became bigger and even more sedentary, she looked forward to these lessons with increased enthusiasm, as if someone were bringing the choicest particles of this universe to her on little plates. When he went to Klegit to investigate tidal creatures, time dragged by. He came back bursting with new discoveries.

"There must be four hundred inches of rainfall a year in those mangroves! You can glide up a great way among the trees. Perciformes

259

hang all over the branches at high tide! They take a gulp of water, you see, which sloshes in their gills. At low tide, it's all mud. I found the largest mengaris, perhaps you know them as the tapang, not a Dipterocarp at all, I see now, but a member of the legume family! Lovely smooth bark, over forty meters tall, often harboring honeybees. The orchids are bigger and more lovely than anywhere else."

To investigate the tidal creatures, he had a collapsible little coracle, wicker and calico smeared with pitch, with a flat hide bottom and strong as iron. In it he could scull into a foot or two of water. The Kelabits were amused at this contraption. He showed it to her one day—she had asked to see it—carrying it in like a cradle and squatting to set it against the veranda wall, and she had a sudden urge to touch the perfect buttocks. She found, half consciously, over the days and weeks that followed, the real object of her studies on those afternoons was the small, perfect body of the naturalist. It made her feel horribly guilty and perverted in her condition, yet she did not stop, realizing with some hidden instinct that she was merely continuing her education in a sensible way; the thunderous organism she had married did not lend itself to study; it was somehow never "still" enough, or its designs on her were too resolved. She would, without her conscious choice or anyone else's, continue her instruction. There was nothing in her that warranted this direction. She was raised to be monogamous. It was perhaps the contrast between the two men that intrigued her: the overflowing energy in that black wool and this perfect balanced specimen, a specimen who, at the age of seventeen, recorded his first sexual encounter in the Sumatran highlands, recording its intensity and duration alongside a description of the lily Fritillaria with a sketch of its rare checkered petals. She would dream, in that rosy nook, of his undoing things, her bodice, her shoes, until she lay naked and huge in the dappled light, he continuing the lesson, counting petals, separating labia with those small, precise hands, droning descriptions, explanations.

In November, Lytton made his last excursion, journeying to Belaga to investigate the gliders. He returned in December with several dried specimens of flying lizards, flying squirrels, and lemurs. He was depressed that he'd been unable to find the most common: a flying fox. He did collect, he said happily, some of the largest, most beautiful Ornithoptera he had ever encountered. He produced a bamboo frame with an immense butterfly pinned inside. The ground of its wings was a velvety black, the rim dipped in emeralds.

"I have named it the Ranee Amelia."

"It's dead," she said.

"It's the first of its kind to be found."

"By whom?"

He put the frame down, looked at her miserably, and left.

For two weeks he did not come. At the end of the third, she heaved herself up and was rowed down to Santubong. The little bungalow had undergone a hideous transformation. Birds of every description hung from the center rafter, waxed labels wired to claws. Gorgeous fruit pigeons, azure rollers, golden-capped sunbirds, kingfishers. Everywhere were drying carcasses, hanging from hooks, pinioned to boards. The air reeked of pickling chemicals. In the middle of the room, several uncured birds lay under gauze, their bed placed on sticks and these in shallow basins of filthy oil.

"I didn't know what to do with those." He smiled, climbing in from the rear. "*Nectarinea auriceps* is strangely attractive to the red ant. I keep a sharp eye while I skin, but they always turn up. I devised a suspended box, but the devils climb down the strings. You see before you the solution. How fine of you to come!"

These devices, the smells, the filthy basins, the very man, repelled her. She thought of her feverish longing in that red room with amazement. Yet there was remarkable order in the hideous little workshop. Pressing plates were hung from nails in graduated sizes, maias head measurements pinned neatly on a wall, sets of calipers beneath; gibbon heads gazed out in sad wonderment from their jars.

She said she had to make the tide. He grasped her hand and thanked her warmly for coming. He promised to come up the following week.

He appeared, clean and polished, a tin of Java cocoa in his pocket and two pretty beads that he said he had dug up outside the bungalow. Santubong was known to have had a Chinese community centuries before, and small, interesting things were turned up from time to time. "The mandrake fruit, I believe, is faience overlaid with manganese," he said. "The rosette has to be frit."

Their lessons resumed. It was, after all, a pleasant way to pass the heat of the day in some tropical backwater, pregnant. It cost her nothing. It was this young man, Barr saw, whom it was consuming. Stepping onto the veranda one afternoon and seeing her, languid, heavy, the boy quietly frantic, he conjured up guides to Semunjan three weeks early.

Lytton left for the Moluccas at the end of the year, after waiting to thank his host, who was up-country, leaving when Barr's return was delayed. "Where is he?" he asked, when he got back.

"Who?"

"The gentle wooer of pregnant matrons."

"He's a gifted naturalist," she said coldly, "with deep understanding and admiration for wild life."

"Admiration for wild life! He was given leave to travel to Semunjan to study the maias. The Orang Kaya gave him two sons as escort, and this admirer of wildlife came back with seventeen of the creatures' heads. To 'measure' them. I'm going to bed."

She watched his lamp ascend the stair. A cecak paused on the tea tray, a small fairy dragon. She sighed and it skittered away, a trail of excrement behind. Lytton was right. Just when you made up your mind something was exquisite, it moved, becoming an object of loathing. Everything eventually moved. Everything moved of itself or rotted or was ingested by a million small jaws. A mantle of microscopic plants covered every undisturbed surface in the wet monsoon—a saddle, a gun barrel, the inside of a boot—lifting in a sickening mist, clogging the lungs. The DO's wife at Lingga, before she left for good, was found one morning with every one of her orifices taped shut to prevent the entry, she said, of parasites. She was all but asphyxiated before the kitchen amah dropped her baskets and tore the bandages off her mouth. Everything left on its own for a few hours, a week, was covered by this crawling layer, or, if left a month, vanished. There was a stench of something always somewhere, and a thick fragrance of something somewhere else. The violent daily cleansing did not matter, for decay resumed before the last bullet of water ceased. In this atmosphere, out-of-body flights were common. She herself flew above the green roof of the little mosque the night the child was born.

"One desires a daughter first." Siti Aisha smiled. "She will watch over her brothers."

She had milk fever very badly. For five days she was delirious and assumed through her delirium that he was away. When the fever broke, she was told that he sat outside the little room night and day. Only when she was out of danger did he leave for Seboyau, where he was overdue.

Special foods, beautifully arranged, were pressed on her. Radii of pomelo, rambutan, loquat, and soursops, and coconut broth for her milk. The datins provided two baby amahs until her mother could send out a proper nurse. Gifts arrived. Embroidered bajus, tiny bracelets and anklets, bags of charms. The wife of the Orang Kaya sent a little boat filled with wooden animals, all armed, with bold expressions, challenging the antus who invade children's dreams. There were a number of ba, woven baby carriers with formidable designs, adorned by rows of coins and polished teeth. One of these was truly exquisite, the complex geometry of its design worked in silver thread, a gift materializing one afternoon out of the air. She found it herself on a little marquetry table in the hall, having passed it merely minutes before and seeing nothing. She stretched her neck to scan the garden and orchard and made out a willowy shape gliding toward the syce gate. She would wonder for years if she had really seen the woman in that retreating figure, the back straight, the head floating a few inches above the neck. Raseh was directed to burn the thing with the orchard leavings.

On the Feast of the Hungry Ghosts, a figure outfitted more like an oblong package than a human being arrived on the *Bintang Rajah* with one large bag and a tremendous crate. Cates' gray drill was buttoned to her throat and secured with a sterling C. Oxfords encased long narrow feet, and spectacles hung from her neck on a purple cord. The woman looked at one so squarely the eyes crossed a bit and this disturbed the Malays, for this was angat and, after the first infant, sabut. She had dark hair swept over her ears in two plaits, a long nose, and a long neck. Yet the brow was clear and the mouth was kind. One found oneself thinking if the nose were shorter and the neck were shorter and the gaze were less intrepid—and to hell with it. The child's nurse had, long ago, decided this as well.

The crate contained her coffin. It was her one aberration other than the usual accoutrements of spinsterhood. If she were to die out there, she would be buried in English oak. In the meantime, this receptacle contained a Bible, a small library of children's books, knitting needles of various diameters, several pounds of wool, a necklace of medicinal amber, and diaries from the thirty-eight winters and summers of her life. She had used a third of her savings on this expedition and departed England as one departs the earth.

Cates approved of Iris Mumm in their two interviews and what she had to share about her daughter. She did not approve of this absurd little despot, who would most certainly be thrown into prison in England and with good cause. Yet over the first days and weeks, she saw there was a saving grace. The man adored the child. At first he had viewed her with fear and awkwardness; and, after the first months, with adoration. He turned into a complete fool, rushing out of the library to tie a handkerchief on the small head, catching the round shape up from behind and swinging it into the air.

Carolina Dewi Sri sat in a little sling outside the cookhouse and eventually toddled through the orchard. Everyone took pleasure in her small, squawking presence. Anything she reached for was immediately brought within range. To reverse such spoiling would be beyond Bibi Miriam herself, Siti Aisha said.

III

Hogg

Allamanda

In November, the Dyaks prepare their padis for harvest. These were often far from their longhouses, and for centuries this had always been the time of the great massacres. Yet Novembers had come and gone for four years without real incident: a small skirmish in Muka, three heads in Oya. Conversations in nipah parlors had long since leapt over the subject of survival to improved packet service, an incipient rail line from the Selantik coal fields, a recreation club. Gossip took up the slack. The town was not so much a half-baked crossroads as a rollicking little microcosm. It stopped with a jolt at six o'clock on a November dawn.

The morning star twinkled when Maureen Dolan walked down between her squash plants to the cookhouse. She had a cook, all memsahibs had cooks, but cooking was her passion and this was a special day. The hut was not much more than a rude pit with walls, tin roof, and smokestack. Nine metal spoons, six pots, a roasting pan, and a stirrup ladle hung on wires, and the book *Enquire Within Upon Everything* sat on a stool, its audacity always lifting her spirits. In the center of the mud floor stood her pride: a Brown's Mighty Mite camp oven.

She picked up *Mrs Beeton's,* lowered herself onto the stool, her big belly resting on her thighs, and opened to where a loquat leaf marked the page. On that morning, thirty-eight years ago, David Martin

Dolan had entered the world, and she was going to bake him a cake. She had rolled from under her nets, urinated in the damned pot, tied back her hair—dry and dull with pregnancy but soon to rekindle like the phoenix—and trudged outside. The recipe called for black sugar, orange bitters, eggs, and sago flour, all ingredients she had. She had discovered the secret of making a cake in the spirit oven. After a year and a half of raw half-charred failures, she realized that if she quickly opened the clap door, spun the pan a quarter turn, and snapped it shut and did this thrice over one hour and ten minutes, she could count on withdrawing something quite edible in the shape of a derby.

She poked in a fagot, and the little demon burst into life. The hut filled with heat and light as she prepared the batter. She slipped in the pan and sat back, sweating profusely. Twenty minutes later she slid the steel watch back into her pocket, opened the door, made a rapid turn, closed it, and sank back. She dozed, heat rising, her eyes suddenly snapping open with the knowledge that she was not alone.

There were three of them along the wall. She had not seen markings like this before, blue crescents and white rings, the faces beneath as expressionless as masks, but she knew they were not local Dyaks and a long way from their river. Parangs hung against their thighs. One of them held a small, beautifully woven basket. She recognized the dukow kelong, and her breath stopped. They glided around like water, regarding her and the stove in turn. She did not know how long she sat, her breath suspended, paralyzed. They murmured to each other; a parang was unsheathed. Black tendrils curled from the edges of the stove. Her nostrils flared.

"My cake!" she screamed, lurching forward and dropping the door, releasing a cloud of dense black smoke. She swung around, grabbing a broom, flailing it in vicious arcs. "Get out! Get out! Get out!"—her hair loose and flying.

Dolan, naked, was on the path with his rifle. He shot the first one dead as he emerged, the two others skirting him and vanishing into the trees. He turned back and was hit squarely in the face with the head basket.

"My cake," she said, sinking in the doorway. A black cloud rolled over her. He dragged her to a tree, checking her everywhere with trembling fingers. Finally satisfied, he walked inside and emerged with the smoking pan on a board.

"Look, sweetheart," he said, burning his fingers. "The inside is quite perfect." He bit into it. "Paradise," he crooned, his mouth on fire. He reached down for the little basket—"This was for you, you know"—but she had fainted.

Boyd Henry Dolan was born that afternoon, a spontaneous delivery, a child who would be addressed for all his natural life as the Mighty Mite.

The dawn visitation was the herald of massacres throughout three divisions. "What a strange way to start," Barr mused.

Si Tundo did not think it strange. "They began with Memsahib Dolan because she has powerful magic," he said. "It resides in her hair. They believe Memsahib Dolan is the Pontianak."

"Well, now they have no doubt. They could only have hoped to disable the woman; you cannot kill a Pontianak. If you follow their reasoning, I suppose they set their priorities straight."

Massacres occurred everywhere that winter. People had no choice but to harvest their padis, no matter how distant, leaving the young and the very old in the longhouses. Raseh's granddaughter returned with her own daughter to help her family during this time. She was an intelligent young woman. Her grandfather had taught her how to detect the smallest signs of danger and to act quickly on them. While washing with others on the riverbank, she heard the nightjar, an unpleasant sound and a gift, for in daylight it is the consummate warning. She gathered up the other women and children noiselessly, herding them into the undergrowth. They waited only minutes before voices were heard on the stream. They were in their own language and the others collapsed with relief, but she cut the air with her hand. The first boat came into view and she at last shared their relief, for it contained people of their longhouse with their own sarongs and palm-leaf hats.

"The Saribas are downstream!" they shouted from the boats. "Come quickly. There is no time!" The women grabbed the children and splashed to the boats. She reached the first dugout, holding her daughter up to the man, his wide-brimmed hat lifting, his hand catching not the child but her own hair, twisting it round his fist, the parang sever-ing her head with two chops, the trunk sinking while the child was cut in two. All who tried to get away were speared and their heads taken. The younger boys were beaten unconscious and thrown into the boats. Raseh had told her they do this: They kill and take the clothes of vil-lagers and impersonate them, to fool those who have escaped. They do not risk their own lives unnecessarily. They call, call, like mimicking birds, to the children and women. It was not considered cowardly. One obtained heads in the easiest way possible.

By the beginning of January, headless trunks of men, old women, and children too young for captivity were scattered about fields and villages throughout the Second and Third Divisions. There was no news except of Dyaks. Dyaks everywhere: at Fort Beryl, at the mouth of the Oya, at Cape Sirik. He relied on Fitzhugh to hold Simmang-gang and stop any movement down neighboring rivers. His main weapon, however, was Hogg.

When the two women returned from the morning pasar, they found dozens of dark shapes gliding below the lawn and through the orchard. Several dozen more sat quietly on the landing stage. These men, she was told, were part of the Tuan Mudah's personal guard. Hogg trav-eled with five hundred.

She left Cates at the foot of the stair and found her husband on the back veranda with a tall, extremely fit young man with golden hair. He was dressed like any other Resident in service. The only extraor-dinary thing was a blue necklace, which, on closer observation, was a tattoo. He turned toward her, unsmiling.

She had never met Hogg but, over the years, had felt the dark counterweight of him to the west—the persistent naïveté of her hus-band, for all his ferociousness, rendered ultimately harmless by this man's existence. Standing a few feet from him, she felt the power and elastic nature of that weight. Before her stood not a well-adapted Englishman but a true denizen of the place.

In the years to follow, she would come to see more. One man, younger, harder, painfully diminishing himself in the presence of the other, yet holding some palpable sway, some very real power: It was a balance struck with Malay flexibility. Except both knew one would die before the other and so there was no balance at all. At what precise instant, at what cracking fever-pitched rage or soft decaying moment, at what cry of a bird, at what "mistake"—a balleh too overloaded or too weak, the balance tilted from that little metropolis on rotting stilts to the inland stockade of this man, this Rajah Ulu, a title Hogg himself never allowed, saying it belonged rightfully to Mua Ari, an enemy chief, and this was true also—at what precise moment doesn't matter. It would happen, and this other, a woefully different man, not a good man or a bad man but a grotesquely efficient one, a narrow visionary, would take the higher ground. The story would simply become Hogg's.

In the course of that visit, he too, dull to most womanhood, felt the queer strength of this girl, gauging her a vessel that could leave substantial wake, reserving the information.

She had difficulty talking with him. She asked the usual questions one asked a man come down for a programmed respite. She asked how he got on at Lundu, a place he had been billeted for twelve years. "I've grown fond of it," he said. He said no more. The business of the day was a joint balleh between them, and she was happy to leave them to it until tiffin.

When Unggat signaled on the gong, she rejoined them and took Hogg's arm. He was light on his feet, all motion seeming to originate in the small of his back, like some gliding animal. At dinner, he did not display the detached, slightly crazy conversation of a man newly come down. It was more like the recitation of some queer list, a list of "things to converse about." He might have been following a guide to human conversation supplied to interplanetary travelers. While the style of speech was spare, there was such unabashed egoism about the man that she was perversely taken with him. He spoke of everything at Lundu in the possessive. "My fort," "my Dyaks," "my boats." He spoke of his DOs, Smalley and Bassett, as his friends, not, she guessed, because they were but because he knew every man had friends: "My friends Smalley and Bassett." He seemed, in some ways, like a child, and some children, she knew, were capable of anything. Even in clean ducks, with that graceful stance, the blue necklace told the tale.

Hogg did manage some of the usual courtesies. He asked after her health; how the climate agreed. He asked after the child. In between, he looked lost, so much so that, at one point, she had the absurd urge to press his hand. It was a fine hand with an ugly scar the length of the forearm to the base of the thumb.

After exhausting his list, he began to impart bits of erratic information. He spoke of a package he had hoped would be waiting for him. "Brown Shield's soap, a coffee grinder, writing paper, Lakey's tobacco." This last he would be especially pleased to see, he said, for it had certain healing powers when applied to wounds. On this bent, he described examples of up-country obat to which he seemed to subscribe wholeheartedly. A bark tea for leishmaniasis; a yam for contraception. Much of what he said should have been grossly offensive to female ears, yet there was such raw innocence about it she was not offended. "I live in a natural apothecary," he explained, capping the dissertation.

The conversation turned to the impending balleh, and she rose. It was not that she did not have an interest. Over the years, she had acquired considerable information on the manner of conducting these things, an exercise involving thousands of men over many months. The face put on it, the words "pacification" and "open trade" slathered over what was simply the systematic butchery of thousands, nauseated her. She saw her husband now in a variety of lights. His naïveté and duplicity. His pomposity. His pathology. He was, she decided, rather good with words. Not the sexually rich simpleton on her mother's doorsill; not the naïf bidding good-bye to the crook Bloch. He came across to these people as one of their own manangs. "It's not pacification," she once blurted out, "it's sport! These people, if left to themselves, would never devise the systematic slaughter you instigate. You extend their blood feuds into the next century!" Four male faces had looked up from their black-rice puddings, regarding her coldly, courteously, a girl two years in-country.

Hogg investigated his accommodations and found everything inferior to the forest. "There is a bark the Punans use for their langkans," he said. "It is soft on one side, providing a capital bed, and the other is repellent to insects. I'll send some down." It would arrive, four months later, in a war boat with his compliments.

As bizarre as his presence was and as heavily as it was felt, his guard taking up much of the town, every trace of the Tuan Mudah vanished with the next dawn. The plan, known only to himself and Barr, was to return with his full force in six weeks' time to make a joint effort against the Saribas, the main perpetrators of the massacres. They would start en masse from Kuching.

Hogg knew little of the town. He didn't like it. He didn't like the filthy pasar or the unruly press of prahus in channel or the ill-built shophouses piled on top of one another along the bank. He found the astana itself a joke, an embarrassment. There was, however, one place he admired, a modest, orderly enclave amid the disorder and squalor. He would walk around this fenced little kingdom before dawn overtook the place. It was a stroll that gave him deep pleasure. He would pass the green-shuttered bungalow, walk the length of her vegetable patch, and stand gazing into the shimmering pea vines until light began to spread.

Maureen Dolan found the thing wired to a post. A wild-armed bouquet of allamanda. Gazing at it in the rising light, she jumped back. A tiny chameleon was tied to one of the stems with a bit of rawhide. He had thought it pretty and so made it part of the package. She knew, of course, who left it. She conjured him as he had been an hour or two before, in the gloom, twisting the crazy arrangement to the stake. She would pry it off and carry it to the cookhouse and lay it on the fire, only afterward remembering the little animal tied to the allamanda stem.

He had identified the branch of the Saribas whose members visited her cookhouse on that morning, a branch which ceased to exist.

He would do this, prowl about the outskirts of her life. Once or twice he slipped in closer, once finding her cutting a child's hair. She was good at cutting hair, doing Dolan, the children, and an occasional clerk. She'd sit them in a bamboo chair, a pile of pillows under a child, and glide around, snipping, easing the steel shears under an ear, along a forehead, all the while keening a high little dirge. Once he found her outside the cookhouse stirring a pot, a book open on a stool, her eyes distant. Another time she was kneeling on the sway-back porch bathing a small boy. He found her before the balleh at Sungei Lang on cleaning day, her skirts pushed into her pockets and fastened with pins so that she looked like some baggy Turk, calves showing shamelessly, her eyes hollow after her latest delivery. "I'm killed," she said rising, not seeing him, rubbing her back, and he wished to rush up those stairs and enfold her in his arms, he wished she *was* killed, on the spot, so he could fiercely revive her, his body burning life into her expired corpse. One or two times he spied only Dolan, a thick, stupid specimen.

He knew what he wanted from Dolan. He wanted him to die. But what did he want from her? Love, but what is that? Filling her with himself, yes. Every day, always, but what? He wanted, he realized sheepishly, for her to cut his hair, to undress him, to bathe him like that five-year-old male, to feed him with something from that book. Once only, he actually had come onto that porch to ask for a haircut, and she acquiesced with a small smile, flipping her hand toward the chair inside. He had withdrawn his anak parang and revolver and slid the ugly American knife from his boot, smoothed his gorgeous hair, and stepped over that vestibule as if entering a temple. He changed his mind and left.

He would dream, in his lair, of a wraithlike shape sliding around him, adjusting his shoulders, the steel shears gliding by his neck, his nose, her tentative eye, her breath as she circled him, appraising her work, he unmoving—he would groan so that his boy thought the bacillus had at last shown up that could bring him down. He would ejaculate at the last clip, and sleep.

There was the time, a momentous event in a two-year desert of nothingness, when she answered him by using his Christian name. She answered his question as to the origin and quality of certain snap beans. "I believe they are hardier, Richard, but the Chinese are sweeter." His name in that mouth stunned him. He rode the rich wave of it, freezing her expression when she said it in his memory, the Chinese beans made to grow at Lundu, served to him every week. Her own name tasted of her. He mouthed it in the night, renaming secret pleasures with it. He once heard Dolan call her "beloved," lightly, uncaringly, and he wished to cut out his heart.

He hadn't touched her except one time, after the huge cholera encampment at Sadok when he came back with only a remnant of the great force with which he left, standing, twenty pounds lighter, in the dappled shade of her six-foot pea vines, and before she could speak, he pressed her against his chest, releasing her almost instantly and disappearing. She would revisit those five seconds for years, so that after a while they meant nothing but a brief constriction within leaves, yet at odd moments, when thinking of something else, a pot burned, a child feverish, she recognized them for what they were: five seconds in which she was enfolded by a love so dense it ate the air she breathed.

Of course, such fire was born of a towering disparity, their preposterous remoteness from each other, and, in fact, if Maureen Dolan had had him under her roof for two years, feeding him regular sensible meals, watching his health, reforming his queer personal hygiene, abusing him roundly for his taste for blood, he would have awakened and stepped back with a shudder, not even a large shudder. That was in the beginning. At the end, she could have been dead and her corpse command the same power.

She sometimes thought on what terrible forms of amusement he created for himself up in that place, sleeping above his inventory of heads, but did not imagine the books in French, the entomological drawings, or the waistlet snatched from a line of wash in her marrow yard and spread in the night on his broad chest, the single strand of her hair on his tongue, the muslin strip washed clean of menstrual blood and hung in the same fenced yard, but he knew what it was and where it had been, decor for his burning, self-stimulated erections.

While he continued sexual relations much the way he drank water, as his love intensified he developed the habit of not sleeping with a woman more than once, this including those eight or nine with whom he already had children. Occasionally one of these creatures loved him enough to trace, through their enigmatic network, the trail of his heart and wonder at the unearthly tastes of white men, then proceed through the usual steps of telepathic murder, steps intensifying over time and to which the C of E stick turned out to be amazingly immune. One June morning, Maureen stooped, in her fifth pregnancy, to pick up a scrap of woven leaves on the little bench by her cook shed, this the most tempting invitation to death devised among Kedayan manangs. She recognized a pungent herb she used with some success in place of rosemary and plunged it into her soup pot, thereby reversing its power in a dry wind, bending the trees to Sungei Katang, setting the hair of the leaf-weaver afire as she slept.

Traveling through that vast territory of his with only his fierce one-night explosions, he was, for all purposes, celibate; certainly more than she. They had succeeded, in those years of queer encounters, in pummeling eroticism into something so strange and bruised that a new emotion would emerge from it.

Six weeks' preparation was allowed for the balleh against the Saribas. Six weeks for people to complete their farming and prepare the boats. There had never been this large a force, so well disciplined, bivouacked in the hills around Kuching. Hogg supervised the final stages when he returned: making cartridges, repairing gear, provisioning. Barr had not worked with him closely before and had never seen anything so systematic in his life. For Hogg, the only unmanageable component was Barr.

Ten days were spent covering the main boats with wooden armor so they could pass the Saribas fortifications. They sat two feet deeper in the water before he was satisfied. He employed a peculiar personal checklist on these campaigns. Before each one, he remade his will. He also made certain to carry several bolts of fine white cotton as part of the baggage of war. There was fear of sickness going this far inland, and the cloth was to bury his dead. The sick and wounded were transported deep within his formation, kept as safe as possible. He never moved without consulting the omen birds. Barr suspected this was no theatrical display but something he would do if he were going off to fight alone. Yet Hogg made interesting distinctions. He subscribed to birds but not to dreams, equally powerful Dyak augurs. "Fear produces disagreeable dreams," he said, dismissing the subject. He regarded other things as infinitely more important. "Never trip on a gangplank," he advised. "The whole bloody bunch will turn around and go home."

On the day the balleh was to proceed downstream, many of his men were seen rubbing their bodies with mercury: "Quicksilver," he explained, "rushing to the point of a blow and preventing mortal injury." You did not know whether he, too, spent the early morning hours rubbing his body with mercury or whether he was describing a superstition he found absurd.

The last afternoon was used to distribute ammunition and tobacco. The fleet started with the sunset gun. Barr rode with Sutton in one of the steam launches, the two lying on the foredeck with their cigars. Everything went by water, including gunpowder carried in long palm leaves, waterproof when sewn together. Hogg's boat displayed greater speed than the launches, having a superb bowman and stern paddler. His personal kit was always the same on these campaigns and included his double-barreled gun, a light Minié, one pistol, two twelve-pound cartridges, two pounds of shot, his spyglass, and a copy of Paley's *Natural Theology.* At five in the morning, they hove to for breakfast and he swam. His coffee was prepared by his boy and he drank it, naked, on deck. All his stiffness and eccentricities seemed to vanish under way. This was his element, his heart's home; all was alertness and grace. He straddled the rail with his cup, his eyes moving among the boats.

There had always been a hesitancy to attack the Saribas River. Even after Kilcane's initial foray, it remained formidable. Its fleets, its strong fortifications, its steep ascents formed a lasting deterrent, yet Hogg's leadership changed the mood of the force. His Dyak lieutenants approached him only when necessary and with cold respect. This was not a movement of men, Barr saw, but of one man in whose body the others found a functional place. "Who am I," he mused, "the one sent before to clear his way?"

There would be a series of these commissioned ballehs over the years, joint exercises with the First Division. Hogg did not like joint exercises with anyone, least of all Kuching, but he came willingly. In the month or two before, the pain would start, dull, deep in his chest, lingering while he engaged in the stuff of his hours, locomotion not commencing for weeks. Then the tramp through mud; days of brown, rushing water; new fevers, sores; the true purpose of this movement not a joint campaign or a caisson desperately needed—there was always desperate need—or anything else, but the point, his heart fixing on it, beyond his arrival and the shower on soft wooden slats and the change into civil attire, beyond the demeaning civilities in that circus tent of a house, her scent now detectable on the river, in the trees, the journey's end and a new misery beginning for it would never end and was therefore a hellish journey, never to call her by the name he wished, never the melting of bone, the lifting of the skull, the convulsive sweetness surging through them both. He would leave after whatever work was completed, leave with his caisson, his mail, his Sakarangs, and hurl himself into the darker aspects of his work as if falling down a well.

Under way, he stopped all boats they passed, taking them in custody so word of their movement would not spread. It was an old habit. If he had enemies not warranting execution, he would haul them along, never leaving anything behind, often arriving at Lundu with a half-starved caravan in tow.

The fleet anchored at the Kalaka. Toward sunset, an enormous flock of bats left the trees and circled the boats, a singular omen of luck. Cooking fires began to glow on the sterns. Jokes passed from deck to deck. By dawn, the current had increased, and the boats slipped into channel cautiously, one by one. Dolan, armed to the teeth, was overjoyed to be part of this. He sat on a gunwale with his plate as his boat swung in. No one saw exactly how it happened. The boat veered into the current, and he lurched backward and was gone.

He was pulled downstream, underwater, then surfaced, floating along rapidly until a man in another boat caught hold of his hair. While this kind of thing could have gone the other way, disastrously, the slightest irregularity in a balleh potentially ruining it, the idiotic smile Dolan wore when he was hauled aboard broke the tension in the fleet. It worked more smoothly from then on, a single animal.

They beached at the mouth of the Seboyau on the thirteenth day, and the bulk of the force proceeded overland. Over the years, Hogg had developed an interesting formation on land. His Dyaks would sweep ahead in two wings while he would remain center and back, as the head, or "beak." It took great discipline to proceed this way through such terrain, but it was remarkably effective. When moving at speed, he could engulf an enemy, his two flanks pushing him back and toward the center. The remarkable thing about this formation was not its ingenuity, but that something so effective had not been used before and, over the years, was never replicated. It was as if it was recognized by his enemies as *his* battle formation, as queer a courtesy as the lock of hair left at the nape to facilitate the taking of one's own head.

He had his own primer for ballehs, and he shared it en route. Europeans must keep together, and extreme caution was necessary when the enemy did not seem at hand. Never stay more than three days in enemy country. The force must proceed in order and, except for guides, no boats were to pass his own. At one point, one of his boats did cut ahead, and he was furious, pitching stones at it, finally leveling his rifle, until it dropped back. When passing through enemy country the lives of women and children were to be spared whenever possible, this seeming more a matter of form, for in the heat of things no one was ever spared. Destruction of enemy longhouses was key to his policy.

There were other peculiar characteristics of his force. While blocks of time in these things are usually spent in idleness and boredom, his men were never idle. Everything was kept in meticulous readiness. Deck space was always clean, ammunition dry, rattan lines ready, and swimmers and divers prepared to cut away approaching booms. His rules were inflexible, yet he had little use for things one would assume de rigueur in battle. One was bravery. "Common sense beats out courage every time," he was heard to say. "Run, if it makes sense. You can regroup and gain better footing later, or maybe you can't, but you've not been a fool."

Various things were heard of the enemy by the time they reached the Saribas estuary. One squadron had anchored in the flats; another had slipped out of a northern stream to strike at Serikei; they had been raiding continually. There was no engagement. While the tide was in their favor, they pushed on to Serikei, fifty miles in one day with paddles alone. At midday, up a small stream, they made contact. An eerie falsetto of thousands of voices began in the valley all around, rising in pitch and intensity in the surrounding hills, then dropping to a murmur before resurging. This sound is a weapon. In the right terrain, it rebounds in horrible answering waves and has the effect of a paralytic poison.

"Let me know when they come," he said, curling up below the gunwales, dropping a topee over his eyes. Two thousand came at four o'clock. The first responding shot splintered one of their own prog baskets. The men on land and those in attacking bangkongs were no match for this fleet. The slaughter lasted three hours. The screw steamers finally moved in, pressing the remaining bangkongs into shallow water and ramming them. Heads were taken wherever possible without guns, saving ammunition. A remnant of the enemy, including the few upriver Malays who led them, sped downstream. They were found two days later, careened up a small creek. Hogg himself and young Eakins slipped over the side and waded to one of the camouflaged hulls. Behind it, a middle-aged Malay looked up from his prayer mat.

"You have recited the ruah selamat a bit early, my friend," Hogg said, and shot him. It seemed a wondrous thing to Eakins, to come upon a man and shoot him as he gazed up at you from his prayer rug.

The pattern was repeated thrice, working eastward. After this, no other encounters were made. The campaign was considered a success. In twenty-seven days, the massacres were stopped, albeit by a monstrously larger massacre, the exercise paid for by heads.

On their return to Seboyau, the edge of friendly territory, they came upon six prahus left damaged on the sand. In the stern of one of these, its forward half burned, were two things: a woman with her arm badly broken and gangrened, and an animal in a cage the size of an ammunition box. They amputated the limb and the woman lived for three more days. The animal seemed healthy. It was very woolly, a marsupial with a small head, huge eyes, and little clawed hands. They took it with them, the creature not eating or drinking during the entire voyage. Lytton later identified it as a *Cuscus ornatus,* a mammal of the Moluccas. It held a look of mute terror, which it never lost, and slept with its hands clenched. It must have been starving, although its thick coat would have hidden it. At the astana, they found it so docile it was not caged. It did not eat and it did not run away. Raseh came upon its husk one morning in the little grove of bamboo, the wool lifting lightly in the breeze, the eye sockets empty.

Sakit Taun

The harbor at Labuan Island always caused a prick of envy in his heart, the waters a more translucent green than his own delta, the onshore elevation providing a lovely vista over several miles. It was a beautiful site, Anna Russell was right in that.

Barr took advantage of the lull that followed the winter's activities to visit this neighbor. Someday he would continue up the coast, beyond all the northern estuaries, beyond Brunei, Marudu, continuing around that point that had risen like a lucent pinnacle in his dreams. "I have been marvelous!" he'd cry to those bones. Yet he could never bring himself to do it. In all his life, he never did.

He passed on to Sulu that spring, concluding a small commercial treaty. It was wise to show his presence in those waters. Marudu, a superb bay beyond Brunei, stood at the juncture of the two great seasonal sweeps of the Lanun fleets and served as their stronghold while on voyage. These people usually kept clear of his coasts but in recent years had worried his eastern estuaries. Kilcane's imminent presence in these waters put his heart more at ease. He returned to Kuching at the end of July. He returned on the eve of his forty-sixth birthday, three weeks before his friend was expected, yet the great spars of the *Golden Grove* loomed above the trees. He was always amazed that a vessel her size could navigate his reaches. Seeing her poised midstream, it seemed more likely she had glided those twenty miles through the air.

Kilcane was gratified to find he had used his own broom with such success and he was delighted to find the astana the abode of a healthy white infant. As usual, he came with gifts. Yet the largest was not for Barr. The morning after his arrival, he took the Ranee by the hand and led her out and across the lawn, saying nothing yet not letting go despite her obvious annoyance. She stood agape when she saw the pinnace rowing toward them, low in the water, its black cargo listing, tinkling in desperate chimes.

Her dislike of Kilcane had not waned over the years. She braced herself for these sojourns, the whole house bending to his will. Yet when she saw the dear, clumsy shape lurching toward her, her eyes filled. That evening, the lead-lined Érard safely braced against the saloon wall, she played a rusty Schmetterlink and some Locatelli as the man sipped his cocoa and laudanum. His presents to Barr on this trip included a new repeating Minié, a Syrian cake of pistachios and honey—supposedly impervious to mold—and perhaps the most wonderful thing he ever brought: a crystal harmonica. It took him a full afternoon to unwrap the little glass bowls from their wadding and set them in proper order. Tiny rainbows glinted everywhere. He threaded the bowls, one inside another, on a spindle that was turned with a little foot pedal. By dusk, all was ready. He tapped the pedal, wetted his fingers from a cup, placed them tentatively at the edge of the spinning bowls, and an eerie, crepuscular music floated on the air, as appropriate to the Bornean night as any kromang. Observing this absurd exercise, one could inch deliciously into this man's soul, the sheer delight in that dissolute face, wetting and rewetting fingers, fragile adjustments, later singing with it, the foot working, high, high, his falsetto waxing into a mad little lieder swathed in glissandos. How happy one was with this individual. And then a note. Not right. The face falling. If anyone from his fleet had observed this exercise, he would have deserted.

The gifts would never cease. He would bring, in future years, a Chow puppy, a *lit-bateau* with Nereids and dolphins, a Burmese masseur. Some he created while in residence. On one visit, he spent three consecutive nights with Lim, perfecting a sabayon, breaking dozens of eggs. He brought two majolica sconces, smiling, corrupt cherubs, which he affixed to his bedroom wall. In one he kept flowers, whatever they gave him; in the other, his vial of vin cocoa. In '54, during the dry monsoon, he drilled a tiny hole in the roof of his room so that a small disc of sunlight appeared on the floor and was discovered slowly to skim along in a gentle arc, the path predetermined in green lacquer painted with a brush at the end of a stick. And then he was gone, the great ship dematerialized, the calendar hole—for that is what it was, the thing a whimsical clock, the months a series of arcs, calibrated into days, the beam of light gliding from arc to arc—plugged up during the wet monsoon to avoid further rot.

Kilcane was obsessed by time. All his life he engaged in quasi-experiments in its manipulation. He viciously resented its constraints and luxuriated in its rare bounty. In his opulent cabin, under Barr's bougainvillea, riding his timeless Chinese, he was always, at some level, occupied with it. He was a gifted amateur horologist and carted about a sizable collection of chronometers, antique astrolabes, water clocks, and portable observatories. He never looked happier than when immersed in this obsession.

Yet he searched, all his life, through books and through those waters, for a society, no matter how small or primitive, that had no use for it. "The semanggat," he said delightedly, when he discovered that Dyak construct, "travels out of time, the rascal, does it most blithely!" He had made arrangements to be buried with his most cherished companion, Kepler's *Harmonice Mundi*. If by chance—as once happened at the astana, when he smelled Lim's egg custard while sitting in a sunlit chair—a small event that did not so much transfer him back to a moment in his childhood when an Irish cook slid those quivering wonders out of an oven as haul *that* sun-drenched time forward so the lines of past and present and the necessity for any future were momentarily obliterated, rendering him immortal—the only condition his soul could truly abide—he was ecstatic. Best was when he himself erased those lines. He would occasionally make the odd maniacal choice, a decision without connection to past or future, standing boldly, insanely alone: accepting a patent liar's word; risking a plan he had worked on for months. He often had about him some colorful idiot or dangerous individual, one of his favorite ways of spiking the mechanism.

Kilcane always had projects. Some addressed "decor." He once organized a team of kulis with spades to duplicate the Sultan's water-reflected audience hall. In attempting to re-create that natural *salon doré,* he had them dig a shallow water trench around the east section of the astana, the Ranee at first admiring the runny gold reflections that resulted, changing her mind when she saw the clouds of mosquitoes spawning in the standing water.

She began to feel in this man something depraved and tender. He unsettled her, yet in his absence she found she missed the queer figure with its moroccan slippers, the inner look of calm and amusement, the errant flashes of despair. A caricature of what? Saint Eustace, she thought one day, observing him. He had been pulling a string to maneuver a metal arm across a calibrated disc. It did not work. His head dropped comically. He walked around. He smoked. He began again. Saint Eustace in the crumbling little temple with his oven, his stag, his bizarre raiment, that tortured, beatific gaze. Years later, when she was old and he was dead, she would lift her eyes to this saint and see the sailor.

So much of the rare lightness that helped to buoy up those years was Kilcane. He had, by then, discarded his haji pantaloons for a silk dressing gown as his house costume. He would sit chatting long into the night and then not appear until noon, languid, refreshed. Yet one morning he stepped onto the veranda with a pale, shaken face. Barr was concerned. In the worst conditions, he had never seen the man unnerved. "I've just seen a howwible thing," he said, pouring a brandy and downing it. "I wan into it in that bathhouse of yours. I've seen Cates naked. It was as if someone had painted little gynecological clues on cardboard. She has an inverted nipple." Beyond his shoulder, a long, angular form shot crosswise across the grass. He was to learn, four years later, that the cardboard played chess, played it with the genius of those who can only walk in one direction and so redesign the earth. To see them moving the soapstone pieces between them on her embroidered tea cloth was like watching an old crone and her surprisingly young son or, when he was losing, a wizened wreck and his aged daughter.

The Ranee's birthday also fell while he was with them, and a soirée was planned. The Boynes, Dolans, and Parks attended, with a local nakodah and another from Rhio rounding out the party. It seemed to her, on this evening, across the candles and noise of supper, her husband looked at her queerly, tenderly and stonily by turns. Later, as she sat at the Érard, his eye still seemed to play over her in this odd fashion, and then the revelation came. *She* had been twenty-six when they buried her. A dull chill enveloped her. She rose after her last selection and retreated to the garden. For eight years, she had not been diminished just by the black creature upstream. The whole place— the house, the fort, the ship, even the child, whom she had secretly wished to call Iris—bore the stamp of that powerful specter. She had called it filial devotion; she had admired it. But it was not. It was something else.

"You've done a capital job," Kilcane said, finding her in the shadows. "The little one is superb. She wields her Da about like a little sultana. My compliments to both woyal ladies."

"Thank you, Homer," she said. "And thank you for the piano. It is truly splendid."

He took her hands. "You're the best thing out here, you know." He kissed her, then turned away, looking suddenly ancient as he shuffled off.

January 2, 1860

Mama,

Today Dewi is four. Her fête was attended by Unggat and Lim's children. She received a simpalili from Tom Lytton, which arrived in a wicker cage with half a cabbage, a form of tarsier with small sticky hands; a batu bangat from Raseh, the gallstone of a black monkey with a white face, very potent magic; a green puggaree and paste bird from the Dolans; a white moon rat from Unggat; and Fort Dewi Sri on the Muka from her father. Cates made two lovely pinafores, yellow and white.

This small being has transformed my life. I find myself seeing everything through her eyes. She delights in so much I found strange and ugly. She resembles the Rajah more and more, a long-legged baby with his burnished hair. He continues to act the idiot round her. A few days ago, he crossed from the courthouse with a basket he would let no one else carry. I assumed it contained documents, Biverts has schooled him to take more care with these things, but instead it held a set of terracotta kitchen toys—tiny cooking pots, a kendi, a brazier, bowls, and a little teapot. With these she now serves him high tea. She orders him up at four o'clock and the man appears!

There was a change in him, she wished to write. His prahu had not pushed upstream for three months. She was pleased to have him about continually, to see that torso turn a corner, to hear his voice from within the house. One evening his hand dropped inconsequentially on her arm at table as he told of a man's court appearance that morning to claim a stone found in a banana. She laughed, and at the same moment heard Dewi and Cates upstairs and Lim scolding in the cookhouse. My God, she thought, I'm happy. There were nights he approached her almost as a lover, a stranger she wished to know. This period she would look back on as the time of the Érard, although the piano would last a decade longer before termites found a way around the lead.

It comes as a red hat; as a comely woman with no pupils to her eyes; as a warrior, resplendent but without tattoos. It comes as a prahu, heavy with cargo, its freeboard miraculously high; as a dry, pleasant wind. Then it is among you and nothing is ever the same again.

Over the course of two weeks, the air became surprisingly breezy and dry, the dryness giving a pleasant respite, especially to the Europeans. One had a little surfeit of energy. Tempers eased; conversations were extended; one did not have the sensation of drawing water with each breath.

The only individual unhappy about this change was Njoman. "It is not a natural wind or a natural heat," he said. "It is the wind of the sakit taun." But he said this only to Unggat.

June 6, 1860

Mama,

I sit on the veranda with my lap desk for there is a delightful breeze. I can hear the children in the bamboo as I write. Each afternoon Dewi plays in the small grove where she can be watched by the wash amah while Cates draws her bath. The green poles rub against each other and sound like a reedy organ. Unggat sits in there too, and Sylvester, Crossjack's son. The dog is stupid, but alert to snakes.

The child looked pretty emerging from the leaves, yet peering more closely at the florid cheeks, the dreamy movements, she had Cates take her up to the nursery. She brought up tea herself. The child was crying and complaining irritably when she arrived. She drank some tea and threw it up. The women regarded each other. Dolan was at Lingga. Michaelis was summoned, but he was at Santubong for the night. Mackertoom, the new pharmacist, came in his stead.

"Summer complaint," he said, clipping his Indian leather bag closed. It was the season; he had seen two other cases that day. They gathered up the soiled frock and tidied the room in relief. By midnight the child was delirious. She complained of thirst, but even a little water brought vomiting and diarrhea.

No one knew why it was the dry, pleasant weather that preceded the cholera. The first case to be accurately identified was a prisoner at the fort. Three days later, a dugout with two blackened corpses drifted downstream and caught in the mangrove below the sago wharves. A Dutch gunboat arrived the next week and anchored in the estuary. It sent a message up, to be opened only by Barr. It was in van Lutyens' hand.

> We have the cholera here. Allow no vessels up nor any exchange of food. If you are strict in your quarantine, it will pass. We've lost Kies.

The sakit taun worked rapidly, first taking the very young and the very old. Within days, dugouts with wrapped corpses passed down the river daily, a macabre flotilla welcomed by the saltwater crocodiles at the estuary. Occasionally, as in the case of chiefs from the higher reaches, a corpse was accompanied by a small bag of uncut diamonds. Certain people waited at the mouth for these. At Lida Tanah, a few bodies were pitched out of their shallow graves by the unstable bank and floated for miles like black gas-filled pillows. In some places where they were in a great hurry to bury the dead, a few wretches buried alive worked their way to the surface. The gates of hell were open.

Perhaps worst, a clear line was drawn between the sick and the well. One regarded the dry pallor, the vacant eye, and knew that this individual, man or child, was now a resident of another universe. He was "other," as dead as if he were in the ground. Simultaneously, death worked a queer elixir on the healthy. Symptomless, one was suddenly immortal.

Dolan returned from Lingga on the ninth day and could not believe his eyes. He found Michaelis in the little dispensary with his head in his arms. "Even the bit I *can* do, they won't let me," he said miserably. "I've been distributing chlorodyne, but they won't use it unless the Prophet himself sends it in a dream! Even when they do take it, they don't take it. They smear it on the support posts of their houses to prevent the spirit from climbing up! With fevers like this, shutters everywhere are sealed! They are not stupid people"—his voice cracked in fatigue and misery—"but they do a fucking fine imitation."

Dolan found his bungalow dark except for one light above. Maureen was in the girls' room. He braced himself on the lintel, staring at the two cyanotic little faces. "What is being forged here?" she said, turning, a strange twist to her mouth. "Nell is still warm. She died three hours ago and her body is still warm! She was wracked by those hideous spasms *after* she was dead!" He reached for her and she leapt back and hit him hard in the face. "Dolan!" she shrieked.

The older girl succumbed two days later. The Mighty Mite, true to his name, survived. She watched him like a hawk, keeping him with her every moment, rising in the dark and watching him sleep. She ignored Dolan, finding her only solace in the boy, all else become invisible.

"The Datin wishes the favor of some flowers from your garden." They would not say they were for the old Datu Imam, who had died. They would not name the sickness, for fear of summoning it. In the kampongs, great tables of food were set up to appease the thing so it would not covet human flesh. At Bau, a naked man was set on a sedan chair made of steel knives and carried about, his head and eyes rolling backward, by order of the towkay.

At the astana, Lim's eldest and youngest sons died in the same night. By noon, the small daughter of the wash amah was dead and the woman shrieked all day, banging her head against the steel tub.

Death had taken possession of the house so thoroughly they searched for some sign of welcome to this hideous power.

And it was a great power. Not a naive antu who could not turn corners and so was foiled by a wall in front of a doorway. It was Sakit Taun, who commanded great respect, a woman with colorless eyes and a decaying breath. Everywhere, shophouses, kampongs, and bungalows gave up their bundles. The disease not only took the oldest and youngest first, it horribly transformed them so that nothing was left to those who loved them. "Truly, evil is greater than good," Ah Moi moaned, watching them wrap the corpse of little Chew An.

Dewi died on the afternoon of the fifth day. He sat on a stool in the nursery, the air still thick with her fever. He gazed at the child, the cyanosis now vanished, in wonder. The small corpse had nothing to do with that merry, bright presence. She was not there. And if she was not there, the mad, joyous thought occurred to him that she was somewhere else. She, a small shade, ate, drank, and laughed at this moment somewhere else. Sembayan. A small shade in sembayan.

Raseh entered the room on the second evening. He had never been inside the house and was afraid. He was an ignorant man, a land Dyak, and therefore of no consequence, yet all in the household had come to value his heart. Lim had summoned him.

"Tuan Rajah," the old man said finally, in a crazy, loud voice. "The Sultan runs out of his house when you tell him. The Rajah Laut sails forth at your command. Your voice turns the Saribas in the stream. You are most wonderful even with our small brothers. Your dog brings the stick to your feet and sits and does not rise. Our dogs do nothing. All these things you can do. Yet I marvel that you cannot do this. You cannot smooth the path for this small foot and say, 'Walk on.' " Barr gazed up wretchedly. Raseh and Lim put him to bed.

They did not comfort each other but drifted, in their grief, to opposite poles of the universe. They came together one night in wordless sexual paroxysm and did not repeat it. Each devised separately his own punishment.

Dewi, at four, had been able to write her name. He had kept the small scrap, her first successful attempt, and he would sometimes stare at it. One day, he placed a pen in his left hand and began to write. He watched as it continued, clumsily, the writing taking on the painful awkwardness of another life. DEAR MOTHER, he read, marveling at the appearance of words he had written over forty years ago, the painstaking loops, the uneven hillocks, all the ancient misery surging back.

She, too, stepped into hell. She had hated the place, and then, through the child, began to delight in it, and now she hated it with a hatred that knew no depth. She saw and heard her everywhere, a sweetness always just out of range, and she remembered over and over again a thing she wished to cut out of her brain. Once, furious at him over something, she sat on the veranda to regain her composure. The child was singing in the bamboo. It was a shrill, repetitive tune, and she called out angrily for her to stop, but Dewi sang louder still, laughing, and she strode down and yanked her out of the little copse and struck her. The child was silent, a look of terror and confusion on her face. That little song tortured her now with its high, off-key strains; she heard it everywhere. "I have a cat. I have a cat. . . ." Of all the times in her life she wished to forget, to erase, it was this, transforming that joyous little face into one of confusion and misery.

There was a small, strange thing. Weeks later, she found Dewi's topee with its paste bird and green puggaree. It had been left in the bamboo and was already rotted out. She took the small mess to her room and placed it on the dressing table. "You forgot," she said dully, "your hat." Through the roil of sleep, a light wind filled the room. She saw, through a silent luminescence, the small hand reach for it, and Dewi went laughing over the threshold. When she awoke, the hat was gone. She did not look for it or speak of it. Heaven and hell played a heavy-handed game in that place. If it was madness, it was a small price to pay to hear that throaty little laugh again.

She could speak with no one close at hand about her grief. Instead, she wrote letters to those far away. She sought communication with strangers, people she had once known but of whom she had lost track, people now living their lives out at other ends of the earth. She wrote nakedly to them, remaining shut to those near her. She wrote of her grief and received no answer. How do you answer a letter like that, out of the blue, drowning in suffering, from a person you do not at first recall? It was as if, she sometimes thought, she could reach her, that the child was somehow closer to those far-flung strangers because she was not here.

Grief poisoned everything. The weather was foul, and she would not rise out of bed. It was fine, and she would think, How can the sky be so blue and she be dead? In the evenings, all the scents and myriad night sounds swept over the house. Cecaks chattered shrilly. The burong hantu called sweetly and answered itself. Yet in all these melodic, mechanical, familiar voices there was not that one, and so it was a music from hell.

Barr continued the cholera rounds. He and Dolan supervised the digging of graves in high ground and made a count of the dead. On the eve of a Gawai, a great Dyak feast, unable to justify staying away longer, he returned downstream. He worked at his desk, accomplishing nothing. He took ledgers onto the veranda, and accomplished less. On one of those afternoons, seated in a chair, he saw Njoman walking along the tree line with a long package wrapped in white wadding. At first he could not believe it was the boy.

Njoman had found Unggat at the end of it all. The boy had taken his sickness to the empty kebuns' shed and curled up with it. There was no other way his kind would have dealt with it. Njoman would not disturb the Rajah or Ranee in their time of grief.

Unggat was placed in a grave on the hill behind the astana. His bajus were hung from sticks, the sleeves and seams torn so that no antu would steal them and impersonate him, but his soul receive them whole on the other side. They placed his small dirk beside him, along with two porcupine quills, a pig tusk, and the lace cuff. This was his baya, his belongings and the gifts he received before his death. To add to it after death was forbidden. Yet a figure came alone at dusk, unseen except by the female maias, and placed a small box atop the grave. It glinted in the last light, the soft, warm glint of tooled silver.

She, who spent her nights drifting through rooms like some nocturnal animal, shuffled out to the veranda in the first yellow light and saw this same figure walking through the garden. It walked slowly through the canna beds and out the iron gates and down past the landing stage. It turned up the river road and did not look back. It was Njoman, and they would see him no more.

She was surprised there was room in her heart for more pain. She never knew how strong her feelings were for this boy, this savage who, if left to his own people, would have moved rapidly away from the sakit taun, leaving everything, often surviving because of it. In the night she saw him, that narrow brown back, hand in hand with the sartorially splendid maias, the two trudging over the rim of the world.

During times of horror, a throb of life persists. A pig will change hands. A coin will be drawn from a purse. After a while, one became aware that the deaths were abating. It was a barely perceptible turning. One day fewer died than the day before. Then it was gone. And with it the dry, pleasant air.

The deluge began. She walked in the garden as hundreds of fountains sprouted back up over the grass. She felt she had set foot in a river and was being carried away, and she didn't care. The great mystery was how death had missed her for so long. For death was all there was.

It was to him, over those weeks, as if she did not exist completely, but a vague mist in the shape of a woman passed through a room or sat beyond the lamps at tiffin. Once, seeing her walk down to the bathhouse, the trees were visible through her dress, the shoe she lifted filled with air. He felt unbearable grief at this. He took her that night in a brutal way, then slipped away like a dog.

Norris' death, a simple failure of the heart, happened in a time so dense with grief it elicited no more than a thickening in the chest. His friend had been in transit to Singapore and was struck on deck, leaving his family of females, his journals, his drafting table and awnings, his star sights, triangulations, soundings, and transit bearings, his encyclopedia of bad lee shores, shoals, bores, and his beloved green notebooks of animals and flowers. A mild friend, departing mildly. Later in life, he would look on the death of this man as something he had somehow missed, a face he could no longer see clearly, until the last day, when the young surgeon appeared again, notebooks lashed under his arm, smiling his shy smile.

Thunder began as it did in that season, darkly, for it came from those unknown regions to the south, a predictable break in the steaming continuum, part of the country's animal habits, its lungs set in the Kadang hills, its alimentary canal the great Rejang, a brain far back in the reaches of Sungei Lang, its feet dangling in the surf of Sirik, its scrotum sunk beneath the mangroves of the Samarahan. How ridiculous Lytton's divisions and compartments, she thought, his genus and species, resting on the belly of this great body. She had borne two of its creatures and so was part of it: a sinew, a talon. No "system" could parse out this living being, label it, and shove it into boxes. Scales of stamen length. Cranial diameters. Lytton's birds did not speak, they bequeathed no message, no warning. The thunder rolled closer and she breathed it in with the unaccountable but certain knowledge that she was again pregnant.

She walked as she did automatically in this condition, anywhere but where she had walked with Unggat. She refused to be accompanied and kept a revolver in her skirt. There were times she seemed to glimpse a figure thirty yards behind or ahead, but as she approached, it dissolved into the leaves. The tracker's presence did not trouble her. It provided a wide, tactful envelope for her grief. He would stay at the circumference of her life, she knew, until some sign that she could once again gaze into a human face. It was peculiar grace in a savage.

"Selamat, Rajah Ranee," he said then. "Makan angin?"

"Do I eat the wind?"

"Do you walk for pleasure?"

"I do," she said, and, from that hour, in a tentative way, it seemed she did. She would look for him at the syce's gate, and he would appear and walk beside her. "I am very sorry for the small one," he said the second week.

It was again September and the Dyaks were burning their fields. They did this for a few seasons and, when the land gave out, moved northward toward the sea. She wondered why they did this, moved ever closer to a natural wall, and what they would do when they got there. Would they build boats? Now was the time, Jawing told her, of the Gawai Batu, the feast of whetstones. A blessing was asked upon the stones to make the parangs sharp for their work. "The gods Pulang Gana, Ini Andan, and Manang Jaban are honored," he said. "Pulang Gana is the god of earth, Ini Andan of heaven. Manang Jaban guards the gate of heaven. It is a great feast that requires much preparation."

"Why all this for a plant?" she asked.

"The padi too has a soul," he said. "With due respect, it will increase. Offerings are made to the omen birds. A petition is made to the spirits of rats and bugs to leave. A small boat is made with masts and sails and a few of each kind of insect are placed on board. A little betel and lime is given to them, salt, small pots for cooking, all is given to them, and they are placed into the stream. Depart ye to Brunei, to Santubong"—he raised his voice—"to Limbang, to Pontianak." There was an ease to the sound. It fell into a rhythm in which his eyes, his smile, his movements were all part. It took nothing from her to spend time with this individual. She knew her husband had once again commissioned him, and she didn't care.

More often than not, Jawing chose the path. They made an odd pair, the large white woman in her European dress and topee, and the long-muscled penglima, naked except for his chawat, moving like water by her side.

. . .

"Of course padi has a soul," Barr said. "So do their jars, their parangs!" He did not wait for Lim but refilled his glass.

"I think not," she said coldly. She had made this effort. She had offered this to him, a word from a universe outside themselves, untainted.

" 'I think not,' " he repeated. "No, I don't suppose any of us agree that padi has a soul."

"What I mean," she said, "is that it is more a force than a soul. If a thing grows, if it changes, there is a force at work independent of the thing changing or growing, a force at one with all other forces. It is less 'apt,' less 'construed' than our idea of a soul." She rose, her eyes swimming. "It is lovely, and I believe it with all my heart."

"Ah, yes, but follow it through, this lovely idea." He would not let it go. "There is only so much of this life force to go around. The Dyak takes a head to partake more fully of it. It is shared by the womb of his wife, by the rice he eats. If one draws from the bank—by marriage, birth, death—one must cover one's withdrawal. I don't frankly know why a head, why not a foot or a penis." She realized then that he was drunk and that he had not at all come to terms with his grief and he never would, and she pitied him.

"Jawing," she said, walking upstream the next month, "what happens to one who dies?"

He gazed at her. "It is said Allah takes him to Himself."

"Do you believe this?"

"My mother believed when one dies, his flesh goes into bamboo and his soul enters the body of an unborn child." He stepped off the path and found a stem of bamboo and notched it with his anak parang. A clear red juice flowed. "After many lives, one reverts to dew, from which all things rise."

The blade had been used so quickly and smoothly it stunned her. She asked to see it. This, too, a simple thing she had seen a hundred times, had a more complex nature than she suspected. The blade had a concave and convex side and was held with thumb toward the concave side. He explained how there were right- and left-handed blades.

"I see. The handle is carved so the thumb may be held one way or the other."

"No," he said. "One blade likes to be swung from the left, another from the right, as one child likes durian and one does not."

It sometimes seemed to her on these ambles she might place her foot at a point on the path from which it had all gone wrong, and continue on again, with another chance. Then there were days when the density of loss, of a deeper loneliness, sat like a rock on her chest. One damp afternoon she mentioned the sameness of everything, the land, the weather, how she missed the English seasons. It was the first time she had mentioned that other world, *her* world, to the tracker.

"This is not true," he said. "There are very great changes in this place that make the heart swell. In summer, the southwest monsoon arrives, a pleasant, dry time with low water, but it is no good for traveling on rivers. In November, the great winds veer and bring the rains and, afterward, all the world steams. The rivers are high and one can speed to see old friends and places." He picked up an ant. "This small man will tell you the seasons of a single day, the time, the degree of heat, the presence of water. The birds will tell you what this day will hold, and the next, down the years."

So began her second series of lessons, which, in many ways, negated the first. There were all kinds of things she had seen or half seen and not understood—signals, tastes, communication between the denizens of that place—that now, slowly, were made clear to her. One day, continuing along a path above the second kampong, they came upon a large fig with an ax wedged in its trunk. No one was in the vicinity. "If one wishes to cut down a tree," he explained, "one must first see if a spirit dwells within. You may give it one chop and leave your ax embedded. If, in the morning, the ax is still in the tree, it is not occupied and you may cut it down. If your ax is on the ground, a spirit is using the tree and you must choose another. It is an easy thing to do."

On another day, upstream on the far bank, they passed through a clearing planted with manioc. In the middle was a solitary spindly tree with only its top branches remaining. Here, two crosspieces were hung with colored streamers. He explained that this tree was left standing as a home for the displaced spirits of the wood in which the clearing was made. Such a network of courtesy had never occurred to her.

At the astana, they were extending the west lawn as far as the dairy, and she had watched them clearing the ground for weeks. She spoke with Raseh, and when the work was completed the last member of a stand of hardwood saplings was left standing. She opened her waxed basket and pulled out several bright strands of wool and gave them to the kebun. It was spread quietly that she had done this, that she had honored the small spirits of the forest.

Only once in their walks was the tracker disagreeable, and it was due to something she considered ridiculous. An old tortoise had lumbered over their path, passing from the creek to the river, and his progress was so slow and labored it made her laugh.

"You must not laugh," he said seriously. She looked at his face and laughed again.

"Why do you laugh? This is his way of going from place to place, and he does it very well. Those who mistreat or laugh at animals may be turned to stone. These stones are batu kudi, and there are many of them in this world." Years later, when nothing was as it had been, her dugout passed an odd formation of rock in the rapids above Klegit. It looked remarkably like the body of a woman and she asked her bowman about it. "This," he replied somberly, "was a woman who laughed at a water naga tearing his skin on the rocks."

With the resumption of these little circular journeys, grief sank into a deeper region, becoming part of her flesh and bone, not something sitting leadenly on her heart. She could move with it, breathe and sleep with it, without the constant wretchedness. She asked the tracker one day if he would be glad, in a few months, to be returning to his family and learned that he was indeed married and had two small daughters and both had died in the cholera. She was astonished and mortified that she had never asked, that he had borne a sorrow equal to hers and never spoke of it.

In her sixth month, she gave off the walks, and he was free for other duty. He was assigned to work for Cakebread, above Bau, and she did not see him for the rest of the year.

Cinta

Dolan was worth nothing in the months following the cholera. He took off with his dogs for the Samarahan, and it was Semple who ministered to all the Christians of Kuching. Semple was, in his own way, a marvel. He had become a force in country. That voice, the faultless biblical quotations, the precise nasal diction, strangely resonant, wafted over water on Sunday mornings, piercing bone.

Nor, in Barr's view, had Delia Semple improved with age. A block of flesh trussed up in a web of interior guys and stays, the immense mammaries jiggling in harness so that, confronted, one was hard pressed to park one's eyes. She was always fit. No vibrio had the tenacity to ride her out.

The Semples had one of those not uncommon marriages based on mutual hatred. They were steadfastly considerate of each other and took regular interest in each other's health, albeit with certain quirks. Semple, unlike most other Europeans in the East, found his bowels perpetually turned to stone, so that a regular dosing of salts was a necessity and often didn't work. Once or twice, Delia envisaged her mate, as he expostulated from the pulpit, filled toe to scalp with excrement. When dosing Arthur Semple or giving him enemas over the big kapok cushions in the bathhouse, she twice nearly killed him with triple strengths of paregoric.

He, for his part, never confronted her outright on any subject, yet tried, over the years, to gently improve her. He encouraged her Bible study, coaching her in chapter-and-verse recitations, refining her grammar the while, her own redolent of the Table Bay cook who spawned her. She was particularly sensitive to these grammatical corrections. It was, in fact, the one way he could get to her. Underneath a thick Christian crust, she no more believed in the Father, Son, and Holy Ghost than in a long shot at Epsom. His main weapon was useless. The only other arrow in his quiver was light humiliation, and he eased it into that mass of flesh with some regularity.

There were other small things in the marriage that, over the years, drove her to the edge of sanity. Semple's habit on rising was to put first his left foot, then his right, out of bed; clear his left nostril, then his right; then stare for a long, dolorous minute at a miniature of a little girl in an inlaid frame, their only child, dead at five of diphtheria. He would then proceed down the path to the water closet, giving way to chronic flatulence. The small room behind the kapok tree was a refuge; he would sometimes sit in it just to escape his wife's clairvoyance.

Life had not dealt generously with Delia Semple. She had taken early account of her thin supplies and was practical about it, thus making her sister at the bone to the only other person in Kuching with whom it could be said she had nothing in common. The Nakodah Dullah was her frequent confidant. She made him pay well for the watered-down, often erroneous information on the raj she supplied over the years, mostly gleaned from conversations with the Ranee. Payment came in the form of extended float on her gambling tab with the Chinese and a Hokkien kebun with diverse talents and singular discretion.

Semple was pleased with the increase in his congregation due to Dolan's absence. He waxed inspired on Sunday mornings, flanked by his wife's carved fruit and vegetable arrangements.

Barr decided to speak to him. It was all right to step in temporarily for a fellow clergyman, but Semple was robbing him blind. Following the afternoon downpour, he cut over on the bajau and left it tied to the water gate. He chose the time of day in which Delia Semple usually hauled herself through the pasar and Semple would be alone. He rarely sent messengers to Europeans; it was his habit to go himself. In this way he found out the damnedest things.

The bungalow was a pretty one, a bright flower garden in front and the house shadowed by huge trees. It struck him that the place, with its overhanging roof, truss of vines, and gaudy flower beds, bore some terrific resemblance to Mrs. Semple herself, trussed and cantilevered under one of her sun hats. The small garden was the loveliest in Kuching, due solely to their kebun, a fat, smooth-skinned Hokkien who always bowed a little too low for his taste.

He was about to call out, one foot in the little entry, when he heard voices. They were softly muffled from well within, male and female, Malay and English, and he thought, My God, the scoundrel. To bring a girl into his own bed in broad daylight. Probably one of those wretched Sunday school waifs. Yet he might do it too, bolted to that slab of meat. He stood on one heel, not moving, and envisaged Semple with his pants around his ankles, pimpled behind pumping over some splayed-out brown child. He was tempted to follow the mewings to the very door and shout *halloo*. He no more thought of it than he stepped lightly across the mat. An inner door up two little stairs was partially ajar, and a flat, pretty face lay beyond with its eyes closed. Delia Semple sat astride the Hokkien, her head thrown back, her mouth open, the great breasts swinging. She gave a low moan, and Barr dropped backward, ricocheting noiselessly between the furniture until he was outside, beyond the garden, and then he started to laugh. He laughed mounting the bajau and trotting down the river path. He laughed climbing the astana slope and going into his bathhouse and coming out, and then he told himself he damned well better stop.

He decided to attend Semple's evensong. Delia appeared next to her husband in gray cambric held to her throat by an onyx cross. "I stopped by this afternoon, but found you out," he said to Semple. She continued to flop a large fan back and forth. There wasn't the slightest indication of panic or even interest. She was to be admired. She was, in fact, a woman who had matter-of-fact needs and satisfied them as one would fill each hole in a muffin tin. She didn't obfuscate or channel anything. Her brain was stripped of useless electricity and her bowels were clear. Yet he now held her by the throat, the only position to be in with such a creature.

These two, he would realize, had done him a service. A day had passed in which he had not grieved or agonized over the mess he made of solacing his wife.

In the spring—along with a newspaper started by Cox, a fifth fort to consolidate the Rejang, two new steam launches, and a vituperative form of dysentery that left its survivors with every organ sore and skin like glass—came love. It was transported on P & O steamers, trans-shipped in the Singapore roads, and hauled the last three hundred miles by packet and naval frigate. It came to Cardhu, the agent for the Borneo Company atop Bukit Merah; it came to Bertha Minjoot, the chief clerk's widow, in the form of a third cousin to her late husband from Malacca whom, on the urging of her relatives, she consented to marry; it came in secret, by prahu from Rhio, for the Nakodah Dullah in the form of a new twelve-year-old concubine, a girl whom no one met until Dolan attended her confinement and death that winter; it climbed the Batang Lupar to join Reventlow and a young district officer so completely and perfectly that it precluded anything more female impinging on the rest of their lives than a Celebes parrot. And it came to one of the two young gods of the Rejang.

With the influx of new blood, district officers were allowed to marry before their ten-year stint was up if their families remained in Kuching. It changed the life of the town. Ross and Connor Doherty arrived three days before the packet to meet Rose Collins Doherty, Connor's bride since his last and only leave. The Ranee regarded the boy laughing with his brother outside the bungalows or sitting on the quay, shoulders flung back, gazing at the sky. To be the target of so much beauty and lust, innocently hurled at you. She felt suddenly ancient, dead.

Ross had not met his new sister-in-law but felt he knew and loved her a little himself because Connor had described her endlessly and shared her letters. She was a widow of twenty-four, her husband, a civil servant in Madras, having died in the summer diphtheria epidemic. She was bringing out a child, a boy of five, from this marriage. Ross was immensely happy for his brother.

He, too, knew something of love. He had an exquisite little Melanau of sixteen whom he treasured like a true wife. He traveled by prahu himself rather than refuse her passage on the launch. She was a gentle creature who made him her whole life. They had an infant daughter whom he named Nora, after his mother.

One or two of his bride's letters Connor did not share with his brother. He considered them too personal, too splendidly unsettling and somehow pure, his blood coursing wildly as he read them. *I do it to myself,* she wrote, *for desperate need of you.* Ross read these as well, seeing them tucked under the moldy blotter, curious that some weren't shared.

The two were glorious specimens, Ross a bit thicker than his brother, with blue eyes so clear you felt you were gazing to the back of his skull. He was nearsighted and often wore spectacles, a way many told them apart. Aside from their embarrassing beauty, of which they seemed amazingly oblivious, and natural high hearts, the two displayed fierce solidarity when either was mishandled. The memsahibs furtively drank them in. The Ranee, despite Barr's explicit warning not to cultivate the young Residents, had them to dine as often as they could come, and they could come, it seemed, all the time. They sat at table like schoolboys, entertaining her with their feats on the Rejang. They regaled her with Dyak fairy tales and sang her songs with the delight and abandon of children, yet she could see, in certain small mannerisms, there was already a natural danger to them. As far as Barr was concerned, they boasted outrageously, ate everything in sight, and should have been consigned to the DO bungalows where they belonged.

His was a shallow objection. He had enough ego himself not to care about them much. Yet their archaic sense of honor, their natural goodwill, left a rancid taste in some mouths. There was a fineness about them; one somehow knew it would propel them toward wondrous feats or hopeless disasters, and they would ride either out to the end. They were simply better than the rest, and because of this one admired them, loved them, and, in a small corner of one's heart, wished them dead.

"Of course they brag!" she said, flying at him in a way that surprised them both. "It's impossible to speak the truth when you're young. Things are too splendid! You mean to say you were late or tripped or thought better of it, but something more brilliant pushes through!" She looked at him stonily, her face flushed. She had lost her last pregnancy to fever that winter, and the ordeal showed. He had forgotten how young she was. She was the same age as those two.

It took no time for her to share their excitement and anticipation in Rose. She envisaged a sweet, lovely creature who would care for them both.

Rose Collins Doherty was a dark, long-waisted young woman with a bewitching tilt of bone from cheek to brow. She had a pale complexion and a tentative, slow-spreading smile, and was immediately labeled the beauty of the batch. Her only fault was a slight separation between the upper front teeth.

An elaborate tea was held at the astana for the newly arrived brides and government employees. The Dohertys walked in with Rose between them in navy muslin, a cool dark stream between two cliffs. She said little, though occasionally she would smile and sometimes laugh, yet it often seemed unrelated to anything said. It was an odd face, Melie thought, reflecting interest, amusement, and vague contempt.

The child she brought with her was undersized and pale. She had only the two big carpet bags and this boy on the quay. She held on to him firmly but, it seemed, disinterestedly, as one would keep contact with a piece of baggage.

Barr took his own account of the "female issue." He was taken with the gold and pink Annie Cardhu at one end of the spectrum and disliked Mrs. Doherty at the other. Alluring with her beveled eyes and narrow waist, yet somehow underbred. Such people possessed a corrosive force that could have the most remarkable effect over time. It was Dawes who perhaps best expressed the unease the girl inspired. "I dunno." He scratched an ear. "She looks right enough. It's just as if you knew when she took off a shoe there'd be only four toes."

Newly married Residents were given three weeks' leave before returning to their stations, and this was extended, as a courtesy, to both Dohertys. Melie was relieved, one afternoon, to see the girl sitting on the stair of their bungalow, watching her young husband bathe in a tin tub. Her pretty lips were parted in admiration and something else, a hot, roiling look, her eyes milky with desire, so that her observer turned away, embarrassed yet pleased that this fiery link existed. She climbed through the canna, yet could not resist one more backward glance, the boy lifting, at that moment, his broad shoulders and wet head above the little nipah screen, unaware of either woman, a set of spectacles held in the air. My God, she thought, shivering.

There are insignificant people who have tremendous significance in hindsight, like a good wheel horse that, one morning, simply does not rise from the straw and so travel is never the same again. John Cox was one of these. He did a very decent job with the Borneo Company's books, providing valuable information if anyone ever had the sense to use it, and basically kept Bigelow's family together by his simple, generous presence. Yet living on the edges of that queer, concocted family, he had begun desperately to want something for himself.

Cox slammed the swollen door to his office, locked it, and walked around to his two rooms. He bathed, shaved, and dressed, his three war decorations in a neat line across his narrow chest, his thin hair carefully combed, topee in hand, the miniature of Hannah Forbes Allen in his pocket. The cannon had rumbled downriver, and now the steam shriek itself as the *Hindoo Queen* churned into the quay. He wrapped two Mokara orchids in a damp handkerchief and went out, every nerve tingling.

The crowd on the quay seemed larger than anything the town could have produced. He hung back, not wanting to be noticed. A woman on deck in a green suit and matching pancake hat looked at him in alarm, then fell into the arms of Nast, the DO at Tegora. There were exclamations and embraces all around, a hot, milling surge of people. The agitated mass, artificial, joyous, moved up the slope, and he stood there. He boarded the packet, now actually higher in the water, and checked with the purser. A Miss Forbes Allen had not embarked in Singapore. He glanced behind the man and scanned the empty deck, the arc of sky.

"Right," he said. He disembarked and walked in strong strides up the hill, catching the tail of the crowd. Halfway up, Herbert Bigelow emerged from nowhere and jerked his sleeve.

"Never mind, Cox," he said. "She was probably a bitch." He looked down at the child, then continued through the cannas. The tea was splendid. An ornate silver service had been produced, and platters were piled with a variety of colored coconut water cakes, moon dumplings, and shortbread. He had never been in a crowd so electrified before except in war. Two-thirds of the newcomers, he surmised, would be raped before moonrise; the rest left stonily under their nets.

He accepted his cup, his citrus wheel, made pleasantries, and withdrew, descending the slope and stepping into his dugout, which he sculled to the opposite bank. When it nudged the shore, tears streamed down his face. The truth was he did not care for Miss Forbes Allen. He did not even know her. Three brief encounters over a single leave. The whole thing, their engagement, her coming out, had been arranged via a cousin in Bath. Yet over those fourteen months, he somehow came to place all the rotting hopes of his life into that signal cannon downriver. When the light began to sink, he walked downstream and slipped into his rooms.

The two Dutch lamps were already lit, the table set. Each simple object had an expectant air in the soft glow. The amah peeked in.

"Go home," he said.

He sprang his collar and sat down. The lamps, the bowl with the rest of the Mokaras, the squared-off cutlery, looked absurd, reconfirming his hopelessness, his idiocy in his hope. "So be it," he muttered. He called back the amah to reset the table for one, picked up the seven-month-old London *Times,* and opened to the society pages.

A lovely woman in white sat between two faux Corinthian columns with a small boy at either shoulder and a large dog at her knee. It was a picture he knew well. She was a stranger, yet he knew the sound of her voice, her innermost thoughts, her body undressed. He did not eat. He poured himself a gin, removed his studs, and began to work on the one volume he was in the habit of returning with in the evening. Gutta: eight hundred and forty-nine kilos; palm oil: five hundred barrels. The revolver in the drawer of the tin desk gave a degree of comfort. There was, at some point, a small, sharp knock, but he didn't stir. After a while, the caller could be heard moving away. He rose and flung the door open, and Tannes Bigelow turned around in an abrupt little jump.

"She didn't make it," he said lightly. "She's not coming." He laughed, rubbing the back of his neck. "She's not coming altogether." He looked at her, then began to close the door. She stepped toward him, her hand outstretched, the fine brows high and sympathetic, and he pulled her in and crushed her in such a passionate embrace neither could breathe for several seconds. He released her miserably, with infinite apology, and she smoothed her dress, turned coldly, and went out.

There was always the spare dovecote. You would think that one of these soft, desperate birds was made in heaven for Cox. But this was not so. There was some mathematical rule against it. Tannes Bigelow, of all people, recognized it. "There is a law of nature that certain people shall love no one and not be loved their whole lives through," she said to her husband. Bigelow belched and patted her hand.

Love was not purely an imported commodity that year. After Dewi's death, Cates made arrangements to return to England. She did this without consulting the Ranee. She felt the sight of her own person, linked as it was with the child, was in itself painful. On learning she was leaving, the Ranee entreated her to stay for the child coming, and Cates unpacked her bags with the same slow precision with which she had packed them.

Emma Cates was not outstanding in intellect or education but she had a sizable share of common sense. And she had it without residing in those flat, spiritless plains where it most often is found. The reason for this was easy. All her life she had been in search of love. She looked for it in every face, human and otherwise, that crossed her field of vision in forty-three years. Despite her tight hair, tight shoes, and tightly pursed mouth, her heart opened wide. She had shared an unconditional, blissful love with someone for the first eight years of her life and the last eight of his, a clergyman and widower. Two weeks before her ninth birthday, her father died. She had not known she was plain and destitute until then, and the news was broken to her without delay. She was boarded with relatives and, as soon as she came of age, was encouraged to go into service. She did this at fifteen, as a child's nursemaid, continuing her search for love. Given her physical appearance and circumstances, she found it most reliably in other people's children. It was not so common a commodity that you did not take it where you found it.

Cates was open to the miracle. Queer things happened to her. Even the way she got her fur, the only luxury of her life, was like tumbling down a flight of stairs. Willy Manse, the seventh Earl of Longham, cut big moon and banana shapes out of her new cloth coat, bought with two months' wages, and Lady Manse replaced it with a moth-eaten rack of stone marten. Cates began early to believe in her star.

She believed in things. She believed in mustard compresses, in airing rooms in winter, in smart-paced walks, in the existence of evil, and the eventual and eternal triumph of good. She dealt with the rest—mosquitoes, kurap, prickly heat, malaria, loneliness, rot. With the onset of the northeast monsoon, she could be seen retiring with two hot-water bottles, one placed under her slatlike buttocks, the other atop her concave chest. "I don't get sick," she said to Iris Mumm. It seemed she did not.

She took exercise each morning, folding and snapping upright thirty-two times behind the washhouse screen, thirty-two flips from toes to sky. She finished by sitting down and rotating her wrists and ankles the same number of times. Observing these precise gyrations, the Dyaks, who quietly observed everything, promoted her from simple witch to manang mansau. After exercising, she replaced, in the sweltering heat, a small wool shawl, pinned in front over her bosom and behind over her shoulder blades, emitting the eternal scent of naphtha.

Cates was given her own bungalow in a natural depression below the DO line. She was delighted. It was her first "personal roof." Yet she found, with her few treasures spread about her, she could not furnish a dwelling the size of a closet. How could, she sometimes thought, the prie-dieu, the great breakfront her father used to catalogue his sermons, the oak settee, all have vanished from the universe and this thimble, this half-filled jar of orris root, this garnet earring remain?

Barr disliked plain, asexual females as much as anything in life, yet Cates had her points. She was useful, and she didn't drag about. Even now, without the child to care for, there was always something to be mended, a book to be rebound, a pudding to be boiled. She was an industrious, silent shade, rising with her darning egg and gliding away so as not to disturb, although he was never sure who was being disturbed.

Yet one afternoon, shortly after the arrival of the bride packet, she knocked on the library door, something she never did, less prim, less self-possessed. "There is someone on the veranda, sir," she said. It was clear she intended to say no more, so he got up and went out. There was no one. He scanned up and down the boards and was about to go back inside, annoyed, when he detected the rank, undeniable scent of Boola Boy pomade.

"Peachy!"

At that same moment, Dawes flapped around the corner with his gin. This man had a queer fastidiousness when reentering civilization. The tent was pulled down and belted so it resembled a child's pinafore with cartridges. The greasy black hair was parted dead center and combed to either side so he looked like a celebratory bat. This hair had puzzled Barr. "Why in hell do they call you 'Peachy'?" he asked one evening when they were deep in a bowl of arak. "Your hair is dead black!"

"*Peachy* had fuzzy red hair," Dawes explained. Barr looked at him crazily. "My mate on the upward trek. My mate wot's dead. Peachy

Donahue, who says to me—at about three stone, for we be a-sail two month and sharing a sort of special diet, 'I got nothing to give you and you been like a brother to me, Albert, so I give you myself, but don't be too hasty.' And I wasn't. 'And I give you my name, too, seeing as you don't fancy yours.' And I took that too, because I never fancied Albert."

Peachy grinned. "Selamat pagi, Tuan Rajah."

"Selamat, you old fool." Peachy was the only visitor to the astana who had free access to the gin cabinet before presenting credentials. The man was "well come." Through the years, he continued to provide the accurate, timely information of a veteran Resident over a vast scope of territory, but that was not all. He would, if asked, throw in a short, brilliant analysis of what he had reported. Yet if one did not say, "What do you make of it?" he never said anything. In his bizarre comings and goings, he had learned to volunteer nothing.

"I've had a chat with Tunku Ishmael on the Bintulu," he would say. "Says all's in order and wrapped up after their little tea party. Had four headmen give reports one after the other."

"What do you make of it?" Barr would ask by habit.

Peachy sat, folding a knee with his hands. "Line o' bloody parrots. We've got three weeks to nip whatever's going on. It'd take the likes of Fitzhugh, but he could never make it over in time. Smalley's the man."

"All right." Barr rose for Sutton.

"No need, your grace. I sent two runners from Kapit. Different routes. Bolted a third off at Lingga. Told Smalley he'd need five hundred men. He'll be four days on his way."

Cates, pinning little wet cardigans to a board on the veranda, heard one or two of these conversations. She turned the bat over in her head. Filthy and bizarre as he was, he was to be respected. In fact, on that first day, he had tried to be civil, to introduce himself. "Peachy Dawes," he said. He said it twice, and when he saw how alarmed she was, he stepped back, falling off the stairs. He fell in a strange way, his body collapsing unlike any other, then getting up brightly.

Over the course of two years, her initial repulsion turned into keen interest. There's no explanation for this, as there rarely is for these things. Except perhaps that they were both peculiar when held up to the rest of mankind. She displayed her interest in the only way she knew how. She made him things. Petit-point suspenders; a portable poultice of mustard and gauze housed in an ingenious linseed envelope; hand-bound vespers.

She appeared to Dawes as a mosquito, a great, flat-chested, sexless mosquito, omnipresent when he put in at the astana, leaving him insane little presents. He did his best to stay away.

Yet he found to his utter amazement, at the end of the second year, returning from the Apo Sut, walking between the Rajah's brilliant canna up to the main house, his good eye was darting around on its own. He was used to his organs and limbs taking on sudden, asynchronous life, yet this was different. He felt a strange sensation in his stomach, "disappointment," on not seeing that boardlike presence flit out of a door. She had been sent to Pontianak to help out with the new van Lutyens infant; he had missed her altogether.

She stayed down there, in the well of her grief, knowing she had missed his turn in and so could not personally give him the fine lemon-colored shawl for at least five months. She left it with the cook, and the small package was flung behind the yam bin. Oddly enough, Dawes himself found it while replenishing his stores from the Rajah's pantry, and Ah Moi rolled it around his rice case. *"Cinta."* She smiled evilly out of the toothed side of her mouth. "Love."

Returning to the watershed, he looked at the yellow thing. It was ridiculous, but it was light. He might as well carry it. One night in a heavy downpour he pulled it out and wrapped half of it around one leg and passed it over his groin and around the other leg and lay this way under his roof of leaves. It felt all right. He spent the next five sodden nights wrapped this way. On the fifth, he found himself visualizing the narrow lace collar on Cates' dress, the way it threw a light filigree on her scrawny neck. The experience so unnerved him that he passed over his next turn in altogether.

When he came down the following winter, she was on the veranda with her sewing and got up, taking off her spectacles. Her bony face was so flushed and happy that he seemed to be seeing her for the first time. Over that stay, he kissed her. She was not surprised. She had done the right things. But when he left, he left without a word and did not return until Hari Raya Puasa tiffin.

"How's the girl?" he said then, uneasily, over a punchbowl where she filled little cups, but once begun, conversation between them resumed in a surprisingly easy fashion. They spoke of the new families in Kuching, the Kanowit expansion, the queer turns of domestic animals on the equator, an old Gaiety comedienne turned up in the *The Times* obituaries, and the curative nature of mustard. Its inclusion, Cates affirmed, had to be useful in up-country medical kits.

"You don't need a *kit,* Em," he replied. "A bit of quinine. Maybe turmeric for the bowel. Stay right as rain. Lingire swears by turmeric. What do you think?"

"I think," she said, gathering every ounce of courage she had and fixing on his good eye, "people like us never have anyone."

He took a gulp of punch and looked away. "Aye," he said.

She was right, he thought, pulling off his pants in Smalley's leave bungalow. And it would not be half bad, and at that instant a full, rolling warmth inundated him from head to toe. He would, he decided in this miraculous spreading glow, cherish and protect Emma Cates. He would love her and protect her and right his life to do it. He fell asleep happy. The next morning he left Kuching like a man leaving a burning building.

As the previous year had been the season of brides, the next was of babies, babies everywhere. Life surged forward with new life, indifferently. Breeding, replacing stock, she thought bitterly, her hands folded over her own swelling stomach.

It was a rain of infants, a torrent of sweet young flesh, to be flushed out in storm drains, gills flapping in the mud. They were everywhere, in cribs, in rattan cradles, stuck hard to teats, the survivors toddling forth in a year like the little turtles at Talang Talang, the vast number to be snatched up and swallowed in their rush to the sea. The Boynes had a new infant, the Dolans one coming, the Michaelises and Parks were expecting as well; there were crabby, dugong-shaped memsahibs everywhere. Lim planted a frangipani tree behind the cookhouse in honor of a first daughter.

Where did all the lust occur to spawn them? she wondered. No one saw it, yet one could feel it, smell it, in the night. The heat above the Dolans' porch; the leaden rhythm in Bigelow's cramped quarters; Cardhu drowning in the moist, pink flesh of Annie; and, at times, in the square upper space in the astana itself when a violent tide washed over him, leaving her sprung.

To be a strange machine, forever in the process of producing children yet not having any, had a dark humor about it. She had spread out early in this pregnancy. There were two sets of twins in her family, her Aunt Pat's and her Cousin Genevra's, and this, she felt certain, would be the third.

One made a point to see babies, ephemeral balls of life at that septic threshold, often to pay a small salutation before they departed. Huge herself, she greeted the new Mary Kathleen Dolan with a set of tiny bajus and a box of cornstarch. Maureen was pale, but her breasts were hard with milk and the baby seemed robust, with Dolan's big bones and her red hair.

They talked of the little girl. Maureen admired the shirts. Yet in between, her eyes were dull.

"What is it, dearest?" the other said, finally.

"I can't see him." She turned away. "I can't see his face anymore." The little girl began to fuss and then to wail.

That afternoon, turned to the wall, deaf to the infant's cries, Maureen Dolan told of the hours of her son's dying. They had known of this death, a death absorbed with all the others of that year. This is what we have come to, she thought, listening, that hell burned so fiercely across the river and she, nursing her own grief, gave no comfort.

Scarlet fever is a disease of cold and damp, a disease of black wreaths placed on door knockers in the snow; it is a ridiculous disease to have in the tropics, but the fall after the cholera, the Mighty Mite had it, his strong, small heart, Maureen could see it in her dreams, contracting with the onslaught. His death was hard, but afterward he looked again like a child sleeping. The queerest moment, she said, was his books. Five, kept in a tin bread cabinet. His favorite story of a magic cow had to be burned. All his clothes, his shoes, everything was burned, until nothing at all was left of the boy and she tidied the crooked room under the eaves and took off her apron and sat in a chair with Dolan's revolver in her lap.

" 'What is happening, Mother?' he said; he was always a bright child. 'Where am I going?'

" 'You will let go of my hand,' I told him, 'and at the same instant Jesus will take hold of your other; you will never, even for a second,

be alone.' I sat with his hot hand in mine and told him this drivel."
In the night, she woke and his free hand was flung far out and she tore
to the other side and clutched it, an object.

This was the bitterest thing, that she could no longer see that face,
that her tired memory no longer held those two blue pools. "Ten days
before, I poured him a cup of milk and he sat at table in a slab of light,
healthy as a little horse."

"You'll see him on the other side, dearest." Melie kissed her cheek.

"Oh, I won't see him anywhere," she said, almost matter-of-factly.
"It's odd. I've pushed all this vile stuff into Dolan and now he is
shackled heart and soul to it and I'm left with nothing." She was
quiet and the infant was quiet.

"You have this precious little lady."

"She's a lump of flesh to me." The voice was leaden, frightening.
"He was a *person*. He was one of those who is a person. You make so
many. Bloody little specks passing through you. Big, healthy eaters
tearing you apart. You make more and more, a gory oven. And then
you have one like him. Do you know what is the worst thing in the
world? The worst thing in the world is that first morning you open
your eyes and know he isn't anywhere, not on his cot or at the wharf
or in a boat crossing the ocean or among the stars, not anywhere
anymore, and you must get up and place one foot in front of the
other and relieve yourself and rise in your stink and begin the day."
She lifted her eyes, remorse sweeping through them. "Of course,
you know."

Does it happen over time? she wondered, lurching in the stern of the
dugout. A boy in a slab of light, suns and galaxies swirling through
him, his lips white with milk, ever existing, all else rotting and falling
away. Moroccan slippers glimmered on the floorboards. She had
come to respect time, its vacillations, its contractions and playful
expansions, its arbitrary cooperation, its hideous tricks. Does it happen in measured steps, so much for a journey, so much for fruition,
so much for wisdom? Not here. Here, even the measurable things,
the growing of trees and flowers and men, happened with great fury
and waste. In this universe of vast, plodding distances, people came of

age, lived, and died, in haste. A man of twenty-three could find himself master of a ship and a hundred men; at twenty-seven he had buried a wife and children on a hill in Malacca or Madras or Bencoolen, their names crammed together in the speed of a diphtheria epidemic. By thirty, he would have a second family, and they and he with them slipped under the same stone during the summer cholera. Sometimes, with such speed, grief was flat. Sometimes it was so sharp it could never dissipate. OUR WILLY it said on a small piece of rotting stone in the Fort Canning cemetery, not an epitaph but a wail down the ages.

Other things stretched beyond endurance. Months at sea, days in childbirth, dying prolonged by a strong heart. Friendships hung suspended for ten years, sometimes longer. Memory failed and imagination filled the gaps and it too gave out. Then there were the tricks, so diabolical they caused one's heart to stop. Mrs. Minjoot kept the letter in her pocket, happily taking it out and reading it to anyone who would listen, folding it, replacing it, patting it like the head of the child who sent it through the freezing night he burned alive in Westbourne Abbey School with nine other seven-year-olds. When they finally thought she was over it, never the same but over it, she set their bungalow afire. They bumped the wharf.

A large shape lay in the gloom on the kapok settee. He had been to Betong and must have quietly returned. She lowered her weight into a chair and gazed at him. He had thickened and it became him. A handsome, dissatisfied man who looked as if he had ruled that world of mud for forty years instead of twenty. They had taken little notice. "A man who rules five hundred miles of coast should be more than a bloody consul general," he had growled to Biverts the year before. With Hogg, he was swallowing a river a year and he needed Whitehall to back him. "Why do more for me than they have to?" he said bitterly. "It's bloody comfortable to control this coast without the expense of a protectorate. They slip me a ship when it suits. To 'that self-styled Rajah.' To hell with them and their parsimonious mincing! I'm sick to death of it." Yet he dreamed in the night of the Queen's plump white arm sweeping over those waters, drawing his rivers and estuaries and mountains to her breast.

He had changed since the child's death. Things that would have glanced off him now drew blood. What had wounded him most successfully, oddly enough, was *The Straits Times*. Its editor had referred to him in print as "an opportunist of the worst cut, given to grandiose posturing and bloodthirsty abuse of the aborigines in his domain." He had never met Mace but felt some admiration for him. To write with such confidence about a man one has never met. Yet the words tore at his stomach. Could they know something he himself did not? And the bastard was prolific. He could count on reading something every three or four months.

In the gloom, he opened his eyes and, by a trick of light and dark, seemed to look at her tenderly.

Sengat

The two gusi tuak stood squat sentinel above the little ladders and streams during all the years of expansion and the plethora of brides and births. He spent less and less time at Na as time passed. Yet those days high above the forest and river were some of the most pleasant of his life. He felt years drop off him each time he climbed into that high, cool refuge. The woman continued to reside there in serene authority.

The mistress of the sumur gamelan was a surprise to everyone but himself. One found a middle-aged, yellowed Malay with a bloated stomach from numerous miscarriages. It was only when she rose and walked in that airy, regal way that one could see what she once had been. She was, by then, over forty and addicted to opium. She treated him more like a son than a lover, and he seemed satisfied with this.

Ajar no longer left Na. She lived the retiring life of a second wife. Yet beneath the stuporous round of days, a hive of astounding energy could stir into life when the need arose and then sink into dormancy when it vanished. She continued to assist him, and it was not a small thing. Over all those years, nothing was ever asked outright, and he never pressed her on the degree or nature of her assistance. If he had and if she had answered at all, it would have been obliquely. He simply rose one day to the rill of water and realized he did not trust her and had not for some time. The thing that had been staring him in the face for so long was this woman's continued involvement with those whose interests were not his own. She did not have spies among the Lanun and Balignini and the kongsis at Bau and Pontianak. She had friends. Yet he liked coming to Na. He liked the cool air, the vistas, the whimsical signs of obat tucked everywhere. He liked resting in those yellow arms.

Over the years, guests continued to be invited. Dolan and Michaelis came up, and, of course, Dawes, and Lytton twice. The priest came, a harmless lunatic yet one who could, it turned out, discourse on a variety of subjects with originality. He invited Hogg to Na. He did not do it because he liked the man's company. He did it to exert a public force over him. There was clear distinction between the summoner and the one summoned in that country. Yet he found that the time spent with Hogg at Na was not unpleasant. The place wrought a change in this man, as it did in everyone. He did not talk of war and ordnance up there in the clouds, but of poetry, animals, and a queer form of pantheism. The one person with whom Hogg developed a friendship, for want of a better word, was equally surprising. Dolan found the Tuan Mudah a queer amalgam, a white man more savage than any Dyak, yet with pockets of generosity and grace. They would have bizarre quasi-religious dialogues that went nowhere.

"Yes, I believe in immortality," Hogg once said. "It's short. A man who knows a death blow has been dealt him but continues to fight is immortal for those few moments. There's not much more to it, nor need there be." Dolan would sit back blankly, a corner of him considering this wretched possibility. It was an odd collection of men. The country found you out and there was a winnowing, and they were what was left.

Conversations at Na began ordinarily enough, encompassing work, newcomers, disease, sex. They would, in the first few days, invariably take a downward turn, spiraling into a litany of miscellaneous, bitter complaints. They would hit bottom, one could almost pin it to the day, then bank upward, expressing satisfaction and enthusiasm with an increasing variety of things, buoyed by the rare air and vista and lack of malaise, leveling off in a high realm of lofty sentiments and pseudo-philosophies. Speech was broadcast with superlatives: the most important quality in a man, the best fighting tribe, the most treacherous, the best sexual techniques. "The greatest thing in the world," Paoluzzi declared one evening, "is wit." This, for some reason, inspired an amazingly fierce crossfire, so that Dolan finally rose in disgust. "What happens to people up here? This place is bewitched. That sorceress will turn us all into swine."

Barr was to think over this rude remark, so unlike the man. He had, in his own way, reached a similar conclusion.

Eight days after he headed upriver, the Ranee was delivered of twin boys. Dolan was in attendance and the births, while a month premature, were remarkable only for the smoothness of labor. The Malays were gracious in their good wishes, yet somewhat restrained, for twins were bad luck. She was delighted with her sons, who gained in strength daily. She had Cates dress them in gold-trimmed bajus and set them in a double crèche to await his return. When he was ten days overdue, she summoned Si Tundo.

"Old man," she said rudely, for she felt this man was privy to all her husband's activities, "the Rajah must know of his sons. Please find him in that place he goes upriver."

"Excuse, Rajah Ranee," the man said. "The Rajah is not upriver."

"Excuse, Si Tundo." She was furious. "He *is.*"

"He is not, Rajah Ranee." The man looked at her steadfastly. "He is in the hills above Penrissan, but we know not where. Already we have parties looking for him."

It was the truth. Immediately after the births, Si Tundo had sent boats to Na. They found him gone. He had gone, the woman said, to continue his circuit, ending south of Penrissan, an unplanned extension, one that made no sense to Si Tundo, except he had said he wished to hunt boar in this country, for the priest had told him of immense specimens. Si Tundo felt this was unwise. The Rajah did not have enough of his own men with him to go into this territory.

The woman also told the truth. He had gone to hunt boar beyond Penrissan. She had given him a beautiful ikat hunting pouch. In later life, he would remember everything about those days except consciously making the decision to go. He had expressed something to her, he could not remember what, but coldly. She presented him with the pouch.

In odd ways, it was a friendly country. Message sticks were everywhere. If you could read them, they would tell you who preceded you, how many, where they came from and where they were going, and their luck in hunting. The Punan, the shy, reclusive people of this region, had no longhouses but sheltered in caves and the buttresses of trees. Entering their universe was like entering a riddle.

To become lost in that country was not uncommon. The undergrowth was thick, and one could quickly lose sight and sound of those traveling ahead. It could happen instantly, and the next voice you heard, often so human, was not. On the fourth day, he and two others lost sight of their vanguard. These men later said they doubled back and found no one.

Never had he been in an atmosphere more deadening, the surrounding green wall admitting only thin spears of light. In the pouch were four smooth stones. The thing was beautifully woven with a serpent image, the double nabau, the most dangerous of all ikat motifs. The second afternoon alone they came across the python. The end of shoulder-high brush, and then the animal moving along the ground. At twilight, an egg held aloft by thin sticks bound with rattan. It spoke a language none could decipher. Fragrant air, a sharp stench—the source of both invisible. His feet were infected. At certain times, their legs and arms were covered with bees, harmlessly drinking their sweat. Message sticks became more frequent. At dusk on the fifth day, they again saw the sinuous double track in the mud. He pulled the pouch from his waist and flung it away.

Thunder rolled up in the afternoon, a dependable companion. Evening descended and his teeth rattled. The two men with him had been reduced to one. They had ceased speaking. By the tenth day, he was two persons, a molten one in his skull and a freezing one crouched below. He did not want to close his eyes, for immediately the visions came. Dreams, sleeping and waking, were filled with animals. On the eleventh day, sitting against a tree, he saw, ten feet away, a small green man.

There are townsmen and officials among the Punan, but no towns. They move to follow small game and ripening fruit in season, so if you greeted a man making mayoral decisions for his group on the Matang escarpment one day, you might find him the next week digging a hole ten miles away and, the week after, twenty miles from there, never to revisit these places again.

The man had sharp cheekbones and small, sparkling eyes. He could have been twenty or seventy. He was naked and carried a sumpit and a basket woven with a fine Greek key design. Even in Barr's hallucinatory state, the design intrigued him, a vestige of some distant Elysium. The creature's flesh was tinged with green, for they avoided sunlight. With three of them, they traveled through that region of twilight, given food and drink before they asked for them. His hallucinations subsided and were replaced by a sense of acute hearing. On the twelfth day, he detected, through the trees, a voice gliding in the upper reaches of a Neapolitan romanza.

Light-footed cherubs twirled in the rafters, toes brushed his face, plump little buttocks, little budding breasts, grazed his lips. Paoluzzi groaned and swung his legs to the floor. The hut was already filled with flies.

The priest felt an eternal carnal hunger and the purest love for the sensuous little Kenyahs. He dreamed of them even while saying mass, but most ardently in his pre-dawn slumbers, slivers of light playing over his head, cherubim, seraphim, powers, thrones, at this level waking in terror for they were no longer children but women with eyes like fiery knives.

He crossed to the middle of the mud clearing in twenty-seven steps. He stopped and lifted his eyes. "Ah, Dio," he murmured, exactly as he had at this hour of the day at this point on the mud for nineteen years. He continued on, dipping under the nipah awning and sitting on the small bench. His food was waiting: a mound of rice, four roasted grasshoppers, and a dipper of tuak. The boy, his acolyte and only convert, accepted his blessing when the priest looked up, took a few steps away, and spat.

Paoluzzi surveyed his world as he ate. He knew every inch of it. It was forty-three steps from his hut to the cookhouse, thirty-seven to the bathhouse. Eleven revolutions around the little "chapel" to say matins. The plank with his food was always the same, each thing in exactly the same place. He had not realized he took note of any of this until the boy changed it one day. He looked at the mound of rice, suddenly in the northwest quadrant, and realized he had been dead for years.

In the first five years, he had actually acquired a small congregation. His sermons were simple parables, and these people are great lovers of stories. After five years, with an increased facility with the language and the irreversible damage of fevers, they became longer and a little crazy. They dissolved into the air or burst into flames. The little statue of Saint Theresa of Avila alone looked startled, her blue eyes rimmed with panic.

To see the Kuching Rajah sitting beneath his awning struck the priest as a small but plausible miracle. He did not seek to understand it. While his own diet was frugal, better fare was produced for this guest. His feet were washed and dressed in moldering leaves, and a rattan couch was placed in the hut. Paoluzzi then began to speak as if they already had started a conversation which had been interrupted by some small annoyance.

"I have gone through this kind of thing as well, Tuan Rajah. I put it all aside. Misplacing the altar stone, even the sacraments, God help me—they steal, they steal everything, not unkind people. What do I have left? Not nothing! Not nothing! Grace. One must merely ask for it. If you ask for it, you get it. In what form? How? You may never know. But you get it." He spoke of both actual and sanctifying grace and a kind he called sengat—a sting—of cooking, infection, music, and cooking again, cooking involving veal sausages and fennel, summer figs, the oily rosary pinched through his fingers.

"When you are rested, the Punan will take you to Tegora," he said.

"They will not go farther. You must keep up with them. They will not harm you, but they will leave you if they are afraid. They are small," he added. "I am not sure they have souls."

He rose. "You know, Tuan Rajah, you have gone nampok. But you have done it wrong. You took no food. You made no offering. An offering must be made if one seeks guidance from the forest. It must be made and no one must know you are going. You could have met the Koklir. To meet her during nampok is a terrible thing."

"Ignazio," Barr said the third night, half in his own skin, "come down with us. There's room for another church. Who in hell cares."

"Thank you, dear Rajah"—the priest was genuinely moved and took Barr's hand, his fingers like worms—"but I must continue my work. If they see I am gone, all that I have accomplished will fall apart." He looked around at the empty clearing, the hut, the youth leaning against a tree.

"Has anyone come besides me?"

"Peachy. Peachy comes. And sometimes I pretend he comes. Peachy is full of grace. He has, you know, one good eye." His face lightened. "He can sing bel canto. He brings me letters. Although in the last nine years there have been none, except those I have written."

Looking about, it seemed the madman did little else but scribble. Stuffed in crates, falling out of rattan cupboards, banked under his pallet, rotted pieces of paper filled with writing formed a gray mulch. Some were newly written, weeks or even days ago; some in another lifetime. He carried on his person, under his soutane, a packet of letters, friable and glued together, the size of a second heart. He wrote things besides letters, sheaves stuck together and tied, crumbling to the touch. When he finished a page of these "notes," he would not go to the next but continue to write around the rim, along the side, over the top, only then using the other side, the writing becoming smaller and more precise. Notes on the nature of Kayan stringed instruments; adaptation of the tomato within ten degrees' latitude; establishing faith in plenary indulgences among people of the Ulu Ai; the use of the diagonal strut in nipah dwellings; methods of exterminating belief in the Koklir; determining virginity without inducing an occasion of

335

sin in the examiner; sixty-seven uses of the ruby banana; Theresa of Avila, saint or Pontianak, a discourse; the failure of the mails in tropical outposts.

In all of this there was an enveloping rightness, Barr felt. Only the boy seemed wrong. A dangerous, untrustworthy boy. What did he gain by staying with the priest? Yet the great wonder was that this soft white creature had somehow dragged itself up to this place and had survived.

He stared at his feet, swathed in layers of clean gauze, dressed morning and evening by Cakebread's woman, knowing, in the midst of Tegora's fish racks and sweet potato gardens, he had been sent out on that murderous journey and hauled back by the same hand. She had struck at him in this way. For what? Perhaps she at last saw the slow weaning of his heart away and toward the great white gravid organism downstream. It didn't matter. It had been a display of power. To pass through such queer hands and finally to Cakebread at Tegora, from one elemental step to the next, belied belief. Yet seeing that quiet, green face in the leaves, he wondered in which way he was traveling.

April 27, 1862

Mama,

All of us here have been through days of grave concern. The Rajah was up-country and did not return when expected. We had three hellish weeks, at the end of which we were certain something terrible had befallen him. No one had seen him since his prahu left Lida Tanah. There was no information. Then yesterday, at nine o'clock in the morning, he walked up between the canna lilies as if he'd just taken a stroll before breakfast. He arrived in a war bangkong from Tegora—this with Hogg sending calling-out spears across half the estuaries—delighted to make the acquaintance of his sons.

She longed to add another line, just one, knowing the burden would be instantly shared ten thousand miles away. She never in all her life wrote of Na, a place halfway up a mountain, the one ensconced there black, perhaps with children "black and lily fair" like van Lutyens' horrors. She would never write this.

September 11, 1862
Next month we leave for Pontianak. The boys are comfortable and, when given full responsibility, Cates is in her element. Diplo-

matically, we should stay out of Dutch territory, but I cannot wait.
Birgit has become my dearest friend, despite the fact that she keeps
house four hundred miles round a wild coast.

"*Daar is zij!*" Birgit's thick strong arms were about her. Dirck
stood back grinning, little Sanneke on his shoulder and Bas by the
hand, one born after the cholera, the other surviving it. Preparations
for their visit had been under way for months. White flour had been
imported from Batavia for Birgit's cakes and soft little rolls, and two
pigs had been butchered. Flower pots lined the walk and bungalow
stairs, and Birgit and the two girls had new rose skirts. Yet, looking
about, even from the water, there was something different about the
station. Everything seemed less square, more skewed in the wind.
Over those years, van Lutyens' compound would appear trim on
one visit, overgrown the next; the garrison itself taking on more of
a native flavor. There were little quirks. A Dyak porter sported a
worsted vest. Natives of the lower classes seemed to have developed a
taste for white cheeses and cabbage soup. Once they were alone,
Dirck explained: The Hague had given up hope of using the base as a
point from which to expand into Borneo and had severely cut back
his outlay. Birgit's kitchen garden and creamery were now used as
barter for labor in their own compound. He refused to requisition
anything. It was, he said, the first sign of rot. It was an odd attitude in
a Dutchman, but she subscribed to it as well. The little cheeses were
her pride, she said, no matter who ate them.

Birgit makes her cheese in collusion with four bony cows. The
little cakes sit in a bath of brine and mature on wooden slats, some
flavored with caraway, some rolled in pepper. Her watercress is a sea
of emerald behind the munitions keep.

In the afternoon, the two women entered the little creamery. "We
think, when we are young, we will do something fine and lasting."
Birgit sighed, stooping for the brine bucket, the pungent air biting
their eyes. She ladled a half dipper over a little toque. "Lasting, that's
the thing. Well, this station and the empire itself will last only a little

longer than my cheeses, if you step back among the stars to look."
She held up a chalky little cake, "a perfect, good thing." Frits pulled
at her skirt. *"Joe!"* She cupped his chin and kissed him hard.

It was Birgit who kept it, all of it, with the bit in its jaw. The station could have so easily gone the other way in these circumstances,
like Banjermasin or the Java districts of Lebak and Parang-Kujang,
where blackmail and corruption festered through to The Hague. Her
rules of courtesy and order for her own household spread outward
like a steel net. Her even rows of big, waxy turnips had some subter-
ranean connection with the neat rows of ordnance. Her well-tended
milch cows, her brilliant squares of horseradish and cress, were the
true, hard inspiration for the still-orderly artillery keep, the civilities
imposed on raw subalterns. Her deeply rooted kitchen philosophy
invaded even van Lutyens' monthly reports.

She asked after the twins—knowing, detailed questions about their
eating, sleeping, and defecating habits—and was satisfied with the
answers. The two women sat alone with glasses of her dark beer. She
leaned back in the gathering shadows and regarded her guest. *"Lieve-
ling,* what troubles you?" There were the steady, intelligent gaze and
new inroads of fatigue in that kind face.

"Nothing." She smiled. "Little things. My mother sent her summer china, a pretty flowered set I remember as a child, and the whole
of it sunk off the Cape."

"Aacch! Dishes! Well, they are worth something. I love the pretty
things too. I did not *grow* here, you know." She gazed about, half
angry. "There is an alley of lime trees at Moordrecht, at my grandmother's house, a house filled with pretty things. At the end of it was
some animal who played high up in the branches, a pet I think,
although it never came down to earth, just this playful shadow leaping about way up high, and the *confituren* set out beneath in a Leiden
bowl and white bread and a wide lap with little yellow flowers marching across like a Prussian army. Here I shared my hopes and shed
my tears. I brought this, my grandmother's apron, at the bottom of
my bridal chest and, when Kies was old enough to run to my lap, I
treated myself to the sight of it and it was a mass of holes." She
sighed. "Your mother's dishes are at the bottom of the sea and my

apron is a mass of rot. Our men do not understand how this breaks our hearts, stronger hearts than theirs. What else?"

"There's a woman," she heard the words leave her mouth. "She resides seven kelongs upriver. It is a creature I believe he knew before I came, and for whom he cares. There may be children." Bats darted. Frits climbed into his mother's broad lap. "How can you stand it?"

"Lada?" Birgit disengaged the child's fingers from her hair. "She's a good girl. The best of a long line. In truth, I could take no more of him than I do, and I suspect I get the best."

"But *here,* under your nose. I would tear out her eyes."

Birgit laughed. "It would be terrible to tear the eyes out of someone who has made your life easier. No, I stay out of the kampong and pray for her continued good health." She leaned toward the indistinct face. "Don't strain everything so. Don't make misery. God knows, there's enough of its own making in this world. Take life and knead it." She pushed the heels of her hands into the little buttocks. "You needn't break anything." The boy slipped like water to the floor.

"It's not only this." As they sat in the deepening dark, even she was amazed at the number and precision of the small, hateful memories that tumbled out, poisonous, unstopping.

"Yes, yes," Birgit said afterward, "the little paper knife to the tidewaiter, the woman upstream, and what all else in between. You keep a close accounting, my girl. But he came to you, not once but more than once, and you received him not in your heart, or even your bed, but in this countinghouse."

She should have known better. Of all people to whom she could bare her heart, she chose a creature imbued with so much understanding it bordered on lunacy. "Dinner was lovely. What was the meat?"

"A form of water rat. I minced it and wrapped it in pastry."

She gasped, then laughed. The sound cleaved the thick air, and she laughed again. They had smoked a third hog, Birgit said, for the *Carolina.*

The evening before their departure, there was not beer but wine, and the older girls made a dessert, *zomerkoninginnetjes op een wolken-troon,* little-summer-queens-on-a-throne-of-clouds, quivering yellow towers in a custard sea. A basket of choice pomelos was left on the stair by a child from the beach kampong.

Rocking out to the wind, Barr regarded his wife, a young woman standing at the rail, waving to figures on the receding shore. She stood upright in the sunlight, clear-eyed, thick brown hair lifted. He gazed at her and had visited on him one of those brief moments when he saw her as through a strange doorway, or walking down a strange street, a woman who could hold his attention for a considerable time. He was simply happier with her than he had ever been without her, yet telling her was beyond him.

They were met by two of their gunboats off Cape Datu. At the estuary, she stood braced firmly in the bow, eyes pinned upstream, a Bayswater matron returning to her brood. She no longer wondered how women like Birgit and Maureen ordered their universes. She was taking hers in hand. If she was an accountant, they were accurate accounts. The bar was under surf when they crossed, and he put an arm around her shoulder to steady her. She gave him a pleasant look with nothing in it.

He returned to the usual optimistic correspondence from Bloch, but no money, and a tortuous list of requests from the ever-growing number of memsahibs.

"They're a plague," he said to Dawes, newly turned up, one eyebrow unaccountably shorter. "There are days I'd like to shoot every bloody one and be done. Reedy's bride has her *bath*water boiled. Mrs. Park has her syce wearing gloves!"

She herself was deeply pleased with the increase in the number of Englishwomen. Things she never would have asked for were now demanded by half a dozen others with impunity. Feminine skills and supplies were shared, a renaissance of "the nourishing little gesture"—a lesson in needles, the loan of a sash—things she had desperately missed. She came down one morning to await the Parks' nurse, a competent seamstress come to make alterations, her girth slightly wider after the twins.

Passing out to the veranda, the blue voile glinting, she found not Miss Dray but the priest, seated, his hands holding each other as if they belonged to separate, nervous people. He sat as if in conversation with someone close, although he was alone. Part of this man's affliction was that everything spoke to him: little wagging tongues in leaves, the steam from a pot, rain.

"Selamat hari, Rajah Ranee." He smiled, rising, flipping his hand as if to dismiss some small presence. "I am sorry, I am waiting all morning to see the Rajah. I was told he had to leave on an emergency, and so I waited, I have taken the liberty of waiting, you see, for you, because I too have something of an emergency. Or maybe not. I hope not, please God. But what a beautiful dress!" He stepped back, admiring the flowing skirts, the ruched bodice. "The color of the evening sea in Naples." His eyes lingered on her breasts.

"Thank you." She brushed the voile briskly. "I didn't know you were here, Father. How good to see you down." She drew him into the saloon.

"It is Joseph. My acolyte," he said. "The boy is a trial, but he is quite gifted. One day, he said to me, 'Father, I can show you a miracle. I can move an object with my eyes.' They do so many absurd things, but here it is, you see. He stared at a little bench, and it rose in the air. He did this many times, with many things. And so I have come ten thousand miles and fifty-eight years to tell a child that he cannot make a little stool move with his eyes. Which he does, Holy Mother! He does it most easily! What does one make of that? Not the stool moving, but the waste! For fifty-eight years I have admired beautiful things"—he gazed at the ruching—"from afar. Afar! I have never done more than stand apart, and the little stool moves. Their prayers are more powerful than mine. They mumble, and He hears them like a cannon." His rosary of the glorious mysteries for the last ten years included Singalang Burong, the keeper of all severed heads from the world's beginning.

"He is worthless, but he is a child. The Punan say he traveled inland, toward the Kayan. He has my monstrance, the Florentine gold that bends in your fingers. They will hurt him. They will take all the time in the world. They are like this. I meant to follow, but I was afraid. And then he didn't come back. He has always come back. The birds, of course, predicted this."

A little sun roller hung in its cage, a gift from the Moluccas from Lytton, and he walked over and gazed at it. "I meant to follow him, but I was afraid. I was afraid when I was six and sent to the convent of Santa Maria della Salute and they cut my hair. I was afraid to travel at night from one mountain village to the next with the old priest. He talked to himself and smelled bad and I was always cold. I was afraid to join the missions and I was afraid to come here. Here I have been afraid every day of my life." He smiled.

She gazed at him, suddenly less put out, less repelled. "Why don't you stop? Why don't you go home and do nothing more that makes you afraid? Surely part of your life should be like this, unafraid?"

"Because," he said with the same puzzled smile, "I am afraid."

"Of what?"

"Of my immortal soul. Of losing it. The Rajah might learn something of the boy."

"I shall inquire for you. Perhaps you should also ask Mr. Dawes. He travels to Kayan country. He may take you with him." Why say this? Some wickedness in joining with life to terrorize him further.

They brought tea. He spoke of tisanes, of an infusion of little Calabrian flowers. "Love and suffering." His eyes burned over his cup. "They do not disappear once they have occurred. They are saved, horded, the only true currencies in the universe. The thing that ruins it all is the suffering of children. How demented and cruel to permit the suffering of children! I cannot abide it. What kind of God is this?"

The man pulled subjects out of the air like a maniac. Once, watching a syce walk her husband's pony, he said, "Do you think it is possible to be God and never to have been a horse? One would think, if nothing else, He would be curious. How can one make a horse if one has not had four feet and sped on them like the wind or pulled a cart and died, a bag of bones, in harness. How? How can one make a man, and test him day after day, and never Himself feel the need of a woman, the pleasure of eating a little cake? Sitting in a chair in the sun and eating a little cake, the kind with many egg yolks and a thimble of anisette, not caring at that moment for anything else but the crumbs in your mouth?" There were tears in his eyes.

She watched the black bulk of him pass under the trees, a hand snapping angrily in the air.

344

Lytton arrived that fall. He was totally unchanged, retaining the fresh face of a boy down from Cambridge on holiday, only his row of satchels and tarps contained not cricket bats and mallets but a great variety of stinking and pickled life.

He admired the twins, recounting the varied ways primitive societies greeted this somewhat common phenomenon. They sat as of old, teapot between them, a jar on the little split bamboo stand containing something that resembled a blue rooster. He described the Moluccas, his fourth voyage, a place he favored for the richness and diversity of fauna. The specimen in vitro simulated the greater pettichaps in every way, yet it wasn't. It was totipalmate. On top of that, it could not swim!

The afternoons fell into the easy expositions of former days. He described those islands, the architecture of the native dwellings, the variety of tides, of his finding, one morning, a large yellow serpent draped over the rafters above his cot. There was so much that just escaped identification, he said, "a climbing bloom so like the wild valerian and yet the stamen too short; a verifiable *Callinectes sapidus,* not blue but electric green!" One afternoon, standing behind her as she gazed at the stream, well into a description of an anadromous fish of the southern estuaries, he pressed against her. Yet lightly, an airy, figmental sensation, so that she could not whip around or muster any outrage. She stayed rooted, facing the river, the rail against her stomach more violent than the tentative caresses that followed in a soft wave, even his intumescence tentative, a finger politely poking through ducks. When she turned, he stood apart, mute. She passed through to the saloon and found Ah Moi seeking her for instructions on tiffin. Her first infidelity, a poor anemic thing, left her wretched.

He tried to catch her alone in the days that followed, but she was out of sight or with someone. He finally began preparations for an expedition to the Tandong highlands and was again given Jawing as guide.

Seeing the two men together on a grassy slope a few days before their scheduled departure, one small and pale, brow furrowed, the other languid, eyes distant, she realized how poor an object Lytton was.

Jawing, in the end, did not guide him. "This Tuan," he said to her, coming up quietly and squatting by her chair, "does not study the orang utan. He kills them and takes their heads and measures them. He has killed thirty-four. I have offended these men of the forest. I will do it no more."

Lytton did not go. He spent another week ordering his data, then left for Singapore. From the veranda, she watched him hoisting his presses up the gangplank of the *Hindoo Queen* in the afternoon downpour, counting satchels, tripping once over Lavransson's big feet. They would not see him again. He will die at ninety walking down some forest path, his heart slipping to the floor of his rib cage, she thought, unaware of the depth of her prophetic powers.

January 2, 1863

Mama,

The pressed spider orchid is from Dewi. Today is her birthday. She would have been seven. She had a yellow pinafore the color of this flower, and she looked so sweet in it. I know what you will say. I know that I now have two wonderful sons. I know this, and yet I cannot walk in the orchard or come round the corner of the washhouse or pass her small grove of bamboo without hearing that sunny little voice. My days and hours are so sweetly haunted, and I wish it unchanged until I die.

The boys are fine. Yet there are always these gastric upsets that slip so easily into horror. Hugh, our little Tuan Mudah, has been feverish. The weather changes a degree and I am a wreck. I will secret to you my plan. It is to return with them. We have slipped into an unnatural attitude here—we regard the children we lose as necessary casualties, as replaceable. If I put it to him right, I believe he will agree.

Things change daily. Kilcane is in England. He has conferred with Bloch, the Rajah's agent, and makes a dismal report. The company was formed to work mines and pay royalties into our treasury, yet to date nothing has been paid. Homer feels we should not expect much. This is a great disappointment, for we planned to begin mining coal at Selantik and to finish a railway to a place lower on the river where steamers can load. The trouble seems due in part to Bloch's salary demands and his failure to raise capital. The original investors were promised a quick return and are incensed it has not materialized. It is a shambles.

Yet, strangely, it seems the Rajah will keep the man. He is too far down the road with him, he says, and he feels Bloch may actually have made some inroads with the Colonial Office. I do not pretend to understand. Thank God for the Chinese and their opium revenues. They never grumble, although one glimpses, at times, the cold, resentful eye. They are a strange race, so thick among themselves.

The days progress apace. We have two new divisional Residents, a Mr. Sturdivant and Mr. Cheeks, and three new bachelor juniors. I have not met any of them, as we were in Pontianak when they arrived and they left for their stations before we returned. We have a new gunboat, escorted from Singapore by the frigate *Hebe* and christened the *Dewi Sri*.

Lim has whacked the gong, so I will collect my monkeys and descend. If things go well, we may well dine together, all four, next Christmas.

She posted this, as she did all her letters, by placing it on the little marquetry table in the hall. A brick of personal mail already awaited her, the packet having caught the tide. It contained a *Godey's* catalogue, a shipment of Manila cheroots and several letters for Barr, and one for herself. It was from her cousin Peg, and she was surprised at how disappointed she felt. Never had she felt so deep a need to hear from her mother.

She waited until the children were bathed and put to bed before opening Peg's envelope. Inside there were two letters, one from her cousin and another from her mother. She was overjoyed. Peg had posted them both. Yet standing in the darkened hall, an ominous, mute wall seemed to rise around her. She thrust the sheets into a drawer and the wall burst, the evening sounds, the kitchen clatter, surging in. Later, after the children were down, she went straight to bed. In the middle of the night, she lit her lamp and descended the stair, retrieving the letters. She reversed their order, reading her mother's first.

The news was nondescript. The usual inquiries after her health and that of the boys, the agricultural crisis, a recipe for trifle in which one could substitute tropical fruits—then nothing. She stared at the page, the familiar slanted hand simply stopping. *Dearest girl,* Peg wrote, *please be brave. Your mother's letter is unfinished because it was her last. We found her at her desk. Spaulding said her heart had been bad for years. I'm sure she shared this with you. . . .*

It was absurd, she would think for the rest of her life. The function of distance on love. She had loved her mother, but it had never been purely expressed until she put ten thousand miles between them. She had loved as a child loves who is treated with great coldness and great affection by erratic turns, a love undershot with resentment and deprecation and pain, and this distilled out by the sun and millions of acres of water. They had gone through this transformation apart, and then one died. How absurd. To live all your life with someone in a crippled position and have it made right when apart, and then for one to die. She felt most keenly the need of hell to spread its misery among men.

Of the things which would recall her mother to her in the years that followed, none would do so more wrenchingly than a piece of that handwriting. It was impossible to believe that the firm hand would not take up its pen and do it again and again. *A wonderful little cake made of carrots; a Turk's head bracelet.* She had taken everything from this woman, her last hope of marriage, her only child, the sight of any grandchildren she may have enjoyed. She had taken everything and what she received in return were carefully copied recipes, fruit salts, and unconditional love.

She did not know how to mourn. She walked down to the amah's quarters in the pitch black, the recipe in her fist, and awakened Lim. She told him to gather up some loquats and sugar and vanilla and eggs and sherry, and the two of them, the frightened Chinaman and the big, hollow-eyed white woman, cooked up the trifle in silence. She took the bowl into the saloon as light began to spread and ate it in great heaping spoons.

One thing living in that place had taught her was not to delay, obfuscate, or fill with salves a sore that is best left open to the wind. She wrote to her cousin, and then to her mother's solicitors, inquiring after her inheritance. She would give the greater part of it to him for his railroad. This place was, after all, the legacy of her sons.

She did not have the sense of her mother being truly lost to her until the end of the summer, when they received word that the merchantman *Mercury* had sunk off Madagascar. A consignment list was forwarded, which he balled up in disgust and threw on the desk. She flattened it out on a wet afternoon and read it with desultory interest:

> One bolting mill, eight hundred and seventy steel rails, ten pairs scales, eighteen plough harnesses, twenty tin troughs, a brake, eighty dozen iron posts, two dozen Yorkshire sows, one boar, two crates crockery (salt glaze), one garden statue (Pan).

She had asked for it: A little lead Pan, a green boy with double pipes, his pointed ears visible above the herb beds, a face at eye level—when she was six—to herself. He had been wrested from his bed, crated, brought down by carriage to Deptford, rowed out and hauled aboard ship and set below on a bed of straw, and now he lay beneath two hundred feet of Indian Ocean. She slumped into a chair and wept.

She did not know how long he had been there. He placed a hand on her neck, a warm, shattering gesture. "What is it?"

"Nothing," she said. "A piece of garden statuary. I'm crying over a statue." She indicated the consignment list. "I always liked it."

In June, at the end of another flat marital winter, she raised her eyes from her book and beheld a hideous face floating over the cassia fistula, progressing sideways in short spasms above a web of timber and guy ropes. "Sweet Jesus." She rose.

It was a gift. He planned to use a stream of gravity-fed river water for a fountain. He had worked on the scheme and drawings on and off for months, enjoying himself, enjoying the idea of surprising her, creating reams of correspondence with an Italian statuary firm, torn between designs, finally asking Biverts' advice and then not taking it. It came eight months later, not a sweet boy with pipes and little hooves but a true Pan in all his cloven priapic glory.

She was appalled and then, for some reason, laughed. She saw his face, confusion and misery instantly disguised. She saw, for a fleeting moment, the boy, a boy who wished to please her, to restore something she cherished. She saw and wanted to beg his forgiveness. She wanted to say she was sorry, sorry for all the years of accountancy that bred more and more rot. Her life had been squared and settled after Pontianak, and now the glimpse of that boy. Could one love the "flash" of someone, seen and then withdrawn, perhaps forever? The ache in her heart said yes. She resolved she would have the thing carted to the orchard, a place he knew was her favorite, a place where the dense foilage would mask its ghastliness. The next morning she summoned Lim to organize for the task and learned the thing had been flung into the river, on his orders, and he was gone to Lida Tanah.

"No, wait."

"I *have to,* damn it!" The Tuan Besar undid two buttons of his shorts, and a pale yellow stream arced into the lilies.

"Father will kill you if he sees you watering them that way." The Tuan Mudah sank on his heels and began peeling a scab off his knee. "Today I met a man." It was suppurating beneath, so he must go to Raseh, who would place on it a little tree mold, not to his Mama and her tin box and then Dolan and his lancets, for the box never worked. "Near the nipah grove, and when he stood up and spoke, a bird flew to his shoulder. The bird spoke too. Oya River talk. There was suddenly a great crowd of them in the trees. Ripping fellows. The man with the bird walked away, and all the fellows in the trees disappeared at the same time. Do you think I should tell Father?"

"No." The Tuan Besar pushed in his little penis. "Let me know if he comes again. Have you seen that naga Si Tundu? He has my anak parang, he says to sharpen it, only he does just the opposite."

"It looked like the old man who dragged me out of the pond in Sibu," Hugh continued that night, horizontal in the dark. "Except he wasn't old. You remember, I didn't know how to thank him. I gave him my rag horse. It was a splendid thing to do. I rather wish I hadn't."

She put off taking them home from one year to the next. They seemed to thrive, darting about like snakes, immune to the usual infantile maladies. On their fifth birthday, Kilcane sent small midshipman uniforms. These, along with two small krisses presented by the Temenggong, became the official attire of the Tuan Mudah and the Tuan Besar at ceremonial functions. Two peas in a pod, very much dependent on each other while independent of everyone else.

In September, the air once again turned pleasantly dry. By the end of the month, cholera was reported in the Rejang. It was believed a Dutch sago steamer brought it in. That same week, she booked passage to England for herself and the children, alerted Cates, and kept her own counsel. She kept it so well he did not realize her plan until a fortnight before the vessel's scheduled departure from Singapore. To her amazement, he acquiesced, but extracted a promise that they would stay away only a year. He planned to return to England the following summer, he said, and would travel back with them.

She agreed. She agreed, but planned to decide what she would do once she was settled in Deanstown. She had meant to discuss it with her mother, to sit in the little morning room with its Boudin prints and watch Iris Mumm play with her grandsons and, only after months of righting her blood, to discuss it. They would, of course, stay in England. They would naturally put off telling him. They would walk the rhododendron corridors and take the carriage to the village and let the boys sit up with Mallow returning. They would ride up Carney Hill on a November night, muffled in American buffalo robes, viewing the bonfires on neighboring hilltops, a ring of fires in the freezing dark, the horses' breath all smoke, a joy from her childhood. They would look into schooling, perhaps Norwich, which might please him. A year would round. And again.

Now she was taking them into a silent, empty house. The monsoon began in the night, the house shuddering into life, Lim and his wife rushing from room to room, slamming, bolting. One of the children cried out in his sleep.

The precise steps of it all she left to Cates, who began counting singlets, socks, and quinine vials. Cates was to be lent to the Dolans. The Boynes' nurse was journeying back permanently and so could assist her on the homeward leg. The boys were no longer infants, and at Deanstown there would be Mary and, afterward, time to acquire a qualified governess. The week they left, cholera was reported on the Sadong. Only when they crossed the bar and passed into deeper waters did the tightness loosen in her chest.

Cates never before had the luxury of time. She was to help Mrs. Dolan with the morning and evening ritual, but had the great center part of the day free. She sat on the astana veranda with her small knives and glue pot, rebinding a stack of the Rajah's books. She had begun the work of rebinding the year before, facing the ridge of Matang as she worked. Just to the left of this escarpment, where it first turned purple at four o'clock, where a branch of a great kapok formed a perfect Old English *E* against the plummeting sun, was the point where Dawes and his Murut would first appear if he came overland from Lundu, a trip of eight days. He would camp at Bidi, leave at dawn, and appear at approximately this hour, a bright flash and a blue ball—the tip of his Minié barrel and Lingire's little hat.

Back then, she had watched the spot daily—and daily, for weeks, saw nothing, her life absorbing this disappointment as it did all others, but after a while she felt the weight of it, cumulatively, and stopped. Three days later, she had started again, disgusted with herself and her life.

He arrived by prahu at the beginning of November and was waiting on the veranda when she came up with the boys in their oilskins, dripping like a great brown moth. "Albert," she said, radiating joy.

"How's the girl?"

"Fine." The word choked out of her because he had her in his arms. He came in twice in the next six months, for him more or less loitering. He shared his plans with her, painting a joint, hypothetical life for them both, in bliss, in terror, the two resembling a pair of Lytton's disparate species who nevertheless find some mysterious interest in each other.

"Have you ever been married?" she asked, serving him tea.

"I think so, yes."

"My God," she muttered.

"None of 'em took."

She took in a deep, slow breath. "Children?"

"None I ever met."

He had left and she heard nothing. In February a packet was delivered to her from the Sut basin—to her alone, the tattooed messenger refusing to leave it in any other hands. She withdrew to her bungalow, sat in a chair, and unwound it. A small filthy thing fell out of the wrappings, a talisman of some kind, parts once alive. She rose, letting it slide from her lap, undressed, and went to bed.

Two red inked hearts had appeared at her breakfast plate the next morning, the Tuan Mudah and the Tuan Besar learning to use scissors. One sat atop a pink moon cake; the other on an embroidered handkerchief. She gazed at the little display, and then they watched the miracle of Cates becoming suddenly young. She did not shake their hands, her usual method of expressing thanks, but pressed each small torso painfully to her bony chest. The feather, the bone, the scallop shells butted hinge to hinge and fastened with some glutinous muck was meant to be pretty. It was meant to be a valentine.

Dawes had secured a house in the Baram, given in payment for a cargo of steel rods from an Australian wreck. "It's lying dogo up the Ulu Ai with holes to take windows." The good eye focused on her tenderly. She told no one. The children found her strange, her voice soft, as with fever.

Dawes did not die from violence or disease but a fall, a long slip down a muddy catwalk, cracking his pelvis, and the Murut, who never said he did but all suspected, who loved him, put a bullet in his brain and buried him half wrapped in that bewitched shawl.

It was, of course, for the best. The idea of such a liaison was cataclysmically absurd, and she realized it. She had never altered her regimen. She exercised and took her hot-water bottles to bed in the new wet. Her heart did not grieve in those weeks and months. It shrank. She managed her charges, was as efficient, exacting, and responsive as before, but with no investment of that leathery pouch under her ribs.

. . .

The *Beatrice* was a new P & O vessel with all the latest amenities, a universe of gleaming brass and order. The children found instant companionship with three yellow-haired van Eycks from Batavia, the five diving below into what turned out to be the games hall, the Boynes' nurse trailing. She remained at the rail, gazing over the immensity of shipping, two Company frigates in their immediate vicinity, three Cochin junks, a small Dutch steamer, and myriad prahus and lighters.

Her eyes took in the glorious breadth of it, scanning east to west, and slowly she realized she was gazing at the most beautiful thing she had seen in her life: a knife, slender and white, its total length reflected in gold corrugations beneath, the *Rainbow* out of New York. She was a new breed of clipper, gorgeous and sleek with a long, concave bow. It was said they designed her for the tea trade now that more Chinese ports were opened by the opium wars. She seemed not anchored but tethered, ready to take wing, the point of her bow giving deep conviction to the rightness of any course toward which she swung. She would be headed north on the tide and was reported to reach speeds of fourteen knots. Gazing at her, she experienced an extraordinary moment of serenity. She took a last long look at the beautiful hull, now completely afire in the horizontal light, and turned away with renewed faith in her own chosen direction.

On the third day out, a serving boy fell over the captain's table with a bowl of mashed turnips. In the night, he died. The ship passed out of sea and sky into a new medium, electrified by a vibration beyond audible sound. Halfway across the Indian Ocean, she was a traveling plague, sprinkling corpses like sowing wheat. By the time she reached Capetown, a hundred and eighteen people had died and been buried at sea. Both children were dead.

Watching those small sacks sink, she felt nothing could touch her again. She saw them descend through green sunlight into a deeper, colder twilight, spiraling downward, tumbling into the endless dark. In the night she prayed wildly for the same retching spasms in herself.

At Capetown, they were placed in hard quarantine a mile out, the yellow flag flying. Provisions were put aboard by pulley, and in one of these wire baskets had gone her letter to him. The *Beatrice* passed into the icy waters of the North Atlantic in mid-December, her brass still bright, the cholera vanished as silently as it had come. She stayed on deck as much as possible, the Boynes' nurse hovering. The spray froze in her hair so that she found she could break it off in chunks, like glass, the exercise providing a soothing pastime.

Ice was everywhere. Bolts of canvas were encased in it on deck, and midshipmen were sent up one hundred and fifty feet to crack it from the yards. She, too, had little midshipmen, their uniforms starched and folded in a studded chest. She had been a fine caretaker. It drove her mad that he did not know. He had his foot in a stirrup or walked grim-jawed under his payong or was straddling his black whore, thinking himself the father of two robust little boys. She had seen them sewn into bags, and he did not know.

Peg met her at Deptford. She remembered nothing of her arrival except intense cold and blinding flashes of ice passing the carriage wheels. Old friends came with sad, confused faces, glad, she thought, finally to go.

She passed through the silent house as a stranger. It was to have been gay, the boys jostling and loud, her mother rising, delightedly, tearfully. In her mother's room, vetiver hung stale, smell the best and worst sense, returning the very dead to us. She sat by the hearth, the bright eye of a porcelain Staffordshire terrier glinting out of the gloom. She had told the boys of these dogs, this house. She thought of the letter traveling toward him, a stone pitched from hell.

The banister glided under her hand, and she turned with it like a blind horse. The room, any room in which one grows out of childhood, throbbed gently, a steady, intimate pulse for the nurtured one, each object breathing a minuscule life of its own, for you. All for you. The cheval glass reflected a haggard version of the eighteen-year-old who last peered into it. She looked, more than anything else, "maternal."

She found she could not see the people she had planned to see. She could not bear their commiseration. She was, she knew, a freak. The three reasons she had come round the world, the two little boys and her mother, were gone. She could go round and round, from steam to ice to steam again, and never find them.

The cold soothed her. She walked for hours, a ball of ice in the small of her back. The tarns gleamed solid, blackening with passing clouds, here and there a patch of winter rye, the fiery green of padi. Death was a quality perhaps "movable" from person to person under incantation. She had not protected them. She had needed a strength she didn't possess. Walking in that freezing world, she understood "heads."

Spring broke through with a flourish. It brought forth strange yearnings for brown swelling rivers and thick, wet winds. How odd for long years to hunger for tender springs and autumn fires and here to have one's every cell infiltrated by lush, heavy scents—Mary's dull tread mocked by a light patter on split palm, the gibbon countersong turning church bells to tin. And him.

Loquat, she wrote. *Pomelo. Mangosteen. Guava. Jackfruit, mango, durian.* Elephants swallow durians whole, Raseh had told her. Apparently their stomachs could not break down the leathery skin, and the fruit sometimes passed through intact. These durians were valued highly because of this singular journey.

The vine obatular, pounded into paste, cures poisonous snakebite. On the other side of the world she had owned a bird called Wipe-the-eyes-and-dry-the-face. Her little sons loved this bird. Under a stone on the bank of a river on the other side of the world a child's hands, small bony claws, were folded over her stomach. And him. No, *you.* You smiling back, rump cocked in the saddle, you deaf and dumb over your egg, you naked in a little veiled hat, sheets of fire washing up your thighs. There was no deceit in him. He never said he loved you.

His letter came, on the whole sheet only two words: *Come home.* The walls, the paddocks and fields and woods beyond, fell away like cardboard props. He who, all those years, had said, in anger, in innocence, the wrong thing now said something so eminently right she put her lips to the paper.

Chachar

The Érard, black and stolid, loomed as his only companion in the evenings, the two of them mute. He could have provided some simple society for himself in those months after her departure, but he did little of it. Dolan, the individual in Kuching he found made for easiest companionship, had been called to India. He would eventually doze, sinking into that murky workshop of his childhood while smooth skirts traveled away. When Lim brought his stengah, he'd sometimes look up with such infantile self-pity the Chinese averted his eyes.

The only light note in those months was a letter from the Bishop of Calcutta. He opened it and it made him laugh. He commandeered a small dinner party to share it. "An honor has been bestowed on one of us." He waved the thing over the heads of Cakebread, Bigelow, Park, and Boyne, who were starting their cheroots. "Dolan, the redoubtable Dolan, summoned to the Indian subcontinent not knowing whether he was to be excommunicated or made a bishop, has found it is the latter." Boisterous round of applause.

David Martin Dolan was consecrated Bishop of Labuan and Sarawak in September of 1867. Charles Rocket, the Bishop of

Calcutta, confided directly in the Rajah. "I have taken the liberty to caution our brother in Christ regarding deportment in his new ministry. Mild gravity, with occasional tokens of delight and pleasure, become the sacred character. You, as his friend, perhaps may act as secret advocate." Two men fell off their chairs.

Maureen received word of this elevation from Dolan himself, but it did not cheer her. She did not do well in his absences. Her face became thinner, her manner sharper. By November, she had undergone a veritable transformation. An even more remarkable one occurred when he returned, his huge, spongy body intact.

"Ah," she said to Meg Park, her cheeks already showing a bit of color, "ever after one of these trips, he needs a bit of weakening. He loves his custards and wicked nighttime ways. He's put on a stone, I swear to God. Yet the lad has stowed in my vanilla and some India silk. To think I asked for balbriggans!"

Fancy, she thought, stirring his double egg spume, fellatrix to a bishop. Well, you'll not get such filth with a shepherd's crook either, my lad. Inwardly, she thought on the salvation of his arrival, the strange terrain her mind had entered, thoughts of that one up-country.

Dolan, riding upstream, somehow expected to see a smaller settlement, the Kuching of six or ten years ago. The sprawling town, spread over two riverbanks and the hills beyond, shocked him. Nine new bungalows crowded the slope of the little chapel. The place now had two European shipwrights, a brewer, a smith, a cobbler, a baker, and a shifting population of jack-tars. The territory itself extended from Cape Datu to Kedurong Point. Up-country, the railway from Selantik was a third of the way to the Lingga River. A German engine had been ordered, along with seven cars for coal and forest produce and a coach for passengers, of whom, in all its history, there would be five. A seventy-two carat diamond had been found in the upper reaches of the Igan, although no stone even one fifth its size would be found again. A new quay was under way, and the little museum now had an avian annex. Most startling of all was something that had existed before he left but that he did not at once recall: a green-and-white pagoda bandstand. The absurdity of the thing, sitting in the middle of a square of mud, made him smile.

Barr loved the little band. He had taken great pains with it, personally ordering the music from Messrs. Hawkes and Bloom of London each season. He was discouraged with the result. In Dolan's absence, he had fired Master de Sousa, the former proprietor of a music school in Bencoolen, and replaced him with Arcadio Metz, the seasonal trader in olive oil and boaters, who had revealed a musical background. He did not wish to confront de Sousa personally and so commissioned Bigelow to do it. "The band was even worse last evening and the program badly chosen," he wrote to the policeman. "I can't stand it. I direct you in your capacity as Resident of Kuching to inform Master de Sousa that he is to do no more duty and he will retire on a pension, if one is due, at the end of the month." How Metz actually inserted himself into this vacancy, no one knew. He did not so much take on new jobs as incarnations. While conducting, somewhat plausibly, he arranged to sell paper cones of sweets and rupiah copies of the orchestration among the crowd. The only drive outrunning the man's need to merchandise seemed to be sexual. It was noticed, over the years, how many half-caste children resembled the hat seller if one simply added bifocals and a cocky walk.

Metz undoubtedly had some knowledge of music, making up in wild flourishes what may have been lacking in training, but his true contribution proved to be economic. In six months he managed to have the little ensemble turn a profit by allowing the Chinese to commission it for their own use at suitable times.

In all, the place had acquired the attributes of a small settled state. Yet Dolan, climbing the river, found his heart yearned for the sparsely studded hill of a decade ago, for those two tiny rooms off the courthouse, the lost paradise of love without paternity.

Dolan's return proved all too short a hiatus to Barr's gloom. Even in daylight, he sank into a strange mental zone. He thought of her and the children as they entered a civilized, temperate region of the earth, a region more favorable to their happiness. Those closest to him kept falling through his hands. It occurred to him that someone like

Dawes had possessed more of a sense of family rattling around by himself. He missed Dawes. He missed the mixture of Boola Boy pomade and gunpowder wafting around a corner of his veranda, heralding the tender bat. The occasional evening with subordinates only half lifted him out of this mood, after which he sank deeper.

Russell's invitation was a godsend. Four days of festivities were planned to celebrate the seventh anniversary of the dedication of Labuan's harbor, culminating in a New Year's Day ball. The man's idiot committees had finally borne fruit. He decided he would make a personal contribution, the full municipal orchestra to be transported with the ladies of Kuching in five gunboats.

Festivities would commence with a prayer convocation conducted by Labuan's newly arrived C of E chaplain. Races were to follow, the little bajau ponies decked out in brightly colored silks; a regatta of sailing longboats was planned for the third day; and numerous private tiffins throughout. These last were central to all effort, effecting the introduction of a dozen young ladies from both settlements to sixty eligible men within a five-hundred-mile radius who had the good fortune or genius to arrange leave.

There was a necessary compression of such things in those latitudes, things life in other areas of the earth would allow a more leisurely development. Contracts, economic and sexual, were settled with brutal speed. One came in from years in some primeval forest and had to ram arms and legs into a suit of manners only half remembered, acting as if white society were something in which one participated comfortably every day. Men arrived with their brains addled, straining to be correct, surveying the small field, choosing one or two prospects—gauging stamina, age, family, as from horseback. Females tried to look as ravishing, in those four or five days, as they would ever look in their lives. The most honest assessment of the male herd took place within the ladies' relief tent, over the hot splash against metal, information and observations coldly shared.

McLeath from the Baram and the Leeds girl, sitting on little palm chairs, discovered a common interest in ornithology, she then having two budgerigars and he a stuffed owl as a child. I have thought of half a dozen ways to rape you as we converse, he thought, in the interstices of this conversation, and so I fear I must leave and return when I am better balanced—thinking he thought it, billeted where he was, speech and silence much the same thing, yet speaking it; and she, agape, watching the handsome retreating figure fling a cigarette into the dark, might have had him in any ditch, two months later marrying Toomby of the Igan bridge.

The Kuching flotilla was received with much cheer. He, with Biverts and Lim, were housed in a bungalow within the Russells' compound, Si Tundo and his men relegated to a nearby kampong. He enjoyed his new surroundings. He adjusted his routine to fit the pleasant empty hours and the festive diversions. He would breakfast with Biverts and then stroll about Russell's garden, receiving friends and supplicants until tiffin. On the second of these morning promenades, he noticed a woman emerging from a bathhouse, a bizarre yet strangely familiar figure. Observing her more closely, he thought he recognized the Italian soprano of a decade before, then rejected the hallucination.

"My dear Rajah!" It was a girlish bell-like sound. He spent the next hour with the woman on a little bench. She spoke engagingly, flirtatiously, of her life since that performance. After leaving Kuching, her path across the planet had stopped when the ship reached Labuan in the last hours of July, the next evening singing the selfsame lament in the Russells' drawing room.

She was, by then, over sixty, with the same silky black ringlets and high grease-paint eyebrows. A dirty piece of lace bound her curls coquettishly to one side. It was the same coiffure she had had when she sang at the astana and, listening to that mellifluous legato, he once again felt the thickness in his throat, the soft weight of robia in his arms.

He had never conversed with the woman in Kuching, but now felt some curiosity in where such a creature comes from and where it goes. She spoke gaily, with confidence, despite her appearance. "I traveled the Malabar coast from Trivandrum to Bombay," she said, dismissing the first half of her life. When the *Principessa Matilda* sailed from Labuan harbor, it sailed without her. She had come down with malaria, and Lady Russell, taken with the bizarre creature, offered refuge. She recovered and was a charming guest, simply staying on. Over the ensuing years, she passed, without design, through several stages: a glamorous new friend who could provide what scarce entertainment existed in the settlement; a little dove to be nursed and petted; a free hand to fetch an umbrella, to prepare the tisane during seasonal fevers; a lady who was actually quite able to earn a bit of her keep; a presumptuous servant; a sturdy pair of legs to fetch the chamber pots during a seige of dysentery.

That was when Alice, the youngest Russell daughter, discovered her, at the age of six, reversing Bassioni's life in a soft crescendo so that, over time, she reached and surpassed the heights of her "capricciowallah" success in one pair of myopic blue eyes. She taught the plain child to sing. She taught her to read the Tarot using a beautiful deck with a full Venetian Lesser Arcana, the Bastoni and Coppes filigreed in gold, leaving a luminous dust on the fingertips. The child felt strangely at home in the dank room stuffed with dilapidated trunks. One afternoon, she opened a small chest and found part of her friend inside, black silky tresses coiled like snakes. With the woman's baldness was revealed a richer beauty, the cheekbones emerging, the brow revealed, more so because it was just for the girl. When she would die, two years after sitting on that bench with Barr, this child would tell no one, placing a hank of her own hair between the stiffening palms. "What on earth happened to your hair?" Lady Russell would ask, the wash amah's nostrils solving the mystery and the child packed off to England a year early.

He had never spent time with an aged female, yet the hour sped amazingly. He asked if there was something he might do for her. She rose with her bucket and laughed. "Make love to me, Tuan Rajah, as if I were sixteen." Halfway down the path, she turned and suggested vin mariani, an infusion of wine and cocoa leaves, for his melancholia, a problem he had not mentioned.

Russell's festivities proceeded, the races a particular success. The sailing regatta had to be canceled due to squalls, but by the evening of the ball the air was clear. Lemon grass had been cut and strewn over the walkways and, when crushed underfoot, gave off a delicious fragrance (how did the idiot know to do that?). A kromang would play first, then the band would begin the reels, quadrilles, and polkas.

There was a richness of women, a richness unexperienced before in that place, although still outnumbered by men four to one. How wonderful they are, he thought. To glide over this caked mud in all the most unnatural colors, the pink of an English rose, the blue of a Devon sky. They complain, they faint, they level their moods like gun barrels, then walk upon the water; he was already slightly drunk yet could not remember drinking.

Sideboards were resplendent with salted beef, smoked fish, jellied ham, and cottage puddings—a complete tinned, potted, and preserved feast. The Russells were proud of the purity of this offering, the absence of anything native excepting two pyramids of blood oranges. These, and the red paper packets of money, were for the Chinese servants to usher in the New Year.

The fiddles struck and people began to rise. Several little midshipmen were hoisted up and whirled about by their mates. The wife of Labuan's new C of E was passed from one set of arms to the next, the most popular night in the plain woman's life. A polka was struck, and another; then the fiddles changed to a waltz and he drew Claire Russell to the floor, followed by Mrs. Doherty. Rose smiled up at him, her breasts pushed high, the long waist supple. His hand braced her back, the slight separation between her teeth making him suddenly weak. Every man who danced with her, he guessed, would imagine pushing his tongue and more into that pearly gap.

He tired, then danced again, with the young Boyne in her first gown, and Mrs. Higgins, the C of E's wife. He seemed to notice things in flashes, with a glazed stupor in between. Delia Semple in rustling taffeta, a sausage wrapped in too little paper, tied through the middle, made him laugh. She was speaking to him. Lady Russell addressed him brightly.

All was gay and swirling. It had been a sparkling four days, gladdening every heart. Russell deserved credit. Some of the women looked ten years younger. It was something his wife would have liked, he thought, deeply regretting her absence. He regretted, too, the absence of Kilcane. He would have enjoyed his old friend's company in this atmosphere, and there was need of him. Concentrating most of the Europeans in the north in one place was unsound. Kilcane had been formally invited five months before and sent word that he would serve as Her Majesty's representative. He had not come.

Others came. Officers of a small merchantman and a Spanish man-of-war down from Mindanao had joined the guests, and strange faces swelled the crowd. As the evening wore on, he felt the worse for it. He passed through the hot swirl of sweat and cooked meats, a buzzing in his ears, and then something else, the smell of something mildly rotten, wafting in and out in nauseating little puffs, little spikes, approaching putrescence and vanishing in a crescendo of fiddles, resounding prettily in each pulse.

"Come away, Tuan Rajah." Si Tundo was at his elbow, actually pulling his sleeve.

"Si Tundo." He laughed. They were separated by a rowdy group of mids. He sat for a while, then rose and propelled himself through the crowd, a wire now strung within his head from ear to ear. It was the first time in his life he felt his age, yet could not remember it. He regained his bungalow on Si Tundo's shoulder and fell into a deep sleep.

The next morning he was better. He ate a hearty breakfast. Later, a light breeze rose up and died as he sat on the veranda, leaving him in a backwash of nausea. His entire skin itched. He wondered if Russell was fool enough to have rengas in his garden. By noon, there was a puffiness about his face and wrists. After receiving the usual friends, he experienced leaden fatigue. He slept through the day and, at dusk, rose and walked to the beach. Stepping into his dugout, a word was uttered by the little Kling oarsman so that only his mate would hear, yet it carried on the air: a strange word that meant nothing to him.

In his dream, he was riding with Kilcane in a small dugout and all was well. They were pulling past the estuary of his own river when his friend turned to him with an expression of love and spoke the same word.

It was confluent smallpox. Labuan, amazingly, had no resident physician, the one they had having drowned, and Dolan had remained in

Kuching with a badly burned fortman. He tried to assess the circumstances while reason was with him. He demanded gawar leaves be hung in the doorway to declare quarantine and would not allow anyone without the scars of a survivor to come near him. By nightfall, he could not raise himself. Lim, with his pitted face, remained. The Chinaman stretched him on plaintain leaves to cool him from the violent fever, continuingly replacing damp cloths on his head and limbs. Biverts was the only individual who had not had the pox who was allowed to stay. He held Biverts' hand tightly in the night; only this way would he sleep. The man's entire arm went dead, but if he tried to remove it, Barr woke.

Two days went by like this. He had tremendous cramping of his feet and fevers that raged. Chills would then commence. In these hours, Biverts, beyond exhaustion, was privy to his dreams. At one point, he could not hear the words being slurred and bent close, his ear almost touching the lips. A fist slammed into his jaw, loosening three teeth.

On the fourth day, a rash covered his face and abdomen. Two days later his body was covered with pustules, his face swollen as to be unrecognizable. Yet his heart beat strongly. The pustules swelled, running together, then crusting over and itching horribly. He dug in his nails and they tied his wrists to the bed.

Seven others were stricken, four Europeans and three Malays, before the actual onslaught. When the pustules emerged, he seemed to have a degree of relief, yet his delirium increased. With the bizarre logic of dreams, he sat at Norwich in Christmas Hall, the heat of the candles on his face and chest, the cold of the walls behind, the beadle droning. "God bless you and keep you. God grant you mercy. God give you peace. . . ."

"God damn it to hell!" The voice, from a million miles away, drawing him back on a thread of steel. "What idiot would put a wug here?" A hand, small, hard, cradled his bursting head. "Well now." The fox eyes gazed into his. "Well now, I've come. I've come, and there's an end to it."

"He is dying," the C of E said.

"Not here, by God." Kilcane was beside himself, tears welling.

"You'll kill him if you move him," the man advised, but four brawny gunnerymen were already at the sides of the cot, raising it with supreme gentleness and passing through the door, Kilcane fluttering behind like a crazed fowl.

"His eyes! His eyes!" He scrabbled into the sunlight, tearing off his coat and holding it over the contorted face.

"What will you do?" Biverts asked.

"I don't know. Sail about. Sail gently about. Sea breeze, you know." Biverts felt true pity for him.

There were over forty in sickbed. Few, except family, volunteered to nurse them. By the second week, Higgins, the young chaplain, imagined the Queen coming to put things right. A hundred and seventy-seven died at Labuan that February.

"There are, at these things," Kilcane was to note, "too many people." This was true. Any major gathering in that climate was liable to have, among its guests, an uninvited one. One knew the risk of human density, the Europeans burning salts beforehand, the Chinese sniffing dried variola crusts. In those years, every tenth or twelfth "kickup" was attended by a venomous little sister.

At sea, no one was allowed to approach him except through Kilcane. And this was perhaps the greatest miracle the little man ever wrought. His men stood fast. He said the fever was broken and the disease no longer communicable and he was right, but the others had no reason to know it, nor did he.

Once the pulse was steady, he gave his friend a thousand drops of laudanum and allowed him to drift away for two days and nights. "We can speed opium to these wretches," he mused bitterly, "but not Jenner's elixir. They are using it for savages in Oklahoma."

On the eighth day, Barr emerged on deck, the pupils of his eyes contracting in agony, his legs crumbling. Kilcane beckoned two brutes, who dragged a chair. Barr asked for but was given no mirror. He stared into a water barrel. "I have," he would write to her, "the face of the buaya."

He gained strength daily, and Kilcane was overjoyed. Conversation began between them, strange and sweet—of childhood, of the habits of cuttlefish, of a particular cologne, purchased only in Srinagar and made with patchouli and water from the Jhelum. One afternoon, Kilcane peeled him a banana and watched him eat it and sat down and wept. They could hardly take so much time milling about on the oceans, he said roughly, without carrying out some of Her Majesty's business. They would start to travel in earnest, visiting Sulu and Balimbangan, where a British ship had been wrecked and sacked. Sough received them graciously. They continued to Samboange, each leg the invalid coming more into his own skin, although the scarring was permanent.

"Do you wish to stop at Sandakan?" Kilcane asked on the homeward trek. "We could find it, you know. Her marker." He declined.

He disembarked that same month in Kuching, where a letter from the Capetown roads awaited him. Over the ensuing days and weeks, holed up in his despair, he sent to Na.

Sadok

I've always loved fine, light things. The gold of that sequined sack, Phil's pale hair. I had nothing but what was in my skull. I felt wild and new and able to swallow anything. Anything could make me feel this way—the whistle of a ship, a man's tongue across his lips, a sausage sizzling. I was always able to leap boldly in the dark.

It was her tongue, pointed, pink, that first arrested him. Young Doherty offered to help with an immense portmanteau on the Gangetic railway, and the little pink animal emerged, slid over her lower lip, and withdrew. Later, Rose did all the talking, a musical cascade. She spoke of the place she had just been and its attractions; she spoke in the singular although the child stood like a plank at her thigh. She spoke of Fatehpur Sikri, her favorite place in all of India for the pink of the walls melding into the pink of the sunset. He answered in the only way he knew how. "I've never been there." The cascade stopped. "It is my birthday," he added crazily. It was.

The first months of their marriage were a blissful stream interrupted by black eddies of despair. Her pleasure transported him; her displeasure pitched him into hell. He did not know who or what he was. He became physically ill. He would heave to at the fort, waiting for the latest storm to pass over, wondering what he had done. At the first ray of light, he reappeared, all hope. She would welcome him lushly or look vaguely through him as if she had never seen him before. It never occurred to him to strike her or even slam her in place with his tongue, but just to let her words, and once her little fists, beat about him, enduring, clinging to the wisdom that females, in their mystery, were like this. Yet it went beyond him. Something slid out of that small bungalow in those months, spreading its spoor in the forests and hills.

Rose didn't know what she wanted, but it was something strange and fine. She knew its scent, its feel. She wished to feel great pleasure, cause great suffering, give and withdraw great favors. Why was this wrong? Her fingers feathered over his neck, her eyes on a distant place. Another woman's triumph could cast her into gloom; her downfall cheer her. And then she would change, baking for the eternally grieving Mrs. Minjoot, weeping, as she did one night, on her young husband's breast for the sheer luck of finding him. She was raised a Catholic and would, on occasion, pray fervently. At thirteen, she had cut off all her pretty oval nails after reading *Lives of the Martyrs*.

Rose gazed at her lovely reflection. She lifted on her toes and turned as if on a wire suspended from the ceiling, her hands cupping each small breast, with its faint marbling of blue, gliding backward under the full buttocks. Eyes, delicious eyes, peered down from the ceiling and up from the floor and through millions of cracks. The door opened and she glanced languidly behind and it was the child. She pushed it shut and plunged a foot into her drawers. Her brother-in-law was expected in from the Rejang—the two men, after coming down in tandem to meet the bride packet, now obliged to alternate leaves for the duration of their contract. Ross would stop at his sister-in-law's as he had done before, delivering his brother's loving messages.

Rose knew something of herself. She knew she was one of those individuals who never loves something but, as soon as she has it, no longer loves it, yearning always for the distant. Yet romantic. Sentimental. She had married the wrong brother. And if she had married Ross, she still would have married the wrong brother. She knew this. She knew the phenomenal luck of the two had run out. For a moment, it made her genuinely sad.

She had married Connor because he was good-natured and hand-some and swept away her most pressing concerns. In the first months of their marriage he amused her, aroused her, then bored her, and now, with his stupid, lovesick gazes and clumsy hands, disgusted her. Ross, in his untouchable virility, his friendliness, his innocence, set her afire.

She prayed. She made Phil pray. "And take care of Uncle Ross," the child repeated after her. "And Papa," he added on his own. One day he had called Connor this, and it was received with so much plea-sure that he used it from then on. This praying of the child for Con-nor seemed for a time to change her attitude toward him, and she herself prayed for him with a fierce spirit. She'd continue her prayers beneath the nets, in vague, unfocused awareness of her own corrup-tion. She'd sigh, smooth her hands over her thighs, and sleep, enter-ing, some nights, polyandrous dreams of embracing one while being penetrated by the other.

It is strange how even the closest souls are separated, a chance com-ment, a gesture, hurling them to opposite ends of the universe, never getting back to where they were in all their lives. Ross told the first lie of his life to his brother, a senseless one, saying it took three days to reach the longhouse of the chief Meneking instead of the actual five. And Connor, who knew it was false and unimportant, recog-nized it for what it was, a blade dropping out of the sky.

Ross felt duplicitous toward his brother for the first time in his life, so that he walked around in despair, planning soon to be correcting his thoughts but not at that moment or his heart would stop in his chest. He would wake in the morning unable to face that clear-eyed gaze. He began to hate him. When it was time for his turn in, he took leave of his little family with guilty, feverish anticipation. He found himself buying presents, Deepavali lanterns, budgerigars, to amuse his sister-in-law and her child. He took delight in his successes. These two, to whom he conveyed his brother's love, reminded him of his own family, and then, observing Rose's white neck as she stretched to coax the budgerigar, a thing that never struck him before, a col-ored family.

The ice was purchased from a prahu then at anchor in the estuary, a dugout having made its way up with a big milky rock under palm mats and he buying ten rupiahs' worth to surprise them. They were not there, and he set it in a pan inside the door and hacked off three small pyramids and placed them in a bowl. And then she was there in front of him, smiling. Without speaking, she picked up a glistening chunk and held it to her temple, then put it in her mouth. He watched as she slowly disgorged it, letting it melt down her chin, running it down the underside of her throat, dampening the dark green cotton between her breasts, her lips parted, his blood pounding so that he turned away. She performed this way in front of him on more than one occasion. Often she did nothing at all. Her voice could arouse him painfully. He wondered what it was in back of her throat to make a sound like that. He would leave, running his fingers stiffly through his hair, the sunlight so glorious, the mud sucking his boots so gorgeous and thick, he wished to ram himself into old Eng Fatima's passing thigh, a tree.

He was impregnated, full of her. When Connor saw him at dockside on Boxing Day—they had never missed a Christmas together in all their lives—he saw half of him was gone.

Her power to her seemed ridiculous, unnecessary, a waste with such a boy. She saw its devastating effect and lost interest. She renewed, in those months, some of her bridal ardor. When Connor came down before the Gawai Burong, he found his ducks in three white stacks, the pomelos he fancied on a little brass plate. In the night, she sometimes woke him with her hand. He went from miserably reviewing all the stupid things he could have done to warrant a year of coldness to finding himself crazily happy, at the center of her loving beam. Marriage, he decided, had its ups and downs but, overall, agreed amazingly. Having the child about pleased him too. Phil possessed a face much like hers, though unlike hers in that it was consistently happy to see him. He was willing to skirt the female mysteries. He was happy again. He came at her in the same inexpert, ardent way, filled with new bravado. There was no subtlety, nothing new; he had no idea what to do with that handsome mouth and, when she showed him, he blushed and then went at it all the time and ruined it. By the time his leave was up, she was sick to death of him.

Ross came down before Ramadan and did not, at first, call in. When he did, three days later, she was cold, not even noticing the gift of a small, perfectly made sumpit for Phil. That evening, when he returned, the door of the bathhouse was cracked, a strip of light on the ground. He heard a childish laugh and water and stepped up, anticipating the pretty sight of her bathing the child. Rose lifted her white legs out of the tub, glistening with little rivulets between the fine, dark hairs, not a blemish, nor on the heavy buttocks. He stood paralyzed, then lurched backward into the dark.

When he returned to his station, he found the young creature he lived with sleeping with their child in her arms, and a pure wind swept through him. He felt, in the following days, a healing balm at work. Yet soon, in the nights, Rose, open-mouthed, her bodice damp, festered in him like a wound. He was caught in the septic flow of her. When he came down the following January, she judged him ripe.

Contrary to the torpor of the climate, he was quick, the act swift, as if hurried by frigid weather, a hand placed out of frozen air up a skirt, almost too numb for pleasure. He returned to Kapit sick at heart. He loathed her, yet she haunted every night.

The poor creature who cared for him had long sensed the power working against her. Before his return, she dressed in her best sarong, the child arrayed prettily with a multitude of bracelets, the two waiting for hours on the little landing stage. He greeted her affectionately, but later, when the child was exhausted and irritable, he slapped it hard.

You could call things forth in this place, he knew. Rose summoned him as if through a window in the air, her eyes unfocused, her thighs wide.

"She's trying them sorely," Mrs. Dolan said, gazing after him on the last day of his leave. "She's swallowing them," Dolan said.

The child was pensive, brows always knit, a dirty yellow cap of hair with two cup-handle ears. That's what he looked like, Cates thought, a little soup tureen, the gold cap a lid, a broth of mystery within. The soup tureen would climb down the three steps of his bungalow each morning, a solemn little animal.

The mother was queer, a sort of unhinged majesty to her, a slight smile in the corners of the mouth. A "disconnected" face. A lamé purse sometimes hung on a string from her wrist. The purse was wrong, but she carried it like a little badge, a glittering oddity. Cates felt this child pummeled not by chance or hardship or ignorance but something else. Who disburses these gifts so wildly? she thought, watching him trudge up the bungalow line. What monster gave her that child?

He had none of his mother's fire, none of her elastic grace, a child who probably would succumb to gastric complaint before ten. "Phil," a cloying name, the voice flat, not at all like that shimmering laugh. The only face she had ever seen that resembled his belonged to a child tethered to a yew behind the most beautiful house in Bath.

He wandered about. But not like the Bigelow boy. Herbert Bigelow tore around like a banshee or crept like a thief. Phil trudged like an old man, his eyes pinned to the ground. He was six, seven, or eight. It was hard to tell. This, along with their both always being alone, was the second similarity between her and the child. Nobody could guess either one's age.

She had seen him sitting on Jiu Keng's wharf, staring blankly at the water, and she imagined she saw then, too, the outline of the father, a dull, good man. What she did not see was the wonderment this small soul had with death, the possibility of comfort in it, he could not swim and so could slip in, slip into a region where that dull, good man existed, a broad worsted lap beneath the water. Watching, she felt a push, like a small strong foot, against the leathery ball in her chest.

Cates took special pride in having her own dwelling and spent a great deal of time sweeping out vermin and rearranging her few sticks of furniture. The child would sometimes watch this swarm of activity.

"What are you looking at?" she snapped one day and he jumped, ready to flee. She riveted him with her eyes.

"At the cat, miss." There was no cat. Then she saw it, slinking between the wall and the caper bushes, emaciated, its tail docked, a perfect being made imperfect by a Chinese cleaver, no longer able to usurp the place of a Celestial in heaven. The cat leapt, and he ran after it.

A few days later, she saw him sitting outside the bungalow line with the animal. It was hard to befriend a cat so fast, especially a docked one. She recognized this kind of desperation.

One afternoon, sweeping her two stairs, seeing his head in the leaves, she went in, opened the casket, and withdrew a book. It was covered with fine mold but she was used to this by now, brushing, face-to-face with the reality that English oak would not prevent her own body from turning into some nauseating green liquor.

She sat on the stairs and opened to a picture of a beautiful woman rocking an infant. There was a large open window behind her head where the sea shone and a star twinkled. It was a perfectly round picture on a square page with a stiff little tab sticking out. She rotated the tab around the circumference and the woman and star fractured into segments and a fairy materialized, barefoot, wand in hand, smiling down at the same sleeping child. It was fifteen minutes before he sidled behind her. There were eight pictures in all, and by the fifth his chin almost touched her shoulder.

He seemed not to be missed. That summer, he went to the bandstand with Cates, he helped roll her wool, he carried her waxed umbrella to the pasar. He did this silently at first, but by the third week he was talking as if a little spigot had been turned on. He talked of his magnificent stepfather and step-uncle, of the remarkable hats of the hagi, of riding out on the ship. He talked of everything but his mother.

One afternoon she shampooed his head, for she had seen a louse, then stuck his whole body in her tub. She regarded the small pale torso, the spindly legs and large kneecaps, his sweet sex, and a grid on his buttocks. He told her of a fire on the boat passing over to Malacca, how he had pressed against something. As he spoke, the sunlight turned his nostrils pink.

She would give him presents to take home, tinned plums, digestive biscuits, bribes for future golden hours.

"If I took a shovel and turned over a piece of this earth, I should find the white sand of Ballyquin clinging to the underside. A salt breeze fills my lungs, I am running on small feet, Con, my hand in yours." Ross Vere Doherty willed his few possessions to the chiefs of his district.

"One uses the big toe with a rifle," Fitzhugh explained. "You brace the muzzle under your chin. The poor bastard had no revolver." It was Fitzhugh who found him, passing through to Kayan country in search of the priest. It had been seven months. No white man, no matter how foolish or useless, could be "forgotten." All kinds of problems resulted. He, his bones, had to be found, an inquiry conducted, and most likely imprisonments and executions. Fitzhugh found the wrong corpse. The boy's fortmen would not touch him for fear they would be accused, and the air was still foul with him when they arrived, flies creating a roar forty feet away.

"That hair," he said to Sutton, miserably, "was the same, you know. Sheaves of gold on either side of an explosion."

The fortman who kept Doherty's guns said nothing until Fitzhugh smashed his foot with a rifle butt. He then said the Tuan went inside and never came out. They told Doherty they found the girl, who had drowned herself and the child, and he went inside and never came out. Fitzhugh knew the brothers. He had spent two months in their territory, bringing coffee trees into the country, trees that flowered abundantly and died. The two were like and yet unlike any officers he had met. He thought of them often after Ross's death. He thought of them perched on the farthest, daintiest limb of Lytton's crazy tree, far from the mud-swamped roots of a Dawes or a Bigelow, from there to give birth to nothing, simply stopping in their own perfection.

One cannot bury a corpse in that place too fast. It starts dissolving upon the last breath. Connor Doherty saw what remained of his brother's body placed next to that of his little Melanau. The child was never retrieved.

He did not weep. The ability to weep, to howl for his brother, was beyond him. He returned to Kapit, ruining work he could have done while unconscious, finally asking for leave. Smythe, a pale, sickly man who was to achieve the longest up-country service in the century, relieved him.

In Kuching, he found his bungalow clean and tidy, a large bouquet of convolvulus on the table. Phil appeared, looking both frightened and delighted to see him. "Where is she?" he asked. "Where's your mother?"

"No need to ask him," Rose said, climbing in behind. "I'm here in front of you." She faced him, arms akimbo. He pulled back and hit her with such force her ear sprayed blood.

"Go home." He dropped into a chair, not looking at her. "I'll provide for you. I'll provide for you as long as you like. You'll be free. Leave the boy, if it's easier."

He heaved himself up and did not return until the next day, horribly hung over. She and Phil were gone. He searched for them, working his way down the line, bashing doors, passing across the river and climbing to the Dolans', the Michaelises', the Bigelows', asking thickly for his wife. He crossed back and passed through the astana gate and came upon that strange creature, the nurse, on the veranda with her darning egg.

"Good afternoon, Miss Cates." He pulled off his hat wretchedly. "Have you seen my wife? Have you seen Phil?"

She was startled by so much beauty and misery in the same face. "I'm sorry, Mr. Doherty," she said. "Come up and sit for a moment."

"I must be off just now." He turned and lurched down the path. The two o'clock deluge began and he was lost to sight. Terror seeped into her chest. She did not resume her chair. She pulled an umbrella from the jar and bolted into the rain.

The bungalow was a gray shadow aligned with other shadows in the downpour. She knocked softly, then louder, pounding, finally pushing the door. It was a neat, small parlor, with no sign of a child anywhere. She stared at the convolvulus, a coral paper fan, some fruit under a net of small flies, an ironing plank—the iron on end, its snout uptilted above a gleaming grid. Her legs weakened and she sat down. At five o'clock Rose stepped in, hair wet about her face, Phil behind.

Cates rose and began her apology for entering, but did not continue. "I know you're going, Mrs. Doherty," she said. "This is no place for a woman in her prime to be buried. No one can fault you." The face registered nothing, no answering glimmer.

"It is my job to care for children, to educate them. It is my life's work." The pounding in her chest drowned out the rain. "You will be alone. It will be hard. Too hard. Please consider it. We get along rather well."

Rose slid her eyes to Phil. "My, what a popular boy."

"I am a qualified governess." Cates heard her own voice as if underwater. "I could bring him through the fourth primer." Rose stared. There was something deaf about the look.

"I have some money," Cates said, and knew then all was lost.

"Why, he's coming with me. What could possess you?" She flipped her oilskin on a chair, pulled his over his head, and pushed the door open with her foot. "What could possess you?" she said again, pushing it wider.

She said she would not, but at the last moment she did. He would look for her, wish to see her. This, at least, she could do. She had heard the whistle ten minutes before. She rushed out and down the slope, in time to see the rusty transom rotate against the tide and rumble downstream, nothing visible but a shape aft coiling a hawser. She envisaged the light head, ears planed out, facing forward, as she had advised.

She felt old. Older than she had ever felt in her life. She sat long after the thing had disappeared, its rumbling vanished on the water. The sun was sinking when she rose and walked back, dragging herself up the two steps and inside—where, in the gloom, she was greeted by an apparition so exquisite it stopped all motion and sound. Two bony orbs glowed in the last ray of light, a pair of small knees.

He sat upright, asleep, a small effigy, rattan suitcase on the floor. She gazed at him, drinking in every cell. She gazed at the gift of him. What this woman was giving up. An individual who never, even for a second, betrayed her. Cates herself had once lashed out about her. "She's all right," he said fiercely, and said no more.

They began their odyssey with Shearing's malt. They drank out of porcelain cups with the book of round pictures between them, twinkling fairy and shimmering sea endlessly changing places. She taught him, in the weeks and months that followed, an expanded litany of prayers, some simple mathematics, and, over that winter, the history of England as she knew it. She told him of great kings and brave hearts. She told him of a courageous knight with one sparkling blue eye that saw more than any average pair. The child liked these stories and occasionally asked a clairvoyant question.

"Do you remember snow, Philip?" she'd say, lowering his nets. "In spring, skunk cabbages come up like tight umbrellas. The skunk cabbage, not the robin, is the harbinger of spring." His education consisted, in large part, of erratic vignettes. Their days were more or less leisurely. He kept himself to a great extent, given small assignments. Her regular employment allowed them to catch the tail of the pasar pagi while a few stalls were still open. At four, the china cups were produced and she spooned out malt, the top of the tin painted with lovebirds holding a ribbon in their beaks.

What would she have? Five or six years? And then he would be apprenticed or put to sea. It was enough. No one else had a claim. The stepfather was a boy himself. Mrs. Dolan with her brood, the Ranee with her sons, had only an "elongation" of what she had.

She believed the woman would write for money. Rose never wrote. Once, a strange set of clothes, a cheap baju and pants, came from Surabaya. The greater fear was that she would change her mind. Every two weeks Cates sat bolted to a porch chair with her knitting, gazing at the landing stage where the blunt nose of the packet would swing in. If he passed, she would clamp him against her, allowing him to work the needles, dropping stitches everywhere, until all the passengers had disembarked. It was a year before she stopped doing this. She felt that if the woman had been gone a year, with no communication, she would never come. She thought of it as a law, something written by the forces of good in the universe.

The two were seen everywhere, the tall flat board muffled up against the sun and the pale child in his too-large topee. They seemed to travel within a ridiculous envelope of bliss. To invite Cates to tea was a bore, it was always Phil this and Phil that.

March can be a strange month in those latitudes. A few bright, clear days may exist, as if transported from some Nordic summer, only to be swept away the next, the world restored to its steaming malaise. It was on one of those rare days, at first distrusting her vision over the dazzling water, that she saw it, the long waist, the black, sun-faded leghorn. Others would have said a pretty woman down on her luck. For Cates, it was an apparition from hell.

"You've lost everything," she said to the implacable face confronting her. "You wish him to share your misery. He doesn't deserve it."

Rose had meant to come for money. In the year and ten months she traveled the region, the only solid perch she found was a boiler-man off the *Ajax*. "Get your things," she said.

That evening, Cates packed for him as meticulously as if they two were going on a long, happy voyage, each sleeve folded, each collar square. "Be good and brave," she said stonily. She shoved a paper into his pocket. "Write. You can do this."

"If you stay put long enough, everything passes through a place like this," Delia Semple said, and Mrs. Bigelow raised her eyebrows. "The first time I saw that one, she was standing right where she is now, dressed suitably enough for a widow newly married, yet with that whorish purse dangling from her wrist. She might as well have stripped naked."

Rose swiveled her neck and looked back at the town. She looked down at the boy, larger, more awkward, sitting with his hands under his buttocks. She had not meant this to happen. It was bloody stupid. She suddenly wished she could absorb him into her body again so that he would be no burden. It was the "closing of a chapter." She was braced to "turn the page." She would use these expressions to steel herself. If she had had the wit to understand the machinery she set in motion, she might have taken some dark pride in it.

Hogg visited the Rejang the month after Doherty's death. It was a routine visit; after a suicide, the most senior man always followed up. He went through the station with a meticulous mental checklist and found all in order. The brother was there, miserable but functioning, his temporary replacement having returned to Serikei.

Yet afterward, swinging into the stream, unease enveloped him. He reviewed the scene in his mind. The place resembled, in every way, a well-ordered, secure station. He feared his judgment was getting weak and this worried him even more. He clapped his bowman on the back and they commenced the pull down. Yet the feeling stayed with him. He had seen something. The only way to discover what it was, was to plod through every second of the visit. He did this and came up with nothing. He closed his eyes and was soon asleep, as he often was on water. At four o'clock he woke, relieved himself off the stern, and remembered his dream. He had been in a large English country house, well appointed and new. Everything was perfectly arranged, as if awaiting an important guest. He passed through spacious well-furnished rooms, and in every container, every receptacle—a sherry cabinet, a bowl of flowers—there was a serpent coiled.

He had been an idiot. The thing that was wrong was that it was too right. There was too smooth an appearance to the place, a place with no seasoned fortmen or reliable chiefs. Of course they would take advantage of the boy. They knew his state of mind. Yet why had they not moved? And here, too, the answer came with shattering ease. They had waited for *him,* it was inevitable he would come; they had waited for him to pass. It was the first tactical error of his life.

He ordered his boats turned around and poled up with all force, but it would take two days against the fresh that had brought them down in three hours.

They had almost not killed him. One of the two Kelabit fortmen involved had changed his mind, and then, a day before the event was to occur, they changed positions. To see the shifting eyes and ticks in these two dullards would have put even the greenest district officer on alert. Doherty was beyond it.

Hogg's arrival terrified them. His harmless departure did not ease their minds. They appeared for the change of guard the next dawn resolved to do nothing and saw Doherty step outside. He stood at the end of the little stockade porch and gazed at the sky. Seeing him like this, face uplifted, decided them.

By the time Hogg returned, Doherty was dead and the Kelabits fled. He sat down and wept. He wept for the boy and for himself, for this unconscionable lapse in judgment. He should have relieved the fool on the spot. The whole place was a glaring message.

He executed every fortman at the station for gross dereliction of duty and called for reinforcements among his own men. He left one of his lieutenants and a garrison of his choosing in charge and went in search of the fugitives. During the next three weeks he attacked and burned every longhouse in a twenty-mile radius. Following the trail, the fort at Ngmah, between Kanowit and Katibas, was dismantled, and he took these men and guns along with him because he did not know how far he could trust them. Everything that came in his way during his passage across country was destroyed or killed. It was a search for two men that would swell into the bloodiest vendetta and redemption of territory in that century.

Doherty's death, in reality, had been a simple thing. Forces related to Brunei had recognized Kapit as a weak link. One Resident was dead, and the other destroyed by grief, a power respected by these people. They meant to discourage further annexation eastward. There had been some coordination behind it, but not much. Hogg would not let go.

This pursuit of two terrified assassins lasted four years, left off and resumed as the rains dictated. The first winter, he killed everyone who could have given shelter to or lied for the murderers and burned every dwelling that could have sheltered them in their flight east. His path was wide and rapid, for he was well able to live on the land. One might be surprised that these people would hold out and refuse to give up these pathetic fugitives, yet they were tired of years of being attacked by his Sakarangs and driven off their lands. During the winter of his second year, he burned his seventeenth longhouse on the banks of the Belaga. From there, he followed his quarry into Katibas country. Flames rose each night marking his route. Whole tribes were displaced. The fugitives sped away, gathering kinfolk on friendly streams, until the hunt produced a prey of hundreds, including women, children, and livestock. Over months, it became clear that this desperate tribe was headed for Sadok, the stronghold of the chief called Mua Ari, around whose upland fortress all dissent had coagulated for over a decade. This was a high eyrie crowning hundreds of miles of hills, a place imbued with the magic and protection such altitudes held for the Dyak. The flight of the two murderers served him well as a rallying cry. Hogg seemed satisfied with this. Mua Ari was a savage of great cunning, humor, and intelligence, a worthy opponent.

He approached the highlands in the spring of 1870. On Easter Sunday, they surrounded the great fortified longhouse at Sungei Lang, two-thirds of the way to Sadok. He was brought there by a child of ten who exacted a promise that all inside, including his mother, would be set free. Hogg agreed and intended to keep the bargain. But it did not happen this way. Any sound would have done it. The boy cried out to his mother and at the same instant bullets tore through the length of the structure, blood seeping through the floor. Within minutes, the building was burning and the roof collapsed. Those who ran were cut down. His Sakarangs wiped their parangs, slung heads over their shoulders, and were ordered to move on, for in all the years of this pursuit he never was convinced he got anyone important.

Sutton had been sent up and caught up with him here.

The two regarded the burning wreckage together. "They've had a lesson they'll long remember," Hogg said.

"I don't wish God nor nobody to remember this," the master replied.

A man may step back after such things, sickened to death, or he may surge on with renewed vigor toward pure damnation. Hogg did neither. He maintained his pace, neither slacking nor increasing it. It was, one would suppose, a talent of some kind. "He's gone mad up there," Sutton said, when he returned. "We must stop him."

"We can't," Barr replied.

"Why not?"

"Because we can't. We have no force as large as his. We must let the bastard burn himself out." It was Fitzhugh, in the end, who was given the task. Bobby found him at Meri, burning the three great longhouses there. The fugitives had once again escaped, continuing on to the high plateau.

Fitzhugh was dumbfounded at the destruction. "It was *one bloody man*, Dickie. *One bloody station!*" He looked into those lead eyes. He tried to reason with him. Hogg, in fact, looked reasonable.

"They are a chain," he replied patiently when Fitzhugh finished. "If one station goes, the others are a hundred times more vulnerable. The damage has to be rectified."

"They are *not* a chain! How in hell could one of us ever help another, hundreds of miles apart!"

"They're a chain *in here.*" Hogg drummed the side of his head. "I shouldn't have to tell *you* that. When one goes, the appearance of synchronized power collapses. They bloody believe it." He was, in some ways, correct. There was no way for the forts to support each other over such great distances but they did appear interlocked, as having some vital, almost magical connection. Severely weakening or destroying one put them all in greater danger of attack. Already signs of instability had surfaced in other divisions.

Fitzhugh persisted. "There's another reason for this spree," he said darkly. "*You* failed. You poked your head in at Kapit, a place where all the fortmen had been pulled out of the trees yesterday, the boy unhinged with grief. There had to be something. You missed it. You missed it, and now you're tearing the fucking universe apart, collecting rivers by the by. You raise your head and you're on the east bank of the Belaga! You're doing what you've always wanted to do!" Fitzhugh was the only man who could speak to Hogg this way. They were unlike in everything but raw ability, and both knew it. Hogg responded with silence. He said nothing, nor did he show the least resentment.

He moved on to Sadok that summer. "Retreat, retreat"—the gongs rang through the high plateaus—"and one day we will turn and all that will be following us will be an ant. We call on our sisters: disease, flood, cold. A little sister travels with them even as we speak." Mua Ari had a poetic bent. His exhortation flowed.

A new cook had been included in Hogg's force at Betong, a forty-year-old man from a longhouse wiped out by cholera. Two men died that first week with all the ghastly signs, yet he pushed on. What followed was disastrous. Of seven thousand men, two thousand died on that summer expedition.

He organized burning mounds of the dead, the stench hanging in the air for there was no wind, the smoke visible for miles. It took less than a day to die. Men who were well at dawn rolled down banks, screaming, and threw themselves into the stream by dusk. There were vast clouds of flies. For two more years he would wage war, losing thousands of his own men, mostly to disease. By the time it was over, forty thousand people would be displaced and the territory swelled to the outskirts of Brunei. By then, he had forgotten or didn't care why it had started.

At times, the high country seemed to merge with the montagne *of his childhood. He would smell the old priest, his damp underwear and stink as they camped in the dark. He would feel himself at the very beginning of his life.*

Beyond the Rejang and the Pelagus rapids lies the country of the Kayans. They are the musicians of Borneo, with a slightly higher civilization than the sea Dyak. They are a religious people. They are devoted to their chiefs, produce exquisite carving and weavings, and excel at torture. Some Kayans, it was believed, were implicated in Doherty's murder. In continuing his vendetta and invading this country, Hogg, by chance, uncovered the fate of the priest.

Paoluzzi had started into Kayan territory with three Punan guides, who took him up past the third rapids. At this point they left him and sped downriver. The Kayan apparently thought him mad and did not harm him but gathered him up and transported him higher. Everywhere, it was said, he asked after the boy.

The time between the priest's coming into the territory and his death was vague. Something happened beyond the Pelagus that made them question his madness. It was that his protection, one day, vanished. They carried him in those remaining weeks from hut to hut, village to village, ever upward along the river, where little cuts were made, many, many, but never enough, by women and girls and girl babies, so that at the end he was finally a traveling scream.

The Kayan chief Dian recounted, years later, that there had been, in fact, two men. The weak fat man, and the other. "The other was very powerful," he said to Pruitt, the young C of E chaplain at Kapit.

"Who was the other?" Pruitt was sick of their fabrications, their contempt for the truth.

"Jaezu."

"An antu?"

"Yes."

Hogg began burning every longhouse above these rapids. He hated this. It necessitated a two-month hiatus from the task at hand. The priest was an imbecile, well meriting a fate any sane man could have avoided by watching the direction in which he traveled. At the end of summer, he resumed his campaign against Sadok.

The person of Mua Ari, by then, had become his true focus, the hand that kept the murderers of Doherty out of reach. In August, a month rarely supporting outbreaks of cholera, he launched another attack. He started out with five hundred boats and fifteen thousand men, Dyaks from over twenty branch tribes. He took with him his usual kit and a McChessy almanac. A partial lunar eclipse would occur close to the time they reached the high palisades. He was known to use such predictions and general witchcraft to fuse his force at crucial times.

He reached the foot of the great Makun rapids at the end of September. It was confirmed that the fugitives had long since made their way to Sadok. During all his campaigns, he employed a little journal, its brief entries later used to recall specific actions and their outcomes. He was always learning. A phrase, usually conjuring a physical picture, alone would be recorded and later would trigger hours of specific conditions and events already stored in his mind.

September 24, 1871

Makun. Enemy reported six days higher. Strong freshet, leaf plates swept away. Honeybees over boats, sweet-scented air for miles.

September 29, 1871

N.N.E. five miles today. Bath makes the man. Read Balzac. Smoke of anthracite coal seen. Large river carp for dinner.

October 2, 1871

Advanced today E.N.E. six miles. Flow shallow and more rapid with many obstructions. Forced to proceed by land. Path steep with magnificent views of countryside. Dragging four-pounders, rocket tubes, and the new McClintock telescope.

October 5, 1871

Clear night, moon eclipsed as predicted. Water fouled all the way up, half force weakened by dysentery. Each man carries a quart of good water. This morning, looked behind and saw force climbing below us for several miles. Sadok is now visible above, its mustering gong never ceasing, a few clouds gliding over in the dawn breeze. Signs the enemy has passed through our camp during the night.

His movements were slow, somnolent in these dawns. He sat with his coffee, grunting to reports. Everything that occurred—the dispatches of his lieutenants, a sudden maneuver on the part of the enemy, the very weather—appeared to move in accord with some plan in his skull. His physical presence had a great calming effect on his men. He need say nothing, just sit with his cup, steel eyes cracked. One of his few regular inquiries was after the men of the line, especially those carrying the guns. For these he had a kind of tenderness.

It took tremendous effort to keep the line of march through this terrain. The last hundred yards were almost perpendicular. A network of rattans was constructed to aid in the climb, and here the vanguard sat on the side of the hill the whole night, angled eighty degrees, with a few cross-sticks to sit on. At least a dozen fell to their deaths.

They gained the summit at dawn of the eighteenth day and began the siege. No matter how large the burst inside, the gong would recommence. By midmorning, they gained the small upper plateau and found it deserted. There were the dead, but far fewer than expected. The rest of the defenders had gone as if flown to heaven, for there had been no sign of the enemy passing through them in the night.

The fortress at Sadok was unlike any structure they had ever seen. The walls were two feet thick, girting an area of three or four acres. At one end of a great inner room was a Dutch breakfront of immense proportions with little cherubs holding garlands in the air and, above it, to the rafters, five tiers of human heads. The other end opened to a smaller room completely lined with yellowed scrolls in Jawi and old Dutch rudders in which fires had been set, but smoldered down. Behind, in a large interior square open to sunlight, a lush garden of convolvuli, canna, and lagerstroemia spread out, kept, it was said, by Chinese prisoners; in the middle, the verdant likeness of a man, small horns protruding from his brow, his hooves and legs bright with lichen. To the north and west, the vista extended to a milky rim of sea.

Within, a great number of excellent chendaum and bulan jars lined a long arcade. Certain smaller items were not so much placed about as treated to miniature "enthronements." A black silk umbrella was braced vertically in a satinwood block. In a corner of the rudder library, a little Indian rag horse stood in the center of a lacquer table, beside it an inlaid meerschaum—recognized as Rosetree's, his head taken twelve years earlier on the Sadong. It was like finding the fissure through which lost objects had passed from one universe into another.

"What do you think, Abang?" Hogg asked his oldest lieutenant.

"I think, Tuan," the man said, "one does not destroy what one cannot make again."

He sighed. He searched each of the rooms himself, finding only the dead. Inside the large cookhouse, his face suddenly changed. It filled with suspicion. He looked intently at every object in the room.

He stared so long into a green glass bottle, they thought he had lost his mind. "He is here," he said.

"The place is empty except for the dead," Abang replied uneasily.

"Yes! Yes! We are blind to him, but he's here!" At that instant, a man became visible at the far end of the room, sitting on the floor and eating out of a pot. He wore a red jacket bound by a piece of turkey twill, and his long hair was neatly plaited. It was said in years to come that the chief Mua Ari was eating and so could not concentrate on his invisibility.

The man rose and greeted them. It was an almost genteel voice and was to reverberate in Hogg's head for years after, not out of fear but something more terrible. It was familiar. For years after this man's death, he would chase the voice down the corridors of his memory, only to have it turn a corner and vanish. Sometimes the language itself was wrong, or the pitch, or the sex. Once, in his dreams, it belonged to an individual who in fact never spoke at all, a mute with whom he sat on a log during the Sibu campaign. Malaria produced the key. The microbe induces a looseness of thought, a waxing in and out of reality which, by some quirk, sometimes allows connections to occur that were previously blocked. He pinned the voice on one face, then another, and found that, in fact, it belonged to at least a dozen individuals he had encountered over the past decade.

He was told that Doherty's actual murderers had fled weeks before to a neighboring tribe. The chief of this tribe was sent a message. This man, rather than submit his people to more suffering, requested the fugitives to give up. They did, and with great sadness he took their heads himself and sent them to Hogg. It was over.

"Your nose," Mua Ari said, when Hogg entered his prison hut. "Did your nurses pull it out when you were young?" He would, on their descent, find this man pleasant company. They had long conversations, and, above Betong, in the beginning of the rains, he taught him to play chess. At Pusa, a traditional place of execution, Mua Ari was placed inside several thicknesses of mosquito net and a cord twisted around his neck from behind. Strangulation was a death reserved for princes, and Hogg honored this savage who, that morning, had won his fifth consecutive game.

During the years of the Sadok campaigns, Hogg came into Kuching twice. He was surprised to find it filled with refugees, unwilling to believe that his maneuvers had caused them. He stayed only long enough to resupply. Society had become more tortuous to him than ever.

The memsahibs made an effort on these occasions, arranging one or two dinners of senior men and their wives. At one of these, a large, white-faced girl, the new bride of the Banting Resident, addressed him. "A great number of women and children are killed in your campaigns, Tuan Mudah." She took him by surprise. "Why is it necessary to make war on women? Surely, they can be spared."

"My war is on women." He found himself gazing into a sea of faces. "These people hunt heads because no Dyak female will accept a man without an extra head. They cannot don their brass rings otherwise. Women are the principal instigators of their bloody campaigns. The destruction of their homes alone reaches them and turns them into advocates for peace. You are the deadly gender, madam," he said, to the aghast young face. It was one of the longest speeches he ever made. After cigars, he walked to the edge of the veranda, urinated off the rail, and left.

On these rare turn-ins, he was always drawn to the secret fulcrum of his universe. Meandering outside her wash yard, along her garden pickets before dawn, he stepped through a strange transmogrification, his heart palpitating, his limbs loosening like a boy's. While he could speak to her openly enough, he still derived intense pleasure from viewing her while invisible, his eyes and mind drenched with her, his fantasies slow and rampant. In daytime, he would sometimes catch sight of her through a doorway or pegging a sheet to a wire or, once, lifting the paw of a dog. As what beauty she had waned, he came to cherish more intensely what was still there, the graceful posture, a quick, delicious tossing of the head.

On this last visit, she questioned him like the white-faced girl but more harshly, stingingly. He became flustered, apologetic, and euphoric that anything impelled her to feel strongly toward him.

"They wear the same headdresses up there, Maureen," he said, amazed himself at this response. "It's hard to tell who's who. We set heavy fines nevertheless."

"Fines!" Her words were tight, venomous, generating the first long conversation they ever had.

"Ah, you kill me," he said finally, desolate. "You'd defend any little hausfrau's domain, whether onions or heads hung from the pegs." He looked at her, and she never in her life felt so intimately caressed by eyes. She stood there, stunned in the rich tide of it, then broke angrily away.

Dolan, stepping onto the little milk porch, had observed them for some minutes, and after more than two decades of marriage was faced with the miraculous fact that another man loved his wife as much as he did.

With Sadok, all but three northern rivers were brought into the territory. Barr was pleased to have the long rampage at an end and the interior so vastly expanded. Hogg did not crow on his pile. He withdrew to Lundu, the two more or less falling into the same arrangement they had before. Yet the arrangement was, by then, truly strained. Over the years, Hogg had become increasingly annoyed, then enraged, at Barr's vacillating, his disinclination to use force at the outset of problems, resulting in lengthy and always somewhat unsuccessful negotiations. A clear and brutal hand was, in the end, the most humane approach. Barr repeatedly thwarted these efforts, dismantling firm decisions by his softer methods. With the Sadok campaigns, Hogg broke free. Yet he went no further, pulling in his neck, settling back and resuming his normal duties. The thing that seemed most likely to put them at loggerheads did not do it. This was done, instead, by a strange and somewhat ludicrous incident.

The night the witch Lehut died by asphyxiation, a bore came higher up the Sadong River than anyone remembered. Two men died crossing the bridge at Semunjan; another was swept away in the castor tree under which the sorceress had taken the shade for sixty years. Lehut, or Apu Indra as she was known in her youth before her father and brothers were murdered, had been beautiful, yet it was a plate of larvae Hogg looked into when he removed the pillow.

She was a powerful interior chief, immensely obese, a superb conversationalist and an avid poisoner. If she desired your services, she lightly detained you, taxed you just enough so you could not pay, and then absorbed you. She rested her hand on your children in passing, owning them equally with the brooks and trees. She referred to Hogg as her elder brother and never stopped plotting against him.

He had not planned to do it. He parted from her amicably as usual, but at the door the child clasped his knee. The little boy he recognized as the son of an upriver chief whom she had poisoned. She had poisoned the child too but, because of a slave's quick hand, he survived. Hogg glanced back, and she waddled toward him, a heavily bangled arm encircling the child's head. "Have no fear. I shall care for him as my own son."

"God forbid," he said genially. She pouted, a flirtatious nightmare.

Walking to his prahu, he reviewed the steps required to finish with her. He would imprison her key people, a few here and there, steadily over time. When she was finally isolated, he would arrest her and bring her to Kuching to stand trial. It would take months, years. He turned back.

She had resumed her seat deep in the gloom of her house and was already dozing. She looked up smiling on hearing his step. It was said she had been lovely well into middle age, when one day she woke up metamorphosed and with the full powers of a witch. Only the lower and medium strata of witches and black magicians are said to assume their powers gradually; this rare species bursts into being. In earlier years, he had noticed vestigial hints of that distant beauty and wondered what it would be like to make love to such a mountain. It would somehow be an experience worth the time, he thought, if one did not die of nausea.

It was a twofold maneuver, tipping her vast weight backward and ramming the pillow over her face. Two of his men scrambled on either side and sat on the kicking legs, Hogg ramming his knees into the pillow, breaking the wrists of both hands snapping around his windpipe. It took several minutes before she stopped moving and did not respond to knife pricks. On the ride downstream, he set the child between his legs.

"Christ." He dropped into a chair and gazed around Barr's saloon. It always struck him as hideous. "It was like killing a rhino." He poured himself a drink.

"What?"

"Apu Indra. I couldn't leave a bullet in her, and poison would never get past that old bitch at her side. How's Smalley's push?"

Barr stared at him in amazement.

Hogg put his glass down. "I sat on her head. The good Abang held her feet. It took forever. There will be no inquiries."

"*We* conduct the inquiries!"

"Look." Hogg gazed at him menacingly. "She was a monster. No one could raise a hand against her except us. She was executed." He drained the glass. "You've sat in this cockeyed 'palace' so long you half believe the Suffolk fusiliers hold drill behind the first stand of trees. They do not. It's very much something else. In this case, I've got it trussed up for good." He was unbelievably tired. "Forgive me." He rose. "I'll apologize properly when I've had some sleep." He walked out.

This conversation turned a corner for them both and was to set the tone for all future intercourse. Fitzhugh, on a rare occasion when both he and Hogg were in Kuching, asked how they were getting on.

"Brilliantly." Dolan grinned, his face all orange and pink under Kilcane's Venetian lozenge. "They're in there throwing each other out of the country."

Ambun

Gardening has become my principal occupation. I have replanted the damned sealing-wax palms a third time, their trunks sprouting up naked and red, then falling over in the first monsoon. Why she likes them I don't know. Maybe she no longer likes them.

The man sitting amidships in the pinnace seemed a grotesque caricature of her husband. He had written of his disfigurement, but she had not expected this. He had aged ten years. Yet he gained the deck of the liner with the same long strides and shocked her entirely by wrapping arms of steel around her. After a moment, she pulled away, but he held on. She stood there, clutched in this vise, feeling a slow crack open in her chest. Passengers gaped at the grotesque old man embracing the younger woman.

She introduced him to Kate Skinner, a young woman come out to wed the new medical assistant, and he was courteous, almost gallant. His features had become coarse, in some ways hideous, yet there was still that peculiar vitality to them. She excused herself to see about a rug bag not among the luggage.

When she returned, he was talking with a short fat man with a surprisingly belligerent stance. "You are the worst of what soils the shores out here." She heard the low words, from a man who turned to her abruptly and lifted his hat.

"Who was that?" she asked, astounded.

"An ill-informed, cowardly worm." He took her arm. She was never to meet Mace, the editor of *The Straits Times,* again.

There was no sojourn in Singapore. They left on the tide. He waited with strange delicacy until she was ready to speak of the children and then listened with tears in his eyes. They spent long hours together on deck. In these she learned of the Dohertys—something he would not write—he would not freight a letter to her with more sorrow. By the time they entered the Muaratebas passage, she felt a deepening pleasure in being in this universe again, in being by his side. There were no cannon, no prahus, only the soft hum of the casuarinas as they crossed the bar.

A sizable throng was gathered to meet them in Kuching, but she saw no children. The datins would have done this, kept the children unseen this day to spare her heart. These women waited, silent and graceful, behind the memsahibs. Aisha stepped forward when her turn came and embraced her. Feeling those thin, strong arms around her, her heart heaved. She and the wives of the other datus were delighted with the behavior of their husbands, the woman said, who had added no wives. As she greeted each one in turn, a shadow lurked below the veranda, among the pomelos. She pulled the jar of marmalade from her bag and stepped down and placed it in Raseh's hands.

Viewed from the large veranda, the compound looked lovely. He had tried for her. The chimpaka she favored now stretched in a fragrant wall to the dairy. The sealing-wax palms destroyed by the monsoon before she left had been replaced by nurselings. A tin roof now covered her old path to the orchard. Ah Moi, a drier, yellower Ah Moi, proudly showed her the new bathroom on the ground level of the astana, far from rat migrations, although the Rajah, she said, still used the little bathhouse.

Inside, all was cool and clean. A soft, familiar rill caressed her ears. She circled a bright cloud of dendrobium orchids and mounted the stair. At the top, she turned, the nursery door ajar, the room absent of their clothes and toys, which were tucked in one corner under a large batik cloth. She passed down the dim high-ceilinged corridor and felt, at that moment, one of the strangest sensations in her life. It was as if a presence moved with her, of deeply malevolent intent. It faded instantly, an illusion of sun and mild dehydration.

In the red alcove, she removed her hat. She removed her blouse and unbuckled her shoes and reached down for a small green object on the floor. It was jade, a stud for an ear or a nose, too fine for a servant. She tossed it on the dressing table and sat down in front of the mirror, and the face that met hers froze her heart.

She rose up, unable to breathe, the glass benignly reflecting her knuckles, the folds of her skirt. *She* had been there. *She* had walked through those rooms, sat at that table. All—everyone who greeted her, who embraced her—knew. She had wept in Aisha's arms and they all knew. She slammed her heart shut with such violence the house shook and he gazed up from the quay.

She did not come down to tiffin or breakfast. Over the following days, her absence at meals became habitual. At first, there were just long headaches. She became listless and weak and finally did not rise.

The fever began in the morning and lasted until dark. In the evening she felt well, at midnight it returned, and at four she was in a delirious sweat. She would finally sleep at dawn, rising a few hours later with no strength. At nine, the fever returned and the cycle would begin again. She went through two crises, emerging from each weaker. It was the usual malarial clock, and yet it was not.

She saw the hateful vision in the glass more and more frequently, a malevolent, sensuous face. There was the day it circled her bed and leaned over her, and she lunged for its throat and would not let go no matter how Ah Kiao screamed. Barr pried her fingers off the poor girl's neck. "Why are you doing this, Melie?" he asked miserably. "Stop it!"

She kept to her bed. In the third week, she had the sensation of rising up, floating off her cot in the hot, dim room, and while she was up near the ceiling, the door slowly opened beneath her and a figure entered. She watched it approach her, for she was also there on the bed, and touch her head and feet. It had the dress and movements of a woman yet with a heavy jaw and thick wrists. The androgynous

409

being reached for her hair and pulled her head back. She thought disinterestedly, Now I shall die. With one hand, it snatched at the air, catching something in its fist and pressing it to her skull. Almost at once, she felt an easing about her chest and limbs.

By morning, she was ravenous. She stumbled down and found some mangoes ripening on the back of the stove and began to eat them. She sat on the veranda in the first light, sucking the meat from the rinds. Sounds sent spasms of pain through her head, a grinding anchor chain, plates clattering in the amah quarters, a puff of air through leaves. At that instant, although she had not been thinking of them, she knew her children were not lost to her. She did not suspect this or divine it or intuit it. She knew it.

He was deeply relieved to see her regaining her strength and sanity. Yet it could go no further than this, as if she put up a hand in the air. They entered the old, familiar deadness. She saw him, in those days, as part of the landscape, moving yet inert. It was not the first or the last time they would live this way. Drifting close, especially when great distance separated them, then surging apart; one revolving toward the other as the other revolved away. It was the key pattern to their lives and they would play it out. And then one would be dead. What would be left after the dross of those decades was burned away? A young girl gazing back at the trot; a man spending happy, earnest hours ordering a stone monstrosity? "Aye," he might say, if they talked of such things, "there's that."

Things happened or did not happen and she did not mind. Kilcane was to come and did not. Lytton wrote from Lombok. She sat for long hours in the orchard, the trees weaving a comforting cocoon around her. She would stay all day, driven in only by the two o'clock rains, then reemerging. She had been needling a stylized foo, with golden eyes against bottle green, and finally stopped for she could no longer see in the gloom.

"You have given him no food," a voice said from behind, a civilized voice that could have belonged to any gentleman in the twilight.

She turned and saw the black chop of hair with its glistening rim against the last light. "Selamat. I am very glad to see you."

"You must place in this tapis some food for the naga," the tracker said, his eyes studying her face. "Two beetles. The benaga will then be content. I am glad you are come home."

"Two beetles?"

"If you do not, he may go hunting in the night, and you will be in danger." He dropped to his haunches, the body unchanged, yet the face older. "Did you dream the naga?"

"I copied it from an egg pot." He looked disturbed. "Jawing, I will weave in two beetles. But how can you believe such things? You are Muslim." How could they resume like this, she thought, how could she pick up this insane dialogue with this man after being halfway around the earth and then manage, as of old, to offend him?

He did not answer. She finished a rosette, pinned the needle to the canvas, and rolled it into her bag. When she looked up, she could just make out his figure moving along the distant tree line. With that aloof, sinuous stride, he had already placed phenomenal distance between them.

"Tapis protect and bestow prosperity." The Moon smiled. "Threads of the finest weavings incorporate dew, the heavenly source of all life." Straight-backed before her loom, old Bulan, the Moon, mother of the caper bush kebun, told how such work can be extremely dangerous. Only women who have borne their children and passed menopause may weave certain dream designs, for they could cause miscarriage and other disasters. Food must always be included if a predatory animal appeared in a weaving, as these are creatures of great power and vengeance.

The Penglima Khaled wore the design of two pythons, head to tail, on his belt, with no food, the Ranee pointed out, no little men or lizards or beetles. "Jawing is a great hunter," Bulan replied. "This nabau is his special guardian."

The next time she saw the tracker, he was with Lim. The two men stood where a few of Lim's pomelo nurselings had been bent almost to the ground by the last monsoon. Jawing had knotted a length of beaten rattan about one of the trunks and, using a larger tree, showed the Chinaman how to work it back to vertical in gentle increments, a little each day. Lim, who felt a natural contempt for the aborigines of the island, respected the tracker. Over the years, they had become friends. She laughed one day on seeing the Chinaman staggering under the weight of a sumpit, Jawing bracing the scrawny yellow arm with his own.

She did not see Jawing again until the fall. Word was that he had returned from the Baram River. She was dismayed, one morning, to see him emerging from the courthouse in a cheap white shirt.

"Why, you have made him a clerk!" she said to Barr at breakfast.

"He's a smart lad." He looked at her. "He deserved it." He rose and lifted his crop from the jar and went out. She watched him walk down to the low wall and mount the bajau and trot off, stone-jawed. He had written, *Come home.* He had held her on that deck and she would never in all her life forget the feel of it, and four days later she gazed into that hellish reflection. Those words, his arms around her, were small derailments. They were back on track. She had never mentioned her vision or hallucination or whatever it was in the glass. He would have ridiculed it, or denied it, or admitted it, admitted the woman's presence in the small room where she had borne her children. It didn't matter. Nor had she spoken of the equally strange illusion from the ceiling of that room. They resumed a flat, dead succession of days, stretching behind and in front, leaving no mark. She would make the best of it.

She saw some old friends. She walked again with Jawing, who had worn the shirt but once and did not speak of it. They took circular walks going nowhere, yet stretching the muscles in her neck, her spine. He held back a branch for her as he had in another life, and she passed through. One day she mentioned her sickness to him, and strange recovery.

"This dream," he said. "Have you dreamed this before? Has someone told you of it?"

"No, and I hope to God I never see it again. It was evil. An evil antu."

He finished coiling a slender rattan around his arm and led the way upstream. Over the years, he had sworn a strange fealty to this woman that he himself did not understand. It was as if he had withdrawn a great white fish from a pool and stood there, not knowing if it were a blessing or a curse. "This dream was no dream," he said, when they arrived at a new little bridge. "What you describe is not an antu. It is a manang. A manang mansau. This is a powerful magician. He dresses like a woman and lives the life of a woman, even to taking a husband. This was not a spirit but a man who came to you. His power is strong, strong enough to cure even this kind of sickness."

She gazed at him. "What kind of sickness?"

"One placed in your path." She had been bewitched, he told her. He asked if any strange object had been left. She told him of the green stone and described it. It was the sign of a powerful witch, he said, to work with so little.

"How did he know to come? Who summoned him?"

"This manang cannot be summoned," he said. "This manang owes a debt only to another of his kind."

"But I never met such a creature before in my life!" Yet she had. Lying in the dark, she saw those yellow eyes in another corner of the universe, the smell of cologne on her fingertips, the nutlike head leaning into her skirts as she sat on the stair. She had forgotten this place, its protean possibilities. Things merged and divided here. Senses switched places. Smells seeped through the eyelids; colors through the fingertips; a clear blue penetrated the soles of her feet whenever she followed Jawing; words of love on Dewi's lips had smelled like warm bread.

"This kind of manang recaptures souls," the Moon said, as if speaking to a slow-witted child. "Your dreams are the adventures of your semanggat as it wanders through the world. Should it lose its way, you will become ill. Should it not return, you will die. It is sometimes enticed away."

*Close your eyes—a narrow skimming of the forearm. What do you feel?
A small lizard, the flat of a blade, a line of pollen dust from a giant
anther.*

The Ambun rapids guard the Apo Kayan, the highland plateau of central Borneo. From here, six great rivers flow to the Java, Celebes, and South China seas. He had spoken of this place many times over the years. His intention was to someday climb above these rapids and skirt the headwaters of all his rivers. It was the kind of thought he nurtured. She heard him speak of it now, to Si Tundo, the rain pelting the roof, the lanterns flickering. She heard and decided that she, too, would see this place, she would do this for herself. Not to skirt rivers but to gain altitude, to see from one point all the seas surrounding her, to glimpse the Chinese Widow before she left for good.

He was at last planning such a journey, and she asked if she might accompany him. She asked it coldly, yet their conversation was not unpleasant. He said it was to be a long trip and would involve unpleasant work, specifically in the Apo Sut.

"A mess. Reedy has dug himself an amazing hole. The idiot should have dealt with things eight months ago. Now we'll have not just reprimands, and fines of jars, but executions."

Her gaze was serene. He might have announced a seasonal dance, a minor feast. She suggested that she meet him afterward. She would like to see this country before returning home, she said, the rain rattling. She would like to go high enough to see Kinabalu.

"You would have to leave four or five weeks later." It was an absurd answer, but he was glad at this crack in their leaden universe. "Only as far as Merirai. I suppose Cakebread could take you up. I could meet you there. Si Tundo can prepare the boats, and Cakebread will haul you up."

He left with his boats in mid-January. Four weeks later, her small flotilla was ready. The number of provisioning chests seemed enormous and, for a moment, made her lose heart. Eighty men were given five bamboo sections each of preserved fowl, pig fat, honey, and three gantangs of rice. Two days before their departure, Cakebread came down with dysentery. He suggested Boyne take her in his stead. She declined. She said the Penglima Khaled could take her up. He insisted on Boyne, as much as he was able. She coldly prevailed. She passed downstream and out to sea on the fourth of February, gaining the mouth of the Rejang three days later, her mother's birthday.

The first two weeks were hell. She wondered why she had ever asked to do it. She was too tired, too old. A rash covered her buttocks from being always wet and the food did not agree. Her feces stank horribly, making her think her insides were rotting. Near Song, they had to wade to lighten the boats. She lifted her skirt on the bank and exposed black lumps up and down her calves and behind her knees. Jawing held a small lighted stick against the animals until they fell off, leaving thin rivulets of blood that streamed for hours.

After breakfast the next morning, he pounded a vine and rubbed the pulp on her feet and ankles and calves in hard, clean strokes. She wore the paste from then on, whenever portage was made through still water.

February 25, 1870
The river has entered a stand of trees at least two hundred feet tall. Breakfast: boiled rice, smoked deer meat, black tea, lemons.

"Lemons!" she said.

"The Rajah Ranee likes lemons." The tracker smiled.

"Thank you." How did he know this?

"You are welcome." He gazed into her eyes, and she realized suddenly there was no barrier between them. Perhaps there never had been. He had let her think it all these years out of necessity. But it had never existed. He settled on his haunches and watched as their two lead boats glided by. "I am half Malay, but in this it is true. The Malay do not know how to pull. They jerk their paddles."

March 6, 1870

Afloat, I now sit on a dry little platform with a trellis overhead to keep out the sun. I feel rather like an idol hauled to some feast. I sit like this and gaze at the back of the bowman for hours, plunging his paddle like a broad, glossy machine.

Greenwood fires are set each evening for the mosquitoes. Wild honey and water are used for the raw throat that results from the smoke. One never sets a sleeping platform under dead wood. One never sleeps on ground that is already clear, for it has most likely been cleared by pig and full of fleas. We gain altitude daily.

As they climbed, her rashes disappeared. She began to breath freely and deeply. She was sleeping well with the trick of the smoke. No one criticized her or looked dismayed at her ineptitude. She sat contentedly in the boat or on shore, waiting hungrily for them to prepare the one true meal of the day, able to understand the sparse conversation about her.

She learned in this way that the tracker had been to Siam. He knew much about the coast and the prevailing winds and some of the language. "How did you go to such a place, so far away?" she asked.

"I was a boy and went in the fleet of the Laksamana," he replied.

"The Lanun?" This shocked her.

"I wished to see the distant sea. The Dyak does not go there."

"Have you been to Kinabalu?"

"Yes."

"Will you take me?"

"If the Rajah wishes."

They killed gibbon from the boats. She was shown the different poisons used for each animal and the meticulous preparation of the meat necessary to avoid poisoning yourself. At Nangabadau they cut a path for her to bathe. At first she would not because the water was the color of dark tea, but he said no, this was very good water to bathe in.

March 10, 1870

We have passed out of the forest onto a plateau. The birds now are mostly birds of prey.

March 14, 1870

The terrain is steeper, with a new clarity and coldness to the water. We have heard the first rapids above us. Nights are cold. This morning we saw a Brahminy kite, a bird of great strength. It is said to be the animal incarnation of Lang Singalang Burong, the first great hunter of heads. We are now in a region of spirits, they say, where great good or great evil may occur. They speak very little.

March 21, 1870

It is raining. I find I forget, for long stretches of time, the meeting we are working toward at Merirai. I do not wonder where he is, how he is progressing, whether he has finished his business with the jars and executions. It seems my destination has changed. This is where I have been headed. I am here.

March 25, 1870

It rains in bullets. Before it is finished, the sun illuminates a far hill, steam rising, rain visible somewhere else. Weather crowds in on itself, one display rolling over the next. Rainbows are plentiful in the afternoon. The river now is shallow, fast and cold. Here, the bowman says, the dream wanderer and your physical self become one.

This morning we emerged onto a broad, sunlit savannah. The sea is a blue haze from east to west. Some of the men are uneasy. To suddenly be able to see so many miles makes them afraid. A dark column slanted across the nacreous light. "It is raining on the sea," one says. "Pansa antu," a spirit is passing.

There is a sweetness here, a clarity. Small footfalls follow mine. I turn and there is no one.

April 3, 1870

In the upper reaches of this stream, where the water turns in icy swirls, Jawing and I speak of cold. The qualities and shapes of cold, which to the Dyak is the embodiment of good. "I wish you cold and plenty," he will say politely. I explain, bored at first, then interested myself, for I have never thought about it. I describe ice, frost, hoarfrost, the myriad varieties of snow—light and airy, geometrically precise, heavy London slush, piercing sleet; the things men make of snow—houses, "men"—the eerie ping and crack of ice breaking up on northern rivers. His face wears an expression of wonderment and intelligence. I continue. I tell how people glide over it—the delicious feeling of finally telling this individual about something he does not know—on knives attached to their feet. I do not elaborate, I make it mysterious so he knows his place. I come from all these things of which you know nothing, which you will never see, I and my kind made the journey, we had the intelligence and courage to make it, I wish to say. I am small to take pleasure in this exercise.

"I have seen snow," he says when I am finished, and I know, as unlikely as this is, it is probably true. We are to rendezvous at Meri-rai in six days.

It rained steadily for the next five days, and they hove to. On the sixth day, it stopped for several hours but stayed overcast. They began to pole upstream once more. Rain began again at midday, but they kept on the river. At four o'clock, a whistling filled the air, a high-pitched hiss above the rain. The tracker's eyes met his stern man's.

Both men shouted, and all six boats pulled powerfully for shore. Within seconds, the hiss became a shriek, electrifying the air.

"What is it?" she cried. They were in the water before they beached, hands brutally yanking at her, pushing her up the slope. The roar was now so intense it sucked in the air around them. She stood on the bank and looked upstream as a monstrous wall of water swung around the upper bend and raged down, sweeping five feet below her feet, the speed so unearthly, it seemed to be surging by in another world. Two men clutching a gunwale were plucked away. A pig sped past. The ground began to soften and someone pulled her, handing her man-to-man upward, heaving her viciously onto higher ground.

She sat in soft mud for hours, her bare knees two skulls in the black ooze, the rain hitting her so hard she expected to see blood on her skin. Twice something moved beneath her. Her whole body was trembling. For a long time, she could see no one and distinguish no voices above the rain and river. She tried to cry out, but her jaw was clenched shut.

She was aware of increasing cold and darkness. In pitch blackness, she was once again pulled by her arms and hauled upward. Through flashes of lightning she could make out others scrambling up, water pulling earth and trees away. She sat for an eternity on this new ground, wet and frozen. It seemed Jawing came toward her but passed by, leaving her. She sank on her side and began a strange animal keening. She dreamed, in blackness, she was again being pulled, her bones parting, someone enraged, shouting, prodding, then easing her down in all her sodden tonnage. The roar continued but the beating on her skin had stopped. She was inside a little closet, the walls pulled and tightened from without. She folded over, her teeth chattering into a comical life of their own. How odd to die here of cold. If she could have unclenched her jaw, she would have laughed.

She did not know how long she sat in frozen misery. Slowly, from far away, a distant, small point of heat entered her back. It seeped down her arms, her legs. Hands raked the soaked garments from her, pushing them steadily down, a flat chest against her back, hands rubbing her arms, her legs, flooding her with warmth. Her jaw slid open. The roar of the river was there, but the rain had stopped and her jaw could move. After a while, she turned into the warmth, fire and sadness leaking through those hands, flowing wherever she wished, clean, insistent, and always with an overlaying sadness. This, she thought, is the beautiful ship. The beautiful ship in the roads before the boys died. The beautiful ship and Dewi singing in the bamboo and Doherty in the sunlit door with his rifle. All clean, good things merged in this man who held her, fire and sadness leaking through his hands. In the gray light, Jawing's hair seemed white.

By dawn, the rain had stopped. The flood lasted for another two hours and then went down as rapidly as it had risen, leaving an ocean of mud and many snakes. "What will we do?" she asked him.

"We will go back," he said, not looking at her. "In three days we can be at Nanga Tiga. We will send two men overland to Merirai to let them know. You may forget this place."

"I will not forget," she said.

"Then I am a dead man," he said in Malay.

All but two of the boats had been lost. She understood his pain in losing these boats, and also understood that if Cakebread had brought them up, one of their most senior, competent men, they would all be drowned. The river was filled with debris, the water muddy so that submerged rocks could not be seen. They stayed close to shore, the two remaining boats holding a slow glide, then dropping, paddles plunging and she sitting forward, feeling she could sleep like this, she could sleep, eat, and make love, while traveling like this.

At Nanga Tiga, a place of many nets and cooking-oil smells, she washed her hair and was given a sarong. He held the boat by the stern. When she placed a hand on his shoulder to climb in, he stiffened. She saw him then separate, a density forming between them. She saw the long flow of water that would carry them down, safely, everything now safe, deposited finally on that quay, opposite the stone wharves and evenly cut lalang grass. I am a woman, she thought, who has lived through the best moment of her life, and it is over.

"Chinese do not travel this way"—the Nakodah Dullah squinted through the shutter of his godown—"alone and old." He watched the Teo Chew crab his way slowly down the gangplank of the *Hindoo Queen,* the late monsoon gusts lifting his black coat. Dullah sipped his tea and peered more closely. He called a boy and secured a tail to the visitor, then dropped the shutter.

The Teo Chew, looking neither left nor right, proceeded over the stone quay and up Blue Lotus Lane like someone who had lived in the place all his life. That week, he visited certain nakodahs' establishments. In the following two months, he visited the forts at Lingga, the Baram and the Rejang, and the gold mining kongsi at Bau. He visited each humbly, through a kebun's door or cookhouse flap. In the district forts he spoke with no one of importance. Except at Bau. At Bau, the towkays touched their heads to the ground before him. The master of Nan Yang's Tien Ti Hueh, the great triad beyond the mainland, was a frail man with delicate health, yet he carried his own messages. It was his hand, in Macao, that had organized the three massive Chinese emigrations to Borneo, seeding each with loyal members of the Hueh. He was to board a junk eight weeks later at

Santubong and sail for Brunei. He left the message of patience, of the need to wait, to gain strength. In the meantime, they must conduct business quietly and lawfully.

The Tien Ti Hueh was a wondrous brotherhood. Members who were loyal were cared for unstintingly. The Hueh gave generous aid to the family of a dead member, providing for all its needs, watching over the growth and virtue of its children. If a member committed a crime, he was hidden, given legal assistance, and provided with false witnesses. If imprisoned, everything possible was done for his comfort. Another code governed offenses. An ear was removed for lack of fortitude, a hand for a running mouth. If a member revealed secrets or committed an offense meriting death, the sentence was carried out by fellow members. The alienation of the Chinese—due to their appearance, their language, and their economic prowess—made invisible strength essential. The Hueh had been originally formed to overthrow the Manchus on the mainland. Yet it had become a powerful force in the effort to drive Europeans out of China and had grown amazingly powerful in Nan Yang, Chinese settlements beyond the sea. Branches of the secret society occurred everywhere there was a concentration of Chinese. Its presence meant instant corruption of established authority.

Barr knew the Hueh and knew there was no evidence of it in his territory. He would have destroyed any sign of it. Yet he knew you could be an honorable Chinese and still be Tien Ti Hueh.

The only sign of the Teo Chew's visit had been a few Chinese murders: a body in Banting, one in Batu Kawa, three in Seratok. This worried some Europeans, signaling that white deaths would follow. Yet the only European death occurring that winter was Semple's.

On the eve of Ramadan, Semple dined at the astana with Dolan and a missionary from Sumatra. He had not been invited, but his wife was in Santubong, and he was a man who felt uncomfortable in his own company for any length of time. He felt, in any case, the category of guest should have included him. He paid a complimentary visit near dinner. The evening stiffened around him. He stayed until cigars, at which point he left. He did not smoke.

Semple died that night, slipping on a mossy plinth in his wife's garden, hitting his head on the side of a great pot of tubers and knocking himself out, drowning in a shallow catch basin.

"The bastard was niggardly even in death," Barr remarked. That a presence which could not be dislodged over decades by any method had been eliminated by a slippery plinth and three inches of larva-infested water was enough to restore faith in Providence.

Delia Semple grieved. It was she who found him, and she could not believe for several seconds that the inert, sodden mass was her husband. She nudged him sharply with her foot, squatted, took up the chin, and let out a wail.

Two weeks later, she heaved herself down Dhoby Ghat Lane, past the Hokkien sweet stand and the Thaipusam wreath seller. She turned into an alley off Jalan Singh and disappeared in a milky cloud. Chandra Das' workshop was always half buried in stone dust. The carving was ready, a thick brick set off in one corner of the yard. She inspected it approvingly, reading the verse that he, Semple, had selected for his epitaph ten years earlier.

> "For the tumpet will sound,
> and the dead will be raised imperishable"
> 1 Corinthians 15:32

She blinked and read it again. "Not *tumpet,* you fool! *Trumpet!*"

" 'Tumpet' is what it is saying on the paper, Memsahib," Devi Chandra Das replied, his head wobbling with shy indignance. He had carved the thing for her in cheap, rotting stone and even then doubted there would be any profit from what this fat white bitch would give him, embellishing it, at her command, with a winged skull, foliate borders, gourds, figs, and flowers, so that it resembled, more than anything else, one of her hideous vegetable carvings.

"So it does," she said, holding the filthy piece of paper in wonder. "Well, it's bloody wrong." She sighed and sat down. She grimaced, smelling the Indian's grease, then slowly, through the powdery haze, a small smile stretched her lips. "Ah, well, never mind, Chandra. Leave it. I will deduct forty rupiahs, but you may leave it." She rose and walked to the gate, stopping to admire the wild banana that had fused itself to the rust. The root seller's booth seemed particularly fragrant as she passed. At the corner of the Parsee lodge, she laughed outright. She could see him turning white. It delighted her the more she thought of the punctilious fool stretched beneath this "mishap" for all eternity. Yet by the time she regained their bungalow, tears blinded the way. "Bloody little bloodless corpse," she sneered, "to hell with you." She bellowed for Lo Quat to take her parcels, but shoved him away when he offered some physical solace. In truth, her own nature mystified her more than anyone's.

Dullah was puzzled that the Teo Chew had not departed on the packet or on any regular vessel. Both the man and a reliable tail had vanished. He asked Lavransson where the Chinese had first embarked, but Lavransson could not remember. Dullah was used to the breed. He mentioned a new consignment of gin. He really couldn't remember, Lavransson said then, sadly, but Dullah was welcome to ask the crew. This man was an enigma, a white man incapable of setting a few pins in his own favor. A case of Bombay Mata traveled aboard anyway, a tribute to the smaller human mysteries.

The Swede always dined at the astana the second night he was in. By the second night he was more or less presentable. He had a face hewn by a chisel and childlike blue eyes. The Ranee liked him, not for his society, for he was absurdly shy. She liked him because he resurrected, in the occasional tender, helpless glance across her table, her father. Her father had been shy and, like the sailor, found solace not in the company of humans but animals. Lavransson usually had some small menagerie aboard. He had for many years a vervet monkey, a black-tempered, ugly creature who nevertheless always seemed "busy," rolling a hawser and catching a line more efficiently than a Siti loader. When the thing drowned, he was disconsolate. The vessel, too, seemed off, nothing wrong but nothing perfectly right about her, hitting a pier stanchion too roughly, swinging out and then smacking back without some fairy line thrown aft. He also talked to fish. He ventriloquized them when lonely. "With that thrashing screw," he complained, for the line had switched, after twenty years, to steam, "no one comes. I once had, off Kerimun, a whale stay with us four days, and all the pretty flying fish and bonito and skates at night. No more." He kept a hubble-bubble in his cabin, and half a Bible, the other half split off as payment in a game of whist in the Dampier Strait.

Lavransson would take her to Singapore. Barr had wished to escort her himself, had pressed her, but she said she preferred the packet. It was there, turned about and ready for the outward journey. Then, too, its wide beam afforded protection against seasickness, and she more prone to nausea now.

When she had told him, his face had changed. It became lighter, as if youth touched his shoulder. "It's best that you be in England for this child," he said, before she asked. "It's best not to delay."

The morning she left, a gray, erect figure stood on the veranda in a straw kiss-me-not. The eyes looked at her squarely from within the deep brim, almost crossing, and she again felt the queer strength of this creature. "He's never written," Cates said. "Please find out what you can for me, Madam. Her married name would be Downs. Mrs. Gerald Downs, a navy boilerman. A place in Hampstead, I think. I've written to him, but there's never been anything back. The child can write."

Lavransson, staying painfully sober for the four-day journey, escorted her to the P & O agent himself. He wore a little blue silk tie, which he tied square under his chin, and held on to her hand as if she were a child.

She traveled as a somnambulist. She had not planned to return, and there was nothing and no one toward whom she traveled. She crossed the endless water as if slipping downhill, rounding Africa without violence, losing the southern stars without ever looking up. She entered the English autumn dazed, gazing at things as she had gazed at them as a child: a storefront, a medical bag, a pair of lips.

She had seduced him. She had walked in and stood behind him as he sat in a chair, placing her hand on the long slope of shoulder, the feel of the muscle strange under the cloth. He looked up, his eyes confused, then slowly filling, as from some deep well, with hope. It was the last thing she expected to see. The heavy arm slowly surrounded her buttocks. It wasn't disgusting. It happened as she wished, in daylight, the nets piled in a cloud, in the arms of an old man. In the weeks that followed, he came to her repeatedly. She felt loathesome.

A month before the birth, she dreamed it was born black and immediately lifted away from her. A figure carried it into a grove of trees, a smooth, languid figure that did not look back.

The twelve moon fasts. Hari Raya Puasa, Hari Raya Haji. Boxing Day. Peg summoned Edmonds, Spaulding's successor. "Sweetest." Water gushed warmly in the bed. The room was cluttered with stupid objects—silver frames, silhouettes, sconces, figurines, all whispering in some soft language. It did not surprise her. The world was a collection of spells, dictating the color of skin, the one who would die next, the one who would be born. Her husband, Lytton, even Fitzhugh took pride in ordering it, improving it. They even believed they appreciated it, its beauty, its poetry and songs. There were no poetry and songs, only incantations.

She was following someone. Wide boulevards of air opened where he stepped. She had never felt as safe in her life as following that blue footprint, slipping into that corridor of air. The pain resumed in racking crescendos. By midnight, the bloody, golden head of her son emerged, an extremity of relief and guilt flooding her being.

She had forced herself on him. She feared she carried a child from Ambun. She had in no way been certain and drove the mounting hysteria away, the possibility of "doing something" away, by creating another possibility. She was a coward, and it was the only way she could carry this child beyond the point when nothing could be done, this last child. Her thinking had been circuitous and mad, and because of it she had the child.

He sent an affectionate letter. Included was a packet of Sarawak diamonds, which fell in a small, hard shower over her lap. She was not meant to have them set, she knew, but to sell them to live on. They were flawed and she would have to implement her income once again with her own money. There was little of it left.

She knew she would not go back. She had one healthy child to show for half a lifetime, and she would keep him. She did not write this, but over the next ten months the understanding of it was transmitted.

The child was robust, no charms hanging from its crib, no bone rattles, but cream wool and Lyle biscuits. She sent him frequent news of the boy, and he responded with thanks. He began with tender inquiries, then usually some sort of news. Word of a new annexation; a fort on the Suai; once, a description of a clearing leveled next to the recreation club, plans ordered and many false starts for Major Wingfield's sphairistike and a precise description of how it was played with a net and paddles and balls. In the second year there was a photograph of himself standing with one hand on the back of a chair—Metz having materialized in possession of Daguerre's black box, a member of a new tribe overrunning the earth, posing Dyaks, Cheyennes, and Maoris against cardboard landscapes—the dazed, handsome face of a twenty-year-old peering through a fierce, sixty-five-year-old ruination. Here, he related something odd; it made her wonder, a thing that would normally not interest him or would elicit, at best, derision. *In the silver plates of certain people, Metz claims to have seen a luminous halo that, as they age and are photographed repeatedly, becomes more intense, heralding, he believes, a new stage of existence.* He had sent the photo, revitalizing all her aversion and queer love.

During that first year, she had not forgotten Cates. There was no Gerald Downs or his family in Hampstead, and she had checked in a widening circle of schools and institutions for Philip Downs and Philip Collins and Philip Doherty. She traced the names, common ones, to a series of dead ends, and then, the following autumn, to a public orphanage, where the records showed a Philip Collins, born of a Leonard and Rose Collins in Madras, placed there by a female relative, had died of diphtheria two years previous. He had been eleven. She found she could not write it. Half a year went by, with two letters from Cates herself, and still she could not.

Dear Emma, she finally began on St. Crispin's day, *I'm sorry I haven't written, but have had no news until now. I've traced your little man. He's gone off to America. A bright, brawny lad, they say, come into his flesh, apprenticed to—*the sharp, earnest face peered out at her from its absurd bucket—*a milliner.*

The little steamer with his ensign flying at the main pitched in the crowded waters. She remembered stooping and adjusting those blue bars in another lifetime, and his sudden flash of pleasure. He had asked repeatedly, and she finally agreed to return with the child in his third year, but briefly. She had acquiesced. The daguerreotype, its awful finiteness, frightened her. He must at least meet this child.

He had on board a small cart for the boy, and he looked with pleasure as he picked up the string and tore around with it. Rain broke through, and he called to the child and steered her under the canvas. She stood in the damp scent of him, unable to believe they had journeyed round the solar system apart and found themselves together once again, the encroaching hours and days inundating her, the place already playing its soothsaying tricks. The squall would accompany them across, sunlight breaking through near the estuary, the river halfway up filled with prahus. Among those on shore there would be chiefs of the Baram, Hogg's latest annexation, in jackets of leaf monkey and cloud leopard. She would be formally told of those who had died and those who had been born in her absence.

The Datin Aisha has died and the Datu Patinggi, now tooth-
less, has a new young wife. Raseh also is dead, found in his shed.

The Orang Kaya di Gadong had died, she was told. And what of
Cates? Her bungalow was empty, the musty air reverberating with
the heartbeats of the old maid and the child. They had grabbed
for happiness, foolishly, ineptly, wholly, and wrested it from some
abyss. There was a light crooning in the walls. She had gone, they
said, to a family with three small daughters in Penang, to work at
the Capuchin hospital in Batavia, to England, no one was quite
sure. Cates had disappeared over the edge of the universe with her
casket and wool.

She asked the new Resident of the First Division, a pompous, very
white youth, of the Orang Kaya's sons and was told they had migrated
to the Kalaka estuary. She asked after the Penglima Khaled.

"Nipped off. These mixed breeds always show their true colors."

June 30, 1874

This week I visited the graves. Dewi's, Unggat's, Raseh's, the
Dohertys', these last not graves but markers in the churchyard. It is
not quite believable that those two bright spirits lie underground. I
sat by Aisha's grave, a modest ironwood marker, for they say the
new wife is jealous even of ghosts.

The astana had been whitewashed and had a new portico on the
west side with some foreign red tiles. The house seemed benevolently
disposed toward her, free of malevolent shadows. They said the
woman was dead.

July 1, 1874

He seems happy we've come, but somewhat afraid of the child,
afraid to draw that awful cheek against the smooth one, yet enor-
mously pleased with the screeches and hoots of a three-year-old son.
You would still find him overbearing—

She stopped, pen poised, and stared at the words. She lifted her eyes. She could understand finally how one continued letters beyond the death of their recipient, for this she now saw was not a diary, not a series of remarks or an intimate history, but a letter. Her diary for the rest of her life would be one long letter to her mother.

She rose with the lap desk, for she could no longer see. The first night breezes blew. She lifted her head to breathe in the scent, the trees feathered over, and she knew she was no longer alone. He was there in the shadows, black hair gleaming, arms hanging loose.

"Makan angin?" A creature of rare radiance. His sleeping body, his corpse perhaps, lay somewhere in the Kalaka estuary, but his semanggat was with her; they had never taken trouble with distance and time, devices of her kind, entering the garden with the serpent. She wished to embrace him and felt herself embraced, deeply, her breath, her pulse, shared with another more present than herself. The breeze rose, her eyes flickered, and there was no one.

Inside, her husband sat as one reading. She saw herself move across the Sarouk and stoop to that bent head. She saw herself do this, but her hands took up a lamp, and she climbed the stairs.

Hogg came down that summer. He came to discuss a change in the territorial relationship between the two newest divisions. On the nights he dined with them, though little outright was said, she could see responsibility shifting into the hands of this man. She was grateful to him. Because of him, the boy would be free. She saw the child closing the yellow payong and soaring above the morass of brown rivers.

She no longer napped in the afternoons, but dozed in a chair. At ten to six she opened an eye and caught sight of a turbaned little specter flashing by, followed, in a few moments, by the dinner gong. The quick and the dead crossed paths smoothly in this house. The hurricane lamps were lit, bats darted, and time, for a breath, seemed never to have advanced.

She left as planned, two days after the boy's fourth birthday, a time of gaudy celebration and noise, celebrated three years in a row without his presence. She left on an overcast morning with much ceremony, feeling again, in every face, every familiar article, a sense of lastness. The last glint of the maranti floors, the last footfall on a dried mud path, the last time she would stand at this green, steaming point in the universe. Her eyes searched for that dark figure in the leaves and did not find it.

She was leaving an old man in her wake. On several occasions she detected a thickness in the air about him, the smell of disaster. There was no reason for it. The territory, even the new annexations, were secure. Prosperity seemed modestly afoot, still riding the tails of the Chinese but welcome nevertheless. Yet, embracing him, she felt the film of it beneath her fingers.

The first confirmation came eight months later in the form of a letter. Bloch had proposed floating a second public company in which they would split shares. The idea was to buy the raj, leaving him to administer it on a profit-sharing basis. The idea was to replace him.

"Ah, the game, the game." Kilcane laughed when he heard of it. "We played it in Bwunei, and they continue it on Thweadneedle Stweet." Bloch had never been able to secure the backing of any respectable merchant house, the enterprise too risk-laden, becoming more so with time and the uncertainty of profits. While Chinese revenues kept things afloat locally, the Borneo Company was out of capital. As an alternative, Bloch had leased antimony, diamond, and coal mines to traders who themselves had insufficient capital to work them. It was the end.

Barr put down the letter and took up his pen. He brought an action in the Court of the Queen's Bench to vacate the charter. It left him ruined. Bloch was outraged, claiming the action was precipitous. Barr ignored his entreaties and threats. Nature, as is her wont, chose to fall in with the downward plunge. Incipient veins of gold dried up; coal and antimony seams worked themselves out in brilliant synchrony. Over the ensuing two years, experimental plantations were abandoned one by one—the areas selected too low for coffee, too high for sugar, too wet for tea. He sat over his ledgers with Biverts and marveled that, after thirty years, bezoar stones contributed by monkeys still provided more profit than timber, which he found he could not bring down in any quantity through the mangroves, or sago, which fermented in his little train, stalled in all its Teutonic perfection on one of the many sections of rotted-out track.

He did not write to her of these things. It was Kilcane who finally wrote. She found it strange to read the words, free of impediment, as if a more graceful creature had been hiding all this time beneath the lisp and tick. His message was not to be ignored. The man rarely delivered bad news. He wrote to her again when the second and worse blow, one in which he had a heavy hand, descended.

IV

Jahanam

It is a place of gardens, growing things unheard of east of the Arabian Sea, one seaside yard completely encircled in a hedge of holly; a place strangely infused with sixteenth-century courtesy; a place of well-brought-up children. It flies no flag and welcomes anything afloat. It is kept in supreme readiness, a place of pungent smells when its own fleets are sighted. They are superb cooks, superb storytellers. Off the sea, there is no treachery in them.

The P & O hotel in Penang served a little cream cake in the shape of a teat, and Kilcane, every two years or so, managed to find himself on the blue mosaic terrace overlooking the great Strait with a plate of these wonders and a bottle of champagne. Three times he invited his friend to perch on this pinnacle and was accepted twice. He introduced him, during these holidays, to cashmere socks, ridiculous, one would think in the tropics, yet keeping the feet cooler than silk; to the subtleties of silat; to the amazing torpor of Penang's temple snakes, the animals said to be drowsy from incense but Kilcane believing they were simply good-natured; and to the pretty Lili Bakra Hotel on Thaw Hill, where seven English ladies educated their clientele in the most imaginative cunnilinguistics east of Cairo. Once or twice the man seemed to flag, gazing for long moments at a blank tablecloth or a moving carriage wheel, but then regaining himself, the copper eyes snapping, the old glitter back. These years, Barr saw, had been wearing.

The P & O was a lifelong favorite. Kilcane loved their large cool stengahs, their teats and champagne, their curry cakes, and the ubiquitous white-capped "boys." The two were in mufti, rubber planters with something a little off about them. As in the past, the Idea was dragged into the light. Fleets from Marudu Bay, Lanun in league with sea Dyaks, had marauded the main sea corridors for decades while keeping clear of his estuaries. In the last seven years, exceptions had increased. A joint strike against them had been repeatedly examined and always abandoned as too politically dangerous. This time, they gazed off in silence. The Chinese had the English on the run in Canton. That winter Kilcane would be called north, perhaps for good. And Barr had precious little else to occupy him, with the Borneo Company in ruins.

The timing, in fact, was remarkable. A sizable fleet had been growing for months in the north Bornean bay, and Kilcane's entire force for the Straits settlements was just then at Penang for practice maneuvers. They finished their cakes, and their communication lapsed into a peculiar jigging code, covering napkins and tablecloth and tracts of the air with cartoon formations, wind triangles, tide tables, age and infirmity sloughing away as they scribbled.

The largest English squadron ever to enter those waters gathered off his Muaratebas estuary that September. The *Carolina* joined the steamers *Semiramis, Dido,* and *June Bug,* two paddle-box boats, two cutters, a steam tender, the frigate *Harlequin,* and three thousand men in two hundred war prahus.

Barr's journal for this campaign consisted of two entries.

September 10, 1875

Started in evening on swift tide. Gongs mark hours on some boats. Cries of many seabirds passing Seboyau.

September 13, 1875

Dawn. Pointing northeast, a spyboat pulling past, gliding silently with thirty close paddles. Two heavy prahus hold the rear, sweeping for stragglers. We are to cut wood for the steamers at the Baram.

On the twentieth of September, a massive fleet passed out of Marudu Bay bearing toward Sambas. It was intercepted in the night off a narrow spit of land. All was black until near midnight, when the moon emerged. Barr's prahus struck their sails and masts to avoid being seen above the spit, called Batang Maru. They lay inland of it, while Kilcane waited on the far side, his boats invisible against the rise. They could not see each other and planned to communicate by rockets. Once having surprised the fleet, Kilcane would set up a flare and drive them toward Barr on the other side. It was a dangerous plan, for it wagered everything on a single surprise and had five or six things that could go wrong. Yet it all went right. Around two in the morning, an endless dark line of war prahus began to pass the entrance to the river, saw Barr's steamers, and swung round toward the open sea, only to find Kilcane's ships emerging from the outer side. There was dead silence, hundreds of prahus riding the swell, then thousands of voices burst into a cry of defiance, borne on the wind. Four hours of heavy fire ensued before the steamers could close in to ram them in the shoals. By the next morning, the Marudu fleet was in wreckage and four thousand men were dead. Almost every well-known Malay and Dyak pirate leader had been present at Batang Maru. Of those who succeeded in running their boats ashore, two thousand died of their wounds in the forest. Kilcane had a picnic basket carried to the beach, where he sat on a wicker chaise and opened his books.

After Batang Maru, no pirate fleet went to sea from that coast for twenty years. It was considered a brilliant naval maneuver. Yet it was more. It was a brilliant financial move for Kilcane. It was common knowedge that in the next parliamentary session the act granting blackbirding bounty to Her Majesty's seamen was to be amended. Batang Maru slipped in under the wire.

Bloch somehow got wind of events ten thousand miles away. He was furious at losing decades of work in Borneo and immediately instigated an investigation by the Admiralty Court, accusing Barr of using Her Majesty's ships to slaughter thousands of innocent aborigines. The outcry was echoed by Mace in Singapore, who gave it continuous press, bolstering his case by printing interviews with European traders whom Barr had thrown out of his territory over the years. *The Straits Times* insisted that the victims were not pirates but innocent natives massacred for the pirate head tax.

The fact remained that Kilcane was thirty thousand pounds richer and thousands of natives were dead. He had missed the repeal of the amendment by twenty days. He sat on the beach with his hamper and his ledger, adding dead and captured piratical persons, rising out of debt like the phoenix.

On the twenty-second of February, a lunatic entered the Singapore roads. Roger Bright, a government agent, was appointed by the Advocate General in Calcutta to conduct a court of inquiry. There was a dearth of civil servants that year due to plague, and Bright, with two mental crises rising from fever in his past, alone could be spared. On arriving, he found that no dispatch or documents had come from the Home Authorities. The man's rage at being transported thousands of miles and then not having the necessary papers to begin his work fell on his myopic assistant, a Mr. Bliss. Over months of waiting for these documents, Bright lost what hold he had on mental health. He developed the habit of rubbing his chin and the backs of his hands raw, resembling someone in the first stages of skin rot.

Yet when the papers arrived and the court convened, it was Barr, with his ravaged face and fierce expression, who looked the madman. When confronted with Bloch's allegations, he said he was not interested in his ex-agent's accusations. He said no more, driving Bright to the edge.

After each morning session, he returned to his hotel on Orchard Road. He would not stay with friends, the taint of the thing too strong. Sitting in the small enclosed garden, he would attempt to reconstruct the morning. Staring at an arm of bougainvillea, at two children playing in a puddle, he wondered whether he was an avaricious mass murderer. He longed with strange intensity for his wife.

Mace's testimony attempted to place the proceedings in historical perspective. "Sir Barr seized upon a territory as large as Yorkshire by murdering and driving out the natives, and then, over three decades, regularly used our fleet to massacre them." *The Straits Times* maintained that the natives slaughtered at Batang Maru were not pirates, and this "cruel butchery of innocents could not go unpunished." The debate reached the House of Commons.

He found himself, one afternoon, sitting in the Tanglin Club holding a cup rimmed with rosebuds. A Miss Jocelyn Beale and Lady Jane Beckwith of the Aborigines Society had invited him to tea. They sat on either side with earnest expressions. Their organization was pointless, they said, if occurrences like Batang Maru went unrebuked. While they were certain he personally had nothing to do with the unfortunate campaign, they were confident he would redress it.

"We cannot expect a sympathetic ear from the world if we are silent spectators of such atrocities," Miss Beale said. He rose in the middle of Lady Beckwith's confirmation and walked away, leaving them with the understanding that he had lost his mind.

It was an election year in England, and Borneo proved a useful issue. It was a long way off and nobody knew anything about it. "Exploitation of natives" and "waste of public funds" were forceful topics. The Chinese followed with keen interest. Hueh taels reached elements in London, a measure of the silver actually finding its way to Spottiswode and Bloch. With universal condemnation rising, they grew bold. Fifty-three Chinese merchants in Singapore signed a letter denying the existence of piracy in Bornean waters. Lavransson too signed, being told the thing was helpful to Barr. When he found it was not, he desperately tried to have his name removed, actually showing up at the proceedings. "I'm sorry, Rajah," he said miserably. "I thought in this thick skull I was helping you by scribbling my name."

"I know where thy heart lies." Barr pressed the bony shoulder and moved on. He walked in a miasmic fog, having long since given up sleep.

There were few witnesses to support him and handfuls to pull him down. It was remarkable to him how many people he had managed to offend or inspire downright hatred in over the years, not just dubious traders he had thrown out of his territory but the Maces and Miss Beales of the planet. Yet the single testimony that did him the most harm came from an unexpected quarter. He had not known Kilcane was in port until he glanced across the green expanse of padang in the second week and recognized the peculiar figure, the distinctive walk. They had not summoned him; it was prudent to establish Barr's guilt before attacking this power, yet he came.

Kilcane was his undoing. With every opportunity to say the right thing, the saving thing, the man said the wrong thing. Barr could not understand it. There were a few things at Batang Maru, and after, which had not been right. It was true that at sea one's mental state could be masked by a deeply familiar world. In this place, his mind had no such props. The run-on style of speech was still there, but while it had always been the signature of a dazzling intellectual agility, it now seemed something else. Barr, sitting in that crowded, fly-blown room, painfully came to the realization that this marvelous individual, this man who had repeatedly heartened him and swept his coasts until he could stand on his own feet, this friend who had pulled him from death, was a senile wreck.

At odd moments, Kilcane seemed to show some vague comprehension of the damage he was doing and a wave of wretchedness passed over his features. Barr wished to rush to him then, to take him by the shoulder and lead him away.

Afterward, walking aimlessly through the steam of the padang at noon, everything seemed askew. An amah called to her small charges in a voice that seemed infused with hatred. An old woman selling moon cakes held up a tray of pink poison. It was like the onset of some fevers. Squinting into the glare, he noticed a boy sitting spread-legged on a far bench, a boy of fourteen or fifteen with a wizened face. Looking closer, he saw it was Kilcane. He feared the man was devastated. He wasn't. He was happy to see him. In the hour of conversation that followed, bits of perspicacity sprung bright and hard out of that mouth, putting the average brain to shame. He waxed into remembrances, diamond-clear on events and dates.

"Ah, there were sweet times." He smiled. "There were my commands, the first, of course, the sweetest. My Esther when she was young, before she spawned that pack of bitches. There was my nonya out at Changi." Here a look of desolation came into his eye. "There were our own wiping times in those jungles of yours. Oh, my dear." Barr took his arm.

Van Lutyens sent Wenderholt, his medical officer, to testify. The man stated that every Dutch official in Borneo knew these people were pirates whose atrocities were well documented. Wenderholt was credible, but he was Dutch. No one believed a Dutchman, especially one who would testify for an Englishman. Yet his testimony could not be completely ignored.

Brunei remained silent, lending neither support nor denial to the accusations. The balance was finally upset from an unexpected quarter. One broiling morning an old Arab struggled into the box. The body was all bone and dust, yet the voice held such authority that, within seconds, only the flies could be heard. The man said that several of those natives killed by Barr and Kilcane were his own people, who had sworn fealty to him for decades. They were pirates by profession, he said. No one breathed. This man himself was a well-known pirate.

When Barr tried to locate him after the morning session, he had melted into the air. When he inquired, he was told the Sharif Jaffar lived with a granddaughter on the Bukit Timah road.

The old murderer kept him waiting in the sun for half an hour and then waved him under an awning and offered him a filthy mat. Barr sat down graciously and, after some conversation, asked why he had supported him.

"Out of perversity." Jaffar's gaze grazed his head. He was virtually blind. "I liked none of you, but I disliked you the least."

The man's testimony did not have a decisive effect, but the energy of the thing was stalled. People began to drift away. Barr was temporarily dismissed. "Stay, sir, where we can find you." Bright stabbed a raw finger at him.

· · ·

She had followed the proceedings in England, five months tortuously behind events. It tore at her that he fought alone. She saw him before them, outraged and sick while they pecked him to death. He'd step forth in his quixotic bravery, his murderous ignorance, his enduring naïveté; he'd step forth from his museum, his pathetic mines, his bandstand, his caper bushes, his toon trees and experimental tragacanths, his Hochstrasse steam engine. Can you love or hate or trust or distrust or admire or abhor such a man? Yes, she thought, gazing over frozen fields, all of that. She loved him again with that queer love, virtually undetectable when close to him, swelling insanely when she put time and distance between them. She sometimes hoped, in a dark corner of herself, he would die out there, the two of them never again near enough to sink into that truculent coldness. The one man who could help him, she knew, who comprehended the nature of these people better than any other and could transmit it to an English court, would never be asked to do so. He would keep Hogg out of it, lest he too be discredited and the territory lost to the boy. He did keep Hogg out of it. Yet it was Hogg who saved him.

He did not wait where they could find him, but left on the tide. "I am going home," he said to the little waterman, who didn't know who he was and understood no English.

Purdy, an agent sent by Bloch under the guise of investigating mineral deposits for the defunct Borneo Company, had crossed to Borneo a month before in a nakodah prahu. He was accompanied by Bliss, Bright's assistant, who was charged with conducting a first-hand investigation on behalf of the court. The prahu was sunk by natives off Tanjong Datu, a particularly vicious region; seventeen heads were taken, one found hanging six weeks later in a Sadong longhouse by a Chinese wholesaler of bêche-de-mère, its gold-rimmed spectacles attached. Hogg advised him of the murders when he returned. The news elated him.

"But *you* sent them there!" he said suddenly, darkening. It was true. Purdy had approached a coastal chief in Hogg's division for geographical advice. Nothing happened in his division without his direct hand.

"No." Hogg considered. "I gave them leave. It's different." It was the only time in both their lives that this man made him laugh.

The court of inquiry exonerated him at the end of summer. The tumult in England took longer to abate and, in the end, resulted in all naval assistance being permanently withdrawn, something the Chinese had awaited for two decades. The verdict did little for him, guilt and innocence revolving smoothly in a new round of malarial dreams.

Sailing from Canton due south by riding on the north wind in the winter for half a month, one reaches Ling-Ya-Men and in another five days enters San-Fo-Ch'i.

Tao Yi Tsa Tchich, A.D. 1225

When Chan Kho spoke of the great junks, the great ships that sailed through his nights, the junks that were no more, whose rudders weighed nine tons and plowed south from Canton, the young man yawned.

The towkay stretched a wire over each ear, adjusted his lenses, and the young man, this firstborn wedge of fat, settled sullenly on his buttocks. Admiral Liu's rudder gave the old Chinaman more pleasure than anything in life. The glory of the past and the degradation of the present struck him as a private failing. The possibility of correcting it in his lifetime gave him his purest hope. It was the Chinese who kept the raj afloat through its pitiful crises, with their never-ending labor, their revenues. Always, the enterprise most deeply gouged was opium. They had worked hard to open new smuggling routes and now were forced to pay for government balls, whether they accepted delivery or not. Directives from the mainland and Singapore had always counseled patience, forbearance. Recently, there had been no mention of these virtues.

In September, along with an increase in lethargy and a lull in inland hostilities, came another seasonal change. Chinese were being murdered over a wide range of territory. Bodies were found in the plantation highlands, in the ports of Selantik and Banjermasin, in the gold-panning rivers, washed up with the bore or down with the ebb. They were mostly adult males and had no marks of the Dyak.

Smythe of the gold-panning Oya was the first to report. "Monkey wars. The buggers do it from time to time. Clears the air."

Cakebread at Tegora did not concur. "It's a Hong thing," he said. "A purge. Something is up."

Barr was certain the Hueh held no sway on his rivers, yet he could not place his finger on the source of this butchery. He knew, as did they all, that a sure sign of the start of activity by a society is a series of murders of Chinese who have aroused its displeasure.

The murders stopped. In the months that followed, things returned to normal. Yet something had minutely changed. The town seemed to respond differently to stimuli. The fact that the Singapore inquiry had left them without hope of British naval assistance, that the collapse of the Borneo Company resulted in near economic disaster, and that the Chinese were successfully moving against the English on the Chinese mainland were somehow lost on it. There developed, instead, a thin, salacious interest in things. Conversations in European parlors leaned toward superficial speculation and gossip. It was the time of the two-year wonders, young officers barely over their first malaria before booking leave. A more formal separation of Europeans and natives had followed the entrenchment of the memsahibs. Ironclad rules governed household servants. The recreation club now had two grass tennis courts and a club saloon. A languid sexuality roiled around the little metal tables.

Barr made his rounds but at times had a bewildered look, forgetful one moment, fiercely precise the next. He had affected a boiled collar, to hide the worst scars from the smallpox, and would spring it after dining, dozing in a chair. At this hour of light stupor, he took to the habit of counting his rivers. The Samarahan, the Sadong, the great Batang Lupar with its branches, the Lingga, the Undop, the Sakarang, and the Baram. The Niah next year. The headwaters of

445

these new streams over the next four years. From there Hogg would extend eastward into Celebes, a world of long peninsulas and volcanoes. Stepping off this last stair, he would sink into that dream workshop of his childhood, a scattering of blueprints underfoot. Lim tiptoed in with his brandy. The Chinese would regard the familiar bulk. For a long time, he would stand there in his neat oiled queue.

Lim's life, over those months, had become a nightmare of veiled reminders, maniacal asides. His spirit held firm. For three decades, he had taken pains to keep this man whole and functioning. After the smallpox, and now the scandal in Singapore, he sought all means to restore him, to lap him in soothing routine. Yet the face under those ruts seemed dead, the eyes rarely regaining their clear focus. Red bean paste soup, carp poached with ginseng, Ah Moi's tender crab eggs were left cold on the plate. A bedding with one of his own fat nieces was accomplished as on a corpse.

It no longer crossed the Chinaman's mind to share the daily problems with godown and orchard kulis or a foreman's surly attitude. He had dealt with slaves all his life. He had been one himself. He would sweep out this offal. With his own extended family—cousins, nephews, nieces, dozens who owed their livelihood to him—he could cover their labor for weeks, months. In the meantime, he would report this shit to the Hueh. These had been his thoughts, strong thoughts, supporting him like young muscles, when Ah Moi brought the child to him.

She dragged her, his small daughter by his concubine Tan Po, holding the palm open, fingers splayed out, the black chop at the center. The warning was the most serious. They had taken trouble to know his heart, a man with four sons, yet they marked the worthless girl.

In October, the Viceroy of Canton doubled the reward for English heads, and the Straits fleet sailed north. Hueh cells beyond the mainland, encouraged by this development, sprang into life. Instructions to north Borneo were detailed. Care should be taken to execute only Barr and his officers and not to meddle with any other English or to obstruct trade. Proceeding in this way, it was felt the Queen, already angered with him, would not interfere.

In November, Fitzhugh intercepted three bangkongs at the Niabor estuary carrying seven unmounted twenty-two pounders. He sent word to Kuching by rapid prahu. "The only ones who can afford them are the Chinese."

Four days later, at Suai, he thought he ingested a bit of toadstool with his midday meal. He dosed himself with a strong emetic and lay on his cot to weather it out. Within two hours, he knew he was dying. It was an absurd, almost comic, revelation. In mounting agony, he found himself performing what he always thought was a fictional exercise: he began to review his entire life at accelerated speed. He saw himself at five, a child sitting in a green pail half filled with water; at eleven, a stiff collar causing a red mark to the right of his throat in a mirror at Downs. He saw with remarkable clarity the face of the first boy he ever kissed, the salt taste of the lips, the exquisite pressure of the buttocks in his hands.

The times I was evil I have forgotten, he thought, in a break in nausea. Can you be accountable for what you've forgotten? The question made him laugh. Cramps rolled him into a ball. He found himself focusing on one small, bright shard from a day in a year he had long forgotten, then another. His gorge and bowel discharged simultaneously. In the years to follow, a housemaid would arrange flowers in a sunlit room, bees would buzz, people would shudder in the spasms of love, and he be dead. He loved it all with his whole being. His boy came in with a lantern and basin to clean him. He reached for the Tuan's fingers, and he let him hold them.

Fitzhugh's message never arrived. Yet Kuching had already become watchful. Barr's precautions were in some ways strange. At one point he thought of digging the paths around the garden into trenches, like Napoleon's, so he could walk unseen by enemy eyes. Later, he was glad he had shared this with no one.

"Wah!" Ah Moi moaned to her husband. "He changes his bed five times a week! He sleeps in a chair with strong drink! He is old and afraid. Are we to share his fate?"

He no longer slept. He would doze fully dressed and wake in the middle of the night. One evening, he would order his camp bed set up in the saloon; another, in the library. When he went out, Si Tundo sent a man to follow the more or less aimless meanderings from twenty yards behind. He looked haggard and bewildered, but when accosted would rouse nastily.

He knew the Hueh did not exist in his territory, yet murders of Chinese were its clear signature. It was an aged widow three hundred miles away who cleared his head, albeit too late. Charlotte Norris' letter arrived by racing packet two days after the Chinese New Year. *The Hueh here says the gold company of Sarawak will soon have killed all white men in the country.* He read and reread the words. He respected this woman's intelligence. The kongsi at Bau had cooperated for years in rooting out the smallest elements of the Hueh whenever they appeared. The kongsi was the Hueh.

"There are two kinds of men," Selladin said, this prince sometimes visiting him in the evening, the baize chair back visible through his beautiful chest, "those who are alone and look oncoming disaster in the face, and those in the company of others who look in every other direction." In fact, the number of people in that year who knew, on some level, what was coming was astounding.

At the end of November, the Nakodah Dullah vanished. One morning, his houses were found boarded up, his godowns and stalls empty. This occurrence, more than any confirmed intelligence, put Bigelow on alert.

"Spend a moment to review the day, pet," he said to Tannes. "You must tell me anything, no matter how small, that seems different or odd. Nothing drops out of the sky."

There were reports of a larger conspiracy to push the Dutch and British out of Borneo. Bigelow discounted them until he found the accused conspirators put to death with such rapidity he got to none of them alive.

While there were no outward signs of alarm, the dream world of the Europeans became wild and colored. People felt themselves strangely impelled to disclose things. Secret hopes, desires, resentments, lifelong fears spewed out at remarkable moments. Some attributed it to the weather: the sudden drop of humidity in the air, the phase of the moon. Those who knew what was happening rose quietly, if they were in company, and left, feeling the looseness in their tongues.

In December, the steam frigate *Vixen* brought Christmas packages and fir branches packed in ice. Musical rehearsals were under way, and small fêtes were planned. The gaiety of the season took hold. Yet the high spirits seemed to shatter with anything, a loud noise, a minor interruption. When Mrs. Boyne's cook boy dropped a pan of pudding at a pre-Christmas soirée, she beat him, then sobbed uncontrollably.

Christmas Eve saw a fireworks display, followed by fiddlers on the astana lawn. Employees of the old Borneo Company—Murdoch, Bell, Gillies, and Cardhu—performed a sword dance, the rhythmic clash and glide in the hot darkness followed by the clear voice of a small midshipman: "The wren the wren, the king of all birds, Saint Steven's day was caught in the forest, although he was little he thought he was great." Young Ponsie flung up his heart.

What a magnificent race we are! Dolan thought. Gifts were exchanged. The new chandler presented his wife with blocks of peat from home for a proper Christmas fire, she flushing with pleasure for she had been so homesick, yet not wanting it lit, not even the little token square, and enraged when he fired it. Beth Gillies trudged back from the children's tiffin clutching a marzipan doll so tightly two pinch marks completely distorted the little head, and seeing this she began to wail and could not be comforted and was slapped hard.

Christmas and New Year's came and went. Red moon cakes and blood oranges appeared in the Chinese pasar for the Year of the Rat. Arcadio Metz set up his daguerreotype in the Tamil arcade with two choices of backdrop: black velvet or cerulean sky and crumbling pillar.

On the eighth of February, the Cardhu's Chinese cook disappeared. The Boynes' Teo Chew followed. By midweek, memsahibs all over Kuching were searching for their cooks. Little else was out of the ordinary. A black chop on a basket floor, another under a load of linen.

"The Parks and Cardhus and Boynes' cooks have all vanished," Maureen Dolan said to her husband.

"They always leave around their New Year to sweep their own houses," Dolan replied. "Pay debts, cook for their own."

"The yellow race has a rare sense of smell." She dumped the boar kidneys and testicles into a pot. He allowed no one else to prepare food for his dogs. That day, the yellow dog did not go near it.

"There is something wrong here," he said, observing the great head. Yet by the next morning the animal seemed fit. Ah Quat, their wash amah, feared the dog. Ah Quat was gone.

Bigelow rolled over, cupping his wife's breasts in one hand, little studs, like sleeping with one of those starving children in Lucknow. His dream became heavy and warm. He opened his eyes in the middle of the night to a fluttery gilding of the ceiling. Shouts could be heard, then an explosion. He grabbed his revolver and bolted to the door.

Flames rimmed the padang upstream, the little bandstand invisible in dense smoke. Dozens of Chinese were running back and forth with torches, some with clubs, some with rifles. One man seemed to have Miss Dray, the Parks' old nurse, by the hair and the two were doing a strange glissade across the clearing, she reaching around and every time she did this he hitting her with a club, but there was no sound except crackling and explosions. Tannes was beside him, wide-eyed, white, and he pushed her back toward the bed and reached for his britches.

"I must get to the arsenal," he said, putting a hand on either arm. "There's only Sutton and the corporal's watch. Fetch May. Cox and Herbert will take you below to the bathhouse." His eyes drilled into her. "Stay there. Don't move until I come." He pushed back the cupboard and slipped into the same bathhouse passage to exit below the yard.

She felt her arms where he had pressed them and stumbled backward, the bed hitting the back of her legs. She scrambled up, crablike, staring at the door, hearing more explosions and screams. As she stared, it crashed open and a man rushed in and struck her with a bat across the chest. He hit her again on the shoulder, hard, and she fell off the bed and he dragged her up. She could feel wetness on the side of one cheek and realized vaguely that an earring had been torn out. There was shouting close by and suddenly he was gone.

The evening before, the Bau towkays had armed six hundred miners and marched them to the kongsi's landing place, where a squadron of cargo barges awaited. The men were told they were being transported to attack a Dyak village in Sambas that had killed some Chinese. When opium was distributed and they began their descent, they were told their true object.

At Tudong, a single dugout pulled past the rear of this fleet. The Dyak paddling was immediately challenged. He said if he didn't precede them and warn his longhouse two kelongs downstream, it would fire on their boats. Oddly, he was allowed to pass. The dugout did not stop until it reached Kuching. The man was familiar with the astana grounds and found it surprising that no sentries were on duty. He was about to wake the house when Lim emerged, a man he knew, and told him that the Rajah was asleep and to wait in the cookhouse. He sat in the moonlit hut, looking at the dimly shining utensils. As he gazed at a line of bowls with their blue flowers, identical to the bowl always packed in her kit, a parang split his skull. No one knew what Jawing was doing in the cookhouse that night.

The Chinese arrived undetected. They split into two groups above the town, half moving toward the fort, the rest concealed near the astana wharf and up the small creek behind.

Barr woke, hearing noises, and armed himself. He crept down the stair, finding no one about, and entered the passageway that led under the lawn to the old bathhouse. At the bend beneath the orchard he almost put a bullet through Biverts, who was racing up by the same route to warn him. As they faced each other, an explosion shook the earth. "The powder magazine," Biverts said. He checked his revolver, the calmness in that pale face amazing Barr. He led Biverts back down the corridor to where it rose to the lawn. Through a grate they heard the shrieks of the dying. Two of the bungalows were occupied—by Reventlow, on leave from the Sut, and Cakebread. They watched from the grate as both men were pulled out and killed.

"We can make it to the river and cross before they come round to this side," Barr said. "Move when I open the door and stay close." Biverts gazed at him.

"What is it?"

"Nothing," he said. "I'm behind you."

A moment later, he found himself crouched in his own lilies, barefoot and sick. The garden was silent; the Chinese were in back of the house. He scuttled down the slope, softly diving under the bow of one their barges and pulling himself across. On the far bank he fainted. He revived later in the night to watch his library fall in upon itself, knowing as he watched the flames, as he had known looking into that long pale face, as he had known sticking to the shallows in a little scull in another lifetime because the boy wordlessly preferred it, Biverts could not swim. The fort and arsenal were ablaze, as well as the company compound. Agonized bellowing rose from the dairy.

Biverts' head was on a pole and paraded among torches throughout the night, for they believed they had killed Barr. Perhaps because of this, he was able to gain the Malay kampong downstream unpursued. From there, with a small force, he made for Seboyau. A large manned warboat intercepted him, Si Tundo at the helm. It would have been almost impossible to escape and ready a boat of this size from Kuching. He stared at the old man, trying to fathom his allegiance. The look of pain in those eyes was enough. "I'm sorry, my friend," he said, but the damage was done. The man would remain aloof for the rest of his life.

In Kuching, the Europeans fled to the C of E compound, farthest away from the mayhem. Dolan was everywhere, herding them in. His plan was to concentrate enough men to hold back the Chinese until the women and children could escape into the forest. He went around gathering them up, assured that his own family was safe within. He did not know that, in his absence, Maureen had gone to attend a birth at the Boyne bungalow. She was struck running back.

The children, a spindly girl and a younger boy, a thin pale child of later life, remained alone throughout the night, the great dog across the door. This animal, even when young, had an odd disposition. It would not run with the others, nor was it partial to the company of humans, even Dolan. It would be seen in his neighborhood, but no more than that. You saw Dolan and, if your eye skirted the area, you might catch sight of the long yellow hide. It looked at the children, huddled together, and lay down across the threshold. When the young Chinese approached with the torch, it leapt in one motion and took the arm at the elbow, grinding until it gave way, and then lay with the bloody mass. The house with this thing in the doorway had no trouble that night.

The universe separated for Tannes Bigelow in those hours into an upper and a lower region. She willed her legs to move, once sliding in her own blood, through the pantry toward May's room. Herbert, on leave from his apprenticeship on a government launch, slept beyond in the records room. She saw herself doing this, believed in fact she made the actual motions, but found her hands brushing the cool, damp walls of the bath passageway, all noise and horror fading, the giant water jar at the bottom. She stayed submerged that night, her head below the rim. Horrible sounds filtered down, muffled and far away. After a while, she thought she heard their voices, strange, high-pitched, the water hot between her thighs.

From her hiding place, she heard Cox's voice, then gunfire, and she did not hear him again. She heard her son being questioned in that hell above and his answers in a brave, hollow voice. She heard him scream and May's shrieking. They had decapitated him, then set the house afire, throwing the girl into the flames. Tannes Bigelow remained in the jar until thick smoke forced her out.

Bigelow was a good man, brave to a point few are. Cox merely surpassed him when the hour struck. It sometimes happens this way. Bigelow made the decision to go to the arsenal, and it was a good policeman's decision. He knew his family would be safest in the bathhouse, and he knew Cox would assist them. He was to review the logic of this for the rest of his life.

At dawn, a rain of ash sifted over collapsed roofs and smoking gardens. The smell of roasted flesh was strongest from the dairy, as if in preparation for some large feast. The body of Miss Dray lay with peculiar formality under a nipah mat, dropped over her by the Tamil sweet seller. Dogs rooted everywhere. Strange tableaux presented themselves. An arm lay next to a grazing cow. The body of a young Chinese sprawled dreamily in Semple's hibiscus. In the charred house of a Portuguese Malay, Arcadio Metz sat upright in the hot syrup of his daguerreotypes. Mrs. Bigelow was found in the creek, her head floating like a great bud. Two Malays pulled her out, and she gazed at them vacantly, sagging on the bank until some Europeans were located.

"Hello, you've come!" she said to Michaelis. "Wipe your nose." She looked at his feet. "You are not to go without your shoes, my chick."

"Tannes." Ruth Michaelis touched her cheek.

"There are horrible things in the ground."

"They are not here, Tannes," Ruth said tenderly.

"No, they're with Cox. 'That fey fool,' Mr. Bigelow calls him. He acts the child with them. But he's not a child." She looked up slyly. "I've seen him naked. We've lain together in his little room. He's put his thing into me. I am with child. Twins."

Beryl Reedy, Reedy's young wife, leaning over her candle and book, unable to sleep in her advanced pregnancy, was beheaded in one stroke. A Malay, one of the prisoners in the fort freed and armed by Bigelow, raised the musket against the first wave of Chinese and shot off his own jaw. Delia Semple was found locked in her bathhouse, unharmed, her kebun vanished.

The victorious Chinese, half drunk on opium, wandered about discharging muskets, accompanied by Biverts' head. Their leaders settled in the courthouse and demanded to see the Bishop. Dolan, after searching for his wife the whole night, presented himself wretchedly. They were courteous. They told him their quarrel was with the Rajah and his officials, not with the missions or the Borneo Company. As he listened, the scope of the thing dawned on him. The local Chinese could never have understood the importance of this distinction. They asked him to go to his dispensary to help their wounded. Their captain squatted on Barr's chair, the white flag of China hanging by his side. He said it was decided that the foreign contingent of the town be ruled by the Bishop; the Malays by the Datu Bandar; while the kongsi, as supreme rulers, would govern from Bau.

Dolan agreed that everything seemed to be arranged. The young Chinese relaxed, slouching backward and smiling. Dolan then suggested that the Tuan Mudah might not approve of these arrangements. A blankness came over all their faces. There was no way to comprehend how they could have forgotten about this man.

"We are doing the Tuan Mudah's work," the Chinese said, regaining himself. "He too wants to be rid of the Rajah." He dictated a message to Hogg on the spot, requesting him to stay in his territory and they would stay in theirs.

Maureen Dolan was found lying in the mud below the Boynes' cookhouse, her rings scraped from her fingers, a horrible gash through her hair and neck. Dolan, led to the place, looked like a dead man, then saw the shallow lift of her breast and was catapulted into paradise. He wiped the blood from her neck and told her all was well, crooning, his words nonsensical, telling her of plans for the second half of their lives. He told her the children were alive. "The dog, you see, 'the filthy beast,' " her name for him.

After cleaning and binding her wound and laying her in their bed, he sat in a chair. He gazed at the bloody braid in his fist, the crazy, preening thing that had saved her. He did not know what to do with his joy. He could not believe his good fortune, their singular immunity to this nightmare. He sat immersed in thanksgiving. He rose and sat down and rose again, a new, redeemed spirit. He passed through the door. The smoking ruins, the misery around him were seen as if through glass. Nothing could dampen his joy. He could think of nothing to do but find and smoke a cigar.

Huat, his old friend, dispenser of Sumatran tembakau and fellow debater on the nature of Divinity, cowering behind a tobacco barrel, saw in his doorway this bristling, terrifying apparition and, pushing his small son behind him, lifted the rusted pistol and shot.

No one knew how to tell her. He had just held her in his arms. He had wiped the blood from her face and neck and told her the children were alive.

"Dolan!" she cried when they brought him. She slid to the floor, and his head was placed in her lap. "You fool, it's not your time!" she roared, words roared before, in another life. He had been thirty, in the fifth day of a high fever, and a startled, childish look came into those eyes and she could see a groping in the dark pupils, his heavy, living weight once again in her arms. Not now. Now the pupils were dull. She watched him disappear in their dullness, a large, sweet-tempered man. Her love.

"You are only a dog," she said to the great head. "You mustn't grieve this way." The yellow eyes regarded her indifferently. The animal had stopped eating and by the fourth day could not move.

"If you don't eat by tomorrow, I'll send you to him."

At dusk the next day, she pulled Dolan's Martini off its pegs and tied the animal to a post and shot him. To see the sudden, lifeless carcass gave her a moment of intense comfort. She saw the great yellow haunches thirty yards ahead, a molten streak, and him, turning. If it works so well? she thought, and then pushed the gun back on its pegs and locked the room.

On the sixth of February, Hogg arrived in Kuching with four thousand Sakarangs. The Chinese, alert to the formidable force moving toward them, had fled en masse. He entered from the northwest, stationing men as he went, giving brief orders, taking stock of the dead and injured, arresting and executing any remaining Chinese, then heading through the wreckage toward her. He mounted the little stair, disarmed himself, and entered the gloom. He examined her wound and then proceeded to search her for further injury, tenderly, intimately, and she let him. When satisfied, he called for linen gauze and re-dressed her neck. The Dyak who brought it gazed in wonder at the gentleness with which he did this. Only after it was done and she was settled did he notice the silent children. He checked them over as well, rendering them paralyzed. He left twenty men in her compound.

His force had grouped itself in orderly units around the town, each cluster rousing silently as he passed. He drew his lieutenants to him with his eyes, making his way to the charred little bandstand, where he gave a terse stream of orders. He never repeated himself, and they knew it.

"Hang all Chinese before sundown who cannot prove they are residents of the town. Execute all Chinese who cannot prove by non-Chinese witnesses that they were in their dwellings the night of the insurrection." He directed his chief lieutenant to take half their force and pursue those who had fled inland. "Do not catch them, but worry their tail. The forest will do most of your work. Half of those remaining will secure the town. The other half will head downstream to assist the Rajah to return."

She was asleep when he returned. The children had been taken by Michaelis to let her rest. He sat in a chair and gazed at her. After an hour, he took off his boots and stretched his legs over her little settee. In the middle of the night she groaned and he rose in one motion. He slipped his arm under her and cradled her, half sitting, in the deepest ecstasy of his life. An unknown power had done this for him, one that had worked against him all his life and now was miraculously aligned at his shoulder. Happiness surged through him like high fever. For the first time in his life he was afraid.

In the first light, his arm dead, she opened her eyes. He began to rise, to set her back, but she pulled him down. She pulled with murderous fingers, drawing him down, and in that gray hour, what she would not do in twenty years for that sweet, larded man, she rushed and seethed to do to Hogg, the crust breaking in bright seepage at her neck, he paralyzed, feeling her recede further and further as she touched him, knowing he should stay clear of this, his body rising without him, knowing she was trying to leap a monstrous gulf, knowing, pulled and clutched and bitten and sucked, he was being shoved into a void as big as the universe; to fill it she would have shoved in the sea, a steeple, and finally ingested herself. He penetrated her like a boy, unable to hold back, tasting the red seepage, exploding. He would live to marry a woman with beautiful hair whom he detested, a woman who would outlive him by thirty years, who would make more money from her novels on life among the headhunters than his annual coal and antimony revenues combined, and never move beyond this hour.

She may have gone to him once in Lundu, in her forty-fifth year, the only inland trip of her life. The Boynes were newly billeted at Sametan, and in her visit to them Hogg could have sent an escort for her. At Lundu, the Dyak women would have marveled at her. They would assume she was a great witch to have such power over him and would steal bits of her clothing to possess part of this power. In Tubau, and later in Kapit, uncaring about scandal or anything previously held sacred, she would lie with her wrists caught in one of those fists, his mouth in her hair, the torpor, the fatigue of wanting her for so many years, the deadness in him surprising her. She tried to encompass it, the inconsolable eyes, the queer grace, the incalculable ferocity, the quiescence, the lack of good—she tried to hold it all, his weight wedged into her with such deadness.

That these events did not occur, or did, or that she had, after Kapit, come to her senses, means nothing. The Dyak would understand, that slipper sideways through time. That his last contact with her would be in a yellowed newspaper, sent anonymously eight months after her death in a rooming house in Cork, one of four gas accidents that winter, her final vision not of him or Dolan or any Divinity but two blue pools, doesn't matter. He would catch glimpses of her in later years: a red-haired apparition on a Reading train; a lone figure in a garden; several times in the person of his wife, faced away from him or asleep on her stomach, the ruby cloud belonging to anyone—he had married, he once said drunkenly, "a head of hair." The symmetry of his love, the purity of it, consoled him. At the end, it balanced out the horror and justified his days on earth.

Sixty European survivors sat at the Muaratebas estuary gazing at the black cloud upstream. By noon, they could mark the channel over the bar. They started to cross when two funnels of smoke appeared advancing eastward along the coast. If the steamers were Dutch, Cardhu warned, they would have to capitulate the country. The gunboats emerging from the screen of casuarinas were unmarked. Van Lutyens had taken care to remove their ensigns.

They were met that same day by ten of Hogg's prahus and escorted back upstream. A strange carnival atmosphere marked the ruins of the town. His Sakarangs were everywhere. They carried strings of Chinese heads, which they cleaned and smoked over slow fires in full view of the Chinese bazaar. Other heads dried between improvised food stalls. In the following days, a common entertainment was to stroll past and recognize someone you knew, a cook, a greengrocer, a baby amah.

Chinese found in hiding were executed on the spot, and in this way most of the Chinese population of Kuching, the Hokkien and Teo Chew and Hainanese and Cantonese, its little stallmongers, merchants, amahs, kebuns, and kulis, met their deaths. The few Bau Chinese left behind hanged themselves from trees. The rest fled through the forest, flinging loot on the path to slow their pursuers.

These men were forest-wise, of mixed Dyak blood. They now included over one thousand women and children, families of Chinese farmers forced to join them, the mass making for the great watershed. In their flight, they sent parties to plunder nearby longhouses for food. An attempt was made on Na, lying directly in their path. Here, amidst the birdsong and little brooks, Hogg's scouts found an old Malay woman, yellow and shriveled but finely dressed, her throat cut, at the foot of a *lit-bateau*.

Half this troop made it over the watershed and crossed into Sambas, where they were met by Dutch guns. Within ten days, thirty-five hundred Chinese were dead.

In March, a gunboat flying the yellow and blue ensign plowed up and down the coast proclaiming the return of order. In the three years that followed, Hogg would continue eastward, swallowing the remaining rivers between the newest division and Brunei. From each he sent back a gift to the C of E widow. From the Bintulu, a carp with scales of beaten silver; from the Suai, a little sun bear in a cage; from the Kalaka, a necklace of spinach jade; and she accepted them shamelessly.

In '79, he pacified the Muara district, the richest portion of the shrunken territory still left to the young Sultan. The acquisition of Limbang left this youth with merely the town of Brunei and two small coastal districts. At the last minute, the young man appealed to the Sultan of Turkey for help, offering all the possessions he had left.

Labuan was enraged by such rapacity. It was her report to White-hall that finally put a stop to his advance. The Colonial Office, interested at last, would assume sovereign powers over all remaining territory, and the Sultan and his heirs would be pensioned off.

Barr sat under a little awning on the charred boards of his house and drank his tea. From his chair he could see the shell of the dairy, the blackened sticks of the pasar. Only the little Chinese temple was unchanged, its fat, colorful gods ever leaping. He looked at the destruction but could not feel it. He did regret, deeply, one thing. He regretted his library. Over the years, Kilcane had brought the best historians, novelists, essayists, poets, travelogues, and erotica. He very much liked to sit among them. A *Parrot* book rested on his lap, its pages stinking of smoke, the only volume left undamaged. He gazed from it to the scorched orchard and the blackened frangipani from which Lim had hanged himself. He had had the man cut down and buried next to his little daughter. That upright bone, that canny guardian. None of us are purely what we are, he thought. In this I may be saved.

On some days, he had the sense that with this thing there had been a burning back, that they had entered a period of queer resurrection. He gazed at the stone quay, its strange beauty undamaged, a white glimmering strip against the charred hulls. Oddities abounded. Green spikes poked everywhere through the ash, one especially lush cluster through the skeleton of a dog. The one thing left undamaged in the smoking ruins of a bungalow was a divan and on it a daguerreotype of its owner in a too-tight wedding suit. Metz, half liquid, was buried in a jar. Yet no piece of this aftermath seemed as strange as what he had witnessed within Dolan's bungalow. He had gone to look in on Maureen when he first returned and in the gloom found Hogg sitting in a chair with her in his arms, his eyes dark with rapture, not seeing him—the pregnant sculler, that bather of children, baster of roasts, nursemaid to bishops, drawn up like a child in those arms. He knew then he understood nothing.

There was, over the next year, a retrenching. Seven new officers were appointed that spring to replace those murdered. Directors of the new Eastern Archipelago Company were elected. There was a surprise rejuvenation of the railway from Semunjan, and reports began to sift in from the new stations at Tubau and Dalat. Midst it all, a strange, short report, a rumor, yet out of all the uncorroborated information passed to him over the years, this he felt instinctively was true: The Pengiran Hassan had drowned. The old man had attempted to molest a child in a village on the Sut, and the child had pushed him.

I love my chair, I love my bed. I love my bowl of porridge. I love the deadness in my groin around female flesh. He wrote to Kilcane, but to no one else. He wrote, *I feel I have lived on this earth six hundred and sixty-six years,* and his friend wondered why a man who did not read that Book or any book, but only breathed their scent in that parody of a library, chose that number. Was *he,* in his hagi pantaloons and rotting bones, alone immune to remorse?

Barr returned to England before Hogg, leaving him to govern in his stead, which he did from two small rooms at the fort. It would take marriage to make him reside in "the palace." In spring, Hogg would follow for his own wedding.

Kilcane had commenced his retirement. That winter, Barr made the trip to see him in Kent, where he lived with his youngest daughter. He found him propped in a chair, swathed in a satin smoker. They spent the afternoon under rugs, talking—the name of a man, a river, a ship pitching them into synchronous reverie. He wrote to his friend afterward, but the letter turned into a pathetic soliloquy and he did not send it.

It was less painful than he expected to be back. A Rajah tuah, a retired rajah, was less of the twopenny tent. The Foreign Office seemed to have altered somewhat toward him. With Hogg's marriage and a new generation installed, or at least a regency, there were hints at protectorate status before his own death.

These were things so immediately, immensely, important, yet he could not keep them in focus; they slipped away, pushed out by an encroaching rim of light. He had to get the tune right, a tune made of the contusions of air through a grove of bamboo; a sudden thick perfume wafting over water thirty years ago; a little topee, its paste bird bobbing through canna; a rich, florid lament, his arms filled with robia. He looked at the formal proposal from Whitehall, when it was put before him, and misplaced it.

"Perhaps I've done enough to these people," he said to Biverts, who often stood beside his shoulder, very much like the gentle specter he was in life. In his dreams, he would give Biverts swimming lessons, the long body agile as a fish, smiling up at him.

He was, he realized, poor. His wife, with the residue of her modest inheritance, was richer. Out there, he was bequeathing Hogg no stream of wealth. After forty years, the bulk of state revenues still came from opium, which was drying up or moving silently through other channels. All they could rely on were dwindling royalties on antimony and coal.

A few clubs made him an honorary member that first year back. Norwich had a dinner with its second-best plate. He watched himself at these things with scant curiosity, as if he were dead and reviewing this last round and finding it dull. He appeared at one of the Queen's levees, placed in queue directly behind a mass of coffee-colored flesh and pearls. Victoria spoke briefly and kindly to him. The last person who spoke kindly to him had been an old Dyak in a room with a dead child..

Hogg's wedding had more substance about it than his own. He married a very tall girl who wore a hollow luster crown and long damask train, as though she were already a queen. Titled, no breasts, no hips, no breeding room. Only Hogg, who had bedded every kind and color of female in that hemisphere, would choose a woman you couldn't even rape. In a small way, he felt sorry for her; he hoped she was as vapid and impervious to sorrow as she looked. The hair was good, a superior, deep red, and abundant.

The bride gave a little scream at something clever. He was offered champagne; the tray had as its centerpiece a small papier-mâché monkey, one of a series of discreet tropical motifs. He walked from one crowded, flower-bedecked chamber to the next, rooms filled with noise and food, devoid of oxygen. "How in hell do you get out of this house?" he asked a man who turned out to be his host.

He was unwell for the rest of the summer. With the coolness of autumn, his strength returned. He hunted, taking a bad fall midway through the season on a borrowed mare. His back was never the same. He stayed in Gloucestershire with Charlotte Norris until midwinter, then moved on to the cottage at Combe Martin, mortgaged in '69 to provide capital for an experimental breadfruit plantation in the Baram.

He took long walks, moving stiffly over the frozen stubble. He found himself alone, his wife and child estranged. He was resigned to his solitude, yet with the occasional sharp stab, hoping to break the silence with a friendly or familiar word. When the odd human turned up, he became overbearing. He kept to the habit of sleeping in chairs. One evening, Kilcane approached in a new costume, more fabulous than any of the old Chinese robes or hagi bags. He had managed to shrink himself, a tremor in all his bones. "You are old!" Barr exclaimed, grinning.

"I am dead." Kilcane smiled. They talked, the sweet impediment soothing, like old, familiar music.

He learned from the woman who kept the cottage by day that Admiral Kilcane had died the previous week, of heart congestion, in his bed. He rinsed his cup and set it on the board and regained his chair. He slept, dropping below the normal strata of dreams, once again in that industrious workshop, laboring feverishly on a little wheeled conveyance. It did not work smoothly and he switched to another, a vehicle of the air filled with gas, little fins for steerage, which, despite their beauty, would not turn.

He woke in darkness with no feeling on his right side. He tried and could not rise. He knew what it was. He gazed down at the skewed arm and leg and was amused that one half of him had died before the other. He dreamed, that night, of the Niah River, a place he'd never been, a place of limestone hills a thousand feet high and tremendous caves with millions of sea swifts. One climbed there with rattan ladders to gather their nests. He would go to those caves with Jawing. He would finish the elusive journey above the heads of all his rivers; he saw the sweet, luminous arc of it, the strange birds, species unknown below, painted in wild colors, someone—the priest—sitting in the midst of their beating wings.

He knew the sun was on his back but could not feel it. Light shifted sideways through the open window. A line of people approached along the strand, their clothes lifted in the wind, some waving. Selladin approached, extending his fingertips. A small Dervish whirled by, an extra pair of eyes in his red jacket. The woman passed, hips rolling smoothly, head high as a water snake, at her back a young man with a familiar shy smile, notebooks strapped under his arm, and then two great muscled angels, a dark specter between them. In the shallow swell, two men rode in a boat, one skeletal, red-haired, the other a human bat, raising his hat in an elegant arc. Why would the dead bid farewell to the dying? Someone slammed a door with such fury that the parade lifted off the beach like a tail, resettling colorfully in the wind, at the end, a woman, tall, auburn-haired, a small boy behind, lips pursed in the purest effusion of sound. Her hand flipped backward and he stepped and grasped it fast, and there was nothing but sky and sea.

GLOSSARY

adat	customary law or procedure, right by sultanate decree
angin	wind
antu	(Dyak) spirit, ghost
astana	large house, palace
baya	(Dyak) grave goods; cherished belongings before death
chachar	smallpox
chawat	(Dyak) loincloth
gawai	(Dyak) religious feast
Hari Raya	Muslim holiday (Hari Raya Puasa marks the end of Ramadan; Hari Raya Haji is the feast of the pilgrimage, the haj to Mecca)
imam	Muslim priest
Jahanam	last level of hell
kebun	gardner
kongsi	self-governing Chinese company engaged in mining or trade
kromang	(Dyak) musical ensemble

kuli	unskilled laborer, usually Chinese
kurap	skin disease similar to ringworm
laut	sea
maias	orang utan
makan	eat
manang mansau	(Dyak) shaman or healer of rank
mĕngail	hooked, as a fish
nakodah	merchant, trader, trading captain
nampok	(Dyak) to perform a vigil; to go to a solitary place to meet with spirits
Nan Yang	overseas Chinese settlements
nonya	Chinese-Malay or European-Malay married woman or mistress
obat	medicine
pasar	market
pengiran	prince of the royal house of Brunei
penglima	commander (Malay title given to Dyak chieftain)
prahu	a Malay boat
pulau	island
Ramadan	Muslim month of fasting
ruah selamat	a prayer of thanksgiving when free from danger
semanggat	(Dyak) vital force, soul or soul strengthener
sembayan	(Dyak) heaven; hereafter
sumpit	(Dyak) blowpipe
surat	letter
syce	groom, driver
tanjong	cape
temenggong	commander in chief
tuah	Retired, old. Also denotes headman.
Tuan Mudah	(Malay title) young lord, usually designating the heir to a rajah

ACKNOWLEDGMENTS

While many of the characters in this book are based on historical figures, and the major events, in some form, occurred, it is in the truest sense a work of fiction. The character portrayals are fictional, and few passages are without a fictional component.

Several resources were invaluable to me in my research. Prime among them were *The Private Letters of Sir James Brooke,* edited by J. C. Templer (1852), and Charles Brooke's *Ten Years in Sarawak* (1866) and *Queries Past, Present and Future* (1907). Also important were Admiral Henry Keppel's *Visit to the Indian Archipelago in H.M.S. Maeander* (1853) and *The Expedition to Borneo of H.M.S. Dido for the Suppression of Piracy with Extracts from the Journals of James Brooke Esq.* (1846) and Spenser St. John's *Rajah Brooke* (1899) and *Life in the Forests of the Far East* (1863).

Events marking the start of the raj and the years of expansion and consolidation, eventually culminating in the Singapore inquiry and the Chinese insurrection, derive from these sources. The description of Hogg's early naval service and the years of his military campaigns draw from experiences recorded in *Ten Years in Sarawak.*

In some instances, dialogue was taken from historical accounts to fit the fictional setting. The question posed by the chief Mua Ari on page 398; Hogg's explanation for waging war on women on page 399 and his speech after the Chinese insurrection on page 459; and the explanation of the killing of the witch Lehut on page 402 have their origins in *Ten Years in Sarawak.* The words spoken by Semple on page 116 are from the letters of Francis McDougall (cited below), as is the line on page 362 quoting a letter from the Bishop of Calcutta. The description of smallpox precautions on pages 369–70 derives from Keppel's *Visit to the Indian Archipelago in H.M.S. Maeander.*

I am indebted to Lady Margaret Brooke's *My Life in Sarawak* (1913) for anecdotes and insight on domestic life and society in Borneo. Passages on marriage, the births and deaths of children, inland expeditions, and Dyak custom have drawn on this history. Certain anecdotes involving Dyak lore and animal behavior derive in part from Lady Sylvia Brooke's *The Three White Rajahs* (1939). The incident of the talking bird on page 212 is partially drawn from it, as are the "insect boat" and the description of Dyak feasts and gods on page 300.

Other important books were Sabine Baring-Gould and C. A. Bampfylde's *A History of Sarawak under Its Two White Rajahs* (1909); Alfred Russel Wallace's *The Malay Archipelago* (1869); Captain Rodney Mundy's *A Narrative of Events in Borneo and Celebes, with the Rajah's Journals* (1848); the *Memoirs of Francis Thomas McDougall and Harriette His Wife* as edited by C. J. Bunyon (1889); and Derek Freeman's paper on headhunting lore, *Severed Heads That Germinate* (published in L. H. Hook's *Fantasy and Symbol*, 1979).

I am deeply indebted to all those who have recorded and interpreted this history and whose work has guided me through it.

The novel was written over a decade in different parts of the world. If I omitted acknowledging a resource due to failure of memory or to simple neglect, I extend sincere apology.

I wish to thank the people of Borneo for allowing me to plumb their past. Thanks also to the Boston Athenaeum, the Bodleian Library of Oxford University, the Beverly Library, Yaddo, and the MacDowell Colony. My gratitude to Gertrude Perkins Godshalk for sharing family letters from Java.

Finally, my thanks to Theodore Chase, Dina McGuinn, Michael Curtis, Marian Wood, and Ellen Levine, friends of the work, and to Maimunah Haji Daud, Robert Oudemans, William Davenport, and Ingrid Ziskind for their linguistic help. And, of course, to E.

A point on language. The Malay words used are for the most part British Malay of the nineteenth century as they appear in the journals and logs of that period. Certain words now common to the region, such as "Iban" for "sea Dyak," were not in use. Some geographical names, too, have been altered by time.

The phrase in italics on page 127 is a quote from *The American Practical Navigator* by Nathaniel Bowditch. Bowditch, Vol. I., Pub. No. 9, 1977 ed. Publ. U.S. Dept. of Defense: Defense Mapping Agency Hydrographic Center.